The Legacy

MELANIE PHILLIPS

A BOMBARDIER BOOKS BOOK
An Imprint of Post Hill Press
ISBN: 978-1-68261-566-9
ISBN (eBook): 978-1-68261-567-6

The Legacy

Cover Design by Christian Bentulan

This book is a work of fiction. People, places, events, and situations are the product of the author's imagination. Any resemblance to actual persons, living or dead, or historical events, is purely coincidental.

Post Hill Press
New York • Nashville
posthillpress.com

Published in the United States of America

In memory of my father

1

THE PLATFORM AT Swiss Cottage tube was crowded. It wasn't quite rush hour, but there hadn't been a train for more than five minutes. Through a crackle of static, a disembodied voice announced that this was due to an earlier passenger incident at Baker Street.

It was hot in the station as more and more people shuffled onto the platform. Russell eyed them uneasily. Would there be room? He had a horror of confined spaces. The Hillsborough football stadium disaster swam into his mind. He had produced a documentary on it for Channel Four, watched over and over again that awful footage of the fatal crush.

He imagined what it must have felt like to be pushed over and then trampled underfoot as the panicking crowd surged forward. How would you die? Would your ribs be crushed, or your skull, or your spine snapped by the stamping feet above? Would you simply suffocate, gasping for breath as the terrible press of bodies shut off the air altogether?

But this was worse. He was underground here, entombed. Ironic, since he was on his way to a funeral.

In extremis, he was often wry. An affectation, it also served as his armor.

He pushed his way to the end of the platform where there were fewer people, for the time being at least. He looked at the arrivals screen. Still blank: no train was yet showing.

The monotonously repeated announcement about a passenger incident grated. It was a coy euphemism that fooled no one. Everyone knew that yet another person had gone under a train. Deliberately, he hoped, looking warily at the heaving crush on the platform. What a way to die, though, he thought. I mean, why would you throw yourself under a train when all you had to do was take a handful of pills?

Morbid. Stop it. Not surprising though, given what had happened recently. He looked at his watch. Christ, he was pushing it. Eleven stops to Stanmore, and then he'd have to get a taxi to the cemetery. Did they even *have* taxis in Stanmore, he wondered.

He began to feel dizzy. Apprehensively, he moved his eyes fractionally sideways. What would happen, he wondered, if he should collapse with a heart attack, right there? Could they get an ambulance crew through? After all, he had been under a lot of stress, he said to himself, well before the events of the past few days.

It didn't help that he had no one to confide in, no one who was that close to him anymore. He wanted someone to reassure him that what he felt was happening was not in fact happening: that his world wasn't falling away beneath him.

Why was it all going wrong? He blamed the BBC. That's where the rot had set in. When it had decided to stop being a national institution and turned itself instead into a free-market enterprise.

Now producers like him had to fight for every commission. His last three ideas for shows had been turned down. Bastards. Of course standards had slid. The cutting-edge journalism he'd specialized in had given way to reality TV. He'd turned up his nose at that cooking show idea. For God's sake, who was to know how many ratings there were in Victoria sponge cake?

And now this. He could really do without it.

He felt the stirrings of a breeze. He looked up. The screen announced a Stanmore train in one minute. The breeze gained force and became a warm wind. A distant rumble grew louder from deep within the tunnel as the train approached.

Russell was near the platform edge. A Tube worker in a hi-viz jacket intoned metallically that passengers should stand back behind the yellow line as the train approached. Russell looked towards the rumble that was rising in volume; he stared into the sooty blackness. He saw the faint flicker of reflected light as the train approached the bend in the tunnel; with a roar it burst into sight as it raced towards the station.

And then he had the strangest sensation, as strong as it was terrifying, of being drawn to jump in front of the train. It wasn't a desire to kill himself, of course not—he of all people. It was a compulsion, as if some force was actively pulling him towards and over the edge.

The platform started tipping up. The ground started to dissolve. He swayed on his feet. A hand roughly grasped his arm.

"You all right, mate?"

A black youth in a hoodie was looking at him in concern. He kept hold of Russell's arm and helped him into the carriage. "Bit too crowded, yeah?"

A Sikh passenger who noticed stood up and Russell sank gratefully into his seat.

"There you go. Okay now? No worries."

And the ordeal ahead of him, Russell thought drearily as he wiped the cold sweat from his forehead and neck, hadn't even started.

2

THREE DAYS LATER, after seeing his father into the clay-clogged earth with what seemed to him indecent haste and absence of due ceremony, Russell Wolfe sat inside a synagogue for the first time in forty years with hatred in his heart.

He hated his sister, Beverley, for making him feel it was all his fault. He hated the synagogue for its rigid complacency. He hated his fellow Jews for making him despise them. He hated himself for having needlessly exposed himself to this irritation.

Most of all, he hated his father for dying.

He had no business dying when he did. There were unfinished matters to attend to. Now they would never be put right.

It was stifling inside the synagogue. He looked around with distaste. Nothing, absolutely bloody nothing had changed. It even had that smell that brought it all back: musty books with cracked spines, cloying perfume and, faintly, fishballs.

The same dreary architecture that managed to convey both grandiose pomposity and a total absence of the sublime. The same drone of background chatter punctuated by sibilant hushing from officious types on the platform where the rabbi, who was reading from the scrolls of the law, stopped from time to time and momentarily silenced the hubbub with a look of pained weariness.

He felt the life draining out of him at the dreariness of it all.

A tiny child rolled around underneath the table that was supporting the scrolls, plaiting and unplaiting the fringes of the heavy, embroidered table-covering hanging down.

Russell's head swam as he swung the prayer shawl over his shoulders and automatically held it over his eyes to pronounce the blessing. Oh God, not here. Not another dizzy spell, not in front of all these people. The words dried in his mouth. Feeling he was being watched, he looked cautiously sideways. Heads swiveled imperceptibly, and bespectacled eyes appraised him up and down before dropping again towards the books bobbing beneath the soft folds of the shawls.

In a sea of Marks & Spencer navy blue suiting, Russell felt as if his trademark black leather jacket was burning a hole in his shoulders. His gorge rose in irritation. After all, he had taken the trouble to put on a tie. A black one.

He had done his best to make it clear to anyone who might have got the wrong impression that, whatever points of genetic continuity or physiological resemblance there may have been between himself and his devotional companions, he was very definitely not of their tribe. Accordingly, he was wearing a black shirt with his black leather jacket, the one he'd picked up in Portobello Road when he and Alice had lived in that flat in Notting Hill. Oh, and a tiny diamond stud in his left ear. Beverley's jaw dropped when she saw him, which was very satisfactory.

"That shirt, Russell! You can't wear that."

"I'm in mourning. It seems entirely suitable."

"But Dad marched against them, for God's sake."

Well, you could see her point. But at least it marked him out as having absolutely nothing to do with his brother-in-law Elliott, sitting in pompous seclusion in the synagogue wardens' box and looking forward to his ritual Saturday lunch and the ritual Saturday afternoon sleep he would have straight afterwards. Prat.

Russell looked upwards to the gallery. Yes, there were the women, even today penned in like a flock of brightly jeweled birds, pecking and preening in their elevated enclosure. Excluded from participation in the proceedings, no wonder they chattered and gossiped throughout. Plump, lip-glossed lips glistened below placid eyes that showed no glimmer of rebellion or even awareness of this demeaning ostracism.

How astonishing it was, thought Russell, that outside these doors modern women—even, probably, many of these comically behatted ones perched above—were daily asserting their equal rights as workers, citizens, voters; and yet in here they took their places docilely and unquestioningly in this cage of decorative uselessness.

Some of them, though, he had to admit, were nevertheless quite fanciable. But how many, he wondered, would be up for it?

They were easily led. After all, the kind of person you found in such a place was...well, not to put too fine a point on it, not the brightest bulb in the box. He knew the type so well. Were not his sister Beverley and her absurd husband Elliott among its members? Small-minded, parochial, above all stultifyingly suburban. Oh yes, they were what demographers would call the professional classes all right, the ABC-1s as the statisticians would describe them; but they were estate agents, high-street lawyers, dentists. Not the kind of world he came from, the intelligentsia.

There really was no comparison. Their world was tiny, introverted, incestuous. Its central artery was the North Circular Road; venturing south of it required major preparation for an expedition into hostile territory, preceded by anxious conversations of cartographical illiteracy with others of similar territorial scope, and producing the kind of travelers' tales upon arrival in Hammersmith or Clapham commensurate with surviving a journey of epic peril.

Russell's life was filled with many causes, testimony to a wide-ranging appetite for ideas—tackling global warming, ending Third World debt and of course fighting racism. They only had one cause. Israel.

It was truly an obsession, positively pathological. They believed with iron certainty that the smallest criticism of that tiresome country would leave them one gasp away from the gas chambers. He, by contrast, placed the whole of the Middle East in its geopolitical, socio-psycho-historical context and so took the more sophisticated view that Israel was merely a byproduct of a discredited colonialism.

His was the world of books and bicycles, of polished wooden floors, of holidays in French self-catering *gîtes* and good conversation over several bottles of decent claret. Theirs was the world of fitted carpets and velveteen lounge suites, in which social gatherings were called "functions," and where the women still had their hair done in rollers at hairdressers' salons with fey French names in suburban parades.

It had been Alice who had pointed out that last observation to him, snorting with derisive laughter after she had got lost in Edgware on her way to meet a client. She'd never imagined that such a place was actually part of London, she declared, shaking her head in mock wonderment. So unutterably dreary! So hideously lower-middle-class! He hadn't felt like telling her that this was precisely the kind of place where he had been brought up.

That was when they were still together, of course. Before she had so bafflingly packed her things one day and left.

What in God's name, thought Russell, was he now doing here. But of course, he knew. He really had no choice. Even before the day he'd gazed flinching upon his father's body stretched out, still on his side of the bed even though he had been alone these past two years, Russell had always known that if he observed nothing else he must say the *kaddish*, the prayer for the dead, when his father died.

Not to do so would be to abandon him, as he himself had been so painfully abandoned. It would have been a form of revenge. God only knew he was angry enough. But he realized he wouldn't have been able to stand the guilt. He weighed up the options: to dip back into this world he had rejected and subject himself to these gruesome people and their ridiculous behavior; or stay true to himself, turn his back on all this and suffer the pangs of conscience forever.

Put like that, it was a no-brainer.

But when it was time to stand and say this prayer, this *kaddish*, he found to his embarrassment that he stumbled over the words. It wasn't just rustiness, but a welling up within him of an emotion for which he was entirely unprepared that made breathing difficult and his head again start to swim.

Swaying slightly, he started to sweat and to panic. He stopped and bent all but double. The men around him gently repeated the words he was supposed to say. He looked up, and saw them turned towards him in a gesture of solidarity. In their black and white striped prayer shawls, they looked like a herd of zebra shielding an injured foal. He swallowed hard and falteringly continued. The men murmured more strongly in response, and when after an eternity he got to the end they turned away immediately as if to indicate tactfully that nothing untoward had occurred. Discomfited, Russell found his eyes were hot and damp.

He wiped his face. A feeling stole over him that he was being watched. He looked along the pew. There was an elderly man at the end in a trilby hat. As soon as Russell caught his eye, he looked quickly away.

Russell noted his black-rimmed spectacles, curiously old-fashioned, and the absence of a prayer shawl; and the way the man's hands gripped the back of the seat in front so tightly that even from that distance the knuckles gleamed white. Physical frailty, maybe, he thought—but then the man, although old, didn't look fragile; quite the contrary. He was a big man, still powerfully built, with a thick neck and a dimple like a cleft in his chin; and those hands were broad. Peasants' hands.

An unwelcome picture slotted into Russell's mind: a woman in a drab council flat, her mouth a toothless grimace of permanent discontent, her enormous hands pressing down heavily on each of her splayed knees under the floral overall that crossed over and tied at the back; the sort of overall that cleaners used to wear. His grandmother. Yes, he knew those hands. Shtetl hands.

The voice of the rabbi cut into his reverie. He was delivering a sermon about the binding of Isaac, when Abraham had prepared to offer up his only son as a human sacrifice. To Russell, the story was both repulsive and incredible. If it was supposed to be true—of course Russell assumed it was a deep-seated cultural myth, although in the spirit of open inquiry on which he prided himself he kept all options open, theoretically speaking, just in case—but if by any chance this story did indeed have a historical basis, then either Abraham had a heart of stone or the prevailing ethos of those times viewed children on roughly the same level as animals.

Russell considered that this was probably the most likely explanation for the whole distasteful tale. Tender concern for one's children was, after all, a recent development associated with advanced civilization. Paternal love, a social construct, was a modern invention.

But then again, he thought in a spasm of fury, it wasn't only in antiquity that parents saw their children principally in terms of productivity or the perpetuation of the tribe. He saw once again Alice's face, washed first by incredulity and then, as the realization sank in, disgust. "As if I'm something to be ashamed of," she had said bitterly. And in that moment he had known he hated her, even as he knew that through the choice he had made for her he would finally break with his father.

Dismayed by the direction in which his thoughts had led, he tried again to concentrate on the sermon. It appeared that Abraham had been set a supreme test which he had passed with flying colors because he had not questioned it but simply set about lashing Isaac to the pyre. Russell stifled a yawn.

The small child who had been rolling around now emerged from behind the lectern and started pulling at the rabbi's prayer shawl, which promptly fell off. Everyone laughed. The rabbi scooped her up and stroked her hair. "What greater joy do we have than our children?" he said. "They are our lives, they are our future, they are our purpose on this earth. What more appalling test could there be than to kill your own child? Of course, the very thought fills us with horror. What parent would not die himself rather than have his child come to any harm, God forbid?"

Oh for heaven's sake, thought Russell; spare me.

The old man at the end of the row blew his nose loudly and wiped his face with his handkerchief.

Russell felt in his pocket for his iPhone and turned it over in his fingers like a comforter. He hoped he had remembered to turn the ringtone to silent.

"So what should we conclude," said the rabbi, "that Abraham was a callous parent, unfeeling, inhuman, a forerunner of those Palestinian parents today who send their children to be suicide bombers?"

Russell looked up, startled. A stillness descended upon the congregation as if it had temporarily forgotten to breathe. Some appeared to be asleep. Others looked shocked. The young suddenly seemed to be paying close attention.

The rabbi shook his head. "The mistake," he said, "is to assume that he intended to sacrifice Isaac. Look at the words. They don't say that. They just say he must take Isaac and prepare a sacrifice. He had perfect faith that the holy one would provide the animal to be slaughtered. Which is of course what happened. Abraham trusted he would not be required to kill Isaac. He had unshakeable faith. That's the point. That's why he passed the test."

Despite himself, Russell was impressed. A clever argument, he had to give him that. Not the usual banal and absurd pieties. Russell looked more closely at the rabbi. He wasn't old, beneath that beard, late thirties, early forties—younger than himself, certainly. There was a brain there, no question, possibly even quite a good one. Yet he had suspended his intellect to believe in fairy stories. As for the Palestinian jibe...well, no surprise there of course.

Not for the first time, Russell despaired of his fellow man.

When he had approached his bar mitzvah, Russell was sent to Rabbi Levene for tuition. This sage appeared to him to be an ancient; but since he was to live for another forty-five years this impression must have been caused by his chest-length beard along with forests of hair sprouting from ear and nostril, not to mention the persistent food stains on his shabby cardigan or waistcoat.

Russell had a good ear and equally good memory, and found it relatively painless to learn the Hebrew passages he had to sing aloud. What he found more difficult was the exposition of religious thought that he was also expected to prepare for his bar mitzvah test.

"So what about Charles Darwin?" he asked Rabbi Levene.

"What about him?" said Rabbi Levene warily.

"Well, how could God have made the world in six days when there was the evolution of species?"

"And why not?" The rabbi had this irritating habit of answering a question with another question.

"Because the universe is billions of years old."

"Here you have missed the point," said Rabbi Levene, plucking loose hairs from his beard. "A common mistake. Look at the order of creation in Genesis: light at the beginning, mankind at the very end and fish and fowl in the middle. Just like Darwin says! Uncanny!"

Russell tried another tack. "So what about the dinosaurs, then?"

"So what about them?"

"Well, they don't even appear in Genesis."

"Ah," said Rabbi Levene, leaning forward so that Russell could smell the onion on his breath, "that's because before the holy one made the world, he made another world first..."

"Uhh?"

"...and that was the world with the dinosaurs, which was quite different from the second world which is our world, the one with Adam and Eve, and that first world was destroyed before he made our world, which is why the dinosaurs died out."

Russell wrote in his draft exposition: "My view of Judaism is that there's a lot in it that doesn't really add up but somehow it manages to find ways of explaining all this away."

"If you were to apply yourself properly to the study of Torah," said Rabbi Levene sternly when he read this, "you would find that everything miraculously does add up *and* that there is no limit to what you cannot understand."

Russell changed his exposition to say: "My view of Judaism is that there's a lot in it which doesn't seem to add up, but the more you study the more you understand." At his bar mitzvah, he was word-perfect and sang beautifully ("Like a choirboy!" said poor Auntie Evie, who was promptly sat upon) while his real, secret voice deep inside him repeated ever more loudly, over and over again, "God does not exist."

And yet, four decades on, he had come to say a prayer in a language he could barely read anymore from lack of use to a deity in whose non-existence he would still have believed as firmly as that boy of thirteen, were it not that after much mature reflection he had concluded that this, too, was a kind of faith which as a man of reason he could not in any sense endorse.

Whatever was he doing there that day, in a synagogue of all places, forty years after he had served divorce papers upon God? And why did he now feel, absurdly, bereft and wounded, as if he had been robbed?

His father had been but a shadowy presence during his childhood and had then shut him out of his life. He had surely done Russell a favor; he didn't want to be part of that life anyway. But now Dad was dead, he wanted him back. He wanted, finally, to win the argument with him, to hear him admit he had been wrong. That he, Russell, had been wronged. He wanted his father to ask him about his life, to be proud of him again. He wanted to give him another chance to be his father, before it was too late.

But now it *was* too late, and he was furious.

At the *kiddush*—the reception following the service—he stood in a crowded hall holding a thimbleful of sickly sweet wine and a piece of bright pink herring on a cocktail stick, feeling conspicuous and uncomfortable as the crowd flowed around him. Elliott, thank God, was on the other side of the room, holding court.

Russell overheard snatches of conversation. The rabbi, it seemed, did not command universal admiration.

"A load of mumbo-jumbo! God this and God that. You'd never think this was the 21st century."

"Well, what do you expect? He's very black. And his poor wife! Looks like she's pregnant again!"

"Is it her own hair, d'you think?"

"Course not!"

"Well, it looks so real."

"The better ones are made of actual hair, you know. Cost an absolute arm and a leg."

"It's the children I feel sorry for."

"One a year from teenage to the menopause. Poor thing!"

What did they mean, "black"? The rabbi's skin seemed to be as pasty as anyone else's—beneath the beard, paler, in fact, than the perma-tans on display. Was it his hair that was black? His soul? Russell felt his head begin to swim again.

Two men started a mild argument over the Palestinian reference.

"He shouldn't've said it. Too political."

"But true."

"*Tsk*, so unnecessary. He's just going to offend people, divide the community. Should've stuck to the Almighty."

"But it's what actually happens. They *do* turn their children into bombs. They *are* inhuman. He's a rabbi. He tells it as it is."

"*Tscha*, you can't go round calling people inhuman. We know where that kind of talk leads. He's been warned before to keep *shtum* about politics. A lot of people here will just leave. We have to keep the community together."

"You mean pipple here actually support Palestinian pipple against Israel?"

It was the old man in the trilby from the end of the row. He had an Eastern European accent of some kind. He sounded incredulous. The other two looked at him. One paused with a glass of whisky halfway to his lips. Then they looked at their feet.

"Well, er..."

"Look, it happens." The man with the whisky lowered his voice. His shoulders rose in a shrug as he spread his arms as if helplessly. "Even here."

"Can't have gone down very well with *you*." They both laughed uneasily. Russell realized with a start that they must be addressing him. He looked uneasily from one to the other. They were looking at him sideways, eyes bright with curiosity and, he thought, a hint of malice. My God, he thought, do they *all* know who I am?

"You like Palestinians? You no think they terrorists?"

The elderly man with the trilby was now gazing at him intently. All three waited expectantly. Russell groaned inwardly. He really didn't expect to have this conversation here, of all places.

"Well, um, I do think they, ah, have a *case*," he said cautiously.

The two men exchanged glances and slid away, leaving him alone with the elderly fellow. Russell swallowed his irritation at having been accosted by the kind of person he was doing his best to avoid and tried to look agreeable. The man was continuing to stare at him.

"This *case* they have," he said. "This *case* include wiolence?"

He couldn't pronounce the letter *v*. Like his grandmother, Russell thought. Polish, then, probably.

"Of course not," said Russell, affronted. "It's their *cause* that I support. Only a few of them use violence. I think it's wrong to judge people as if they're all the same. People here may think they're all murderers, but many Palestinians are victims."

To his surprise, the man nodded slowly. His eyes never left Russell's face.

"This something pipple don't understand. You wery unusual young man. Wrong to judge everyone as if all same, as if all equally bad."

He was disconcertingly intense. But why did a man like this not damn all Palestinians? Maybe this was what the other two had been getting at, that there were indeed divisions in the community over the issue. If so, that would indeed be a level of sophistication he hadn't expected.

"Are there many here who don't unquestioningly support Israel?"

"To tell truth," the old fellow said ponderously, his tongue peeping out pinkly as he paused, "don't usually talk to many pipple here. Is hard for me. My vife..." he gave a little shrug, "my vife not come. Everyone here is in family. So is hard for me to make friends here."

Russell felt a twinge of sympathy. "To be honest, I don't come much either," he said.

"We both strangers in Egypt, no?" said the old fellow, and gave an odd kind of leer. His eyes behind his spectacles roved restlessly round the room as if he was searching for someone. He had piled a plate high with the bits and pieces you get at a *kiddush*—fishballs, crisps, that dreadful pink herring again, crackers—and was tucking in at speed.

He seemed really quite agitated. Russell wondered if he might have one of those weird neurological problems written about by Oliver Sacks, who said he spotted evidence of them all around him every day in the street; not that Russell could say he had ever spotted any, which was a bit of a worry since he was supposed to be a close observer of social phenomena.

"Everyone here is blessed accountant or lawyer! You are accountant, lawyer?"

Russell ground his teeth.

"I'm a TV producer."

The man put down his plate and looked at him. His eyes were watery behind the glasses, and little veins on his nose and cheeks were broken.

"*Ach, Bake-Off*! This wery good. Mary Berry! Her I like. She remind me of Mrs. Tetcher! You work on *Bake-Off*?"

"Er no, I do documentaries mainly..."

"*Ach*, BBC! You work for BBC? You think is bias? I think is wery bias. I think is communist."

Russell recoiled.

"They think only black pipple, brown pipple have suffering. We all have suffering. We all have tragedy. No one have monopoly. Me, sure, my family have suffered. Many, many of them dead. Mother, father, brother. Bad times in past. We all wictims. We all suffer."

Russell badly wanted to move away, but such was the crush it was difficult. The last thing he needed right now was to be cornered by a Holocaust obsessive, and a bigot to boot.

Apparent salvation arrived in the unlikely form of a woman in a navy blue suit with white edging, matched with navy and white shoes. Perched upon her hair was what appeared to be a lace doily. She was bearing a tray of cake, from which the doily had surely escaped, and an expression of professional sympathy.

"Such a shame about your father. A lovely man. Such a *mensch*. So quiet and unassuming. You couldn't help but want to look after him. Go on, take two slices. But so independent—well, what can you do? Beverley was marvelous, of course. Nothing too much trouble. What a heroine, don't you think? Still, that's how it goes. You must be so proud of her."

Russell backed away, but in the process trod heavily on a foot, which turned out to belong to the rabbi.

"My condolences," said the rabbi, wincing.

"I must congratulate you," said the old man, who was now ploughing through a plate of cake, "on your address. Beautiful vords. A pleasure to hear educated man."

The rabbi paused and inclined his head slightly in acknowledgement.

"Too much complaining these days. Everyone wants it easy. Who knows today abaht hardship? Understand me? Not like in old days, eh. But now everyone says what hard life they had. Blame, blame; all they do is say is other fellow's blessed fault. But we all to blame! Know what I'm saying?"

The rabbi rocked back and forth on his heels. "Well, sometimes some of us are maybe a bit more to blame than others, Joe," he said laughing, and patted the old man on the arm. "I'm really very sorry about your father," he said to Russell. "I know you're not a habitual visitor, but if there's anything I can do..."

"Not a habitual visitor..." He could just imagine the conversation he would have had with Beverley. "My brother the heathen," she would have said. "The heathen nebbish TV producer." And they would have smirked together in a conspiracy of small minds.

"Maybe you'd like to come for a meal? We always have visitors; you might be interested. I'm Daniel, by the way."

These people! They never missed an opportunity.

"Of course, Elliott and Beverley are mainstays of our community. Trojans, nothing too much trouble. We are so fond of them. We were all so fond of your late father, *alav hashalom*, and of course your mother too is always in our thoughts. And we go back a long way. You know I knew Elliott at Oxford. We shared law tutorials for a while. I was at Balliol. After your time, I'm afraid."

Balliol! Russell gaped at him. "You're a lawyer?"

"Well, only first degree; never actually practiced. Then I did an MBA at the London Business School, but that seemed very dull; bit of a gadfly, I'm afraid. My doctorate was a little more rigorous: philosophy. Nietzsche, to be precise. Smart guy. Just a bit nuts! Great training for rabbinical exposition."

He laughed again. Russell wondered uneasily if he was being sent up. He thought again about the sermon the rabbi had just delivered. He looked at him again, and noticed now the steady brightness of his gaze.

"I saw the TV documentary you did on ancient Mesopotamia. Fascinating! I admired the way you unearthed so much that was new from the distant past. New to me, anyway."

"Well, it was all in published sources," said Russell modestly.

"Even so, the skill lies in extracting what's important from the historical documents. The language issue must've been a bit of a challenge. Although I gather you're a bit of a whizz at languages yourself."

Russell's eyes widened. "Medieval French and German aren't quite the same as Sumerian cuneiform script," he said. "We used translators and academics, of course."

He was taken aback. How did the rabbi know what he had studied at Oxford? It could only have been Beverley. How much else would she have told him about her errant brother?

"And the photography was simply glorious, of course. My congratulations on a terrific show. I wish you long life." With the customary words of condolence, he shook Russell's hand and plunged back into the crowd.

"You do research into the past?"

To Russell's intense irritation, the old man was still standing there. But now there was a slight change in his demeanor. He was a little more upright, more alert. Now he was staring at Russell.

"Sometimes. For documentaries, if there's an appetite."

In fact, historical subjects were the one thing TV program controllers couldn't seem to get enough of.

The man was looking down at the floor, obviously thinking. Why did this guy find him so fascinating, wondered Russell. He badly wanted to get away. He knew this type well enough, those with some bee or other in their bonnet. Once they fixated on you, there was no escape.

"You know Hebrew? You study writings of great rabbis, Jewish thinkers?"

Russell felt as irritated as he was embarrassed. He didn't want to confess his inadequate knowledge. Why should he, anyway, to this stranger? He'd had enough of this.

"Sure," he said breezily. "Although I haven't yet made a program about any of that."

The man nodded slowly and looked up. He smiled as if he was now satisfied; but there was something else in his expression, something unsettling that Russell couldn't quite place.

"Wery good," he said.

For a moment, Russell thought he saw calculation. No, he must have imagined it, he decided, and dismissed it from his mind.

3

RUSSELL SHIFTED IN the hard, low little chair. It was hideously uncomfortable.

The physical discomfort, though, was hardly the worst of it. His sister Beverley was wedged into an identical little chair next to his. She seemed to be radiating waves of silent fury in his direction.

They were sitting *shiva*, the customary week after the funeral when mourners sitting on low chairs are comforted by visitors, in Beverley and Elliott's front room—or, as they would call it, Russell registered with a shudder, the thru-lounge.

It was furnished, he noted, entirely in beige and cream. Beige fitted carpet, cream leather sofas—settees, they called them, just like his parents had done—beige curtains with stiff pleats covering the runners, recessed gas fire shaped around beige pebbles, abstract prints on the walls in beige, black and orange, pieces of black modernist sculpture on the mantelpiece and sideboard. This was considered good taste, he thought, by someone who had no idea what taste was; by playing safe, all that had been produced was a bland negation of personality.

Although those sculptures definitely had fascist overtones.

How relieved he was to have escaped all this. He could so easily have been trapped. And yet, remarkably, he still felt a tug somewhere deep inside him. He felt again as he had done as a little boy, before it had all gone so sour. It was, he was embarrassed to admit to himself, a feeling of safety. A feeling of home.

A steady stream of people shuffled towards them, their faces arranged into a rictus of sympathy. He knew none of them. They murmured a few words of condolence, nodding towards him and glancing quickly at the unresponsive form in the armchair nearby, and then sat or stood and talked to Beverley.

He tried to tune out but the same repeated words and phrases floated into his hearing.

"How sad...very sad...a good age...lovely man...sad at any age...did everything you possibly could...how did it, you know, finally...heroic, Beverley dear, heroic...a blessing she doesn't know...really so sad..."

As if operating outside his control, his eyes kept turning to the figure in the armchair next to him. Her frame was painfully thin, her head slightly bowed so that she stared at her lap. Her body didn't move, but her long fingers twisted constantly round each other. Her hair, once so neat and bobbed, had been allowed to grow long and was swept back from her forehead;

it was clearly not thought worth the bother any more even to try to give it a style.

He had hardly recognized her as his mother. He stared at her in horror. He hadn't seen her since she'd got so bad. She hadn't recognized him at all.

His father was no more; but his mother wasn't here either. This shell, this husk—this wasn't his mother. Sylvia. He spoke her name clearly. No response.

He tried to conjure up the mental image of what she had once been, that domineering character who had run the family. How could that possibly be the same person as this shrunken figure? This was why he hadn't been to see her, he whispered to himself. He had flinched from seeing what he was now being forced to see. And now he couldn't stop looking at her, and he felt stabbed with a physical pain deep in the very core of his being.

She hadn't been taken to the funeral. "No point," Elliott had said briskly. "Not worth upsetting her. For what?"

He had lifted his shoulders slightly and spread his hands. Russell had bristled. This was his mother whom Elliott was shrugging off so casually. How dare he. Smug prick.

At his father's open grave, he had looked at the plot next to it, the empty patch of earth that was waiting for her, for his mother. He took hold of the shovel and drove it with all his force into the heavy clay; and on hearing the terrible thud as those first clods of earth hit his father's coffin, he shuddered at the inexorability of it. His father; his mother; himself.

For twenty-six years they had not spoken. His father's choice, without a shadow of doubt. Not Russell's fault. His conscience was clear. He knew who the victim was in this affair and it wasn't his father, that was for sure. Hadn't Russell tried to repair the rift in those early years? Hadn't he done what he could, shouting at his mother down the phone at the nastiness, the narrow-mindedness, the sheer bloody perverse irrationality of it?

He had expected her to lay down the law to his father as she did a dozen times a day. After all, Sylvia was the one who ran that household, ran her husband. She was the one with the brains, the social class that was a cut above, the ability to get things done. She had never stopped telling him so.

"You're such a funny boy, Jacky," she would cry, applying her fingers to her scalp as if it might lift off under the pressure when Jack dared suggest that perhaps they might take their annual holiday this year in Bournemouth, a destination she considered wholly unsuitable in comparison with Rimini which required the sophistication of air travel.

She was not complimenting him on his amusing qualities.

Jack had what would have been called in later decades a phobia about airplane travel. He shook with white-knuckled terror from the moment he was strapped into his seat until the plane touched down. He also avoided traveling on the Tube and going through revolving doors, and refused point-blank to use a lift.

In any confined space, he was like a trapped animal pleading to be put out of its misery. Attempts to bring the evidence of science and technology to bear on the problem foundered on his unshakeable belief that all human agency was potentially and lethally flawed. "I don't trust 'em," he would mumble darkly. For Jack, life was a continuous conspiracy against his safety and security and required permanent vigilance.

They went to Rimini.

So when Alice came on the scene, and his father behaved so badly—no, let's not mince words here, outrageously, despicably—Russell expected that his mother would sort it all out.

"You've broken your father's heart," was all she said instead.

To Russell's feelings of bewilderment and outrage was added an aesthetic distaste. To speak in such clichés! "Broken his heart"? What, simply by living his own life he was being cast as a villain from a B movie? Wasn't he entitled to find his own happiness in his own way? Who did his father think he was? Who did *she* think she was? His father had retreated into some kind of ethnic primitivism, and his mother—normally so quick to slap down the slightest evidence of social or cultural backsliding—was suddenly struck dumb.

How could they behave like this? This was 1998 Britain, for God's sake, not some 19th-century Polish *shtetl* or whichever benighted backwater his father's family had come from. And his father, of all people, who as Jack Wolfowicz had marched against Mosley's fascists in the East End in the forties, and leafletted against the National Front in Notting Hill in the fifties, and demonstrated against Enoch Powell in the sixties, and proclaimed his resistance against racial prejudice almost daily—his father refused to have his daughter-in-law's name mentioned, let alone her presence entertained in his house, because she happened not to have been born a Jew.

Even when Rosa had been born he had still refused to bend. Sylvia, though, couldn't resist it, and from time to time she'd turn up by herself. Did she tell him where she was going? Russell didn't know and he didn't care. She would coo over Rosa, and bring her silly toys made of garish plastic of which Alice disapproved, since Rosa's toy cupboard was stacked with improving jigsaws and tasteful wooden railway sets; or she'd buy her dolls, of which Alice disapproved even more. As for Russell, he would retreat to his study while she was there and was relieved when she left. Once or twice, Beverley came with her, but since she and Russell always ended up having a terrible row, she stopped coming.

It wasn't even as if religion actually mattered to his parents, he thought furiously, not in any real sense. True, neither Jack nor Sylvia was actually an unbeliever; they had an unthinking, superstitious assumption about some kind of mysterious primal force. "*Pfeuh pfeuh pfeuh*" went his mother as she threw salt over her shoulder.

But they were hostile to anyone who advertised a way of life they scorned as primitive and which, since it was one they associated with their own forbears, they feared would tarnish them by association. They both had a horror of the *frummers*, rolling their eyes whenever they saw the ultra-orthodox in their sidecurls and long gabardines.

"Just look at that!" said Sylvia one day in horror at the spectacle of a young woman with a tired, pale face, attired in the usual uniform of drab, mid-calf skirt, long, shapeless anorak and a snood covering her hair, struggling with a push-chair and seven children under nine, all of whom wore spectacles and four of whom were staggering along with shopping bags suspended from stiffly extended little arms. "In the last century they're living!" said Jack in deep scorn. "And the men don't even work," sniffed Sylvia. "All they ever do is study while the women have to do everything."

Despite the socialism and the horror of backwardness and the contempt for actually believing what was written in the five books of Moses, an important part of Russell's childhood was spent accompanying his father to the synagogue on Saturday mornings for the Sabbath service. Jack, who was fluent in reading Hebrew even though he couldn't understand a word, read the prayers as his own father, who had taught him, had read them—very fast, always with the same tuneless melodies, with much swaying back and forth and absolutely no comprehension or wish to comprehend other than that this was how it had always been done and always would be done.

Russell had found the whole business immensely tedious and would sit kicking his heels against the seat and staring vacantly into space, despite his father's attempts to make him follow the service. "You want Hitler should have his victory after all?" he would hiss into Russell's ear.

Neither Sylvia nor Beverley generally accompanied them on these weekly excursions. From the moment they left the house until they returned for lunch, this was the one time when Jack had his son to himself. Because for once he was in charge, he would fuss over Russell's clothes: press his jacket himself, make sure he was wearing a clean shirt and that his socks were pulled up to his knees.

Tentatively—because all conversation was normally mediated through Sylvia—he would ask Russell, as they walked along, how his schoolwork was going and what books he was reading. Russell would launch into an animated exposition of set theory or a recitation of Latin third conjugation verbs. "You don't say!" Jack would whistle, beaming and shaking his head in awe at his son's accomplishments; Jack who had himself left school at thirteen. "All this he knows already!"

For his part, Russell would look at his father's tall, broad-shouldered figure in his fly-fronted navy blue overcoat and the bowler hat Sylvia insisted he wear to make him look like the accountants, opticians and GPs amongst whom he would be sitting, and swelled with happiness that, for this moment at least, he had a father of whom he could be proud.

It was Sylvia who had insisted that the family change its name from Wolfowitz to Wolfe. (The final "e" was an afterthought, but she thought it a masterstroke of social mobility). This was done when Russell was very small and Beverley wasn't yet born. Young as he had been, Russell remembered hearing raised voices one night when he was in bed. He heard his father only indistinctly down the hall, but recognized the unmistakable note of cowed inarticulacy in the face of one of Sylvia's important and unanswerable points. Then his mother's voice, in the exasperated and weary tone she used whenever one of her important and unanswerable points was meeting incomprehensible resistance:

"You want he should go through life with this round his neck, like you?"

So Jack meekly surrendered his name, in the interests of English sensibilities and domestic harmony. Under the covers, Russell pulled his knees up to his chin, the position in which he could keep his fingers wedged in his ears to drown out the sound of his father's humiliation.

A young boy of about sixteen now appeared at Sylvia's side bearing a mug of tea and a plate with two shortbread fingers. He knelt beside her chair so that he could look into her eyes. With her head still bowed and unmoving, her eyes lifted fractionally towards him.

"Here you are, grandma," said the boy. "I've brought you some tea."

Gently and carefully, he lifted the mug to her mouth and she drank. Her eyes never left the boy's face.

Russell looked at him with interest. This must be Anthony, Beverley's youngest. He was very unlike his three elder brothers. They were all beefy and hearty, their voices loud with self-confidence, carrying themselves with a certain swagger even in this *shiva* house. Anthony was physically different, slight and slender with a shock of untamed dark curls. A certain pre-Raphaelite look, thought Russell.

With small, delicate actions Anthony gave Sylvia sips of tea. Putting down the mug, he broke off a small piece of shortbread and folded her fingers round it. Slowly, he lifted her hand to her mouth and slid the fragment through her parted lips. With infinite care he removed her spectacles and shook his head.

"Don't know how you can see anything at all, grandma, when these are so dirty," he said cheerfully, as he dipped a napkin in a glass of water and wiped the spectacles clean.

"Big improvement," he said with satisfaction as he replaced them on her nose. And he lovingly caressed her hands.

Russell heaved himself to his feet, mumbling he had to stretch his legs. He stumbled for the door. The boy's tenderness had touched him deeply. What had gone through him like a knife was the dirt on his mother's spectacles. Had no one noticed it at the nursing home where she lived? Had no nurse, no doctor, no carer observed that Sylvia's vision was clouded by a layer of grime? That meant no one was looking after her. Was she even being badly treated? No one knew because she couldn't tell them. As the shadows deepened around her, his mother was absolutely alone.

He emerged from the bathroom with reddened eyes and the start of a throbbing head to find himself face to face with the elderly man from the synagogue. He was still wearing the same trilby hat. Russell stared at him. The man put out his hand.

"I come to wish you long life," he said. "You and your family. May you know no more sorrow."

"Thank you," said Russell, stiffly.

They were standing alone in the hall. There was a curious tension around the man, an unease. He stood there staring at Russell. Once again, Russell wondered whether he was quite right in the head. He certainly didn't want to engage him in conversation. He made as if to go back into the room but the man put his hand on Russell's arm.

He put his head closer to Russell as if conspiratorially. There was garlic on his breath and a whiff of something more sour and decaying. "I want to show you something that will interest you wery much," he whispered. "I show it to nobody else. You clever man. Only you I trust."

He put his hand inside his jacket and pulled out a photograph from the inside pocket. It showed what appeared to be the frontispiece of a book, written in Hebrew. It had clearly been taken by an amateur since the page was at an angle.

"So what you think?"

Now it was Russell's turn to stare at him. "Think about what?"

The man jabbed at the photograph with a stubby finger. "These wery special vords. Holy vords."

Russell looked again, baffled. "Well, many Hebrew words are holy words." What was he getting at?

"You know Hebrew. So read here. This wery special book."

This was getting tiresome. He squinted at the photograph again. The frontispiece featured three Hebrew words and a number, 4940. He tried to decipher the words. For some reason, his brain wouldn't register them. Laboriously, he spelt out the Hebrew letter by letter, like a small child: *le-se-te-oo-air; de-le-ah-chem; de-ah-bo-ra-k.*

It sounded familiar, but at the same time strange. Russell couldn't quite place it.

"Wery, wery old. Must be wery waluable, no?"

He had his face very near Russell's own and kept jabbing at the photograph.

He looked at it again. Once more the words meant nothing to him as he spoke them out loud.

The man suddenly looked sly. "Now I tell you big secret," he said. The tip of his tongue kept flicking out from between his lips. "This is precious document, has been in my family for generations. Handed down from father to son; kept hidden through pogroms, through Holocaust. And now I am guardian. To me is duty to look after it."

"Woah, just a minute," said Russell. "This is some, ah, very old manuscript? That you have in your house? An original?"

"Exactly, mister director."

"Which no one has ever seen?"

"No one. I keep it wery safe, oh yes."

Russell digested this for a minute. Just how likely was it that such a man, coming out of the ghetto in Poland or wherever, would possess a genuine ancient manuscript? But on the other hand, Jewish families did sometimes possess treasures that had somehow survived centuries of flight and persecution.

"Uh...so why tell me about it? Why don't you take it to, I dunno, a medievalist, or the British Museum or something, an expert who can really tell you what the book is about?"

The man carefully put the photograph back inside his jacket pocket. "All these years I look at it and vonder vot is. My vife said it vos cursed, always brought misery, it vos trash. She wanted me to throw it in fire. But I knew it vos important. This book, it went through many fires. The vords I didn't understand. But I said to myself if it vos hidden so well all these centuries, something in it vorth hiding. You know vot I'm saying?" The pink tongue flicked out again. "If I take it to authorities they may take it away from me."

"Why'd they do that? It belongs to you."

The man shook his head. "I not trust authorities. Never they are keeping their vord. Always they have robbed me. Believe me, I know what I'm talking abaht. Everything I lost. Everything."

His voice rose, and his face reddened. "Please don't upset yourself," Russell said hastily. The last thing he wanted at this moment was a scene from this old man.

He took out a handkerchief and wiped his face. "You I trust. You are clever man. You understand old vords. You are not rip-off merchant, make quick buck. Now I come to point. I am now old man. I would like to know, before I die, vot is in this manuscript I have kept safe all these years. I vont to know what it says. I vont to know secret. You help me?"

Russell's first instinct was to walk away. How likely was this? It would almost certainly turn out to be a worthless old book, just as the wife had said. He had encountered this type before—Holocaust survivors who unfortunately had long ago lost all sense of proportion in the never-ending nightmare of their memory.

On the other hand, if this man was telling the truth, if he really did possess an undiscovered medieval manuscript—well, might that not make for a truly original piece of television that program controllers would die for? An unworthy thought; but once conjured up, it sat in his brain and refused to budge.

He remembered how his father had refused to trust anyone, how that had shut off any opportunities he may have had, even his ability to live his daily life free of fear. Yes, the similarity with his father was striking.

What would it cost him, after all, just to take a look?

"Of course I'll help," he heard himself say, as if from afar. "If I can."

What on earth was he getting into here? More to the point, how would he get out of it? He wanted to get involved with a Holocaust survivor like he wanted a hole in the head. But one visit surely wouldn't be too onerous. One visit, just to see what this was all about. If it was, as he fully expected, a book of no value at all he would just walk away. At least this fellow might then get some peace of mind.

Now the old man gripped him by both arms. His grip was surprisingly strong.

"I vont you to make solemn promise, that you tell no one abaht this. No one."

"I understand."

He gave Russell his hand. It was clammy to the touch. Russell recoiled.

"It vos *beshert* that I should meet you. I am Kuchinsky, by the way. You can call me Joe."

4

WHEN RUSSELL TURNED up at Kuchinsky's house—somehow Russell could never bring himself to call him Joe—his resolve nearly failed. It was an anonymous-looking semi-detached with bay windows in Cockfosters.

Did anyone actually live in Cockfosters? It was just the blob on the far end of the Piccadilly line at the top of the Tube map. Russell always imagined anyone who did live there was just about to fall off the edge of London, and therefore civilized life, altogether.

This feeling got stronger as Russell had to hike a tedious distance from the station to get to the house, down one long, featureless road after another with identical 1930s housing and a total deficit of originality, imagination or charm. All the roads looked the same. Russell got lost twice, but there wasn't a soul around to ask the way. Ah, suburbia. How could any fully functioning human being live here, so far from any signs of life? Not so much as a newsagent in sight, let alone a coffee shop.

By the time Russell finally got to the house he was depressed and irritated, a mood that only deepened when he noted both the shabbiness of the exterior and the fact that the bell didn't work. He knew he had been spotted because a grimy net curtain had twitched in the bay window as he pushed open the broken front gate. Kuchinsky had clearly been watching out for him, a fact that made him nervous; he didn't like being watched.

Anyway, Kuchinsky seemed pleased enough to see him when he opened the front door—a little too hearty for his taste, frankly, from the way he clapped him on the back. "I am honored that you should come in my house, mister director," he said, smiling broadly. He ushered him into the front room. There was a sickly smell of air freshener. "You must excuse," he said, gesturing around him with a slight shrug. "I am modest man. I do not have fine house, big car, expensive this and that. I am ordinary, vorking man. Not intellectual like yourself."

"'It's fine," Russell said in his most sensitive tone, his toes immediately curling inside his desert boots. "Very cozy."

He sat down gingerly on the small sofa, which was covered in brown uncut moquette. There was a hole in the fabric and the stuffing was poking out. Kuchinsky grabbed a cushion and covered the offending spot.

"Please forgive...senior citizens don't have it easy, know vot I mean? This neighborhood..." He waved at the window. "Not ideal, not ideal at all. Wery mixed, wery mixed. Lot of children running up and down street all day, shouting. Always on skateboard. Vot happened to parents these days?"

"Nowhere for the kids to play. All the playgrounds have gone because of government cutbacks."

"Government? Vot government? Children need discipline. Six of the best. Is nice phrase. Very polite, like English pipple. My father, he had strap, like this..." He pointed to his leather belt. "I got them often, six of the best. I tell you, after that you didn't want to do it again. Now they just got everything they vont. Computer. TV in room. iPad. iPhone. And bad vords they use, very bad vords all the time. I am ashamed for myself to listen. My English not so good but these vords I know. So who can be surprised when they knock you down and rob you?"

"You've been robbed?"

"Thank God, not yet."

Typical, Russell thought. Another one just parroting what he had read in the tabloids.

"Me, I don't cause no trouble. Joe keeps head down. Joe says nothing. Joe don't trouble neighbors and they don't trouble Joe. I say hello over fence, and they say hello back. That's all. English way. Joe like that. Joe like English garden. You have big garden in your house?"

"Actually, I live in a flat."

"Not house with garden? But you bigshot TV director. Sure you have big house."

"Look, I'm hardly Steven Spielberg."

Kuchinsky looked blank.

"I produce TV shows, that's all. I'm afraid I live from one commission to another."

He looked astonished. "But you clever man. You important person. You know important pipple, celebrities, politicians. Me, I poor man, uneducated. You have family, children in this flat?"

"One daughter. But she doesn't live with me any more. Actually, she hasn't lived with me for years. I'm divorced."

He nodded slowly. "And your daughter, she is close to you?"

"Afraid not."

"Aiee aiee aiee, such *tsores* we have." He rocked back and forth on a wooden armchair. "You speak *mammaloshen*?"

"A few words."

Of course Russell didn't speak Yiddish. Not even his father had spoken Yiddish. It was his grandmother's tongue, the language of illiteracy and dispossession, and the sooner forgotten the better.

"I have garden with fruit trees, roses, everything," said Kuchinsky. "Now I show you garden and then we have tea."

Russell followed him as he shuffled down the hall. It was dark and narrow. It also smelled and not of air freshener. Russell happened to be sensitive to smells. There was a sweetish, cloying smell in his father's flat in the last days of his life. For a while, Russell couldn't place it, even as it turned his stomach. He had thought it was something the district nurse was using on him, some cream or lotion. But then he realized the smell was coming from inside his father himself. It was his body already beginning to rot.

This was a faint odor of damp carpets and mold. A whiff of neglect. Russell wondered about Kuchinsky. He clearly wasn't poor; too smartly dressed, too well-fed. But a certain slovenliness in the housekeeping department; yes, there was definitely an element of that. Russell put it down to the effects of age. He felt sorry for him.

The garden was long and narrow. It wasn't much—just a small strip of grass. But here someone had taken a degree of trouble. In these dreary streets, he thought with a rush of sympathy which surprised himself, a dream of Arcadia. The flower beds were free of weeds and stocked heavily with rose bushes, which had been neatly pruned. Clumps of azaleas flanked a small pergola laden with honeysuckle. There were banks of lupins and hollyhocks. There was a tiny pond with a rock garden, and a couple of hideous gnomes. And along the fence, apple and pear trees were trained in the espalier style, linking arms as they sidestepped neatly down the flower beds.

"So who's the gardener round here?"

Kuchinsky gripped his arm. That steel clamp again. "They say Englishman's home is castle, yes? Well this is real McCoy. My little bit of paradise. Every day I come out here to see to plants."

It turned out that, before he retired, he had owned a dry cleaner's.

"My parents also had a little store. They sold household goods. We lived above the shop."

"You lived there? You didn't have house, garden? All English have house!'"

Russell thought of the little flat where they'd lived cooped up, falling over each other. A rented flat, because his father never had any sense about money or property. He wouldn't entertain the idea of a mortgage because he didn't like getting into debt. And anyway, he never had enough capital for a deposit. So while other boys climbed trees in their gardens, swung in hammocks or kicked a ball around the lawn, Russell played in the shop in the large cardboard boxes that housed the regular deliveries. He would climb in and pull the flaps closed over his head, and then listen to his mother shouting for him, or Beverley whining, and feel safe.

Anyway, he never liked houses. Too bloody bourgeois. And you have to talk to the neighbors over the fence. No, give him the anonymity of flat-dwelling any day. The idea of being neatly stacked, with other tenants above and below you, made him feel as safe as when his mother used to tuck him up in bed so tightly Russell could barely move his arms.

"Things were tough in those days. The business didn't make much money." Nor did his father's taxi-driving.

"For sure, is hard running business. Long hours, vork fingers to bone."

"Still, people always need their clothes cleaned." Russell absently fingered a leaf. How much longer was he going to have to put up with this?

"I didn't do so bad. My shop wery high class. Hanower Square. Lot of important pipple my customers. Pipple from embassies, tings like that. Sometimes they send chauffeurs to collect clothes. I go out myself to hang them up in back of Daimler, Jag. I know how to handle fabrics, when to fold, when not to fold. Their most delicate silks they would send me; animal skins, suede, leather. To me they trusted these precious tings. This attention to detail, it no longer happens. Standards now, ach! And you, you also come from pipple in trade. You know vot it's like to watch pennies. You not one of these blessed snobs with silver spoon in mouth. But you now TV director."

"Producer, actually."

Different, goddammit.

"I was lucky. I went to a good school."

"Ah, English education system, best in vorld."

Russell was finding all this English ra-ra tiresome. There was a certain type of British Jews of a certain age who never stopped touching their forelocks at Britain. They were so grateful to have been granted admission, so starstruck by fabled British characteristics like cricket, bus queues and stiff upper lips they never stopped behaving like foreigners frozen in time somewhere around 1957.

The way Kuchinsky himself was dressed! Grey flannel trousers, a red paisley cravat tucked into his white shirt collar and a double-breasted blazer, all in immaculate condition. Savile Row out of the Łódź ghetto.

He was stooping down, filleting the odd leaf or tiny weed from the soil. Russell watched him sieving the earth through his fingers. For some reason, such absorption in his plants and attention to detail touched him. Truth to tell, he had always been fascinated by people who could actually make things grow. No sooner did he stick a geranium in a pot than it folded up its petals and died. The fact that Kuchinsky had an affinity with the natural world made him warm to him a little. It showed that he may have been a prize bore out of synagogue central casting, but at least he had a green soul.

A certain camaraderie settled between them. Russell thought he could have been one of his uncles, pottering about. He knew where he was with this man. He knew the type.

"Look what I grow: beans, tomatoes, cabbage. And these fruit trees—you like how I train them?" His thick hands tenderly cradled the blossoming branches. "See buds that will be fruit, growing again every year, no problem. No matter what happens, it all comes up again. Regular. Nothing can stop it. It was here before us and will be here after us. That gives me comfort. It reminds me of home."

"Home?"

"I was brought up on farm. In Poland."

"My grandmother too." Really, the similarities were striking.

But now his face had suddenly closed up. Something seemed to have snapped shut. Russell realized he had strayed into sensitive territory. An entire way of life had simply been obliterated in Poland in the Final Solution. For those few who survived, the past was often now a forbidden country. Not that Russell personally had any wish to visit it; he had had enough of hysterical survivors to last a lifetime.

"We go in now and have tea."

Back in the front room, Russell looked at his watch. When was he actually going to get to the point of his visit? Kuchinsky seemed to have forgotten all about it.

Russell found he was shivering. The room was dark and quite cold, despite the sunny spring weather. In the street outside, the cherry blossom trees foamed pink. But the room was gloomy and dull. The furniture was heavy and old-fashioned. The faded, threadbare carpet had a large floral design marching across it in regular lines. A large television set stood in the corner on a stand. A gas fire was set into a surround of greenish tiles, some of which were cracked. Roses and clematis clambered across the wallpaper, which was brown and stained in places, and on which hung two prints in cheap but ornate frames: the Tretchikoff of the woman with the green face, and Constable's Hay Wain. There were some ornaments on the mantelpiece, but no photographs at all.

In the street, a car went by with its radio blaring. Russell fancied he heard raised voices from within the house, but when the car had gone all was quiet, and he decided he must have imagined it.

Russell prowled round the room, staring at the hideous Tretchikoff and the equally hideous china figurines and plastic flowers on the mantelpiece. The contrast between the care bestowed on the garden and the dreary, worn interior was striking. Russell paused before a large, walnut cabinet with glass panels. Inside was a collection of silver objects. Russell looked more closely. There was a pair of tall candlesticks, quite ornate. There was a set of wine goblets, and what looked like a Passover plate. There was a tall, conical-shaped object hung with silver bells and flags, which Russell recognized as a container for the spices which are handed round in the ritual ceremony marking the end of the Sabbath. And there was something Russell had never seen before: a kind of silver upright panel from which protruded a row of narrow scoops.

"You vont to see these as well?"

Kuchinsky's voice behind him made him jump. Russell hadn't heard him come in. He was carrying a large cardboard box, which he put down on a chair. His voice was a bit sharp, Russell thought.

"They look like fine pieces."

"These all wery precious. To me, you understand? Precious to me. Many memories. Some sad, some happy."

Anyone would think Russell was sizing up the stuff in order to steal it. Kuchinsky laboriously unlocked the cabinet with a key attached to his belt. He was wheezing slightly. He took out one goblet, then another. They were thickly encrusted with bunches of grapes, leaves and flowers, all picked out in relief.

"This craftsmanship, you never see now." He turned one over admiringly in his large hand.

"What's that?"

He took out the upright panel, and Russell realized that the scoops were receptacles for burning wicks in oil. It was a Hanukkah menorah, in a style Russell had never previously seen. At home, they'd just had a standard eight-branched candlestick in tarnished silver, which had been stuck in a cupboard and then dutifully brought out every year when they had all tunelessly and self-consciously sung songs round it in a cursory fashion.

But Russell had never seen one as beautiful and ornate as this. Behind the scoops were arranged tiny silver tableaux of flamingos and palm trees, monkeys and parrots, while on the upright panel supporting them were carved elaborate crowns, trumpets, flowers and rampant lions of Judah. What must it have taken, Russell wondered, to make just one of these sumptuous objects, to hammer the silver into these delicate figures and shapes? For what these objects spoke of was love, a passionate feeling poured into every grape and branch and feather of these molds, an emotion felt for a people and a faith which had been passed down through generations of silent witnesses in a faraway country—an emotion which Russell had never known.

He thought back to the rituals enacted in his own family. For them, there had been no objects of beauty crafted with love. What had been used had been as anonymous and perfunctory as the family's observance itself. And yet these fabulous pieces spoke of a spiritual life of richness and depth that had once been lived on an impoverished Polish farm.

Of course Russell wasn't jealous, or anything like that. Religion was bunk. He was just interested.

"And these objects weren't just for show, but they were really used in your family all the time?"

Kuchinsky fingered the menorah. He seemed to be far away.

"At night during Hanukkah in our village, every Jewish house had one of these flickering in vindow. Through it, you would see faces in candlelight, and as you walked home there would be faint sound of chanting from house to house to house. No street lights, just black sky full of stars and these vindows glowing. As I walked down street, I thought I heard angels singing. Those were magical times."

He faltered, and swallowed hard. "These sacred treasure. If they could speak...they have witnessed too much terror, too much sorrow."

To Russell's horror, Kuchinsky's face crumpled and he let out a gasping sob. At almost the same instant, the door opened and a woman came in carrying a tray set with a teapot and cups. For a moment, she was framed in the doorway as she paused fractionally to take in the scene: Kuchinsky holding the menorah in one hand and shielding his eyes with the other as he wept, while Russell was rooted to the spot in a rigor of embarrassment, clutching the Passover plate.

A look of intense irritation crossed her face, and she set the tray down so hard the cups tinkled in the saucers. She was a small woman, thin and wiry, with a sharp nose and chin and untidy brown hair. She took the plate from him and put it back in the cupboard, without even looking at him. She detached the menorah from Kuchinsky's hands, stored it and the goblets in the cupboard and locked it carefully, feeling for the key on his belt. Then she led him to the sofa and sat him down while she remained standing.

"You promised you wouldn't do that," she said coldly. "You mustn't upset yourself. You know what the doctor said."

Kuchinsky didn't move, but sat slumped on the sofa.

"I've made you your tea, like you asked," she said. She had the faint trace of an Irish accent. There was a pause.

"That's very kind. Thank you," Russell said, to break the silence. "I'm very sorry if I...I had no idea..."

This time there was no getting away from it. She was deliberately ignoring him.

"So I'm away to the hairdresser," she said to Kuchinsky. "I'll be back in an hour. You'll be okay now."

It was not a question, but a statement. She was dressed drably: brown trousers and a shapeless grey cardigan over a black jumper. She seemed on edge and yet at the same time reluctant to go. She stood staring at him. Eventually, she clicked her tongue in annoyance and abruptly left the room. The front door banged.

Russell poured the tea. The cups had fussy little handles that you couldn't get your fingers through. Eventually Kuchinsky roused himself.

"My vife, she doesn't understand." He shook his head. "No one who vosn't there can understand. No one."

"I understand. That we can't understand, I mean," said Russell hastily. "You met here in London?"

"She vos my presser." He made an ironing motion with his arm. "She vos lonely. I vos lonely. So ve got married."

In the silence, Russell heard a clock ticking. Kuchinsky's unhappiness hung like a pall between them.

"I don't think my ex and I ever understood each other. But then, she wasn't Jewish and that does make things more complicated."

Russell couldn't believe what he had just said. Of course it wasn't true at all. The fact that Alice wasn't Jewish had had nothing to do with it. They were just incompatible. No, they became incompatible. No again—she made herself incompatible with him. So why had he said such a thing? The words had floated into his brain and then onto his tongue like a bubble and before he could stop them had popped into the air.

Clearly, he had only uttered them because he was so embarrassed that he had managed to revive such unbearable memories for this poor old soul, for whom thinking about his family's religious heirlooms had not surprisingly revived the agony of the carnage in Poland. He had instinctively blurted out something to indicate his solidarity and sympathy with him, to show that he was not alone and that Russell knew from personal experience what it was like to go through life with a soul mate who wasn't a Jew. Because Russell was pretty sure, having seen his wife, that she wasn't.

On second thoughts, however, maybe it wasn't so tactful considering he and Alice had actually got divorced. Maybe he had merely made things even worse.

Anxiously, he eyed Kuchinsky over the teapot. To his relief, he appeared untroubled by what Russell had just said and did not betray by so much as a flicker of the eyes that Russell had indeed rightly assessed the ethnic composition of the Kuchinsky marital ménage. Clearly, this was an area of his life that, for the time being at least, was to remain off limits.

Kuchinsky pushed his cup away, wiped his hands on his immaculate white handkerchief, shot his cuffs and drew the cardboard box to him. "Now you see what you come to see," he said. "Now you see jewel in crown."

He opened the box and withdrew something wrapped in a grubby blanket. He peeled off the blanket to reveal an object wrapped in a piece of deep blue velvet, embroidered round the edge with silver flowers and leaves. It looked like the kind of fabric often used to clothe the Torah scrolls in synagogues.

Carefully, he unwrapped the velvet to reveal a book. It was about as tall as a modern hardback, but a bit wider. Russell picked it up gingerly. Its front and back covers were made of wood, and the pages between them had been sewn onto bands running horizontally across where the spine would normally be. The whole effect reminded him, incongruously, of the ice-cream bricks between two wafers he used to consume as a child.

Russell opened the cover. The pages were hard and crackly, brown and discolored in places. Every page was covered on both sides, in two columns, with regular black rows of script. The pages had been neatly ruled in brown ink, with margins down the sides. Every so often, words were crossed out and another, different hand had written above them. Some of the pages seemed to have tears that had been sewn up; others had small holes with stitch marks round the edges.

The writing was for some reason difficult to read. In front of the book was what seemed to be an inscription, the words Kuchinsky had photographed, with that number, 4940.

Russell sounded out the Hebrew letters again. *Li-se-te-oo-air; de-le-a-chem; de-ah-bo-ra-k.* Part of the second word looked familiar. The letters were *dalet, aleph, lammed, yod, samech.* Russell tried the previous word, *listooar. Lammed, shin, taf, vav, aleph, raysh.* Russell spoke it aloud. *Listooar.*

It almost sounded French, he thought. Wait a minute, though—*listooar deliachim.* He spoke it to himself several times. Supposing it *was* French—but in Hebrew characters? *L'histoire d'Eliachim.* The story of Eliachim. The next word was *de-ah-bo-ra-k.* If the first Hebrew letter *dalet* actually stood for the French *de,* it would be "the story of Eliachim of Aborak"—whatever that was. Could that be it? That would explain why it was so difficult to read. And if so, well then could 4940 be the Hebrew year? What was the Hebrew year now, for heaven's sake? He had noticed it on the front page of Beverley's *Jewish Chronicle.* It was 577 something or other. He did a rough calculation. That would make 4940 somewhere around the 12th century AD.

Could this really be a French manuscript of some kind written in Hebrew characters by some medieval character called Eliachim of Aborak?

Kuchinsky was watching him closely. His tongue flickered out from between his teeth. "You never seen book like this before, mister director. This one in million. You think it priceless?"

He leered greedily.

Russell was stunned. Okay, he had been curious to know just what he'd got, but Russell didn't really think he actually possessed a valuable antiquity. Of course, the thing could still turn out to be totally worthless, a piece of junk, a forgery, a fake. But as Russell turned it over in his hands, and looked through the pages again, and then picked up the blue velvet cloth and examined that, and then looked through the parchment pages again, he was suddenly possessed of a deep certainty that he was holding something unique and extraordinary. Was it really possible that this man Kuchinsky was sitting on a priceless relic of Jewish history? Stranger things had been known. But what was it? Russell had to find out.

"How did you come by this?"

"It was hidden good."

He stamped his foot on the floor.

"Under the floorboards?"

He nodded. "Kept secret in family for generations. Survived centuries of persecution, pogroms, killings. Somehow it vos kept safe, thank God. All those years he vos looking after it. Is holy book, yes?"

"Well no, I don't think it's religious. Could be some kind of journal, or history.'"

"Not holy book? But must be wery wery special, to surwive such terrible things—God himself protected it. So must be wery important book, sacred."

"It looks like this might have been written by someone called Eliachim of Aborak. Was this one of your ancestors, perhaps?" What Russell didn't understand was how a book written by some medieval French Jew could have ended up on a farm in pre-war Poland.

Kuchinsky shrugged. "Who knew? All ve knew vos surwiving. No one knew vot vos in book."

"But there must have been someone in your family who knew something about it, how it had got there. I mean, they knew it was valuable enough to hide, to pass on from generation to generation in who knows what conditions..."

Kuchinsky brought his hand down hard on the coffee table.

"Enough with these questions! I did not inwite you to my house to ask all these things abaht family!" He snatched the book from him and, with his hands trembling, wrapped it again in the blue cloth and then in the blanket.

"You don't believe? You think I don't say truth? Is enough the book is here. If you are interested, that's good. If not interested, you go away."

As soon as he took it from him, Russell had an overwhelming desire to look at it again. He found that he was intensely curious and, to his slight embarrassment, more than a little excited. He had to find out whether this was the genuine article or not. He hadn't come all this way, given up his afternoon and endured the maunderings of a dry cleaner with an obsession in a hideous suburban semi in order to depart with the question unresolved of whether he did or did not have in his possession a manuscript of historical significance.

"I'm very sorry," Russell said humbly. "Of course I believe you. Of course I do. I wasn't trying to pry. I know how difficult this must be for you."

"This vos period of life I never talk about. Ever." The look on his face suddenly made Russell's blood run cold. For a brief moment, Kuchinsky's eyes registered a hardness, a blankness, that Russell had not seen before.

"Of course I understand." Russell was anxious not to upset him again. He did understand that what Kuchinsky had been through was beyond anything that could be grasped; that he had stood at the very heart of the European darkness, had experienced the most inhuman extremities of behavior with which survivors could only cope by blanking them out of their minds altogether.

"May I see the book again?"

Kuchinsky was hugging it to his chest inside its blanket.

"You translate it now?"

"Well not now, you must understand, these things take time, a lot of time; it's not an easy job, even for me..."

Even. How easy it was to slip into the wishful thinking that someone else creates. Russell had no qualifications whatever to decipher such a document. Ok, so he had done French and German as his first degree, but medieval texts like this were above his pay grade. All he could bring to this was a certain linguistic skill and his native intelligence. A small voice inside him warned that he was getting into something that was way over his head. Was this really something that he could in all honesty undertake?

Kuchinsky unwrapped the book again and gave it to him. Russell turned it over and over, looked through the pages again. It looked real enough, had the smell and feel of the genuine article. But who was to know? Not him, that was for sure.

"You need to get this looked at by someone who can verify it as authentic. Tell us exactly when it was written. Date the parchment, the script, that kind of thing."

"This is real ancient book! Kuchinsky tell you truth!"

"Yes, yes, I'm sure you are, but the trouble is no one else might believe you and if you want people to read this, if it's going to be published..."

Russell was obviously running way ahead of Kuchinsky. "Not published! No one to see this book! No one come here to see it! No experts, no dating of any parchment, nothing, nothing!"

He was wheezing more heavily now, and beads of sweat stood out on his forehead. Russell was perplexed.

"Look, if you don't want it published why do you want me to translate it at all?"

Kuchinsky took from his breast pocket a paisley handkerchief and wiped his face.

"I am 93 years old," he said. "All my life I want to know what this book said. In every generation people risked their lives to hide it. So Kuchinsky say to himself, must be for reason. Its pages must be blessed by Almighty himself to keep it safe. So I ask, vot are these vords here that have power to cheat death itself? I would like to know this before I die, to answer qvestion. I vont you to give me answer. Only me. You must promise—no experts, no publishing, no TV, no one must see it. It must not leave this house. This you must promise."

Not take it out of the house! That would mean Russell couldn't take it to a library but would have to decipher it by bringing in dictionaries, grammars and what have you. And at the end of the whole process he would have to walk away from it without finding out precisely what this manuscript was and whether or not it was valuable. Of course it was valuable; he knew it in his bones. And he had to confess that this was an important factor to him. To stumble across a historical find like this, a possibly priceless contribution to scholarship that might unlock knowledge of an obscure period in history.

And what might follow from that, for him? For sure, it would transform his life, his reputation, his career. He would stop being a run-of-the-mill television producer and would move into a different league altogether.

No longer would he be merely a vessel for the ideas of others. He would himself become an opener-up of worlds. He would become a Columbus of scholarship. He would create something unique. No more derivative trawling through the ramblings of pretentious intellectuals. No more scrabbling for advantage amongst shallow TV production companies. He would turn into an original, just like the manuscript itself. He would bask in its reflected glory.

A happy daydream engulfed him. He would make a prestige show for the BBC, bypassing altogether its byzantine labyrinth of supercilious commissioning editors and program controllers to get a personal stamp of approval from the Director-General himself. On the back of that he would publish the manuscript, jetting from one prestigious international conference to another to discuss its meaning and significance.

Of course, the problem of Kuchinsky's refusal even to entertain the thought of publication would have to be overcome. But having thought himself into this happy frame of mind Russell was quietly confident that, when it came to it, Kuchinsky would offer no objection. He was agitated now because he didn't know whether Russell could be trusted. Hardly surprising, after all, given the way this book had been hidden for so long. But once they had worked together for a while and he came to have confidence in him it would be a different story altogether.

There remained the question of whether Russell could actually do the translation. It would be tricky, no doubt about that, particularly with the restrictions Kuchinsky was imposing. But with a bit of boning up and the purchase of some decent medieval lexicons, Russell should be able to cope. The image in his mind of the finished translation, artfully packaged inside an exquisitely illustrated jacket and on prominent display in the front window of a discerning bookshop to the admiration of one and all, overcame any qualms he felt about his ability.

Inside him a small voice said, Wait! *Wait!* What if this is a fake? How would you find this out? You could end up like that history don who made a complete idiot of himself over the so-called Hitler diaries.

Russell told this voice to pack it in. As he worked on the translation, he would surely be able to sniff out any telltale inconsistencies; and he could always take discreet soundings about what it was that he was working on. No doubt he could eventually persuade Kuchinsky to let him take the book to someone for them to look at. If he came with him, what objections could he possibly have, once he had come to know Russell and trust him?

Anyway, Russell was fed up with being predictable. Time to branch out, to live a bit dangerously.

He felt a buzz of energy of a kind he hadn't known for years.

When can I make a start?" he said.

5

AS SOON AS Russell got back home, he sat down at his computer and Googled Aborak. If it was indeed a place, the net would surely tell him where it was. He was so fired up by what he had seen that he didn't even notice that his iPhone was registering four missed calls.

In response to Aborak, up came a series of Google references to pesticides, Italian psychoanalysis, comic books and stuff in Czech and Cyrillic. No joy there. He tapped in instead "Aborak place name" and hit the bullseye.

Up popped a genealogical site that revealed that Eborak had founded the city of York. He Googled York, and discovered that the Romans had named it Eboracum and that medieval Jews had transliterated this into Hebrew as Eborak. York! His hunch had been correct. Kuchinsky's manuscript had been written by someone called Eliachim of York. He wasn't French at all. He was a medieval English Jew.

Of course! In medieval times, English people had used French interchangeably with English. Jews would not have used Hebrew, the sacred language of the Torah, for everyday use—but they would have used Hebrew letters to transliterate the language of everyday, which happened to be French. That was why the words were written in Hebrew letters but didn't look like Hebrew words; that was why Kuchinsky didn't even have any idea what this book was, let alone understand what was in it.

Russell sat back in his chair and tried to contain his excitement. If it was indeed a medieval English Hebrew manuscript, some kind of medieval Jewish traveler's tale perhaps, it must be extremely rare. Medieval manuscripts by European Jews were themselves few and far between, but how many secular accounts by medieval English Jews had ever seen the light of day? He couldn't think of any. Had he stumbled upon a priceless treasure?

But along with this excitement came a redoubled feeling of dread. Suppose it was a fake, a forgery? Suppose Kuchinsky was either a fraudster or—more likely—he genuinely believed he possessed a rare manuscript but had himself been duped; or even that his family had been duped generations back? And how could Russell be certain one way or another? After all, translating Hebrew was bad enough. But translating a transliteration, deciphering a bastardized form of old French written in Hebrew characters—the more he thought about it, that was a challenge he doubted that he could meet.

But if he could do it, and if it was genuine...then, the prize! The prize!

He couldn't sit still. He needed a drink. He got up to fetch a beer from the fridge, and it was only then that he noticed the missed calls. He played back his messages.

"Hey Dad," said Rosa's plaintive voice, "I, like, needed to ask you something but, er, as you aren't there s'pose it doesn't matter?"

If it didn't matter, he thought, why did she ring in the first place? And why was there always that hint of accusation in her voice (along with that idiotic upwards inflection)? After what had happened, didn't she know that a call like that was bound to ring an alarm bell or two? Why were the young so... immature?

The second call was from Kim, the secretary at Pollyanna Productions, letting him kindly know that his interesting idea for a documentary called *Whither Turkey?* was thought to be too derivative, but there might be an opening soon on a Channel Four show about suicidal vets which was coming down the pipe and they'd be back in touch.

He played the message again to check she hadn't said suicide vests.

The third message was from his last girlfriend, Helena. She'd lost an earring which had some sentimental value. Had he by any chance come across it buried down the side of a chair perhaps? A description of the earring then followed.

He'd had some hopes of Helena. She'd seemed a bit different from all the others who'd passed through his bed since Alice. They were usually rather drunken one-night stands; the following morning both he and they had discreetly reassessed and the girl had disappeared, sometimes with a cheery wave and sometimes, to his embarrassment and mortification, appearing a little scornful. Worse yet were the ones that suddenly looked at him with a certain compassion.

Helena had had a slightly ethereal quality that reminded him of Alice. She had moreover stayed for more than one night, indeed seemed quite enthusiastic about what he did with her; which made him feel for the first time since Alice that he hadn't completely lost it. But then one day she'd sighed and said he was a sweet guy but she wasn't ready for all these complications, packed her things and departed.

It was simply, he decided, so much easier to be alone.

The fourth message was from Michael Waxman.

He grabbed a Budweiser from the fridge, pushed a pile of papers and books off an armchair to join their fellows on the floor and flopped down into the leather cushions.

Waxman! He hadn't thought about him for years until his old life had started to reclaim him. They'd been at the same school where Russell had disliked him. Hadn't everyone?

Waxman had been an attention-seeker, an exhibitionist. Everywhere he went, whether in the classroom or the playground, he had to make himself the center of attention. He would insinuate himself into every conversation; his hand was always the first to go up in class. Not that he ever had anything very interesting to say; indeed, the sight of his upwardly springing fingers usually induced a sigh from whichever teacher it was.

Was that why no one liked him, Russell now wondered, or did he behave in that manner because no one liked him?

Either way, Waxman seemed to have no friends. Physically weedy and with a voice a high-pitched whine, he was conspicuous by his absence of sporting prowess. He was the boy no one wanted on their team. On the rugby pitch or cricket field, he seemed to lack any vestige of coordination, fumbling every ball; in the swimming pool, he would rapidly fall several laps behind.

"That boy will never make anything of himself," said Sylvia with what Russell thought was ill-disguised satisfaction. She didn't like Waxman's mother, who she thought gave herself airs and graces.

Waxman's mother certainly didn't do her only child any favors. She collected him personally from school every day even after he was in long trousers; he caused incredulity by bringing smoked salmon sandwiches to school for his lunch; when they went on a school outing to the Roman ruins at St. Albans and were allowed to wear their own clothes, 12-year-old Waxman caused widespread sniggering when he turned up in a waisted coat with a velvet collar and clutching an embroidered cushion to prevent him from having to sit on hard ground.

Inevitably, Waxman was picked on by the others. First it was insults; he was (inevitably) called waxwork, wankman; then pansy and poofter. Then his belongings started to be stolen. His homework books went missing, then a fountain pen; then his rather valuable watch.

Russell was on the fringes of the group that was picking on Waxman. Warily, he watched what was happening. He was uncomfortably aware of certain similarities. Russell also hated sport and was bad at it; he also found it difficult to make friends.

He had learned to get by, though, by making himself largely invisible. He wasn't too showy or too loud; he wasn't outstandingly brilliant at anything, nor was he a duffer, but he coasted along comfortably and unremarked somewhere around the lower middle of the top set. He also developed a dry wit through which he displayed a fashionably cynical view of the world, both of which afforded him a certain credibility. So the most powerful boys in the class let him tag along with them.

He wasn't going to jeopardize any of that by coming to Waxman's defense. When he happened upon the scene behind the bike shed where a couple of them were giving Waxman a good thumping, he shrank back into the shadows and hurried away. Not, though, before he heard one of the assailants say, as he kicked Waxman's prone body on the ground, "Take that, you filthy little kike."

He had put Waxman completely out of his mind. So when at the synagogue a thin, grey-haired man with a neat beard had stuck out his hand and said, "Long time no see," he had done a double take.

"Fancy meeting you here," said Waxman.

Even after all these years, Russell still felt a flush of guilt as he stared at him.

It turned out that Waxman was a regular at this synagogue. He had married, late in life it seemed, a woman who was divorced with three daughters. He had become a clinical psychologist, and worked for a firm of management consultants advising firms on motivational employment practices.

Now he had left a message to suggest they meet up for a proper chinwag. He had one or two ideas that might make great TV shows.

Meeting him again had plunged Russell into a morose mood. He had written Waxman off as a loser. Yet from the sound of it he had been rather successful; you certainly didn't end up working for a big management consultancy if you weren't regarded very highly. How had he managed it? Had he just bullshitted his way in, like he'd done at school?

Undoubtedly he would have a nice pension pot somewhere or other, an income for the rest of his life prudently squirreled away. Whereas Russell was reduced to scrabbling round for commissions, never knowing if the current show would be the last, always at the mercy of the media's fixation on the latest cultural fad. Waxman seemed to have managed to make something of his life. Why hadn't Russell?

His stare, from those piercing blue eyes, had been as intense as ever. Dogged, Russell thought. That's what Waxman had been above all else. Whatever was thrown at him, he just never gave up. That was what you needed to get on.

It was a character thing, wasn't it? It had very little to do with intellect. He himself had been clever enough, but never seemed to be able to settle down to much. "Butterfly mind," his mother had said, not fondly.

He knew he had disappointed them. They had wanted him to have a profession. All their friends had children who had become doctors, lawyers, lecturers. The idea that you had to get a professional qualification in order to move upwards in life—and no less important, to fit in—was hard-wired into those who, like his father, had left school without passing a single examination.

Russell had loathed such mindless conformism. He had regarded it as the product of narrow minds. He had resented feeling the pressure of such expectation. He would be a free soul, a poet, a romantic, a radical in life as well as in his politics.

But now he worked for a medium that, in its own way, was as conformist as any of those despised professions. It imposed its own form of drudgery, trapping him into accepting commissions for shows in which he either had no interest or which he actively despised. When all was said and done he still had to earn money to live; and he had to admit that he hadn't been very good at that at all.

Above all, though, he had wanted to do good in the world. "My son the dreamer," his father had said in disbelief, torn between love and impatience.

That's why he'd become a producer of TV documentaries. He wanted to harness the power of television to uncover what was being hidden from public view, to expose abuses of power, to help the vulnerable. When he'd started at the BBC, even his father was quite impressed; he regarded the iconic broadcaster, after all, as a secular Bible, the template of truth and the daily proof that Britain was the most civilized and safest place on earth in which to live.

But then everything had changed; investigative stuff was out, Russell's face didn't seem to fit any more and one day he found himself rationalized and downsized and outsourced as a freelance producer, a desperate supplicant at the door of the myriad production companies which mushroomed in the new competitive environment that was the digital marketplace.

And what good had he actually done, after all? Yes, he'd made a few documentaries of which he'd been proud, like the one about what life was really like on benefits (dreadful) or how the police treated black youths (worse). And the one on the drug companies had even been short-listed for a national television award. But none of them had changed a thing. Worse, by the following week virtually all had been forgotten. The ephemerality of television applied to those who worked for it, too. He had improved no one's life. Nothing he had done had left his imprint on anything.

Unlike Alice, of course. She was fighting all the time for real people, defending their human rights in court, saving them from injustice and worse. Now that was real achievement. How he had admired her. He couldn't really blame her for not feeling the same way about him.

His mother had wanted him to be a lawyer. He had raged against the very thought. Now he winced at the memory and wondered whether she had had a point after all. He'd probably always been too quick to dismiss what was valuable.

He thought about his parents. Sylvia and Jack had been married for more than fifty years. A great achievement. He knew now what it took to keep a marriage going. He hadn't managed more than nine years before Alice left him. He hadn't even been able to make a success of that.

The evening had closed in and he realized he was sitting virtually in the dark. He snapped on the light and blinked. He thought again about Eliachim of York. My Eliachim. He hugged his secret to himself. If this came good, he wouldn't have to worry anymore about such things. Tomorrow he'd make a start on discovering Eliachim's story. There was no time to lose.

6

EVEN BEFORE THEY arrived at the flat Beverley had started organizing.

"You'll need to bring bin bags for what you want to take. Make sure they're the thickest ones. Clothes to the charity shop, crockery ditto, furniture to the dump. I'll take the silver—presume not quite your style? And we'll divvy up the photographs between us. Assuming that is you want any of them at all, of course. But I want the wedding one."

It all seemed more than a little...well, cold.

Back when they were children she had bossed him around, even though he was the elder of the two. He thought their mother indulged her. When she did anything wrong it was he who invariably got the blame. That was because Beverley wasn't very good at anything. She had to be protected. He understood that. But he resented it a bit.

She fussed around, bustling from room to room with rolls of plastic sacks.

"At least I made sure it was all spotless. Of course I had to do it all myself. The girl was useless. Apparently beneath her dignity to get down on her knees and scrub the floor. Quite the little madam. And we had to pay through the nose for her. Social services was a dead loss, *quelle surprise*. Of course I went to the very best agency. I mean, you can't skimp on something like that, not when it's your own father and he's so completely helpless, poor old soul."

She dabbed at her eyes. Russell sat miserably on a plastic-covered stool in the kitchen as his sister pulled crockery savagely out of cupboards.

This was Beverley's place, her territory. Her existence was framed by the twin pillars of family and synagogue life, both of which she ran with volcanic energy. At home, she shopped, cooked, sewed tapestry, mended the puncture on the Volvo estate herself and supervised an endless stream of workmen performing home improvements while she snapped at the cleaning lady or au pair (pull the beds out to vacuum beneath them, please! Ironed tops folded inside out again!) in the same tone she used towards the children (homework, messy rooms, enough with the bongo drumming!) while making endless to-do lists for everyone on sticky-backed Post-Its which she stuck around the house.

At the synagogue she chaired the functions committee, served on the welfare committee and the new building committee, ran a course on "How to keep your kitchen kosher" for 12-year-old *bat mitzvah* girls on a Sunday morning and was the Brown Owl to the synagogue's brownie pack, in which capacity she periodically spent unlikely weekends under canvas, taking care not to interrupt her stream of to-do notes by remembering to tuck a waterproof pen inside her ample uniform.

So when their father died, there didn't seem to be any way Russell could question her assumption that he would attend the synagogue with her on that first Saturday after it happened to perform his duty as the son and say the *kaddish*, the prayer for the dead. He might as well have lain down in front of a steamroller as argue about it.

Of course, he had always known that regardless of all that had passed between them this was one duty he had to observe. Simple cowardice? Maybe. But if he was being honest, it wasn't just that either. It was rather that death, dammit, changed the rules of the game once again in a way he had never anticipated. He had thought he was free of all of it; and then he realized he was still hooked as securely as one of Rosa's nose rings.

Death is when it hits you: the primal attachment, the bond of connection, the thing you finally can't shake off because it's calling to you from somewhere deep in your gut. He had turned his back on him in life; he couldn't bring himself in his death to turn his back on what had bound both of them together. He came back like a wretched homing pigeon, cursing all the while.

And if he was really honest, it was more even than that. Because when he looked at his father in death, willing him despite everything that had happened between them to breathe again, not believing that he had finally gone because he was still there, lying in the bed large as life except of course he was dead, he just had one thought. "Is that it?" Was that really what it amounted to when all was said and done?

He was still recognizably his father; and yet he was not that thing at all. He was lying in the bed in his old blue Marks & Spencer pajamas, with his bushy eyebrows and his strangely long fingernails and the hairs curling in his ears and nostrils, all of which made him his father, and yet he wasn't there anymore. The room was overwhelmingly occupied by him in the bed; and yet it was empty of any human being.

Now Russell slipped tentatively into that bedroom again. He looked at the bed stripped down to the mattress, and he shivered in loneliness. He looked round the room, and he saw that nothing had changed and that everything had changed.

It still had the same furniture, even the same carpets and curtains that he remembered from his boyhood: the same bedside photographs of Russell and Beverley on his mother's side of the bed; the same pink ruched lampshades, now grey with age. All her taste, of course. Nothing of his father at all. And for the first time he noticed that the fitted wardrobe didn't fit very well, and that the bed was cheap and thin.

He wandered in a kind of daze into what they had called the lounge. In front of the television sat a small sofa and two armchairs covered in patterned velvet, all so familiar to him. His father's chair, where he had sat every evening of his life, still had a depression in the cushion. There was a cocktail cabinet, reproduction Georgian, and a side table with curly legs on which rested a reproduction antique silver tea service on a silver tray. His father had loved that room as fiercely as Russell had loathed it.

He sat on one of the chairs. Beneath the velvet pile, it felt like sitting on cardboard stuffed with sawdust. It was desperately uncomfortable. But Jack wouldn't have known it wasn't comfortable because he didn't know there was any better to be had. He was eighty-one when he died, and yet he had never known what it felt like to sit in a well-made, comfortable armchair.

Russell went from room to room. There were a few books, biographies mainly (his mother had been the reader), a few photographs, some Premium Bonds, his clothes (now being ruthlessly snatched off their hangers and stuffed into the bin bags by Beverley), folders of bank statements and bills. Jack's life seemed to have been measured in manila. Of the man himself, of what had made him interested, engaged, a unique human being, there was nothing. He had left nothing of himself behind.

What did Russell expect? Was there anything to be left? Jack had been a taxi driver. His life had consisted of car journeys, rows with traffic wardens, exchanges with passengers; just coping from day to day. Blink, and there was nothing. But then, what does anyone leave behind, he thought? Certainly he himself wouldn't have anything to leave, the way things had gone.

He rifled through the papers, looking.

You live on through your children, people say. But that didn't provide much comfort either. Rosa would be at best an unenthusiastic steward of the paternal memory. Who could blame her, given the fact that for most of her life he hadn't been around?

And anyway, memory does not endure. After Rosa, he thought gloomily, there would be no one who would remember him. And if she had children or, at the very outside, grandchildren while Russell was still alive, once they in turn were dead there would again be no one left to remember him. The only evidence of his existence would be a few faded photographs to be looked at with detached curiosity and with no more purchase on the future than a statue or a picture in a history book. He would not even be a distant memory. He would have simply vanished from the human imagination.

Was it for that reason, when he realized that the undertakers had left behind his father's prayer shawl after they wheeled his body in its black zip-up bag (what indignity!) out to their van, he ran into the street with it and banged on their window for them to take it? It wasn't just that it was the custom for a Jew to be buried wrapped in his own prayer shawl. It wasn't just that it would have mattered to his father. It somehow mattered, desperately, to him.

He had always had a horror of death. It was the obliteration of himself that was so...preposterous. Rosa talked vaguely about becoming one with the universe and everyone merging their atoms with those of the earth and the trees and the air. She appeared to find comfort in this, but it just freaked him out even more. Thinking of himself as a bag of atoms did not reassure him in the slightest.

He told himself that being dead was going to be no worse than not having yet been born. But that didn't help either, because if he hadn't been born in the first place he wouldn't be worrying about being dead.

Strap-hanging on the Tube, he would marvel that the entire carriage appeared not to be preoccupied by the fact that every single one of them was going to disintegrate. In bed at night, the sheer suffocating horror of it got so bad he would sit bolt upright, trembling and gasping for breath. "For Christ's sake, Russell," Alice would hiss, furious at being woken up, "it's being you that you should worry about, not being no longer you."

Even when woken in the middle of the night, he marveled, she still managed to snap into full advocacy mode.

"You looking for something?"

Beverley's voice cut into his reverie.

"No, nothing."

But he wondered if somewhere there was a letter. Some kind of farewell, some expression of regret, a still flickering spark of affection? Something to show he had not been erased, not totally.

"He missed you, you know. He spoke about you just before he died. He said he wondered whether you still played the piano."

As if she had read his mind. But that wasn't what he wanted to hear.

"The piano? I haven't played it since I was a child."

"He was always very proud of you."

"His mind had gone."

"My God Russell, you are one cold fish."

Why was she so angry, he wondered.

"Just look at you. You come swanning in after all this time, not so much as a peep out of you, never picked up the phone to see how I was coping with it all..."

"Coping with what? You seem to have it all very much under control."

"Coping with wha...? Let me tell you what. His mind came and went like a mobile phone signal. You'd be talking to him quite normally and then suddenly he'd say something barmy so you never knew where you were. If you talked to him as if he couldn't understand he would get very upset. He would cry and say I'm not going senile, don't behave as if I'm going senile. And I couldn't get any decent care for him. He was on the waiting list at the home where Mum is. The girls I hired were *dreck*, had to be constantly watched like a hawk. I was in and out of here, cleaning up, cooking for him, trying to work out whether these girls were hurting him because that's what he was saying. A nightmare. And all this time not one call from you, not one visit, nothing. And now you say I had it all under control!"

Mechanically, Russell humped sacks full of clothes out to the Volvo to take to the charity shop. Someone had been hired to come and take away the furniture. A shabby van was parked down the street and two shifty-looking men went in and out carting away tables and chairs.

Russell watched with every nerve jangling as the Georgian reproduction wine cabinet with the interior light and the little cocktail sticks with plastic cherries tinkling in their tray was heaved unceremoniously into the van. He stood and gazed through the open back door at the furniture with which he had grown up, and which he had loathed, now stacked in the back of the lorry, waiting in silence for its last journey like a group of condemned French aristocrats in a tumbril.

A cold fish. He thought of Alice. She was always very focused. That night when he got back home shattered from filming in Melbourne he found Alice waving a chart at him and insisting that they must "do it now" because it was the optimum time for conceiving and they couldn't afford yet another month to go past; and so he obligingly pumped away while feeling quite detached from his brain, let alone any other part of himself.

Afterwards he must have passed out from the combination of exhaustion and too much whisky on the plane. Three hours later he was wide awake again. In the morning Alice slammed the coffee mugs down on the table and wouldn't look at him. Halfway out of the front door she paused.

"Emotional literacy. You really have to do something about this. *Can* you feel? Or is it all just me me me with you?"

He gazed at her through a fog of fatigue. He supposed she must be right because he didn't have a clue what she was talking about.

Back in the flat, he found Beverley on the floor in the dining room surrounded by photograph albums. He picked one up; its stiff, cracked and musty cover reminded him of Kuchinsky's secret find. His secret.

A few photographs fell out, small and sepia-colored, some with deckled edges. He squinted at them. The faces of two carefree people laughed up at him: the man thick set with shiny slicked-back hair, a cigarette between his fingers and his arm round a ravishing younger woman, her hair piled up carelessly in a dark cloud above her head, in sunglasses and tight trousers. His mother? His father? Surely not. These people were strangers to him. He turned over the photograph. Scrawled on the back was "Biarritz, June 1956."

"Didn't know the old man smoked."

"There's a lot you didn't know."

"Quite a looker then, wasn't she."

He idly turned the pages of the album. Picture after picture of Jack and Sylvia with uncles, aunts, cousins at weddings and bar mitzvahs, with Russell and Beverley as babies and then as children.

There was one man he didn't recognize who seemed to appear in a number of photographs, usually walking and smoking alongside Jack. He appeared nonchalant, debonair; he loped along with hands in his pockets, cigarette dangling from his mouth and with his jacket slung over one shoulder. In one, though, he was pictured with Sylvia alone, both of them sitting at a table drinking beer. He was looking at her, serious, his face in profile; she was smiling at the camera, her hand shading her eyes against the sun. She looked radiant.

"Who was this?"

Beverley busied herself with emptying shelves of packets of tea, sugar and porridge oats. After a while she said: "That was Uncle Eddie."

"Uncle who?"

"Don't you remember him? He wasn't a real uncle."

"Never heard of him."

"He was a chartered accountant. He used to come and do the bookkeeping for them, for the shop. They met on holiday, and then after that he came and did the books."

She paused and seemed to brace herself.

"He was in love with our mother and wanted to marry her. She was infatuated with him. It was a holiday affair, which went on afterwards. Several years, actually."

Russell stared at her.

"What on earth are you talking about?" Was this her idea of a joke?

She looked at him for a while over the top of her royal blue Dolce & Gabbana spectacles. There was a glittery motif on the side.

"You never saw how unhappy she was, did you. Mum was highly intelligent. No education because she had to leave school early and look after Gran. Found herself on the shelf in her thirties and so married Dad out of desperation, I suppose. But she married beneath her. Realized she'd made a terrible mistake when she clapped eyes on Uncle Eddie. By all accounts, they were both smitten. But by then she had had you and she was trapped. That's why she resented you."

His mother! No no, he thought wildly, not possible. Not his mother. She was the rock, the anchor, the still and unchanging center of this world he had put to one side. It was his father who had pushed him away. How could his mother possibly have loved someone else? She didn't have the imagination. With that unchanging life in this humdrum little flat, this tomb, where even the windows had been stuck fast against the outside world since being painted shut years previously?

"Did he know?" He was in an agony on his father's behalf.

"Do me a favor! Went on right under his nose—all of our noses—and he didn't know a thing."

"She betrayed him?"

"Dear God, pots and kettles! Just listen to you!"

"I can't believe it. Resented us? All those years?"

"Not us," said Beverley cruelly. "You. When I came along she was already trapped. Besides, I was a daughter and she thought I would look after her. Which I certainly have done."

She sniffed and flashed her eyes. She certainly had a sense of timing, he thought. Who would have thought she had it in her?

"How long have you known this?"

"She told me years ago. It was as if she needed to get certain things off her chest. As if she knew she wasn't going to be with us much longer."

"What else did she say?" Russell asked in dread.

"She said she wished she could have been a proper grandma to Rosa. That really upset her."

"Was that all?"

"Yes."

No, that couldn't have been true. His mother must have talked about him. About what happened.

"Well she could've...but this...this is just too...banal, for God's sake."

He looked at the photograph again. He studied first his mother's face and then the face of this man Eddie. He had never seen her look so carefree. Eddie's expression was intent but inscrutable. So his father had been cuckolded, made a laughing stock, all behind his back. Could there have been a greater demonstration of contempt, he thought bitterly. He felt wounded to his very soul.

"How come you remember this character and I don't?"

"Not sure if you ever noticed anything that wasn't about you. You never saw what Dad made her put up with. You were always his favorite because you were clever. He never so much as looked at me. I also could have made something of myself if I'd had any encouragement. Not that she gave me any, either."

He closed his eyes and pinched the top of his nose between his finger and thumb. His head was beginning to throb again. A picture floated into his mind of Beverley as a schoolgirl with her skirt hitched up over ungainly thighs and ladders in her tights, giggling over cosmetics and teen magazines with her friends. The idea that she had ever had any ambition was news to him.

"I had some talent for art, you know. And I'd have loved to travel. Could even have got to university if anyone had taken any trouble with me. But I was sent to rotten schools. Unlike you."

That wasn't quite how he remembered it. True, he had got into the grammar school and Beverley had not. But hell, she had never been cooperative, not even before that. Never willing to concentrate for five minutes together—and bolshie with it. She was always in trouble, always doing detentions and the like. So she kept being moved from school to school until at last, to everyone's relief, she left for good.

For a while, she hardly got out of bed during the day, and then slopped around in tracksuit bottoms eating tubes of Pringles. Then she had got herself together, smartened up and gone to work as a secretary in the solicitors' office where Elliott worked; and to general surprise, not least her own, had ended up marrying him.

He had always wondered what Elliott saw in her. He assumed he had wanted a doormat. He had never given much thought to what Beverley may have wanted.

Now it was as if a tap had been turned on and left running. "She just wrote me off. Always screaming at me to do my homework, why didn't I get better marks, why were my reports so bad. She never took my side, even when they bullied me, even when the teacher threw the blackboard rubber at me. My God, how she used to shout."

He remembered the screaming. It was true their mother had had a volcanic temper. But generally it had been used against Jack.

"Well you've done all right now, haven't you."

She looked away. For the first time he wondered about her and Elliott. They seemed such a perfect fit. Everything was just so—the big house and garden, the solid husband, the four sons all of whom had been to or were destined for Oxbridge and were slotted into careers in the law, medicine or the city. So unlike the mess in his own life.

Of course Elliott was a total joke and a lump of lard to boot. Russell had assumed that was what Beverley had wanted.

Was Beverley capable of a grand passion like the one their mother had had for Uncle Eddie, and he for her? Was he himself capable of such a thing? He thought of Alice, her perfect oval face set hard and white beneath her glossy blonde bob, her entire body taut as a piano string flinching away as he reached out for her.

"I fancy a bit of hot chocolate. Want some?"

They both sat cradling the steaming mugs. He tried not to think about the powder he was spooning from the half-empty tin that his father would now never finish. The neon kitchen light buzzed incessantly.

"Funny how certain tastes or smells bring things right back. When I was five I ran away. It only lasted an afternoon. I opened the front door and went upstairs and said to the woman in the top flat, I want you to be my mummy. I can hear myself saying it even now. She said, but you've got a mummy, and I said, I don't like her, I want a new one. She gave me hot chocolate and toasted raisin bread and we watched TV on the sofa together. Then I went back downstairs."

"I'm sorry. I really had no idea."

"Oh, you were the little prince. At least you gave her something to boast about to her friends. On me she took it out, all the rage that she had been trapped in and that had ruined her life."

What was it with the women in his life, he thought dully; all of them saw him as the enemy. Was he really so inadequate as a human being? He suspected he was.

He thought of Rosa, of the razor blade slicing silently into her soft skin—swift, rhythmical, deliberate incisions.

"Ridiculous!" he had shouted down the phone when Alice had rung from the hospital. "Just attention-seeking, that's all! It's just a fashion! Stupid, stupid girl!"

Afterwards, though, he had wept copiously, great hot scalding tears.

7

IN THE WEEKS that followed, Russell's life took on a new pattern. At the beginning, he would slog up to Cockfosters in the evening. But then, bit by bit, he would find ways of going there for a morning or an afternoon.

Gradually, he was spending longer and longer at Kuchinsky's. The story of Eliachim of York had got under his skin. He was hooked. He couldn't wait to open those crackly pages between their stiff covers and reveal the next section of the story. At first, it seemed like a kind of game. After a while, though, he felt, strangely, that he himself was being changed by what he was reading. He felt as if the book was somehow physically pulling him in between its wooden boards.

He wondered whether it was some sort of traumatic shock after his father's death. But he didn't feel disordered. He felt exhilarated.

Not that it was easy—far from it. Maybe that was part of its appeal, as an antidote to the cultural semolina through which he had to paddle every day.

Until this point, he hadn't realized just how intellectually lazy he had become, how little mental challenge there was in the work that he did. So he supposed he was bored. But it took Eliachim to shake him out of his torpid state. It was as if he'd stepped through a looking glass.

To begin with, he couldn't believe that it actually was what it seemed so alluringly yet implausibly to be—a medieval English narrative in an old French dialect written in Hebrew characters. There was, however, enough in books he dug out of the library to confirm that yes, given the culture of twelfth-century English Jews, this was an entirely plausible literary mode of expression.

But then it was far from easy to translate it, particularly given the constraints Kuchinsky had laid down for him. After all, translating a transliteration, in two languages with which you are by no means familiar, is a tall order; and to do so in someone's front room with that person breathing down your neck hardly helps.

At the beginning, he was daunted by the task and several times nearly gave up. He brought in more and more dictionaries, lexicographies of Old French and Middle English, histories and other reference books, until Kuchinsky's grim little front parlor started to resemble a corner of the London Library.

He recalled that an old friend, Toby Pritchard, whom he hadn't seen in donkey's years, had gone off to do a doctorate in linguistics. Well actually, he had been more a friend of a friend—amiable enough, but a bit of a library lizard. One of the saddos. Through buttering up the warden's secretary at his old college, he tracked him down and rang him up.

Pritchard was more than a little surprised to hear from him after all those years, and even more surprised to hear his request; but Russell spun him a line that he was writing a work of fiction and needed a strong measure of verisimilitude and so could he possibly help him out with the odd word; and Pritchard was full of admiration and only too happy to help.

Kuchinsky flatly refused to let him make any phone calls at all while he was in the house; he sat over him, watching and wouldn't even let him text on his iPhone. He was frightened Russell was about to give away his secret. Absurd, obviously, since there was no reason why Russell would not do just that when outside his house. And there was no doubt that Kuchinsky's hovering, paranoid presence was unsettling. Anyway, Russell just took a note of the words or phrases where he was stuck or unsure and then when he got back home rang Pritchard, who patiently pondered the linguistic puzzles he was giving him.

Russell soon found he was savoring the challenge of it all. As a child, he had always enjoyed making and breaking codes and all those brain-teasers which involve pitting your wits against a problem. Now he was being given permission once again to play.

It certainly didn't feel like work. For the first time in his life, he was actually creating something. What satisfaction it gave him to work out how all the pieces of the puzzle fitted together and to see the shapes and patterns in language that they formed. It was also strangely soothing; the intense concentration took him out of himself as surely as a shot of whisky. Cracking the word codes gave him a feeling of being in control, an antidote to his increasing feeling that his livelihood was sliding away from underneath his feet.

He would sound out the letters, roll the words around his tongue and hear the music they made; and slowly, word by word, piece by piece, the jigsaw started slotting into place as he tapped it painfully, painstakingly into his laptop.

∞

Eliachim's story (1)

I write these words in the stillness of night because I can find no rest in the house that shelters me. My heart will surely burst with grief. My darling, my most precious love, is no more, most cruelly struck down. And I, I am the cause. It is my misdeeds that have brought about this calamity, my transgressions for which I have brought down the terrible wrath of heaven.

My body shakes continually as if with the ague. I wrap myself in the coverlet but I remain numb as if frozen into stone. Only my fingers still move across this parchment, guided by an unseen hand so that all posterity can know what has happened here. I write in secrecy and in haste, lest my attempt to bear witness to these terrible events be discovered and my testimony be ripped from me along with my life. What have I done! What have I done!

My name is Eliachim, son of Meshullam ben Moshe, may his beloved soul rest in peace, and I was secretary to the renowned

Yosef ben Aaron, also known as Josce of York, may his memory be for a blessing.

My father was an importer of cloth. I still feel prickling in my nostrils the dry, musty scent of the bales of silks and other rich fabrics that had travelled from the east. How exotic that sounded! As a small child, how I loved to hear my father's tales of his travels to the strange, far-away lands where they were woven and from which he always brought us sweetmeats or trinkets for our delight.

My mother Belaset, may her soul be among the angels, who brought to my father a rich dowry on account of her father Yehezkiel ben Salomon who was a trader in spices, was blessed with nine children of whom six lived and of whom I, having lived these fourteen summers, was the youngest.

It was to my mother that people came from around the town on account of her great learning which was equal to that of any man. It was from her that I was said to have gained my skill at letters which brought me to the service of my master Josce.

My brothers Menachem and Isaac worked in my father's trade, my brothers Jechiel and Aharon studied in our great yeshiva while my sister Zipporah had married Eleazar, son of Rabbi Yehudah ben Yisroel the cantor, whose elder daughter Genta of thirteen summers was betrothed to me. I was the most studious of all my family. Like others of our kind, my life was set out for me. I would enter the yeshiva to study and I would marry Genta to whom I had been promised some four summers past. We were due to be married when the omer had been counted, and her bridal garments had already been sewn.

But my soul was restless. I wanted to sail the seas in search of adventure, to discover new worlds. I was enchanted by the beauty of the universe and I gave expression to it in poetry and song. My mother would clap her hands in praise and delight. But my father disapproved of my enthusiasm. Such activities, he said, were profane and would lead me into grievous error.

Alas, he spoke more truly than he could have known. For in truth, I wanted to marry for love; and I found it not with Genta but with her younger sister, Duzelina. With what great agony of mind I now write that beloved name. Whereas Genta had sunken eyes and sallow cheeks and was of gloomy disposition, always dissatisfied and complaining about her lot, Duzelina was as sweet and as joyous as her face and form were fair.

After I walked with Genta, accompanied of course by a chaperone, my head would ache all over from her constant whining. There seemed no end to what she would require of me, in dresses and jewelry and fine furnishings, after we were married. My thoughts would turn instead to Duzelina, to whom my eyes were irresistibly drawn for her beauty and her gaiety. For all her modest demeanor, her eyes would dance with mischief. With her, I knew for certain I would venture into an unexplored domain.

My heart lifted whenever I saw her. And I was sure my affections were returned. When I stole glances at her, her eyes would raise towards mine as if a silken thread stretched between us and my very soul melted at her shy smile. I knew our fates were intertwined. But I was betrothed to her sister. It was at this time that the thought came into my head that Duzelina and I might run away.

My God, Russell thought, this boy could write. From the very first words, Eliachim of York sprang into life: a boy of 14 in a ferment of love and, for some reason, grief. Russell could smell his urgency and his passion. As the words slowly came into focus, it was as if Eliachim was reaching out from the past and dragging him into his story.

And what a story it was. A love affair between two children—well, they married young in those days. A tragic love affair, obviously, to judge from Eliachim's agitation. Why had it ended in tragedy? Almost certainly because the love match was forbidden. Irresistibly, Russell identified with their plight. A love match which pitted children against their fathers, which was forbidden because it transgressed religious codes and which tore families apart—the centuries simply rolled away as, word by word, Russell found himself looking at a version of his own story.

He was entranced; he drove himself on to find out what had happened that would finally, tragically, thwart these children's happiness. Steadily he worked on, decoding word after word and watching them form themselves into line after line of narrative on his laptop screen.

A story was now taking shape that was as unexpected as it was vivid. A whole way of life that he never knew had existed was now being revealed, letter by letter, word by word.

This was Jewish life in Britain, medieval Britain, where Jews had worked out, through both force of circumstance and their own skill and cunning, how to live and even thrive in the face of primitive hostility and resentment by making themselves indispensable to the king and the nobility.

How well these Jews had understood the English people. How deeply they had despised them. But what pressure they had lived under. Taxed to within an inch of their lives. The frenzy of the mob always just kept at bay. The murderousness of those early Christians, the boiling, unfathomable hatred. Ah yes, he thought, Christianity. Well, that was religion for you: it turned people into murderous fanatics. It made them crazy.

But these Jews were also religious, very religious. And what he also saw for the first time was the amazing richness of their lives; not material wealth—although it seemed that there was indeed plenty of that—but the inner life, the spiritual strength they derived from their relationship with their God.

And how intimate this relationship was, how everyday, how woven into absolutely everything they did: into how they ate, how they dressed, how they washed, how they loved. This was not religion as Russell knew it, corralled into dead rituals in a formal institution, something you had to make a point of going to and then leaving in order to get on with your life. This *was* their life; this was what they indivisibly were. They really did walk with their God.

He found himself envying Eliachim, envying the richness of that inner life. This in turn disconcerted him. Here he was, a highly educated member of an elite and, above all, rational social grouping in the most civilized and materially comfortable society known to man, living exactly as he pleased free of all such oppressive and idiotic constraints on his behavior. Why on earth should he feel the smallest twinge of envy for a pious Jewish youth given to mumbling mumbo-jumbo and living in barbaric times?

He could not help but marvel, though, at this faith of theirs. These people were hardly ciphers, brainwashed into credulity. They argued with their God, begged and pleaded with him, berated him for hiding from them. But not for one moment did they question that he was actually there. To call it faith was itself to miss the point. It was a living relationship, as real to them as any other.

What comfort there must be in that, he thought. Not for Eliachim any night sweats over *his* ultimate extinction.

But this wasn't some ascetic abnegation of this world in anticipation of the ecstasies or torments of the afterlife, that dreariness he associated inevitably with religion. No, these people delighted in the physical delights of this world, in the pleasures of eating and drinking, of wearing fine silks and jewelry, of music and dancing.

And they also loved with all their senses—but with a purity and an innocence that came from tremulous restraint, so that sensuality and spirituality became rolled into one. For Eliachim's story told of a passion as delicate as it was overwhelming, and whose consummation would be as poignant as a rose whose full bloom signals the point at which it starts to die.

He was embarrassed to think it, but he was stirred by this in a way he had not felt before. Eliachim's voice—anguished, desperate—now echoed down the centuries like a reproach. How could he not have known about this?

But then, what did he know even about his own forbears? His grandparents, his father's parents who had died when he was a child, had come from Poland at the turn of the 20th century. When he had asked his father about his parents and those who came before them, he got only a shrug and a grimace.

What did that grimace mean? He had never asked, but he knew that, together with the shrug, it meant: "Who knows, who cares, I don't want to know because they were foreign and probably backward and would make us ashamed of their lowly station in life, and we want to put all that behind us because that was then and this is now and this is all that matters."

Or at least, that's what Jack would have said had he been able to string two coherent thoughts together.

And why hadn't Russell persevered until he had got some kind of answer? Even to know just a few of those names would surely have been something, fragments of debris from the great river of the past to which he could have clung. Except that he hadn't actually wanted to cling onto anything like that, not until now.

And he knew why. Because he had been ashamed: ashamed of his father, ashamed of all of them. Just like his father he had not wanted to go there, had flinched from opening that door into the past. Now he was ashamed of having been ashamed. But now it was too late ever to find out.

He worked steadily on. Sometimes he could only manage to get through a few sentences; sometimes he had a good run and was able to translate several pages at one sitting.

And, for that matter, what had he known about Judaism anyway? Jack's parents had come from the harsh bleakness of farm life in Poland. There seemed to have been no education, no culture, no deep Jewish knowledge. A barren, joyless heritage: just the daily struggle to survive punctuated by a few mumbling superstitions. But the life of the Jews of medieval York now shone in Russell's mind like jewels glowing against velvet. Why had he never been shown such riches?

So he pondered. He sat back and stared at the hideous Tretchikoff glowing greenly on the wall opposite. Something else was troubling him.

He certainly was not of Eliachim's tribe. What was unfolding on his laptop was a way of life which was as exotic and foreign to him as a colony of Indian peafowl. The Jews in twelfth century England were eastern Jews who originated in Africa and the Middle East and came to the west through Spain and France and southern Europe. They were altogether different from the Jews like Russell's own family who came from Poland, Russia and Eastern Europe—different clothes, different food, different appearance, different customs. And yet despite all these differences Russell felt an affinity, a sense of connection, with Eliachim of York. And suddenly he felt as if the world around him was a picture that was beginning to blur, even to dissolve.

At work, in the pub, even in the streets, he felt different. Self-conscious. He felt as if he was carrying some kind of mark on his forehead. He looked in the mirror and noted with fresh distaste that fleshy mouth, that bony nose, the deep-set eyes. Unmisbloodytakable. Whom did he think he was kidding?

Combing the newspapers for ideas, he started to notice the repeated calls for an academic boycott of Israel, the endless stream of protests against the "settlers" or the "apartheid" wall. None of this was new. He had just never before given it a second thought. The Middle East had been as much a matter of indifference to him as, say, Burma or Tibet. There was a whole range of worthy causes, all of which he knew were broadly right and principled even if he knew nothing about them because all of them lay within an implicitly agreed world view. He didn't even have to think about them. He just knew they had to be right because otherwise they wouldn't have been part of his world, the assumptions shared between the people with whom he identified. Yet now this one was making him uneasy. Why?

He had no time for Israel at all, of course; but for the first time, he wondered why there was so much about this and so little—no, nothing at all, he suddenly realized—on the persecution of people in the Arab world. Strange. Anyway, none of that was his concern, thank goodness; he could ignore it, and he put it out of his mind. He had plenty else on his plate. And he certainly had no intention of making himself any different from anyone else. He didn't want even to feel different. But feel it, to his irritation, he now did.

He found himself thinking more and more about Eliachim. He became a kind of ghostly companion. How would he have reacted to the boycott motions and the campus demonstrations, he silently asked him. More to the point, how would all the people in Russell's world have reacted to Eliachim?

He thought of how the Jews of his time had been forced to outwit religious hatred and bigotry in order to live; and how cleverly they had done so. An absurd train of thought, he told himself. There was absolutely no comparison between then and now. None.

As he worked steadily through Eliachim's story, the more sharply he veered between elation and fear. He became increasingly convinced that he had stumbled upon an extraordinary find. This was a rare contemporary account, in the vernacular, of a vanished world of which virtually no firsthand evidence had survived. It must surely be priceless. What's more, it was in itself a notable piece of literature. Eliachim may have been one of the pious, but for all his religiosity he wrote with a freshness and vividness that suggested a remarkable creative imagination along with high intelligence.

Yet that made Russell nervous. He was aware that he was far more excited than was prudent. Was he being played for a sucker here? Was this not just too perfect, too sparkling? It could so easily be a forgery. He couldn't be sure, since Kuchinsky was making it impossible for him to check it out.

He was taking this all upon himself, unable to consult or confide in anyone. He was flying blind. Dangerous, far too dangerous. He broke out into a sweat thinking about the risk he was taking. The debacle years earlier over the Hitler diaries, when a distinguished historian had verified what turned out to be a not-even-very-good forgery, preyed upon his mind.

Kuchinsky would sometimes shuffle over and peer over his shoulder as he worked. He was beginning to get on Russell's nerves.

"You know vot these vords say now? Is prayer book, holy book, yes?"

His rasping breathing emphasized the silence in the room. The sickly aftershave he wore made Russell's stomach heave.

"I think it's some kind of diary or chronicle written by a young Jew hundreds of years ago—a kind of snapshot of the times."

Instinctively he downplayed it. Kuchinsky looked disappointed.

"Don't tell me is ordinary. This cannot be. Has holy vords in it for sure. The Almighty himself guarded this book, saved it from terrible dangers, saved it for reason. Saved it to send message to us. To us! It was meant that I should meet you, that you do this. Is holy vork, God's vork."

"Oh, but it's an astounding find, really, a priceless chronicle of the Jews who lived here in England, centuries ago; and it's also a love story, some kind of tragic, doomed love affair..."

Kuchinsky waved him away. He didn't seem interested in what was actually in the book, only in whether Russell could prove that it was the mystical source that Kuchinsky was convinced it was.

When he wasn't pressing Russell for evidence of the book's divine origins, he would hold forth about politics and the state of the nation.

"Too many immigrants! I go out to blessed shops or on underground, is not Britain any longer! I think I am in foreign country, in blessed Pakistan, Saudi Arabia! Politicians—ach, always they make promises, out of both sides of their mouth..."—here he would point to each side of his own mouth; he also had a habit of touching it with the tips of his fingers to signal the importance of the point he was about to make, almost as if he was telling the other person to keep it secret—"...no one speaks God's honest truth, no one stands and fights for vot he believes, all they want is to get power, all the time they tell us nonsenses, vot, they think ve children? Now Mrs. Tetcher, ach, there vos woman, there vos leader. None of this rubbish she would say. You know she vos only one viz balls in government!"

He would wait for a suitable reception for this original sally. Russell's toes curled inside his shoes. This hero-worship of Thatcher was really quite pitiful. Why were so many Jews so right-wing? And why were so many of them so embarrassingly naive?

"You know, we really must get this book properly examined and dated."

Kuchinsky's face darkened.

"No one is to see this. Never."

"But if no one sees it, I won't be able to tell you whether this is genuine or not. And then you won't be able to publish it."

"I tell you already, is not going to be published! No one else will know! No one else's business!"

Well, that seemed to rule out his being a bounty-hunter, at least. And clearly there was no way Kuchinsky could have forged it, no way he could have constructed this elaborate linguistic puzzle. But someone else might have done so. Someone else could have forged it and then played Kuchinsky for a sucker—or traded on his own willingness to believe. Just like that middleman in the Hitler diaries fiasco.

He tried again to find out about how Kuchinsky had come by the book.

"You see, we need to find out for sure whether this really is authentic, whether it really is as old as we think it is. For all we know, it might be a forgery."

"Not forgery! This special book, protected by God. Believe me."

"But how can you be sure? You need to tell me this. I need to know."

Kuchinsky rolled a cigarette between thick fingers stained yellow. His hands shook slightly.

Russell worried that he would start crying again, or worse still have a heart attack.

Once, Russell opened the door to go to the lavatory and heard whispering. A woman's whispered words.

"More quickly...taking too long."

And then raised voices, and some hushing, and a door clicking shut.

He rarely saw Kuchinsky's wife and felt sure she was avoiding him. When he did encounter her moving from room to room in the house, she dropped her eyes and scurried away. He could feel the hostility lying thick in the air.

"Your wife...she doesn't seem to like my coming here, is that right?" he said to Kuchinsky one day. She had just left the house abruptly and Kuchinsky had run after her; when he returned a few minutes later, his face was set and closed.

Kuchinsky sighed deeply and took a moment to reply.

"My vife...she wery vorried about this book. She wery religious. She think it bring bad luck. She think it cursed. She vant me to burn it. I say to her no, no, is good book, is holy book. Will bring us good things."

Ah, that was the difference between a Jew and a Christian, thought Russell. The Jew worships the book; the Christian wants to burn it.

There was something else. Kuchinsky had not lifted his eyes off the floor. Now he put his face in his hands and hid it completely.

"My vife...my vife, she also think *you* bring us bad luck."

"Me? Why? How?"

"She think you might steal book, or...or tell people, tell museum or government abaht it, and then there will be big commotion and it will be taken away from us."

Russell pondered this. Kuchinsky still had his face buried in his hands. What he had just said made no sense. If the wife was so terrified by the malign forces she thought resided in the book, why would she care if Russell or anyone else made off with it? Clearly, that last bit was not her own fear but Kuchinsky's. But she clearly didn't want him in the house, of that there was no doubt.

He felt uncomfortable and that made him nervous. He wanted to believe that his find was genuine, but Kuchinsky was making it as difficult as possible. And all this whispering and the wife's silences hardly helped inspire confidence. There was something else behind the wife's hostility. She had taken against him from the start—and he just didn't buy the idea that she thought he was an emissary from Satan.

Back in his flat, he poured himself a large Jack Daniels—and managed to smash the ice cubes so that they spilled off the draining board and rolled around the floor while the argument raged back and forth in his head.

It was all too risky. The vibes from Kuchinsky's wife were making him feel jumpy. Kuchinsky himself was clearly an obsessive and possibly a little cracked. On the other hand, the book looked genuine, smelt and felt genuine. No one, surely, would have gone to such elaborate lengths to forge such a thing.

But he was out on a limb on his own. His head was aching again. Why was he getting all these headaches? Perhaps a brain tumor?

He went into his bathroom and gazed morosely at himself in the mirror. Tired, heavy-lidded eyes stared back. God, he was looking old. His hair, a thinning nimbus of wiry strands, framed a fleshy face with a mouth whose corners seemed to suffer from a permanent droop. And his chin seemed to have multiplied. He stuck out his tongue and observed to his alarm a grey-greenish coating. Maybe it was a virus rather than a brain tumor. He opened the bathroom cabinet and a small avalanche of pill packets and bottles fell out. He extricated some painkillers and stuffed the packets and bottles back.

He poured some more whisky to wash down the tablets. He had to do something to take his mind off this or else he would go crazy. His eye fell on a box of stuff he had retrieved from his father's flat. He picked up a scrapbook and started leafing through it. It contained apparently random items pasted onto its pages: odd newspaper articles, mostly, some stamps with hinges on the back that looked like a collection had been started and then abandoned; some loose photographs.

A letter fell out, without an envelope. It was folded around a small photograph of two young men in uniform. Russell unfolded the letter. It was dated June 4, 1956, and it was from someone called Bob Falkner who lived in Peterborough. The handwriting, looped and extravagant, was strong and clear. Russell read the letter in growing puzzlement.

Dear Jacky,

Thought you'd like to see this snap from happier times!!! Wondering how you've been keeping after all these years; heard you hadn't been too grand. But gather you're now spliced and with a couple of sprogs! Hope things are easier for you now. You were the best, you know. Wouldn't be here today if it wasn't for you. Well, got to run now but if you're ever in Peterborough do look me up and we'll sink a jar or two for old times' sake. Best regards and do look after yourself.

Your old chum, Bob

Russell looked closely at the photograph. One of the men in uniform was his father; he recognized his younger self from the Biarritz holiday photos. The other he assumed, was this Bob Falkner. He thought hard. His father had never talked about the war. He and Sylvia had both given the impression that Jack had been unable to do his military service because of some unnamed physical weakness. Yet here he was in army uniform, with this man Bob Falkner suggesting he had behaved in some kind of admirable fashion. No one had ever suggested his father had ever done anything admirable or memorable in his entire life.

There was a telephone number under the address. Of course, this man might not still be alive. But Russell resolved nevertheless to ring the number.

He went to bed and dreamed a recurring dream; he was wandering through a railway terminus desperately searching for the right train, and when he finally got on one he found he had no idea where it was going.

8

"WELL, NEITHER OF us looks a day older," said Waxman.

Russell's heart sank. Stupid of him to have imagined that Waxman would have changed. Still speaking in clichés. He had certainly acquired a veneer, though. That non-stop loquaciousness now gave him a plausible social patter doubtless designed when pitching for business to put employers at their ease.

They had met in a coffee shop near his office. Waxman had talked a bit about his family and some of his insights into workplace psychology. He didn't seem very interested in Russell's life over the preceding twenty-five years. He had an agenda.

"So, what's it like in the media these days?"

Russell sifted through the daily trials of his working life, wondering how best to present his own achievements in the least negative light. It was, however, a question that Waxman was himself intending to answer.

"The bias against Israel is shocking. I've got lots of stuff that would make a great TV show—really wake everyone up."

It turned out that Waxman spent much of his free time attending anti-Israel demonstrations and meetings on university campuses and elsewhere, filming them and asking provocative questions until he was thrown out.

Russell looked at him in astonishment. Waxman occupied a senior position in a large management consultancy. Yet here he was boasting of being a troublemaker.

"Isn't all that a bit, you know, dangerous?"

"Well I've had my camera smashed a couple of times by these thugs. But these people are getting away with murder. They're spouting lie after lie about Israel, spreading hatred, inciting violence. People need to know what's going on here. Taxpayers' money, after all. Here, this will amaze you."

Waxman tapped at his phone and swiveled it round on the table so that Russell could see. There were photographs of an exhibition, posters and placards mounted on easels in what looked like a foyer. There were close-ups of these posters under the rubric of a London university Palestine society. One carried a long list of Arab names. There were pictures of Arab families weeping over the bodies of young men and children. On one easel, a placard announced that these were events that were happening in Palestine, where dozens of Palestinians had been killed in their "resistance to Israeli occupation." Another poster proclaimed: "Today we commemorate you: we stand shoulder to shoulder with your resistance."

Russell looked at Waxman, baffled.

"You know who all these names are?" said Waxman. "'Resistance my foot. They're all Jew-killers. This is a list of the terrorists who for months now have been stabbing Israelis or shooting them or driving trucks into them at bus-stops or throwing rocks at their cars to kill them. Women, children, tourists being picked off for slaughter every day. And here's a university hosting an exhibition that glorifies and sanitizes such mass murder!"

He jabbed at the phone as he spoke. He trembled with intensity. Russell recoiled.

Waxman scrolled along the upside-down phone. A video sprang into tinny life. Students dressed in Israeli army fatigues and toting outsized cardboard replica machine guns were stopping other students as they went into a building, shouting abuse and pretending to shoot them. Some of the students running this gauntlet looked shocked and frightened. Others ignored it.

"See, this is supposed to replicate an Israeli checkpoint. But some of these students being harassed by these idiots are Jews. Charming, eh? Of course, any truthful replica would have kitted out the supposed Palestinians with knives and suicide bomb belts. Instead the defenders of the innocent are portrayed as monsters."

Waxman looked at Russell expectantly.

"Exactly where do I fit into all this?" asked Russell cautiously.

Of course it was obvious.

"The university should be prosecuted for permitting this incitement. Here's the evidence. I want you to put it on TV, nail these bastards to the floor."

The sheer impossibility of bridging the chasm between Waxman's agenda and the reality of the world beyond him left Russell opening and closing his mouth like a stranded fish.

"That's just not going to work," he eventually managed.

"I've got loads more footage like this," said Waxman eagerly. "A real gold-mine of incriminating material. Some of the stuff that's being said, the open antisemitism, the lies and intimidation, you just wouldn't believe. No one else has got any of this. It's a unique archive."

Russell needed no convincing that this was so. He took a deep breath.

"I'm afraid there's really just no appetite for this kind of thing."

"You mean the bias? But you're in a position to make a difference. You could get a TV channel interested."

Suicidal vets, thought Russell.

"It's all a bit...well, niche, frankly, for your average channel controller."

"*Niche*? This is incitement against Jews. It's the medieval blood libels all over again. It's open antisemitism. Doesn't that mean anything to you?"

Waxman sounded shocked and upset. Russell looked at him in dismay. The years rolled away. He saw again that look of mute perplexity in the face of unfathomable prejudice, the expression he had seen on the face of the bullied boy of twelve when Waxman was called a filthy kike and beaten to the ground. And Russell watched himself once again slink away.

"Criticizing Israel isn't the same thing," he countered.

"*Criticize*? These are the new Nazis," Waxman fumed.

Russell shook his head, more in sorrow than anger.

"You destroy your own case by making such a ludicrous comparison," he said.

Waxman's eyes narrowed.

"And the difference is...? Look, the Palestinians use Nazi images of diabolical blood-sucking Jews. What, Israel shouldn't defend its people against being wiped out by the same bastards? Turn the other cheek, I don't think! Well sorry, we're never going to lie down and be slaughtered again."

He looked crestfallen, and Russell couldn't help feeling uncomfortable. Waxman was up against forces he had no chance whatsoever of defeating, just as he had been at school; and he was displaying the same combination of mulish obstinacy and being pathetically outclassed and outnumbered.

It had been Waxman's own fault, after all, for being so bloody stupid, for not taking proper precautions with his own safety, for making himself the victim. And yet Russell felt guilty. He could have stepped in. He could have helped stop the bullying. But he had kept his own head right down, hadn't he. He had tried to pretend there was no connection between them. But there was.

Later, he looked up Waxman on the internet. He seemed to be all over it. He featured on YouTube, on anti-Israel blogs, on the *Jewish Chronicle* website.

He appeared to regard himself as a kind of one-man instant rebuttal unit. He appeared at the anti-Israel demonstrations outside Marks & Spencer or the Israel embassy, standing behind placards announcing "Peace not hate" and bellowing through a megaphone about "Fascist fellow travelers!" and "Apologists for genocide!" Clearly, he was in a state of permanently boiling rage. He even appeared to be in trouble with his fellow Jews, who regularly denounced him as a dangerous extremist and even a lunatic.

So Russell was on safe ground, he told himself, in keeping Waxman at more than arm's length. The man was clearly unhinged.

Yet Russell found his mind returning to the pictures on Waxman's phone and the video he had shot. Was it really true that all those Palestinians on that list had murdered innocent people in cold blood, including women and children? If so, why hadn't that even been acknowledged on those posters? Could it really be the case that the university authorities permitted an exhibition glorifying terrorism? Could anything excuse such savagery?

This was just too troubling, and so Russell put it firmly out of his mind. But his father's severe face, most annoyingly, kept floating into it.

9

HE FOUND HIMSELF back at his father's flat. To general bemusement, Jack's will had listed certain items that were to be given to Russell: some religious books, the *tefillin* that observant men wear during morning prayers, some vinyl LPs of dance-band music in faded, dog-eared sleeves. It all sat on the kitchen table in a forlorn and poignant pile.

"I can't think why he wanted you to have these," said Beverley, fingering the phylacteries. "They would have done very nicely for one of our lot. And you're hardly going to use them, are you."

"I'm surprised these hadn't already been shoveled into the bin bags with all the rest of the junk," said Russell lightly.

She bridled. "I started with the stuff that it was obvious no one would want. And I actually don't see any of it as junk. I treated it all with great respect. More respect than you showed him while he was alive, I have to say."

She was obviously still steaming with rage. She stood leaning against the kitchen cabinet, arms folded.

He picked up the largest book, a *chumash* containing the five books of Moses. The spine cracked as he opened the stiff cover. Inside was written in a flowery, looping hand: "To our beloved son Jacky on his bar mitzvah, from his devoted parents, August 1931"—and then in Yiddish, "*zol zayyin mit mazel*!"

Russell sat down heavily on the plastic-seated chair. *Zol zayyin mit mazel* roughly translated, meant "have a lucky life." His father had hardly had a life marked by luck, he thought.

A picture swam into his mind: he and his father together filling in the football pools coupon. Football was Jack's passion, and he shared it with Russell. They both supported Tottenham Hotspur; on a Saturday they would come home for a quick lunch after the synagogue service and then, if their team were playing at home, go off on the Tube to the Spurs ground in White Hart Lane.

He remembered blowing on his hands as they sat in the stands in the freezing cold, and his father pulling out the flask of tea and pouring him a steaming cup. He could still taste the plastic on his tongue, and the hot sweet tea. He remembered huddling with his father over the pools coupon, with Jack allowing him to list the guessed-at results. "It's all luck," Jack would chuckle, "no skill in this at all." It was a ritual, a treasured moment of companionship between them. And every week, when the pools results came up on the TV, Jack would sit agog checking off his numbers; and every week he would whistle softly how close he had come to winning.

Russell thought, I haven't thought about this in, what, thirty years. It was a memory he had simply closed off after the great rupture. How sad it made him now.

He had also hardly thought about his grandparents, his father's parents, those Polish peasants about whom he had never wanted to know. He had certainly never known his grandfather, who had died well before Russell was born. What a born loser he surely was, Russell thought; he hadn't even had the wit to sell anything but had hired himself out instead as a knife-grinder. A knife-grinder! The kind of creature upon whom his mother had shut the door firmly when he had come knocking for work.

He remembered his grandmother as a permanently sour, complaining individual who couldn't even speak English properly right up to the day she died. He had written them off as near-imbeciles, a baleful blot on his own father's life—so poorly had they valued education that Jack had left school at 13—and a source of deep shame for his own.

And yet here in this simple inscription he saw two people of flesh and blood who had felt, and loved, and hoped, and even had the wit to use exclamation marks—and to whom his father had been precious. He had never asked his father about them, and Jack had never spoken of them; now they would be forever a blank page, like this flyleaf, with only this inscription to give them any personality at all in his mind.

He picked up the prayer book, a *siddur* that was used for daily synagogue services. It was scruffy, and the cover hung precariously by a few threads. Inside he read, in his father's handwriting: "To dearest Russell on your bar mitzvah; very proud! With fondest love, Mum and Dad, March 1963."

With a shock he realized it was his own *siddur*, the one he had taken to the synagogue every week when he had gone with his father. He had had no idea it was still in existence; he hadn't had any need of it for more than four decades. But his father had not only kept it close by him, he had chosen to give it back to him now, despite all that had happened.

Not just that, but he had very deliberately passed it on with his *chumash* with its own almost identical inscription. From the grave, therefore, his father was giving him the gift of continuity—the unbroken connection not just to his family but also to that ancient ancestry Russell had so forcefully renounced, which had caused his father to renounce him.

It was an act of love. His father had not wiped him out of his life after all. Russell brushed away tears.

"Bit late for that now, isn't it," said Beverley.

She was spoiling for a fight, to have it out with him at last, Russell thought dully. But having nudged open the door of his memory that had been shut tight for so long, he did not want Beverley to destroy the tremulous images he had discovered lurking there and that he wanted to take out, dust off and look at again and again. He had to head her off.

"Your boys seem fine lads," he said. It came out too heartily, but still.

He saw a struggle briefly pass over her face between her need to unburden herself of all the anger pent up inside and the irresistible instinct to boast. The latter won.

"Oh they're all doing terribly well. Scholarships and prizes all the way. Stu and Alan both got double firsts at Cambridge, Stu's already a partner at McKinseys and Alan's at 5 Stone Buildings..."

"Five Stone...?"

"Top set at the Chancery Bar, didn't you know, well not your world, I suppose. Simon's running his own web service provider company while still at Trinity—he was head boy at Westminster, by the way—and Anthony's just about to do his interview for Corpus Christi. And so what of Rosa?"

"Rosa is...well, she's still trying to find herself."

"I suppose you sent her to some dreadful comp? Poor little mite."

Westminster! Since when did they have such pretensions?

"Elliott still stuck in that same little firm in Wembley?"

She glared. "He's involved in a great deal of charity work these days. Jewish Care. Cancer Relief. And he's been told he's in line for a CBE for his interfaith work."

"Impressive! I had no idea he was interested in such things."

As soon as the words were out of his mouth he realized his mistake.

"Hardly any wonder, is it? We never heard from you from one year to the next. How could you do that? Don't you have *any* feelings for your family?"

"It wasn't my fault. You know what happened."

"You could have made a gesture."

"*I* should have made a gesture? He wouldn't acknowledge my wife. He wouldn't see his own granddaughter. He wouldn't even pronounce my name."

"He was grieving. He had lost his son."

"He didn't lose me. He wanted nothing more to do with me."

"Oh, and I suppose you didn't put two fingers up to him and everything that was so important to him. And anyway, you divorced Alice."

"She divorced me, actually."

"Same difference. Fact is, you split. Nothing then to stop you coming to see us. But you didn't. You wanted nothing to do with us. Too grand for us, that was the problem wasn't it? All your smart friends. You always were a snob, ever since you went to that grammar school."

God! he thought. Still banging on about that after all these years.

"Well, at least I didn't send my child to Westminster."

"Some of us care about our children more than our politics! Some of us care about our families and want them to make the best of themselves. We actually love them. Do you even know what that means? You had a good education at that grammar school; it got you to Oxford and just look at you now. But you wouldn't give the same advantage to your own daughter, would you, just dumped on it all from a great height, turned against it just like you did against being Jewish. You knew what that meant to Dad, didn't you. How could you have been so selfish?"

Selfish! Russell marveled at his sister's twisted values. He had devoted his entire life, had he not, to principles: to fighting privilege and the class system that kept working people powerless and stopped their kids from going to university and getting decent jobs and treated them instead like shit.

He and Alice believed in equality and he was bloody proud of that. Selfish? These principles had cost them. They'd both had to join St. Saviour's, hadn't they, and even go along to Sunday services in order to get Rosa into the church school where loads of academics and politicos and media people sent their kids because the standards were higher than the other schools in the area. Alice had had to put aside her principles as an atheist just to do what was best for Rosa.

Sure, the comprehensive left something to be desired. Rosa was bullied, the teachers were inarticulate and the kids seemed to spend every lesson just ticking boxes. But they'd got her a tutor, hadn't they, and congratulated themselves on the fact that Rosa was going to school alongside kids wearing gym shoes because their single mothers couldn't afford proper ones. Because they had a conscience.

"Dad was a socialist all his life. That was his religion. The Jewish thing was always very superficial."

"Superficial? It was everything to him. How can you just dismiss it all? It's part of you as well, whether you like or not. Why do you try to pretend you are something you are not? Why do you hate this part of yourself? If you hate that part, then you hated them too."

But the fact was that his parents had not spoken with one voice on this. His mother had regarded his father's attachment to religious rituals as a sign of a weak and uneducated character.

Indeed, Sylvia had been quite hostile to religion. Her parents, who had emigrated from Berlin to Britain in search of work during the 1920s, had been entirely secular. Like other German Jews before the Holocaust, they did not see themselves as any different from other Germans. They were German. That was their national identity. The Germans were cultured, educated, with great universities, venerated literary figures, a keen appreciation of art and music. They were the acme of European enlightenment. So there was no place in the assimilated German Jewish world for the primitive rituals of religion. Religion made them different. It was accordingly disregarded, despised and largely dumped.

Like her parents, Sylvia looked down upon those Jews who came from the backward, uneducated villages of Poland as bumpkins, whose religiosity was merely further proof of their low intelligence. It was her misfortune, she thought, to have married the son of just such individuals. She made chicken soup and lit candles on a Friday night on sufferance, merely to pacify Jack. And she was impatient with Jack's socialism, which she thought was the surefire mark of a loser.

"Mum was never religious; none of that meant anything to her at all."

"She was just a snob, that's all. She thought religious people were backward and narrow. What mattered to her was being educated and getting a good position in life."

Unlike you, of course, thought Russell.

"Anyway, religion isn't the point. Sure, she knew nothing about it. But it was being Jewish that mattered to her. It mattered that her granddaughter wasn't Jewish. It mattered that her own heritage would now come to a shuddering halt with you. It wasn't ever about religion. It was all about being part of a people, a history. She knew something priceless was being lost."

Jew, Jewish, every other word. What was wrong with these people? Did they really never think about anything else? Was there really nothing else in their world, their experience, but this constant scratching at the existential wound? Get over it! he wanted to scream.

"You mean she was a racist."

"That's just disgusting. Mum didn't have a racist bone in her body."

"Oh really? Well she looked down on Dad as being some kind of *untermensch*."

"*Untermensch*? What, now she's a Nazi all of a sudden?"

"Why are you sticking up for her? You said yourself that she was horrible to you."

"Because you are worse! They did their best, for heaven's sake. They poured as much into you as they possibly could. How can you spit on their memory like this? I'm not a bit surprised Alice left you."

So now Alice was being used against him. Even she might have enjoyed the irony of that one, he thought.

"You still have no idea what you did here, do you? So wrapped up in yourself and your little world and your own importance. You think the world revolves around you. It never dawns on you, does it, that what you do has consequences for anyone else.

"Well this is what you did to them. When you went off and married Alice, Dad changed. He kind of just shut down inside himself. He had always been so chatty; now there were these long, long silences. He would sit just staring into space. Mum just didn't know what to do with him.

"Then he started to get confused. One minute he'd be perfectly lucid and then the next his mind would start wandering. He would turn up at breakfast without his trousers on. He forgot how to play kalooki. And his personality changed—he became irritable, for no apparent reason.

"Turned out he was having lots of mini-strokes. Vascular dementia, it's called. It was all too much for Mum; she was run ragged. No wonder her own mind gave way. After that Dad went steadily downhill. But here's the thing, Russell. One of the factors that's said to cause vascular dementia is the pain caused by bereavement."

"He wasn't bereaved. He still had Mum."

"He had lost you. You were dead to him. And you were his special boy. She never loved him. He knew that. That's why you were so important to him. And then he lost you."

Dead to him. Wiped out. Erased. No longer existing, no longer a person, no longer even a speck in the universe. Obliterated.

"And some of us had to pick up the pieces."

Beverley the martyr. Jesus, what a cow.

Her accusation was completely over the top, he told himself, bred merely of bitterness and venom and designed to cause as much hurt as possible.

"You're talking total rot. For fuck's sake, Beverley..."

"I'm sorry, I just won't listen to that kind of language..."

"...God dammit Beverley, all I did, *all I did* was dare to live my own life in the way that I wanted to live it—oh, I'm so fucking sorry—and you're telling me that because I behaved like a normal adult, unlike certain people I could mention, this killed Dad and sent our mother out of her mind?"

This was what he had wanted to get away from. How this brought it all back to him—the introversion, the narrowness, the obsessiveness; and on top of all that the paranoia, the belief that they were all at risk of imminent extinction, always fighting to prevent the next genocide, always terrified of their own shadow.

He was sick of it. It stifled him, it sucked all the air out of his life. He had had to get out just in order to survive. He had loved his father—he knew that now—but he simply had to escape from that suffocation. He resisted that kind of living death with every fiber of his being. He wanted to live, he wanted to be free of this undercurrent of terror, this constant apologetic cringing. He didn't want to be different anymore.

He simply wanted to be just like everybody else. And Alice, golden Alice, with her blonde bob and her freckles and her effortless air of superiority and her entrancingly talented and cosmopolitan friends, had been his passport to normality.

And yet he couldn't stop returning to it, like scratching a scab.

He rang the number on the letter. It rang for a long time. He was about to hang up when someone finally answered. A woman's voice, impatient. When he asked to speak to Bob Falkner, he gave his name as Jack Wolfowitz's son.

There was a muffled sound as the woman placed her hand over the receiver, and then a pause. Eventually an old man's quavery voice came on the line. Again, Russell introduced himself as Jack Wolfowitz's son. There was a long pause.

"Jacky? Wolfowitz? Jacky Wolfowitz? Did you say Jacky?"

It took a while for the old man to grasp that yes, this was indeed Jacky's son who was on the other end of the line. He kept repeating the name over and over again, in wonderment, as if it were Jack himself who had rung him.

Russell began to wish he hadn't started this.

"You knew my father during the war," he said somewhat desperately. "Tell me where you were, what you were doing."

After some more difficulty and a number of false starts and repetitions, Russell learned to his astonishment that Bob and Jack had both been in the D-Day landings and then their regiment had fought its way inland from the beachhead. There, on a road through Normandy, they had run smack into a formation of German tanks. The carnage was frightful as they were cut down by artillery barrages.

"I was hit," said Bob, "in the shoulder and the leg. 'Hold on, hold on,' Jacky shouted to me, 'I'm going to get you back.' I screamed at him to leave me but he kept going, crawling on his belly into the guns, and dragged me out of there. So you see, I owe him my rather long life."

He chuckled down the phone, and then there was a bout of wheezing.

"But he saw some terrible sights—well, we all did, but Jacky was very badly affected by seeing a mate of his blown to bits in front of his eyes and all kinds of other horrors. That's why he got ill."

"Ill?"

"His nervous breakdown. Had to be invalided out of the army. Was in the hospital for a long time, wasn't he, more than a year I think. And afterwards, well he just wasn't the same at all, poor chap. Nervous as a kitten. Very sad, after what he'd been like in the war. Fought like a lion, he did. A real hero. Anyway, I heard he'd eventually got married and had a family, so I wrote to him. But I never heard from him again."

After he put down the phone, Russell sat very still for a long time. He thought desperately hard about his father. How could this be true? There had never been the slightest hint of any war experience. Nor had there ever been any mention of a nervous breakdown.

He had just assumed that his father's excessive fears and fantasies were part of his character. He had, it seemed, misjudged him totally. He could have had a father to be proud of. Why had this been kept from him? Did his mother know? Had she ever shown any concern for Jack's well-being?

He tried to claw through the mists of his memory. All he remembered was his mother's distant contempt. A contempt he had shared. He went cold at the thought. Had his father been silently suffering all those years? Did the wounds in his mind remain raw, or had they healed? Jack had been a badly damaged hero; both Russell and his mother had treated him as an imbecile.

Russell wept.

10

ELIACHIM'S STORY WAS engrossing him. Russell's knowledge of how Jews had lived in medieval England was non-existent. This just hadn't figured in anything he had ever been taught. No one had ever mentioned it. Now he thought about it, he realized that it was as if the Jewish past in England was an unopened book. No one had said anything because no one had wanted to know.

What, indeed, had they all talked about all those years? The price of kosher meat. Football, cricket. Slights and insults. Anything of substance, ever? It was all such a blur in his mind. What did he have to hang on to? He felt like a piece of driftwood in the open sea.

Yet there had always been a backstory, there had been real people hundreds of years earlier making their way in a hostile land. His land. To his astonishment, Eliachim was telling him that the Jews of medieval England had been a force to be reckoned with. He drank in the rich detail. And then, to his deep pleasure, the story took off in a new and delightful direction.

∞

Eliachim's story (2)

My father was a man of substance; we lacked for nothing. We knew that whatever foul lies and oaths assailed us from the priests and the common people, our community would be protected by our great usefulness to the King of this realm of savages. To him and his nobles and even to the priests of their accursed church we provided the means to support their wasteful and extravagant luxury. None contributed more than we to their coffers to build their great houses of worship and to fund their wars.

My master Josce, may God avenge his memory, in whose house I served as secretary and commanded his correspondence and the times of his appointments, held many estates in the county of Yorkshire in pledge. He numbered among his familiars all the nobles of the county, the sheriff and the constable of the castle, the abbot and monks of the cathedral and many more besides. To them he advanced money to buy their corn and their armor, to build their estates and their monasteries. To his house they came to profess false friendship, may they be cursed for all time, as they took his money and caroused at his table with hatred in their faithless hearts.

His house was like a palace, fashioned of the thickest stone and with vaulted rooms and minstrel galleries and filled throughout with the finest plate and hangings. His drinking vessels were of purest gold and his table was laden with every kind of fowl and beast that is permitted under our laws.

For many years we lived and prospered under the protection of the former King. The violent humor of the common people was restrained by his edicts, and at those times when the mob was enraged against us the sheriff of the county would grant us the shelter of his castle until the danger had passed, in exchange for gifts of money or precious objects of which our community had an abundance.

Life was good to us. Indeed, such was the fame of our town for its learning and piety that it attracted the greatest Talmud sages from far and wide. The yeshiva in our town of York, may its name be cursed for all eternity, where Rabbi Yom-Tov who arrived from the great yeshiva of Ramerupt some eighteen summers past when our people were expelled from that land by the Frankish king and who sat at the pinnacle of its scholarship with Josce the magnificent as its patron, was renowned for its brilliance and its piety.

Every day I would accompany my father to prayers in the house of the cantor, Rabbi Yehuda. It was my father's custom, after prayers were finished, to tarry and discuss matters of business with others of our faith who were there. I was supposed to be studying my books until he was finished, but I would often while away the time composing songs or poems in my head. One day I stole from the room to pursue a kitten that had run in and looked around desperately, maybe for its mother, before running out again. To my joy I spied Duzelina tenderly stroking the kitten in her arms.

She beckoned me into another room. There we sat and gazed at each other. She was very shy. I told her of my longing to spend my days in poetry and song instead of Talmud study. Then she spoke most affectingly of her own yearning to be free of the stifling embrace of her family, and of her fate in marrying someone to whom she had been betrothed these past two years but whom she had never even seen.

How eagerly I now looked forward to accompanying my father to our daily prayers. No longer did he have to drag me out of my bed, and he spoke of his pleasure at my sudden enthusiasm for piety. As my father tarried to converse with his friends and business acquaintances, I would slip into another room where Duzelina was waiting for me.

We talked as if there was no end to the interests we awakened in each other. She had a quick wit, and was well versed in literature and in history and also in mathematics and astrology. How much she yearned for another kind of life, one in which she would be free to follow wherever her restless, inquisitive mind might lead her. The world was full of wonders, she whispered; they were waiting for her, she felt she could almost touch them, but they were all just beyond her reach. She was destined instead for children, running the household, rules governing every single action of her day: a fettered life.

I was bewitched. Her beauty, her gentleness, her zest for life which sparkled as brightly as her eyes, all enchanted me. I had never before imagined I could feel such allure. I wanted to hold and possess her forever. May the Almighty forgive me, this led me to destroy what I most deeply loved.

We had never so much as touched each other, as our faith strictly prohibits any such contact until marriage has bound two souls together. One morning, I read her a poem I had composed expressing my adoration of her. When I finished, she wept. I reached out my arm and my fingers brushed her hand. Instantly I was on fire. I was consumed with such desire as I could never have imagined. I thought she might snatch away her hand, but she did not. Instead, she reached out her other arm and gently touched my cheek. We looked at each other in wonderment. We drew closer, and my mouth pressed down on softly parted lips. My whole body shuddered with longing. I felt the downy softness of her cheek, smelled the fragrance of her hair. We clung to each other as if nothing should ever part us.

But then the door opened; and standing there was my father. I felt the world around me stop, fixed as if in a tableau. On my father's face there was first amazement; then horror, and then rage. We flew apart, my beloved and I, and my father dragged me from the room.

My mother this time did not save me from his wrath. I was forbidden to leave the house until I was to be married. I was told never to say a word about what had happened to anyone lest the family be exposed to shame and disgrace.

My heart was full of agony. I knew full well the enormity of my crime. It was unthinkable that the younger daughter should marry before the elder. I had risked exposing Genta to humiliation and ridicule. And I had exposed my beloved Duzelina to the danger of becoming a worthless match. For by my impetuous act I had according to our laws made her my wife.

But worse, so much worse, was that I had desecrated God's own laws of family purity. My father told me I had betrayed my people and my faith, brought shame upon our household and exposed it to the wrath of heaven. In great tumult of mind, I fell on my knees to beg forgiveness from the Lord of the universe. But my heart was instead full with my love for Duzelina and the words died on my lips.

Then it was that I knew I would be punished, that the Holy One would make me pay for the crimes I had committed and for which I could not fully repent. But I could never have imagined how terrible that punishment would be.

Kuchinsky, however, was now getting on his nerves. Russell needed to concentrate hard on translating Eliachim's story. But Kuchinsky wouldn't leave him alone. He would shuffle into the front room where Russell was working, surrounded by piles of dictionaries and reference books, and come and peer over his shoulder wafting a pungent odor of garlic and sweat that made Russell's stomach heave.

"When you finish yet? Is taking long time. Too long."

"Well it isn't easy to do this, you know. Can't be done in five minutes. Takes a lot of work. And you're not exactly helping me. All this secrecy, not being able to take it to any experts."

Kuchinsky breathed more heavily.

"You the expert, Mr. Director. No one else see this. You gave me your vord. This book of secrets. You tell only me what it says. Only me."

Just what did he think was in it? His intensity was tiresome. The intensity of the obsessed. Whatever. It was just getting in Russell's way.

"The story that's being told is really fascinating, you know. It's a love story, timeless really, two young people finding each other against the background of all the obstacles of their culture and all the violence of the times."

"Love story? What I vont with love story? You find love story in women's magazine, in blessed cinema. I don't vont with sentimental rubbish. Is something else this book telling us. You find it soon, for sure."

There was a hard edge to his voice that Russell didn't like. He began to feel uncomfortable, even a little intimidated. Absurd; what could an old man like this do to him?

Lose patience and stop Russell from coming to work on the manuscript before he got to the end, that's what.

The wife, Veronica, clearly didn't want Russell in the house. She would open the front door to him and let him in without a word even of greeting, standing with a surly expression and with arms crossed in front of her while Russell was forced to push past her into the gloom.

Kuchinsky would prowl round the room while Russell thumbed through the dictionaries and puzzled over the construction of the sentences. Periodically there would be an outburst about politics.

"This country not vot it vos. Wery sad, wery sad. You go in street, on bus, walk round supermarket, more and more of them you see. What, we're not supposed to notice what's happening? Everywhere you see these vimmin, all in black from here to here" (he gestured from his nose to his feet) "only their eyes they let you see. Who know what they have underneath?"

"Designer jeans and sexy tops, most like," said Russell lightly. A man of a certain type, a certain class, he told himself; but he ground his teeth. To have to listen to all this half-witted bigotry; really, it was intolerable. But he was trapped.

"Enoch Powell! Now there vos clever man. Like you—he also knew Greek and Latin. And he vos right! He vos right! What they did to him; said he vos racial prejudiced—he vos not racial prejudiced, this vos Britain losing its vay, losing its blessed mind. Look around: everything he said come true. They should have listened to him. Now everyone racist if so much as peep against terrorists, vimmin in black veils, wiolence in street. Ve all racist! Unless ve blow pipple up! Then ve untouchable!"

Russell sat frozen in horror.

"This country, when you think vot it once vos, it make me wery sad, a tragedy. Once it had empire that went round vorld, you know? Everything down drain after empire. India, that vos high point, jewel in crown, that vos ven Britain had power. Then it knew how to deal with pipple who were backward, primitive, it knew how to turn them one against the other; those wery clever leaders, those British, but now...now British on their knees begging and pleading. No more British lion. Mrs. Tetcher, now there vos lioness. You liked Tetcher?"

"Well, I..."

"Vot a voman! She strong voman, powerful voman. She understood who were real enemies of her country. Not like now, namby-pamby milk puddings in blessed government. Boys, children—ach. She brought down communist Soviet

Union. You realize that? She knew, she understood. Soviet Union evil, evil. These wery, wery bad pipple. They kill thousands, millions of pipple. They send to labor camps, Siberia. Secret trials; no justice. Now they all scream about human rights. Ach! Secret police knock on your door in middle of night, drag you out of bed, children screaming, they beat you, shoot you. Many, many pipple just disappear. Communists, these were animals. And they vanted to take over vorld. Mrs. Tetcher, she knew this. She destroyed them."

His hands, his whole body trembled. He was most passionate when he spoke about communism. About Nazism, he was silent. That figured, Russell thought. The Holocaust was just too raw for him. So he projected all those feelings onto communism. A man like that—simple, not sophisticated—maybe to him it was all much of a muchness, whoever was taking freedom away. He thought of his own grandfather, who had been in the Bund when he arrived in Britain as a penniless refugee at the turn of the 20th century. He thought of his own parents who had met at meetings of the Young Communist League.

"Well, we all were in those days," his mother had said. "If you were against the fascists, you were with the Communists."

His father remained a socialist all his life, but Russell suspected that Sylvia may have voted Liberal.

"There were many reasons why the Soviet Union fell. I don't think Mrs. Thatcher can claim the credit for winning the Cold War all by herself."

"Vot! You don't like Mrs. Tetcher?"

It was as if Russell had suggested the sun would not rise the next day.

"You are also communist?"

Not for the first time, Russell contemplated the sheer cliff-face of intellectual limitation among the lower classes.

One day, he was left alone in the front room for a long time after he arrived. Kuchinsky was nowhere to be seen. He heard raised voices; a door slammed shut. Eventually, Kuchinsky came in with the manuscript in its usual box. He wouldn't meet Russell's eyes.

"My vife, she vorried you telling pipple about this book. She think you make trouble for us."

"No, I haven't told anyone about it. Really." Russell said. "But anyway, you're not going to get into any trouble over this. You may make a lot of money from it, you know."

"My vife, she say you make off vis money, you cheat us."

Russell was becoming increasingly alarmed. Kuchinsky was restless, distracted; his mind seemed to be elsewhere. It was as if he had suddenly got bored with the whole business of translating the book.

The atmosphere was worsening almost daily. Russell sat at the table, his body now tensed against Kuchinsky's querulousness. The possibility was now uppermost in his mind that Kuchinsky would snatch up the book and order him out of the house.

The old man didn't want to know what was in the book. He wanted only to hear that it was what he thought it was, a prayer book—more than that, it seemed, a book with mystical, even magical qualities. The more Russell tried to tell him what he was actually uncovering and which was so entrancing him, the amazing detail of how the English Jews of the 12th century had lived, the richness of their interior lives, the poetic quality and literary gifts of Eliachim of York and his tender love story, the more Kuchinsky's face darkened.

The unprompted political ramblings dried up. Kuchinsky would sit silently staring at Russell, which was worse. He developed a calculating look, as if he were weighing something up. Russell was pretty sure he knew what that something was.

He had to do something.

One day, he pretended to start at what he was reading. In an instant, Kuchinsky was by his side, breathing heavily.

"You have found something?"

"Well, I'm not sure exactly yet, but...well, yeah, Eliachim seems to be saying here that, um, God is guiding his hand to write, and, er, um, that his words are a blessing and that anyone who reads them will be blessed, along with all in his house and his children, and they will heal all sickness and bring wealth out of poverty and turn swords into ploughshares..."

He knew he was going dangerously over the top now, but the effect was electric.

"I knew it!" cried Kuchinsky in triumph. He clapped his hands together and danced a little jig on the spot. "I knew it! I knew this vos holy book, sacred writing, vord of God!"

He fell to his knees and looked up towards the grimy ceiling, his face radiant. The door opened and his wife entered.

"What's happened?" she said in alarm. "I heard shouting. Joseph, are you ill?"

Joseph. It sounded strangely formal to hear him called by his full name. The more homely Joe suited him better.

"Is all true, just as I thought! The book is vord of God! Is miracle in our house! All this time it vos protected, I knew it was for purpose! Now it vill bring us good fortune!"

Veronica looked keenly at Russell.

"Is this true? Is this what you have found?"

He was disconcerted by her gaze—startled now, not hostile, but still wary.

Under cover of shuffling his books and papers, as if to refer to the words in question, he dropped his eyes to hide his insincerity.

"Well, the language is really...remarkable," he said with as much conviction as he could muster. "Very striking...there's clearly the feeling that this...that this is, ah, inspired, ah, inspired by a higher power of, um, some kind, no question."

She was still staring at him.

"And that the book will bring good fortune to all who read it?"

He set his chin. "Sure," said Russell. "Certainly. It's all there."

He could see she didn't believe him. Still, after that the atmosphere eased. Kuchinsky stopped looking calculating and sat looking expectant and excited instead. Every so often, Russell threw him a few more such verbal bones. Once embarked upon the lie, he found it quite easy to continue.

Meanwhile, the worm of doubt that had been there since the beginning was growing. Was the whole thing a forgery? To have such a treasure fall into his lap...it just all seemed too good to be true. Kuchinsky's story was plausible enough; family heirlooms did get passed down through generations. But just how had a 12th century English manuscript ended up on a Polish farm?

The risk he was taking was enormous. The world in which he lived revolved entirely around reputation. You had to be one of them, and for that everything had to fit. The right kind of people needed to talk warmly of you, to want to drop your name as "very bright" or "mega-talented" because the right kind of people kept referring to you in the right kind of papers or websites. It produced a consensus of approval, this golden club, a penumbra of protection; but there could be absolutely no backsliding. One misstep and you were out. Making allowances would reflect too badly on everyone else for any of them in the club ever to take that risk.

Of course, he reflected as he jogged doggedly round Parliament Hill Fields, he didn't have to expose himself to any risk at all. He could just do what Kuchinsky wanted, translate the manuscript, tell him what it said and then walk away. No one would be any the wiser about whether it was genuine or not.

But he knew he couldn't do that. The lure of revealing this to the world, of being hailed as the discoverer of a medieval masterpiece, the fame and respect that would accrue as a result, above all the chance to break out of dumbed-down broadcasting schedules and put an end once and for all to the sinking feeling that he was now being left behind by younger, more hungry film-makers—this was a temptation that was too strong to resist. The manuscript just had to be genuine.

11

RABBI DANIEL WAS as good as his word. An email suddenly appeared in Russell's inbox inviting him to Sabbath dinner on Friday night. *Shabbos!* No way, thought Russell in horror. He'd had a bellyful of religion in the week after his father had died. He had no wish to be drawn back into that world he had briefly been forced to revisit. Although he had to admit the rabbi's message made him smile.

"Can we tempt you to venture beyond the pale of rational thought?" he had written. "As a piece of anthropological research you'll probably find it quite rewarding. I can guarantee that the chicken soup will be medicinal, even if you find the food for the soul less digestible. And do bring your daughter too."

"Cool!" said Rosa when he told her as a joke that he was facing a choice of entertainment on Friday evening between God and the Manic Preachers. A colleague had a couple of spare tickets for a concert at the Roundhouse. Russell assumed Rosa was impressed by the Manic Preachers; to his astonishment it turned out that she wanted to go to dinner at the rabbi's.

"But he's the real thing," protested Russell. "He's not some trendy feminist who thinks Moses was transgendered and who signs round-robins to *The Guardian* about boycotting Israeli apartheid mud packs. This one has, you know, beard and sidelocks and fringes hanging outside his trousers."

"Wicked!" said Rosa dreamily.

"You won't be able to do anything there. You'll be bored. You won't even be able to turn on a light."

"God, Dad, you're really sad, you know? Everyone's into religion these days. I'm definitely going, even if you're not."

So Russell found himself one Friday evening standing with Rosa outside an ugly pebble-dashed, thirties semi in Hendon. He rang the bell.

"Shouldn't've done that," said Rosa. "Electric bell. Not allowed on the Sabbath. Should've knocked."

How the hell did she know that? When the door opened he was covered in embarrassment.

"Russell! So good to see you. Welcome to the other side!" laughed Rabbi Daniel. "And you must be Rosa. Great that you are here. My children are dying to meet you."

The house was a blaze of light that streamed into the drab, dark street. Russell was dazzled as he stepped inside. The air was warm and heady with the fragrance of cooked chicken, vanilla, spices. Small children raced around excitedly. There was an atmosphere of expectation. Through an open door Russell glimpsed a long table round which chairs were crammed next to each other. People were standing around chatting animatedly and laughing. Every few minutes there was a discreet knock and more people flowed through the front door.

Two older girls of about eight and ten came and stood next to Rosa, staring shyly at her nose and eyebrow rings. They were wearing demure dresses that almost reached their ankles. Russell noticed that unusually Rosa was not wearing her habitual vest top but had sleeves that covered up the tattoo on her shoulder. But he could still make out the faint scars on her forearms.

A tiny child in blue trousers and striped T-shirt and with her long, light brown hair bunched into a ponytail on top of her head held out a toy bus to Rosa. She smiled a sweet smile that Russell had never seen before, took the bus and rolled it towards the child. Then she darted out a hand and tickled the child's tummy. There was a delighted squeal. Russell looked more closely. The child was a boy. He danced away shrieking with laughter and Rosa gave chase.

"Looks like Rosa's already made herself at home—I'm so glad," said a warm female voice. Russell looked round. A young woman with a ravishing smile and with a kind of black crocheted snood covering her hair was standing nearby. "I'm Samantha—everyone calls me Sam."

Russell held out his hand. She hesitated and then extended a limp hand of her own. Too late he realized his mistake—she wasn't supposed to touch a man.

He snatched back his own hand, leaving her own awkwardly stranded in the air. He was embarrassed again. God!

How was he going to get through the evening if it was all going to be like this?

"Pinchas! Go help Bracha bring in the wine glasses! And Rafi, please clear away that Lego now before someone breaks their neck on it!"

More and more children materialized to finish setting the table. Christ! How many did they have? Seven? Eight?

Sam moved serenely from kitchen to dining room directing the children in a kind of military operation. She was calm and unhurried. He thought of his own mother, always in a noisy panic whenever they had had just a couple round to tea; getting a full meal on the table so that the food didn't go cold before everyone was served had been quite beyond her.

He noticed how slim Sam was, despite the bump signaling the forthcoming arrival of yet another child, and how carefully she had dressed; her short, coffee-colored jacket had artful pleats and tucks and her ears and neck were hung with pretty artisan jewelry. This was a woman who, while demure and indeed covered from neck to mid-calf, clearly did not believe in abjuring the demands of appearance. He found this unsettling. Surely, given both her obstetric record and the belief system which had trapped her into it, she should look... well, oppressed?

Everyone finally gathered at the table. Russell found himself seated next to a woman in a bright red dress who appeared to be something in the arts, and on his other side a professor of molecular science. There were several couples but also, he noted, a number of single people. At the far end of the table Rosa had a toddler on her lap who seemed heavily engaged in plaiting her hair, while another hung round her neck and explored the piercings in her eyebrows and nose. Russell stared. He had never before seen Rosa give a second glance to a child.

After the rabbi had made the blessing over the wine, most of the table mysteriously disappeared for a few minutes and then drifted back.

"Do you live far from here?" Russell asked the professor of molecular science. He did not reply but grimaced and shook his head and waved his hands. Why couldn't he talk? Was he suffering from some terrible affliction? Had Russell been seated for the entire evening next to a mute? Now, however, Russell noticed that all round the table conversation had ceased, and that the children were making extravagant sign language gestures to each other, snorting with laughter as they did so.

Rabbi Daniel leaned over as he too got up to leave the table, and said quietly:

"After we wash it's the custom not to speak until the bread is passed round."

For the third time in the space of thirty minutes Russell was embarrassed. Just how many more of these rules were there, for God's sake, to trap the unwary?

But once the pieties were over, the mood became festive and jolly. Dish after dish arrived, fragrant and steaming and altogether delicious: sushi to start with, then clear soup with little pasta pillows filled with meat, chicken in a herby sauce, sliced beef in savory gravy, sweet potatoes scented with cinnamon, tomatoes stuffed with rice and herbs, three different kinds of *kugel* or vegetable cake, something garlicky with squashes and peppers; and then later on cake and fruit, chocolates and nuts. There was a more than decent Cabernet, Russell noted appreciatively, and after the soup was served, various bottles of whisky appeared on the now groaning table.

"If you're a whisky drinker, may I recommend this one," said the rabbi, lifting an obscure Scottish single malt and looking ruminatively at the label. "Someone brought it back from a holiday in the Hebrides. Has quite a kick."

He wasn't wrong. Russell felt an altogether unfamiliar benign sense of well-being stealing through him. Through the pleasantly warm stupor of food, wine and whisky, he was surprised to discover that he was beginning to relax.

He felt a tug on his trouser leg. He looked under the tablecloth and saw the small child—boy? girl?—peeping mischievously up at him. Before he knew it, he was under the table too, pretending to be a monster while the delighted child squealed and returned for more. Up above, no one seemed to find this at all unusual.

Children climbed onto the rabbi's lap and hung one on each leg when he stood. He was strong and muscled. Russell stared at the children in envy. What riches they already possessed. He was suddenly all too aware.

Afterwards, when he looked back on that meal the word that floated into his mind unbidden was joy. Every few minutes someone round the table burst spontaneously into a

Hebrew melody; unselfconsciously, most of the diners joined in at the tops of their voices. Russell found himself tapping away with his foot to the rhythm of it all. At one point, various men jumped up from their chairs, linked arms and danced in a circle as they sang.

"Please treat us to one of your family ensembles," said one young woman, her eyes shining with anticipation.

The rabbi laughed and inclined his head in a gesture of modest acknowledgement. He tapped his wine glass and hummed a note. Then he, his wife and their children all sang in harmony. The sweet, piping voices of the children soared above the rabbi's strong, mellow tenor.

Everyone else round the table sat transfixed. Rosa's eyes were shining, her face alight with pleasure in a way Russell had never seen before. He suppressed a lump in his own throat. What on earth was happening here? Had they simply been bewitched?

The talk turned to what Rabbi Daniel called "Jewish geography." It seemed that just about everyone round the table except Russell was related to someone else in the conversation. Sam, it seemed, came from an enormous family. The woman in the red dress had a husband who seemed to be something in finance and was an important donor to the synagogue, and who was a second cousin of Sam's mother's uncle. The professor of molecular science's brother-in-law on his wife's side had been married briefly to Sam's father's niece—who happened to have been the obstetrician who had delivered the red dress's first child.

"We really are one tribe," someone laughed.

"Well, we do all go back to one father in Abraham," said Rabbi Daniel.

"Not to mention our father in heaven who is responsible for the miracle that we continue to exist at all," said the professor of molecular science, whose name was Sternberg.

"Figuratively speaking, of course," said the red dress, who was called Sophie. "Unless you're talking about the State of Israel, which is hardly a miracle, is it, more a reincarnation of Sparta. Without the charm."

There was a pause.

"On the contrary," said Sternberg, "Israel's survival certainly is a miracle. There is no other way of explaining something that defies all known odds, and not just that but does so over and over again."

"Oh, come on," said Sophie. "America's got something to do with it, surely. No miracle in brute military force, is there. I mean, just look at the way they behave! And anyway, miracles aren't rational, just a metaphor at best. Merely credulous folklore. How can you have something which goes against nature? It's just not scientific."

The lively chatter around the table died away. On his left, Russell felt Sophie's bristling hostility. On his right, he felt Sternberg stiffen and brace himself. The rabbi stroked his beard, his eyes bright and watchful.

"But the whole point is that God stands outside nature," said Sternberg quietly. "You can't use natural criteria to judge His actions. It's a category error."

"Well, I'd expect the rabbi to say that," said Sophie with a brittle little laugh, "but not a scientist. I mean, it's not a very scientific thing to say, is it? Your discipline is all about the natural world, surely?"

"Indeed it is," said Sternberg thoughtfully. "And from the study of that natural world, I have concluded that there are undoubtedly limits to its scope and therefore to what we can ever know about existence. Thanks to science, we now know that we can never know all there is to know."

Sophie opened her mouth again and then thought better of it. She contented herself with shaking her head pityingly. Russell, who agreed with her—or at least, he thought he did—found he was actually rather glad she had been squashed.

"Afraid my wife is rather...*left-wing*," said Sophie's husband with theatrical emphasis. He looked embarrassed. There was a small titter of nervous laughter round the table.

"Well it's no use hiding our heads in the sand," said Sophie, tossing her sharply cut, silvery grey bob. "Israel's behavior does us Jews here enormous harm. I mean, *really*, their Prime Minister! *So* extreme! And those settlers—look how they behave! No wonder the Palestinians are driven to act as they do. How would *we* all feel if our land was occupied and stolen from us?"

"But it was," said Sternberg. "By the Palestinians' ancestors. Those, that is, who didn't themselves only arrive as immigrants in the last century on the back of the Jews—who were, and are, fully entitled in law to live in Judea and Samaria, then and now."

"Judea and Samaria!" exclaimed Sophie, pronouncing the names with an expression of extreme distaste. "Right-wing talk. That's why there's no peace! Really and truly, is it any surprise that people hate us so much?"

Russell looked steadily at his plate. He and Sophie were on the same side, after all, and he suspected that that made a grand total of two around the table who thought like that. But he was unsettled by the argument. He was disconcerted there had even *been* an argument. This was the first time Russell had heard it said, calmly and rationally, that the facts were simply not as Russell had always assumed them to be.

For Professor Sternberg wasn't another Michael Waxman. Sternberg was a scientist, a renowned one at that. He had not spoken from emotion. He seemed to have spoken on the basis of evidence. And now Russell wondered for the first time whether the assertions made by Sophie were in fact true.

"So where did your own family come from originally, Russell?" asked Sam from further down the table. Russell suddenly realized that, while appearing to be dealing with the children and talking animatedly to Rosa, Sam had also managed to pick up the tensions that had developed and was now intent on defusing the situation.

Where *had* they come from, his grandparents and great-grandparents? Russell was aware of faces turned interestedly and sympathetically towards him. Including Rosa's. Oh God, he groaned inwardly; he didn't know. Russia? Poland? He wasn't even sure which. What were their names, the villages from which both sides of the family had fled the pogroms?

Something incomprehensible. He had never paid much attention, and his parents had not exactly been forthcoming.

Once again, he was embarrassed. He heard himself start desperately to gabble.

"Oh you know, somewhere beyond the pale at the turn of the last century, pogroms, Cossacks, usual kind of thing, so many of us like that, weren't there, but you know, what I'd like to know is how we got there, beyond the pale that is, I mean, where did we come from before we went beyond it, as it were, into Poland, Russia, Belarus and so forth, presume we were all pretty Teutonic really, all Germanic really."

"Well, real Jewish geography is really fascinating," said Sam. "If you look at a map of the movements of Jews over the centuries, you can see that they really did roam the world. They went from one country to another and then another as one after the other persecuted them or threw them out."

"My wife is too modest to tell you herself," said Rabbi Daniel proudly, "but she did her PhD in European demographic change 1100 to 1900."

Sam leaned forward, her elbows on the table, her face alight.

"If you draw the migration patterns as lines across the globe, you can see that it's not so much straight lines as great loops. From the Middle East and Africa up through Spain and France, and then into Germany, Poland, Russia and even Britain, and then back, some of them, into Africa—Maimonides, for example, had to flee the so-called Golden Age in

Spain for Morocco—and then out again; always jumping from one geographic frying pan straight into yet another fire."

"You say even Britain," said Russell casually. "But the British Jews were forced out, weren't they, in the thirteenth century. So where did they go then? Back to France, where many of them had come from?"

"Well yes, in the first instance," said Sam, thoughtfully. "But don't forget the Crusades were slaughtering Jews across Europe. So they had to keep moving, from France to Germany, from Germany to Poland and Russia."

"You mean British Jews could have ended up in Poland?"

"Of course," said Sam. "Many Jews from Britain, France, Germany and elsewhere ended up in Eastern Europe. You can see it in the language."

"In the language?" Russell's heart beat faster.

"Sure. A number of Polish Jewish names, Yiddish names, in fact, which you find in Poland, reflected the influence of French words. 'Bunem,' for example, came from the French word *bonhomme*. 'Schneuer,' another very common Polish Jewish name, came from *seigneur*. 'Yentl' from *gentille*. And so on."

"And presumably, since the Jews of England at that time spoke a kind of French dialect, some of those French words could have been imported into Poland by English Jews?"

"Very probable, yes indeed," said Sam.

And they could have brought other things with them too, thought Russell in mounting excitement. Like a refugee's diary.

"If you are interested in this period," offered Rabbi Daniel, "I have a number of books here that I can lend you which might be helpful. If you are sure you have the stomach for it, that is. That was a particularly terrible time for us Jews."

"When is it not?" said Sternberg morosely.

"Oh come *on*," said Sophie. "This is the kind of thing that gives us a bad name! It's not terrible to be a Jew in Britain today! It's wonderful! We have everything here we could possibly want!"

Sternberg looked steadily at her. "Except acceptance as Jews," he said quietly.

"Well, I'm a Jew, and I'm accepted!" said Sophie.

"Jewish kids at my school are being given martial arts training to stop them being beaten up," said Rosa at the other end of the table.

There was a shocked silence.

"Really? Who is beating them up?" asked another guest in alarm.

"Black kids, mainly. And Muslims," said Rosa.

There was a sharp intake of breath around the table. Guests looked down at their plates. Russell's face felt as if it was on fire. He stared at his daughter. What on earth had got into her?

"I'm sorry," said Sophie, drawing herself up in her chair, "but this is just racism. Sheer, naked racism. And particularly shameful to hear it from one of us."

"But I'm not actually Jewish," said Rosa. "Although I'd like to be."

"Time for some more *Shabbos* songs, I think," said Rabbi Daniel.

It was all very strange, thought Russell. First there was Rosa's behavior, showing a side of her that he had just never seen before. Had it always been there? He stole another look at her. Her habitual sulky pout had vanished. She actually looked happy. He was astonished.

And then there were Rabbi Daniel and Sam. How on earth did they reconcile these two sides of themselves: the rational and the credulous, the educated and the obscurantist, the modern and the primitive?

To Russell, you were either in one camp or in the other. Religion simply repelled reason. But Daniel and Sam sounded like people he knew, people in his own world; they had intelligence, to be sure, but more than that they were demonstrably connected to the wider culture. They were, literally, down to earth.

As if he could read his thoughts, the rabbi interrupted his reverie.

"So Russell," he said teasingly, "do you find us as weird and Moonie-like as you thought you would?"

Russell blushed deeply. "I'm just a bit amazed, really, how you keep all these balls in the air at the same time."

"Well, stereotypes rarely bear much relation to reality, do they," smiled the rabbi.

It was now or never.

"But you do believe, don't you? In, you know...God."

"Of course."

"But you seem so...normal."

Rabbi Daniel threw back his head and laughed.

"When Sam and I met at Oxford, we weren't religious at all. Wasn't how either of us was brought up. At Oxford, I was a rowing blue; and you may find this hard to believe, but in those days Sam ran around in tiny micro-skirts and even hot-pants. I was into heavy metal music..."

"Heavy metal?" Russell was incredulous.

"Sure: that and psychedelic rock, you know, Black Sabbath, Led Zeppelin, all that lot. I played electric bass guitar myself. We had a little band and used to do university gigs. All of that led me to...this."

"How..."

"Two ways, really. First, what that music did to me was crack the shell around me, open up my emotions. Once your emotions are released—I mean real emotions, not sentimentality—that allows your spiritual imagination to flower. So that was happening, but at the same time, the people I was mixing with in these rock circles, the musicians and the fans alike, they were all heavily into the drug scene. I saw my friends being really messed up, saw the way they were frying their brains, and I just got frightened. Religion was where I went for safety. We both did; Sam was floating around on the fringes of that scene, and, well, she met me and we kind of stared into the void together. The rest, as they say, is history."

Russell stared at this man in his black silk Sabbath coat, with his dark beard and sidecurls neatly tucked behind his ears. The words just didn't fit.

"But how could you then start believing in something beyond this world?"

"How could we not believe in it?"

"But it's just not rational. There's no more reason to believe in God than in the man in the moon. It's all based on miracles, on things that just couldn't happen."

A pair of warm brown eyes twinkled merrily at him. "Now I'm going to say something that really will annoy you—that's a very Christian attitude you've got there. Christians have this great hang-up about 'faith.' We don't obsess about it like that, we just get on and live it. What's more, Judaism is actually based on evidence, on what is the least unlikely proposition. You know, I bet I can persuade you!"

"No thanks," he said quickly. What was he afraid of exactly? He couldn't really say, when he thought about it. After all, if he really believed it was all total nonsense what possible danger could there be that he might be persuaded it was true? But why on earth was he thinking this way anyway?

Sam collected his plate.

"Rosa is a remarkable young woman, isn't she: so sharp and yet so soft, and with courage too. You must be very proud of her."

Russell opened his mouth and shut it again. Truth to tell, he had always been disappointed in her from the moment she had been born. He had been sure it was a boy. But then he had realized, and he was disappointed.

It was a pattern that was to be repeated as Rosa grew up. He assumed that any child of his would be clever, successful, graceful. He had married an English rose and expected his daughter to resemble her mother. As a child, however, she was short and spherical, almost swarthy and with a fine down of dark hair on her upper lip. A regression to that gene pool that he had thought he could obliterate, he thought in disgust. And now just look at her, festooned with piercings and tattoos and all in black, even on her lips.

"The children have really taken a shine to her. We hope we'll see her again: we have open house here."

"But Rosa's lifestyle...we aren't...I mean, we don't practice anything."

"It takes no practice," said Rabbi Daniel dryly. "Just enjoy it."

"And Rosa isn't even..."

"A child with a sad heart is a child with a sad heart. I counsel a lot of young people from every walk of life—orthodox, non-orthodox, religious, non-religious. If they feel they get something from me, that's great. I'm happy to give it to them."

When they finally left, the front door shut behind Russell and Rosa and extinguished the radiance of light and warmth in which they had been bathing. Darkness and shadows enveloped them once again.

Rosa hunched into her leather jacket. "How come you don't even know where my great-grandparents came from?"

"You've never asked before."

"You never told me there was anything to ask about. It's really cool to know about my family and what happened to them all so many generations ago. And you never told me about any of that."

She waved her hand at the house they had just left.

"They want me to do some babysitting for them. And Rabbi Daniel says he'll teach me about kabbalah—real kabbalah! Not that Madonna rubbish. Real mysticism. Not crap magic, spirituality."

She strode ahead. "They really are getting beaten up, you know," she flung back over her shoulder. "The Jewish kids. And that's real racism."

He stared after her.

12

HE WAS ACUTELY aware he needed to diversify. The gritty social documentaries just weren't cutting it any more.

"You know, heritage always goes down very well," said the commissioning editor at Pollyanna Productions.

She was new. Her name was Damia.

"Heritage? You mean history?" he puzzled.

"Social history, actually. Things like, oh I don't know, how the poor lived in the Victorian era, or the English countryside idyll. Smaller-scale, more intimate. Viewers connect."

He looked at her. Her skin was dark, and her black hair was cut very short, elfin. He guessed Pakistan. Yet she clearly had an instinct for English susceptibilities.

"Immigration?" he ventured.

"Mmn, too angry," she demurred thoughtfully. "You want to avoid rage. You want people to empathize, identify."

Instantly, he knew.

"How about a history of the East End?" he said cautiously. "That's seen waves of immigrants—French, Jews, Asians. You could do it from the perspective of the buildings, the streets.

It's pretty well untouched round there, apart from a bit of gentrification."

She tapped her teeth with a pencil and inclined her head slightly in acknowledgement.

"That could work well," she nodded, with a smile. She was slightly built, with high cheekbones. She really was very attractive, he thought. How old? Early forties? But no ring.

"I once saw a play about that, a comedy," she said. "The writer got into no end of trouble. Accused of racist stereotyping. Utterly ridiculous."

He adjusted his mental view of her. Clearly, she herself was determined not to be categorized. He wondered about her own background. She had a plummy English accent. Like Alice.

"Well, my father came from round there, actually."

"Ah! Is there a story to tell about him, maybe? We could do an authored piece, you know, your reminiscences. Oh, but only if you wanted to..." she added hastily when she saw his face.

"He just died," he said by way of explanation. Which of course, it wasn't.

"Oh, I'm so sorry," she said sympathetically. "Were you close?"

Absurdly, he found himself wanting to tell her everything.

"No, not really," he said.

"How sad," said Damia. There was a quietness about her, a stillness that he liked. She didn't seem brittle like most TV types.

"That must be so difficult. I'm still very close to my parents and they're in Pakistan."

"My father was a Jew."

As if that would explain anything! But he felt he needed to say it, to get it out in the open, cards on the table. He held his breath.

"Ah, hence living in the East End," said Damia. "You know, I'd love to know about Jews and Judaism. I know virtually nothing," she said apologetically.

He was touched, despite himself, by her artlessness. It was a new experience for him altogether to meet someone who really seemed to have no preconceptions. He felt strange, and he realized with a small shock that he had relaxed. Suddenly he saw for the first time the state of tension under which he normally lived in England. Under which they all lived, the British Jews.

They were always braced, always anticipating, always ready to deal with whatever would be flung at them, from a veiled insult to an actual blow; even when there was nothing at all to cause any alarm, there was always the assumption, the knowledge, the certainty that behind the social pleasantries, friendships even, lay centuries of dislike of the Jew, or worse, that was ineradicably embedded in the social DNA. Chaucer, Shakespeare, Dickens, T. S. Eliot, Agatha Christie—it was in the English cultural bloodstream. It was the default attitude, and the Jews of Britain had adopted an automatic cringe as a result.

Yet until this moment he had never realized that his own life had been lived in precisely this defensive crouch. He had only seen it now because for the first time he had met someone who really seemed to be totally free of it. Someone from, of all places, Pakistan.

He wondered if he might break his golden rule and ask her out.

13

"DAD," SAID ROSA, "can I ask you something?"

She was playing Lara Croft GO on her iPhone with her legs draped over the arm of the chair.

Russell looked up from his laptop. Rosa seemed to be spending more time with him these days. This unsettled him. He was glad she wanted to, of course; but she disrupted his world. When she was there he felt obliged to tidy up his flat, pick up his dirty underwear from where he customarily hurled it on the floor. He'd gotten used to being able to slob about without having to think about anyone else. And he always had a nagging suspicion that Alice was using Rosa as a spy.

"Did you ever say to Mum she should convert?"

He stared at her. Why this all of a sudden? And why on earth should Alice ever have done so? It would never have even occurred to him to raise it. The big issue had been whether to get married at all or just stay living together. They had both thought marriage was supremely bourgeois and really quite irrelevant to a relationship, which didn't need a piece of paper in order to make a solemn commitment to each other; but then

Alice had talked to her colleague who did matrimonial at the Law Centre and decided that unless they did get married she would be left without various legal rights if it all went wrong, so they had ended up at Camden Register Office.

"Mum didn't—doesn't—believe in anything religious. Nor did I, really. Wouldn't have felt right."

"Really?" Where had that come from?

"But then I might have known my granddad. I never even saw him."

Irritation welled up. Not this again. He'd had a bellyful of this from Beverley. Not from Rosa as well now.

"Well yes, that is sad. But that's life. These things happen."

He wondered nevertheless how they would have got on, Rosa and the old man. They had certain things in common. Mulish obstinacy, for starters.

He took a large Tesco's pizza out of its cardboard box. From the fridge, he extracted a Budweiser and an opened can of Coca Cola. He fished out some knives and forks from the sink, picked off the congealed food, rinsed them and put them on the table. He brushed crumbs onto the floor.

"Why don't you ever cook real food?"

"No time."

"Mum doesn't have time either but she doesn't eat out of cardboard. At least not all the time. If she'd converted, would you still've split up?"

"Wha...you think that...that didn't have anything to do with it at all. Your mother and I...your Mum just wanted to live in a different kind of way, I suppose. She was very focused on her work."

"Might've made you have more in common, p'raps."

"We had plenty of things in common. We had you. And we've still got you."

"Maybe you'll get back together one day?"

She was resolutely looking away from him, her eyes fixed on her plate. But her voice had trembled. Surely, he thought, she couldn't still be hoping?

"I think she still fancies you."

"How d'you make that out, then?"

"She's always sad."

"So she's got no one else then." To his irritation, his heart lifted.

"I never said that."

He had always known that Alice had never loved him as much as he had loved her. He had been smitten the first time he saw her, taking part in a panel at a conference about miscarriages of justice. She was a young human rights lawyer and had already made a name for herself in some high-profile cases. She was elfin, with porcelain skin. He couldn't take his eyes off her.

Russell couldn't believe his luck when she agreed to go out with him, and pinched himself when they moved in together soon after that. She said she found him exotic, that she'd never met anyone quite like him. She called him her big cuddly bear and said he had a certain smoldering quality. He didn't think he had ever smoldered but he took it as a compliment.

They moved into a terraced house in Hackney, an area that was scruffier and therefore even more cutting-edge than neighboring Islington where you couldn't move for politicians, barristers and journalists.

He was aware that as a mere TV producer he was riding on the coattails of his high-flying wife, but that didn't bother him. They had a smart house, smart friends, smart opinions. They lived in a golden bubble, basking in the reflected self-esteem of a shared commitment to social progress and the betterment of the disadvantaged and deprived.

For Russell, Alice had been his passport into the land beyond the rainbow. Through her, he had escaped the drab and vulgar world he had once inhabited. Now embraced by the elect as one of their own, he had been able to forget the humiliating limitations of his former life and assume instead the identity of the English upper-middle class. In this glowing company, with its effortless superiority, witty cleverness and artful elegance, it felt to Russell as if life was just one long mellow party—one that would moreover never end, but was an enchanted land suspended in place and time.

At what point had it all gone so terribly wrong? He really couldn't pin it down. There had always been a part of her that she seemed to keep hidden from him. She had never quite let down her guard. Sex between them was straightforward and serviceable enough. Afterwards, satisfied, he would fold himself around her back, like spoons in a drawer, and fall asleep straightaway. The fact that she never turned spontaneously to him passed him by.

He put her moodiness down to the fact that she was highly strung. She lived on her nerves, and seemed always to be at the center of some drama or other. Her life was lived at a pitch of intensity that he found simply exhausting. Even on holiday she would tap away at her laptop into the night. He admired her enormously, but he felt rather wistfully that it would be nice if she could just relax.

He himself liked to be cozy, safe, stretched out comfortably in front of the TV of an evening, slippers on, beer to hand, while she was out at meetings or receptions. From time to time, she would pop up on *Newsnight* or the *Today* program, her voice trembling with controlled anger as she earnestly explained the unique evil of the latest government initiative designed to deprive terrorists, illegal immigrants or burglars of their rights.

She presented herself as a freedom fighter for the wretched: if not of the world, at least of North London; and her weapon was the law. "No one is above the law," she would harangue some cowering politician in a TV studio, "because the law is made by Parliament and Parliament is the voice of the people." She was the people's tribune, thought Russell in admiration as he crumpled further into the sofa watching these performances; he was all too aware (not least because she occasionally told him) that, in the war in which they were both fighting, she was the active combat unit while he was merely an armchair general.

He was, however, proud to be her husband, enjoying the reflected glory in which he could bathe as they both systematically worked the room in the fashionable salons to which her stellar reputation gave them automatic access. They complemented each other, he thought; he found her slightly terrifying and ultimately a mystery, but there was no doubt that they made a terrific team.

So it came as a shock when one day she said she wanted out. To be more precise, she wanted him out. He must have realized, she said, that things just weren't working between them anymore. No, there wasn't anyone else, she said. She just felt stifled. She needed more personal space.

"I've never stopped you from doing anything," he said, winded.

She sighed.

"I'm shocked when I look back and realize how much of myself I have had to suppress in our relationship," she said, nodding her head slowly to indicate the significance of the discovery.

Something rose up inside him in revolt.

"And what about Rosa? Have you thought about what this will do to her?"

"Just too boring if you're going to get emotional. We need to discuss this reasonably, as adults."

"What, you're reasonably throwing me out?"

"Well let's face it, Russell, you wouldn't have had any of this if it hadn't been for me."

She swept her arm in the direction of the rest of the house.

"I just can't believe this. Don't you feel anything for me anymore?" he said. The pain was unbearable.

She scuffed her toe uncomfortably against the parquet floor. "Look, I'm not blaming you. I'm just in a different place from you, that's all. Shit happens," she shrugged.

So she shrugged him off, and he found himself in a different place. She never made it difficult for him to see Rosa; on the contrary, periodically he would open his door to find the child deposited there like a parcel because Alice had to fly abroad as a matter of urgency to lecture on human rights.

She hadn't been altogether upfront about one thing, though. A few days after he moved out, he read in *The Guardian* diary that she and an actor with floppy hair and a louche reputation were now an item. Too late, he realized that his real crime had been to be dull.

Russell and Rosa chewed their way through the pizza.

"How's school?"

"It sucks. I wanna leave. The teachers treat you like shit. All we do is play games and tick stupid boxes. They treat us all as if we're thick."

"We got you a tutor, didn't we?"

"Yeah, but she's boring. It's like jumping through hoops. Just to get through GCSEs."

"Well, you've got to pass your exams if you're going to university."

"But university is crap. You say so yourself. All those thickos who're 'only there to get them off the unemployment register'—that TV show you did, remember?"

"Come on, you'd go to a..."

He stopped himself. Rosa narrowed her eyes and sat up.

"You were gonna say 'real university', weren't you. Such as Oxford, I suppose, just like you went to. God, Dad, what a fucking snob."

"But you need qualifications to get a good job, to fulfill yourself. And don't swear."

" 'Spointless. All jobs are just a grind. Most people, doctors or lawyers or...or whatever, like they're all just trying to get through the day, get through to the weekend, have a laugh just like everyone else."

He couldn't resist it. "Like your mother?"

He regretted the words as they left his mouth. She turned her face away from him, but not before he saw the look of... disgust, he thought; but afterwards, turning it over in his mind, he decided it was pain.

"Don't want a career," she mumbled. "Just want a job, like in a bank, or something."

It turned out that Sam had been as good as her word, and Rosa had indeed been doing some babysitting for the rabbi's children.

"Rabbi Daniel's going to see the head to see if he can stop these attacks on the Jewish kids at school," she said as she demolished the remains of the tub of Ben & Jerry's Chocolate Chip Cookie Dough ice-cream that she had dug out from where it had become jammed into a small glacier of nameless brown gunge at the back of the freezer compartment.

"How's he going to do that, then?"

"He wants to talk to the school about what being Jewish means."

Good luck with that, thought Russell.

"Don't you think it's terrible that these kids're getting beaten up? In broad daylight too."

"Well of course all violence is wrong...but it's more important to understand this kind of behavior than just mindlessly condemn it."

She stared at him, a spoonful of Chocolate Chip Cookie Dough ice-cream suspended halfway to her mouth.

"You kidding me or something? This is, you know, like real antisemitism, Dad!"

He winced. That word. Uttered only by the truly paranoid, the undereducated and the suburban. So simplistic. So overused, as if the entire world was against them. Of course Waxman used it all the time, totally failing to understand that it was so very stupid to use it at all because it was the one thing you just never, ever accused someone of, because it was obviously so insulting to them, unless of course they were right-wing.

"Were you ever attacked because you were Jewish?"

He poured milk into his coffee; whitish, curdled lumps immediately formed on the surface. He smelled the milk and gagged before pouring it down the sink. Shit. He desperately wanted some whisky, but thought he'd better not in front of Rosa. He sighed.

"Loads of people have something horrible done to them—if you've got red hair, or speak with the wrong kind of accent. There's nothing special about attacks on Jews. Blacks and Asians have it much worse."

"That's what mum says. She says the Jews are always whining about the Holocaust, as if they're the only people in the world who ever suffered. And now they're doing the same thing to the Palestinians, keeping them locked up like what happened in the Warsaw ghetto."

"She...er...um, your mother said that? About doing the same thing? And that comparison with the ghetto?"

"Yeah. We had like a totally major row about it."

He was startled. Reversing the roles of Israel and Nazi Germany was precisely the kind of claim that he knew characterized far-right websites. How could Alice, of all people, possibly be spewing far-right poison?

Now other memories swam into his consciousness through the sluice that he had kept shut but which Waxman had opened. The playground taunts of "Jew-boy" and "You killed Jesus." Being called to the front of the class to explain Fagin when they were doing Oliver Twist. The history master describing Disraeli to the class as being "of the Mosaic persuasion" and to the 14-year-old Russell as "one of your brethren." Being hauled before the headmaster at age 15 for having stood silently during the Lord's Prayer in assembly because he considered himself to be an atheist, only to be told there was no justification for any Jew not saying the Lord's Prayer since it did not actually mention Jesus. And that Saturday lunchtime when, as he and his father walked back from the synagogue, a man yelling at them from across the street:

"Go back where you came from!"

"Don't look, keep your head down," his father had hissed at him as they had hurried away.

To all such incidents, his mother had merely sighed and then shrugged. "What do such people know? Nothing. Just ignore them. It's just something we have to put up with."

But she closed the curtains when the Sabbath candles were lit so they couldn't be seen from the street.

Why, though, brooded Russell, was there always this awful thing, this visceral dislike, which never seemed to have any explanation, nor any end to it, but which they were expected always just to accept as a fact of life? It must be because, he eventually decided, Jews went out of their way to make themselves different from everyone else. This made people suspicious and resentful. And who could blame them? So the way to avoid this dislike was obvious. It was to be the same as everyone else. So simple! And so perverse not to be!

"I read this book about Anne Frank," said Rosa. "I'd like to go and see her house in Amsterdam where they all hid in the secret room."

"Our family also had relatives who were murdered by the Nazis," he said.

Rosa's eyes widened.

"Another thing you didn't tell me!"

He had known this, somehow, all his life, although it had never been talked about at home. His father's family, lost in the hell that had been visited on Poland's Jews. Who, precisely? Uncles? Cousins? Great-aunts? He didn't know even that, let alone their names. Jack had never wanted to talk about it, for obvious reasons, and Sylvia had had no interest in drawing attention to the primitive stock from which her husband had sprung.

But in recent years, he had been proud to feel connected to that great, defining tragedy of the Jewish people. Those Jews who had died in the Holocaust were pure and noble, innocent victims of the monstrosity of fascism. They had never oppressed or killed anyone. Their culture that had been erased, the *shtetls* and *shtiebels* of Eastern Europe, could now be viewed through the retrospective soft-focus of history as quaint and picturesque.

Moreover, since the Nazi genocide had been directed at the Jews as a race rather than as a religion, Russell could safely bypass Moses altogether and feel himself to be linked instead, through his exterminated if unknown relatives, to a persecuted ethnic minority, thus securing him instant access to the protected and coveted status of a Victim Group. Indeed, *the* Victim Group.

This status helpfully served as a suit of invincible armor.

14

DESPITE HIMSELF, RUSSELL found he was thinking about that Friday night meal at Rabbi Daniel's house more than he cared to admit. He had to acknowledge that, to his astonishment, he had actually enjoyed it; more than that, he had been touched by it. Something in him had stirred that evening, something that had lain so dormant he had never suspected it was there. When he thought about that evening, he found he was actually smiling.

What he brooded about most was something that had struck him in that house like a stray shaft of sunlight. It was a quality of what could only be described as innocence.

There was an openness about Rabbi Daniel and Sam, an artlessness. It was certainly not stupidity—far from it. But their attitude towards the world brought him up short. What they were was out in the open; nothing was hidden. This was the source of their calm, the fact that they were solid and sure inside their own skins. And they displayed the same expectation of others, that they too were assumed to be straightforward and essentially benign.

What these two radiated, in other words, was trust and hope. They believed the best of other people and of the world, until and unless they had evidence to the contrary. Russell could see why Rosa had in effect fallen in love with them. They made those around them feel better about themselves.

And Russell found he himself was looking at his own world through different eyes. Suddenly, the people in it looked mean-spirited and dismal. Their carefully affected cynicism, which they adopted reflexively in order to make themselves appear smart and sophisticated, was actually based, he now saw, upon a deeply sour and distrustful view of human nature.

They instinctively believed not in the good in people but the bad. Accordingly, their habitual position was defensiveness. What he had assumed was sophistication was in fact nothing less than an ingrained belief in the worst about others.

He thought about himself, about his work, about his life. How callow it all now seemed. He had thought he had stood on the side of open-heartedness, of generosity of spirit, of making a better world. But now it was as if the people with whom he was associated, his colleagues, his comrades in this great endeavor, were frozen, atrophied, petty.

Yes, yes, that was it—petty. How trivial they suddenly seemed. How small their preoccupations, how limited their horizons. Now he saw it all so clearly. How could he ever have thought he really was like them? How could he have thought any of that actually mattered? To his horror he saw how second-rate it all was, how derivative.

He could so easily have just slipped into the easy assumption that this was all there was to life. But now he realized that he was cut out for so much more. He had the wherewithal to make a true mark, to register an impact upon history itself with a unique and original discovery. And he owed it to society to do this. In the unprepossessing person of Joe Kuchinsky, he felt that destiny had tapped him on the shoulder. Yes, he owed it to scholarship, to history, to...to Rosa to bring to light the story of Eliachim of York.

Ah, Rosa. He hadn't been a good enough father, he knew that. What he had seen at Rabbi Daniel's table was another side to her, one he had never suspected. It had stung him, her reproach. Why had he never shown her any of this, her own ancestry? Because he himself had never known it, he thought morosely.

Well now he had a chance to make good all of that. Now he had a chance not just to pass on that knowledge but actually to expand it. He would not just be recycling ancient myths and the wisdom of sages—he would himself be adding to it. At a stroke he would redeem his own ignorance, his own marginalization. He'd like to see Elliott's face when he triumphantly unveiled Eliachim of York. That'd show him.

He was aware of a new unease when thinking about the book: his book. He hadn't actually been at the house to work on it for a while. Time had run away with him; it must be, what, three weeks now. Too long.

He had called Kuchinsky a couple of times but had gotten no reply; he hadn't thought much about that. But now he thought of the last time he'd been at the house. Kuchinsky had been even more nervy than usual. At one point he had gone to the window and twitched a curtain.

"Is car parked a few doors down. It comes now twice, three times. Two men inside it, just watching."

"So what? Could be anyone. Not likely to be a burglar." Russell had tried to be reassuring, but he had probably sounded a bit too irritated. Kuchinsky's paranoia was getting to him.

Kuchinsky had made no reply but just stood there by the curtain, totally still, looking through the crack.

Since then, there had been no contact. Now who's being paranoid, he thought. He tried to shake off the unease.

15

THE HOUSE WAS not as he had imagined it.

He fumbled in his satchel and checked a crumpled bit of paper on which he had scribbled the address. Yes, this was it: Folgate Street, number 12. Where his father had said he lived.

But this couldn't be it, surely. This was an expensive street. Although the terrace looked a bit crooked and rickety, these were still grand houses with fine tall windows. They boasted well-kept wooden window shutters, carefully chosen to be in keeping with the age of the houses, some of them painted in tasteful colors.

A buried fact swam into focus: ah yes, these were the famous Huguenot houses, which had first accommodated French weavers in the 18th century and then waves of immigrants after that.

Nowadays they'd be worth, what, one point five minimum? More, even. But his father had never said anything about Huguenots or historic houses. All Jack had told him about where he had been born and spent his early years was that it was in a slum in London's East End, where his parents and he and five siblings had been crammed into a couple of rooms in some hovel with a privy in the back yard and a tin bath in the kitchen.

"That landlord, what a swine," he would say. "The place should've been firebombed as a health hazard."

Jack had never even known that the place had a history, let alone any innate grace. If he saw it today, he would be astounded. But then, he was a fool when it came to money.

Time changes things out of all recognition, thought Russell, as he wandered through the neighboring streets. Signs of gentrification were all around: here was a little coffee shop displaying French *Poilâne* loaves and cupcakes with brightly colored fondant icing and cherries on the top; there was a tiny chic boutique selling expensive leather goods. But he hadn't come here to enjoy such yuppie delights.

He had come to scout out the East End in order to work up his proposal to submit to Damia. Of course it was personal: she had been right. It wasn't just an interest in social history. It was a desire to connect for the first time to the nearest thing to a history that he himself had. To go back to where his father had come from, to anchor himself in that reality.

He had never paid it the slightest attention in the past; he had never asked about it, never wanted to know. Now he was frantically scrabbling in his memory for the shards of information lodged there from Jack's often maudlin reminiscences about his childhood.

Maudlin, but also bitter. Was that just because of the poverty, or had there been some deeper misery? Was it because he had been so ill, because of his breakdown? He had presumably come back to these streets a different person altogether from when he had left them. What had he been like before, when he'd been a character who would run headfirst into danger in order to save an injured comrade? Had he then, in these streets, been seen as a leader of men, as a man who would inspire followers? Russell would never know. And now he wanted to know.

His father's face loomed up in his mind. He dreamed about him; twice he was sure he had seen him in the street. He had a deep yearning to talk to him. But of course it was all now too late. There was so much he didn't know about his father, about his family, he thought to himself, stricken. If he went back to those mean East End streets where Jack had lived as a boy, maybe he could fill in some of those gaps in the picture, connect himself to his father, close up that enormous gap in which there was only silence, anger and rejection.

But the East End had changed.

It was still dingy, dirty, poor. But the streets were now full of men in long jubba coats and galabiyya tunics, women in every kind of veil, hijab, niqab, burqa, and of course the ubiquitous shalwar kameez. There were Bengalis, Pakistanis, Indians, Turks, Somalis; the shops had signs in Arabic; racks of cheap clothes and stalls selling fruit and vegetables and household goods spilled all over the pavements; snatches of Punjabi and other languages he didn't recognize floated in the air as he passed by.

"It really is a different country," Russell thought, and immediately felt guilty. How could he of all people have had such a thought? He detested with all his being that crabbed, sour, intolerant attitude that saw multiculturalism as a threat. Hadn't his father fought that very attitude all his life, first in Cable Street and then in Notting Hill?

What would his father himself have thought of these changes in his old stamping ground? Well of course he would have welcomed them. How could he not have done? After all, weren't these latest arrivals following exactly the same trajectory as the Jews of Eastern Europe who had preceded them, and the Irish and the Huguenots before them? Didn't people like his grandparents and great-grandparents themselves wear strange and even outlandish clothing, and weren't they too treated with disdain and dislike; didn't his own grandmother wear a headscarf and speak no English? Weren't these veiled women exactly the same?

This fear of the other, he mused as he walked through Spitalfields market, this suspicion of the stranger, the outsider, just because they were outsiders, yes, that really was the most pernicious thing.

His phone buzzed. Text from Alice. What now?

Govt ever more shitty, prisoner torture, racist immig plcies. Am being lined up for imptnt role advising Labour P on creeping fascism. R involved unsuitable boy

Unsuitable how? he tapped out in dread. Drugs, maybe? Police record?

Israeli wrong sort

She meant he was not a post-Zionist, an Israeli who hated his own country. He knew that because that's how he also would have thought, not that long ago. He deleted the text in irritation without bothering to reply.

He found himself in Henriques Street, gazing up at a building called Bernhard Baron House. Suddenly he had a clear memory of his father talking animatedly about the Oxford and St. George's boys' club to which he had belonged, and which had been housed here.

"They taught me to box, to use my fists to defend myself," his father had said, "but they also taught us something else, us poor Jews from the East End. The club was divided up into four houses, just like the public schools. We were Britons, Danes, Normans and Saxons. Saxons! Can you believe it! This maybe was to make us feel we weren't only Jews, but Englishmen."

And how proud his father had been to become one, thought Russell. He had forgotten this memory until this very moment. He had boxed; he had used his fists. It had never before occurred to Russell that this hardly fitted the timid, terrified father he had known. Whenever his father had talked about this club, Russell had rolled his eyes. Boxing! How primitive. And he had dismissed it with a shudder.

But now he saw it differently. His father had been tough. He had learned how to stand up for himself. He must also have been physically nimble, adroit. And brave too. How he wished he'd know all that. How he wished he'd been a different person back then, to have been able to be proud of his father for the boxing instead of always feeling so ashamed.

He felt a great weight of sadness descend on him. Come on, he thought, no point in wallowing. But the melancholy persisted. He turned a corner and came across a church, its whiteness shocking against the surrounding drabness; somehow incongruous, as out of place as a lily in a coal hole. Its solidity comforted him. He went inside.

It was a beautiful church, light and airy, with a magnificent ceiling picked out in gold offsetting the poignant simplicity of its cream walls and magnificent, tall, clear-glass windows. A workman was busy with the thick wooden front door, apparently sanding it down. Russell walked round the church, lost in thought.

"Nice, ain't it."

Russell turned his head. The workman had come inside and was messing about with buckets and sprays.

"Beautiful. And so tranquil. A real oasis."

"You can say that again, mate." The man jerked his thumb back towards the door. "Wicked, what some people do, i'n't it."

Russell looked. Now he saw the door had been defaced. "Christian scum" had been scrawled on it in black paint.

"Terrible. Anyone know who did it?"

"Youths," said the man, darkly. "Thass all we're allowed to say, isn't it. *Youths.* Prob'ly the same *youths* what smashed up the gravestones out there a few months ago. And maybe the same *youths* what smashed up the vicar a year or so back."

"Lot of vandalism round here, then?"

The workman straightened up and wiped his hands. He gave Russell a steady look. "Well, less put it this way. These 'ere *youths* what smashed up the graves painted on 'em 'death to infidels,' yeah? Another church round 'ere, what got a brick through the winder, people heard these *youths* screaming 'shouldn't be a church, should be a mosque.' And these *youths* what beat up the vicar 'ere, who kicked and punched 'im in the 'ead, they shouted 'effing priest' as they did it. Those ones, they got caught but they were let off, weren't they, 'cos the prosecution, like, they said it wasn't racially or religiously motivated. And the vicar himself, he said it was only stupid drunken *youths*, and that community cohesion was very important round 'ere. Well, something missing 'ere, if you ask me, and it ain't no community effing cohesion.

"Now the vicar, 'e's a good Christian gentleman, like. But there's attacks going on round 'ere all the time. They want to force us out, to make everything so shit we'll just give up and leave. They're even attacking them Asians as well. And the police they don't do nothing about it. There's Muslim women working in shops what've been threatened if they just show their hair. There's white girls being sworn at and set upon, knowwhattamean, just for wearing a mini-skirt. And there's these gay people being beaten up just for being what they are. One young guy drinking at one o'them gay pubs or what'aveyou down the road from 'ere, he was left paralyzed he was so badly hurt. Now don't get me wrong, they're not my cuppa tea, but they should be able to have a drink without getting beaten up, like. But all we're told is, it's *youths*. No one's joining up the dots, knowwhattamean?"

Russell finally got away. Useful, he ruminated. Nothing to beat getting this kind of feedback. To hear such attitudes from the horse's mouth, so to speak, in all its exaggerated... well, yes, sheer bigotry, of course, it really was so valuable. Maybe Damia would rush a camera crew down here to film this? Then again, probably not. It would only detract.

Nevertheless, as he resumed his walk he began to notice things he had not noticed before. A sticker on a lamppost depicting a rainbow-colored band inside a black circle with black line across it proclaiming "gay free zone"; a billboard with a model in underwear advertising a deodorant, over whose torso black paint had been smeared; the girls' school he passed at going-home time, with crowds of young girls in veils spilling into the street but where one young girl tore off her black face-covering as she turned the corner out of sight of the school.

He had been walking a long time and had a raging thirst. Too early to go for a pint, so he nipped into a small grocery store and bought a bottle of beer. He twisted off the cap and took a long swig. He walked on and came to Fieldgate Street. Fieldgate Street! He was sure that was where his father said he had gone as a boy. Was the synagogue still there?

The whole street, the whole block, seemed to be filled by an enormous mosque, all red brick and large white dome and minaret; and there, alongside this vast and domineering edifice, stood the fragile, tiny synagogue now closed down but still bearing its name and a Hebrew inscription carved in to the stone above the door, the only sign of what it had been below the two stories of flats above.

It seemed to tremble alongside the mosque like a mouse in a lion's paws.

Russell took another swig of his beer as he stood looking at its blue door and inscription. There was a shout from down the road.

"Hey man! No alcohol!"

Three young men in hoodies were looking at him, pointing and gesticulating angrily.

"This is Muslim area! No alcohol! Respect, man! This is a mosque! Is against Islam!"

The three started to run towards him. There was a glint of a blade. Russell turned and fled. He ran down a side road and kept going, across one road and then another. Then he got to a junction with a bigger road, and ran down that.

It was only when he eventually stopped running that he realized he had been running away down Cable Street.

16

"SO, NO MAN in your life, then?"

They sat companionably over coffee and a fragrant Muscat. She had attacked her treacle tart and cinnamon ice-cream with a childlike concentration.

"Mnn, nursery puddings," she had sighed in artless satisfaction as she finally put down her spoon.

It was very easy between them. Russell felt as relaxed as if he'd known her forever. Yet he didn't know the first thing about her.

She lived in Stockwell, it turned out, with two cats called Beatrice and Benedick.

"Why...?"

"Because they're always teasing each other."

He looked blank.

"*As You Like It*?"

"Ah..."

She was that into Shakespeare? He adjusted his view of her once more.

"But they love each other really. At least, I hope they do. You can never be sure, can you?"

He was disconcerted by her direct stare.

They had agreed to meet in the National Theatre restaurant, which seemed a reasonable halfway point between them.

Now she pouted coquettishly. "Does there have to be a man?"

"You're not..."

"No, no," she laughed, "I'm just pretty self-contained I suppose. And you?"

Once again she held his gaze. With her almond-shaped eyes, he thought she had a look of a cat herself.

"Was married but it didn't work out."

"I'm sorry. And you weren't close to your father?"

"No, there were...well, issues."

"Sad. My family's very close. I thought Jews were close?"

He bridled, despite himself. She looked at him thoughtfully, her head on one side.

"You know, I really liked your East End proposal. It's...it's really quite moving."

"It is?"

"Sure. The father you never really knew, the vanished world in which he grew up, all that, it really makes it all come alive, you know. Draws the viewer in. Makes me want to know more about you, about your background."

He shifted in his chair. Was this a come-on, he wondered. She steadily held his gaze. No giveaway there.

"Well it feels a bit, you know, solipsistic."

"No, viewers really love this, to get a little glimpse of what's burning away behind the presenter's mask."

"Not sure anything's burning," he said uneasily.

"Oooh, I'm getting a whiff of scorch marks," she said softly.

He stared out of the picture windows. White fairy lights were strung out along the river, their reflection twinkling in the black water. He wondered what she would say if he told her about the boys outside the mosque.

"I went into a church there. It was beautiful, but it had been vandalized. There was graffiti saying 'Christian scum.'"

"How awful. Do they know who did it?"

"Just youths. Apparently."

"Ah."

She looked down at the table. There was a pause.

"Apparently the vicar was beaten up too."

She shook her head.

"I think we want this film to be very positive, don't we. We want to create...a certain atmosphere. Poignant buildings, streets of memories, nostalgia for transient worlds, that kind of thing. We don't want to get sidetracked."

"Absolutely not," he said fervently. He decided not to tell her about the beer and those other youths.

"Hope you won't take this the wrong way," she said, "but, well, can you tell me about Judaism? I've always wanted to find out."

He was taken aback.

"What do you know?" he parried.

"Well nothing at all, actually. I've never met a Jewish person, you know, that I could actually speak to about it. Where I came from in Pakistan there just weren't any. Now I hear them talked about all the time. I just wonder why, and why it's so difficult to get any of them to talk about it. And now there's you."

It turned out she had been educated at Cheltenham Ladies' College and Bristol University. Her parents had sent her to Britain when she was eight.

"They sent you here alone?"

"They admired Britain, wanted me to have a British education. They're very open-minded. They've had to be. My mum is Hindu, my dad's a Muslim."

Was such a thing possible in Pakistan, he wondered.

"Sounds very dangerous for them. How come they're still there, that they've survived at all?"

She shrugged.

"They've always had periodic attacks and scares. My dad was beaten up; they've been threatened many times. But they're very obstinate. They love Pakistan, it's home to both of them and they don't see why they should be driven out by fanatics. They've had to move around a bit, but basically they were determined to stay put. For me, though, they wanted something different. They wanted me to look outwards, not in."

He thought of his own wedding with Alice, that cursory, slightly shamefaced affair in a drab register office. As if a camera had clicked, he saw a clear image of his father's face.

To his shock, he saw him weeping. No, that didn't happen. Couldn't have.

"So how did this work between your parents?"

"Wasn't a problem. Dad practiced his Muslim stuff and she did her Hindu thing. They are very respectful and tolerant of each other. I grew up with both traditions."

"So what does that make you?"

When she laughed, her whole face lit up.

"Well nothing, really. I don't think I believe in anything, not in the religious way. But I suppose it's why I'm interested in religion. It doesn't have to divide people, and yet it does."

She twirled her spoon thoughtfully.

"What's now called Pakistan was once the center of the ancient Vedic civilization. That turned into Hinduism. Now it's a Muslim country. That doesn't bother me in the slightest. What bothers me is that people kill each other over it."

"Well you're a long way away from all that now."

She waved her spoon at the restaurant. It had been empty when they arrived, but had now filled up with people spilling out from seeing the plays, clutching their programs and talking quietly to each other. The women had stylishly bobbed hair, much of it unselfconsciously grey or white, and had clearly dressed up. Most of the men were wearing ties, although there were some corduroy trousers and a certain amount of tweed.

"This is what I love," she said quietly. "The English middle class. Order, tolerance, self-restraint. No hysteria, no extremism, no violence. People like you take all this for granted. But for me, well, it's precious beyond price."

It was true he had taken it for granted, even despised it as the mark of a privileged establishment. But that was before Eliachim of York had come into his life, before he had begun to see that for the Jews of Britain nothing could be taken for granted. Before he had begun to feel different from the rest.

"But is it home?" he asked. "Is it where you feel you belong? Or is that still Pakistan?"

He had never wondered about such a thing before. She looked at him keenly.

"Home? I just don't think about it. Pakistan is where my family still is. Here is where my life is. The word doesn't really mean anything to me. What does it matter, anyway? I suppose I feel myself to be a citizen of the world. Home is where I feel comfortable, where my friends and loved ones are. But that can be different places at the same time, can't it?"

He stared at her as if she had just performed a magic trick. What, indeed, did it matter? There was no reason at all why it should. He could slough off his past, the stuff with his father, all the baggage about where he belonged. Damia was offering him nothing less than his freedom.

He realized he fancied her rotten.

"I really like you, you know," he said to her as they emerged onto Waterloo Bridge. She reached up and kissed him on both cheeks. He pulled her closer and kissed her deeply on the mouth.

"When can I see you again?" he said thickly.

"New Broadcasting House, three o'clock tomorrow to discuss the East End idea, remember?" she said gaily. "I've got a really good feeling about this proposal. I think they're going to absolutely love it."

Then she kissed him again, this time on the mouth.

"You still haven't told me about you Jews, you know," she said. "I won't let you off the hook."

Hunching into her jacket she turned towards Stockwell and walked off into the night.

17

"ROSA CAME TO see us," Beverley said, a barely suppressed tremor of triumph in her voice floating down the phone.

"She wanted to know about our relatives, the ones who were lost in the you-know-what. And she was quite desperate to know about the rest of the family too. Well, of course we were delighted. Surprised, to put it mildly, but delighted. Somehow gathered she hadn't told you she was coming. We looked at all the old photographs together. She's quite intelligent, isn't she?"

"Why should I've told you?" said Rosa sulkily when he rang her to complain. "You'd only have made, like, a total fuss about it, insisted on coming with me or something. Wasn't Gran just beautiful, though, when she was young?"

He could just imagine what Beverley had said to her as she showed Rosa those photographs. Had she also shown her *that* photo, he wondered dully? Even he probably hadn't seen some of the images of his parents that Rosa would now have seen. Now she had her own independent mental picture of them. He felt as if his personal space had been violated.

"Hey, Dad..."

"What now?"

"Anthony's really nice."

"Anthony...?"

"Anthony. My cousin. Your nephew. Honestly, Dad! He hates school too. He wants to be a photographer but his parents won't let him. They're making him go to Cambridge."

Alice rang in a cold fury. She had sneaked a look at Rosa's Facebook page and discovered a link to a terrible website.

Russell thought: Satanism? Pedophiles?

"Worse," said Alice. "Some weird Jewish sect pushing something called *Moshiach Now*! They sound like the Taliban. For all I know they could be terrorists."

Russell laughed out loud in relief. "Terrorists? They're not capable of blowing up a balloon. They're just pious Jews, no threat to anyone."

"No threat? What about the threat to Rosa's mind? These people are primitives; they are against reason; they take the intellect hostage. The women cover themselves up to their ears! Female servitude! And you find that funny?"

"Well it's better than using a razor to slice open her arms."

A low blow, he knew, but even so. The target was irresistible.

"This is all your fault," hissed Alice. "For some reason you've started filling her mind with all this Jewish rubbish."

He rang Kuchinsky repeatedly. There was still no reply.

18

THEY WERE TO meet at the Wigmore Hall for a concert. Beethoven and Schubert, Damia had told him, but the real draw was that the performers were the latest sensation on the classical music scene: a string quartet that had been winning international prizes and rave reviews even though all four members were still in their twenties.

He hadn't paid much attention to the details. He was just savoring the fact that she had agreed to go out with him again. Walking down from Cavendish Square, he saw some kind of commotion outside the concert hall. It seemed to be a demonstration. There was a lot of shouting and chanting and waving of placards.

Oh *shit*, he thought. The placards read "DEATH TO ZIONISM," "ISRAEL APARTHEID" and "NO PLATFORM FOR CHILD-KILLERS." One depicted the Israeli flag with the Star of David replaced by the Nazi swastika.

"What the..." Then he saw the billboard outside the concert hall. The string quartet was Israeli.

No, no, *no!* he shouted inwardly. Irritation rose up in his gorge like acid reflux. Couldn't he even take a woman out on a date without bloody Israel forcing itself into the picture? Couldn't they have found another orchestra from anywhere else in the entire world for this, the first concert he had chosen to attend for more years than he cared to remember?

Other concert-goers, he noted, were having to run a gauntlet of jeers and abuse as the police cleared a path for them through the shouting protesters. He didn't fancy that at all. More to the point, wouldn't this be tantamount to supporting Israel? Might there be someone out there who would spot him doing so?

He badly wanted to turn round and walk away. But of course there was Damia. Was she inside already, perhaps? Had she not yet arrived?

Anxiously he scanned the crowd. Then he realized there wasn't just one demonstration. There was a counter-demonstration as well, and both were being held back by rows of police.

The other one was smaller, comprising a few ragged protesters. These were waving Israeli flags and placards reading "NO PLATFORM FOR GENOCIDE," "STOP PALESTINIAN KILLERS" and "PEACE NOT HATE." One of these protesters had a megaphone through which he was chanting Hebrew slogans. Russell looked more closely, and saw the unmistakable figure of Michael Waxman.

Oh no, he thought.

The larger group was mainly but not entirely comprised of Asian and Arab youths. They were punching their fists into the air and chanting something unintelligible in Arabic. Some wore green bandannas round their heads; others had their heads wrapped in Palestinian keffiyehs covering everything but their eyes.

As if in slow motion, Russell watched one of the bandanna-ed youths, a tall, muscular boy, dodge through the police lines and punch Waxman's megaphone out of his hand. He lunged towards Waxman and there was a scream.

"Stand back! Stand back now!" shouted the police as the green bandannas surged. Through the melee, Russell watched as Waxman staggered backwards clutching the side of his head.

Waxman sank to the ground and Russell hurried towards him. A policeman got there first and pulled Waxman upright with what Russell thought was inappropriate roughness. The police had struggled to reform their lines and were pushing the two groups apart again. To his horror, Russell saw that the hand Waxman was holding to the side of his head was covered in blood.

"Michael, you're hurt," said Russell in horror. "We need to get you seen to."

"Tell that to this cretin," said Waxman.

"Any more talk like that and I'll book you for insulting a police officer as well," said the policeman.

"As well as what?" asked Russell.

"He says he's going to charge me with assault," said Waxman weakly. He looked as if he were about to faint.

"Death to Israel!" screamed the green bandannas. "Fuck the Zios! Nuke Tel Aviv!"

"*Charge* you? But you were attacked! I saw it! I saw it happen!"

"Move along now, sir," said the policeman.

"I saw him being attacked, officer, I saw who did it. It was that guy over there. Aren't you going to arrest him?"

"There's no justice anymore in Britain," said Waxman, and passed out.

Russell and the policeman both caught him as he crumpled. Someone brought water.

"No platform for hate speech! Zios out!"

"Hamas, Hamas! Jews to the gas!"

"Hear what they're shouting? It's incitement to murder!" Russell couldn't believe his ears. "Why don't you stop them instead of picking on this guy who's been attacked?"

"I'm asking you again, sir, for the last time, to step away now, please."

Waxman, who was half sitting, half lying, suddenly moaned and threw up.

"He needs treatment, he needs to be taken to hospital," said Russell.

"Shut it or I'm booking you for obstruction..."

"Fucking police state!"

"...and insulting a police officer. Any more lip and you'll be down the cells with him."

"Wild horses wouldn't drag me away," said Russell furiously.

He felt a tug on his arm. Half pulling him, Damia propelled him towards the entrance to the concert hall.

"We're not going to be pushed out by these thugs," she said fiercely. Her face was set as she steered him by the elbow through the police corridor between the screaming demonstrators. He kept his head down as if he were some kind of criminal.

Inside, the audience was fluttering with dismay. The Israeli musicians walked calmly onto the stage. The audience applauded them with feeling. The quartet played serenely and sublimely as if nothing untoward had happened. In the interludes between movements, Russell could faintly hear the chanting from the street outside.

At the end of their advertised program, without preamble, the musicians stood and started playing Israel's national anthem. A few people at first and then the entire audience rose to their feet and stood silently as the poignant melody swelled round the hall. Slowly and reluctantly, Russell heaved himself up. When the last notes had died away, there was a second or two of total silence. Then the audience erupted into a storm of applause and cheers.

Damia blew her nose and turned a tearful face towards him. "You see," she said, "they're still here. They still exist. They haven't all died out."

"Who?"

"The people who believe in decency and tolerance and fair play: all the things that make Britain so special to someone like me. And to you..."

Was that a question? He didn't know, and didn't want to know. He felt confused.

He looked at the wildly applauding audience. They weren't neocons. They weren't American evangelicals. They didn't come from Golders Green. They were the kind of people he knew well: the cultured English middle class, the listeners to BBC Radio Three and Four, the stalwarts of Lord's cricket ground and the Women's Institute. The kind of people who would give to Christian charities, who cared about animal welfare and would campaign against ritual slaughter and the circumcision of baby boys.

He would have assumed that they would find Jews distasteful and Israelis at best uncouth and at worst belligerent and ruthless in trampling down all who opposed them. Yet here they were, these circumspect, buttoned-up, very proper English, clapping and cheering approval of these Israelis because they were under attack.

"I thought you didn't approve of national divisions?" he said later, stroking her hair.

She rolled over to face him. Her skin gleamed like warm honey against the rumpled pale blue bedclothes.

"I don't."

"Yet you take the part of Israel. And you identify with the über-English."

She propped her chin on her hand and gazed at him. Her hair swung softly against her bare shoulders. He wanted her again. Her sweetness had been overpowering. He wanted again to lose himself inside it, to erase everything but this moment, this now, this consolation.

"The *über-English*?" she repeated wonderingly. "But it's not a bad thing to be able to identify with others who share your own culture and traditions. It's everyone's right, surely. I know what division really looks like. I know what it's like to be the object of fanatical hatred. I lived with that in Pakistan all the time. I saw the unbelievable savagery, Muslim on Hindu, Hindu on Muslim."

"Exactly. So you'd surely want to minimize differences between people. Otherwise you just get more hatred, more war."

"What, like Gandhi, you mean? Like his pacifism meant cozying up to Hitler and Mussolini? Sometimes you just have to stand up against bad people."

"But that's a recipe for more aggression, more war. Things are never so black and white. There's got be room for compromise."

"Hey, that's not the man I saw earlier on wading in to defend his friend. Wasn't much room for compromise there. You were very upset by what happened. Hardly surprising. You must feel it more than most, all this bigotry against Jewish people."

"Well it's actually against Israel..."

"Really? I can't see the difference. Why are they all so obsessed by Israel? Why do they pick on it all the time? It seems quite mad to me. I mean, spin the globe and all the murder and mayhem going on has diddly squat to do with Israel. Why aren't people demonstrating against the killing of Christians or Hindus and Sikhs in Africa or Indonesia, or Saudi Arabia or Iran torturing and killing women and dissidents, or making my mum and dad's life hell in Pakistan? I can tell you, back in their village we could have done with a bit of what Israel has when people were being disemboweled and having their heads sliced off."

"Well, two wrongs don't make a right," he said, but he knew it was lame. There was a good reason for the difference in reaction. But what was it?

In truth, he was deeply unsettled. It wasn't just the injustice of what he had seen happen to Waxman. After all, he hardly needed telling that the police were often out of control.

No, what was nagging at him was that he had found himself on both sides of the barricades at the same time. Damia was identifying the Israelis as victims. But Israelis couldn't be victims. That was just Waxman talk. The Palestinians were the victims in the Middle East. Israel had nukes, for God's sake. Yet he had watched those green bandannas attack without provocation. Yet again, though, if he had been amongst the demonstrators he would have been with the bandannas, not Waxman.

So what did that make Russell: victim or victimizer? Of course, Damia was starting from the wrong premise, wasn't she?

"It's bullying, that's all it is, and I can't stand bullying," she said. "The English can't stand it either, and that's what I love about them, don't you? I loved the way you stood up to that policeman."

Yes, but it had had absolutely nothing to do with Waxman's cause, he thought fiercely.

"I just thought it was outrageous picking on someone like that who'd been attacked and was obviously hurt."

"Just like they do with Israel," said Damia.

He stared at her.

"It's the same thing, isn't it? Beating up on the victim. And if other people take the part of the beater, then the victim just doesn't stand a chance. It's so clear, isn't it? Isn't that why Jews defend Israel?"

"Well...it's not quite that simple. Jews are in fact pretty complicated. You said you wanted to know about them..."

"Not now," she smiled as she rolled on top of him and pulled the duvet over both their heads.

Rosa rang. She was being bullied at school. No one liked her. Her teachers were crap. She wanted to join the Israeli army. All this in a jumble of tearful half-sentences.

Waxman rang. He'd been in the hospital overnight; they'd patched him up and sent him home with a fractured cheekbone, bruising and shock. He was going to plead not guilty to charges of affray and assault. He assumed Russell would give evidence on his behalf. And how about a first-person account of what had happened as part of a documentary about antisemitic violence on the streets of London?

Beverley rang to say her emails to him had been bouncing back. Upon investigation, he discovered that his computer had been corrupted by a spam attack and was now unusable.

The six o'clock radio news reported the arrest of a Nazi war criminal who had been living unnoticed in London for more than seventy years. His name was Joszef Kuczynski.

19

OF COURSE, IT was simply a coincidence. So the names were similar. Unsettling, of course, but obviously not the same person. Couldn't possibly be. Obviously. One was a Jew. The other was a killer of Jews. Too absurd. Don't even think about it. But still.

Details were sparse, but this Kuczynski was said to have lived in North London since 1946, to be 93 years old and to have taken part in atrocities in Poland in 1941 when hundreds of Jews had been murdered in a town with a name Russell did not recognize.

He listened to the next news bulletin holding his breath. There were now a few more details. A Liberal Democrat peer was complaining about the "waste of sparse police resources" in mounting such a prosecution. "This poor old soul has been leading a blameless life in this country, working in a laundry and paying his taxes," she said. "Is this justice or vengeance?"

A laundry! No, it was impossible. Completely, totally impossible.

But icy fingers were spreading inside him. He had made assumptions. He had not been careful enough. He had wanted it too badly. Even so, this simply couldn't be true. Yes, the book might be a forgery and Joe Kuchinsky a fraud: that he had always had at the back of his mind. But not actually to be a Jew at all but a killer of Jews instead: no no, that just wasn't credible. He would have had to fool too many people.

But would he? How many people had Russell talked to about him for any kind of corroboration? None. How many others had assumed he was a Jew? Had anyone else? Maybe only one person had formed this conclusion: Russell. *No!*

He tried to call up a mental image of Joe Kuchinsky, but he found he couldn't do it. There was a blank where his face should be. All he could see in his mind was the sour, resentful face of Kuchinsky's wife.

In dread, he turned on the TV news. A picture of Kuczynski was flashed up, but this was of a young man. Was it or wasn't it? He couldn't tell. He thought not.

The tension started to retreat. But then there was another, more recent picture, said to have been taken at a reunion of Polish wartime émigrés.

It was him. Or was it? The picture had only been up for a few seconds.

No no no no no, he screamed in his head. His eyes had been playing tricks on him. Impossible, impossible. He felt as if he was outside his body, looking on in disbelief. This just could not be happening.

He called Kuchinsky's number. The phone still rang out emptily. He paced up and down. He desperately needed to talk to someone, for that someone to tell him it was all a terrible misunderstanding and of course it was a totally different guy. How could it not be, he told himself.

A spasm gripped his torso, making him gasp and double up. Too much stress, he thought in agitation, all this upset, one thing on top of the other, this is the kind of thing that kills you. Now he had this pain. What was it? Heart? Gut? Which bit of the gut? Ulcer, or lower down? He staggered to the bathroom and opened the medicine cabinet. Packets and tubs of pills promptly tumbled out once again onto the floor.

He poured himself a Scotch. His hands were shaking. Think, think. He scrolled back in his mind to where he had first met Kuchinsky. In the synagogue, of course. He was there praying. He remembered the veins standing out on the hands gripping the seat back, the tears that were wiped away when Rabbi Daniel had talked about a parent's love for a child.

But he had not actually been praying at all, had he. Oh God!

But then, neither had Russell himself been praying, he said to himself. So that could hardly be conclusive, could it. Kuchinsky had not been wearing a prayer shawl. Well, so what? He wasn't married to a Jew. That hardly made him a war criminal, did it. And what on earth would such a person have been doing in a synagogue at all? It made no sense.

With his heart in his mouth, he rang Rabbi Daniel.

"This guy Kuchinsky who was at your synagogue..."

"Yes, yes, terrible, shocking, a dreadful breach of our security. So embarrassing. I am mortified, just mortified. Rest assured we are now reviewing all our procedures."

Russell went cold, and his dry tongue stuck to the roof of his mouth.

"He told me he was interested in learning more about Judaism, that he knew a lot of Jewish people and wanted to understand the ceremonies and rituals..."

"What? You...you knew he wasn't a Jew?" Russell stammered.

"Well of course; that much was obvious. But we pride ourselves in making our synagogue an open space where we welcome the stranger. Now I suppose we'll have to be more careful. Such a pity. But really, a war criminal, I mean, who on earth would have imagined such a thing..."

Obvious. Of course. Only he, Russell, had believed he was a Jew. Kuczynski hadn't pretended any such thing to the rabbi because he knew he could never have gotten away with it. But he had understood somehow that Russell was easier to dupe. Indeed, he was possibly the only person in that entire synagogue who could have been duped in this way. That was why he had made such a beeline for him.

"He only came along from time to time, but even so... When I think of what he did to our people, and then actually to offer him our hospitality—well, we must all learn from our mistakes, mustn't we."

If only he could confide in him, Russell thought dully. If only he could tell someone and thus relieve the burden. But with a sinking feeling he realized he could never tell anyone. His reputation! If anyone should ever know...He would become an instant laughing stock. At a stroke he would be judged for all time as sloppy, careless, credulous. He would never again be taken seriously. He would always be the idiot who had been duped.

But had he been? Even if he had been taken in by Kuczynski, it didn't follow that the manuscript was not authentic. He could have genuinely come by it somehow in Poland, stolen it like so many other priceless artifacts were stolen from the Jews during the Holocaust.

He lay miserably on his unmade bed. All the certainties of his world were going down like bowling pins. He had somehow lost his broadcasting touch; it turned out that he had failed to understand both his parents and his sister; and now he had managed to mistake a Nazi war criminal for a Jew. How could all this be happening to him? Why was he being picked on in this way?

There was no relief from his thoughts. The whisky bottle was now all but empty. If only smoking was an option—but he had always been far too worried about getting cancer ever to try it. He had once accepted a cannabis joint but had been too terrified to inhale.

He rifled among the pill packets on the floor, found some Valium and downed two tablets with the dregs of the whisky. Finally, he dozed off.

When he awoke, it was with a single, very clear thought in his mind. He had to finish the translation. He could do nothing with a half-translated manuscript. If he finished it, at least he would have something he could publish. And who knows, maybe in the wake of the arrest the original manuscript would become public property. Or maybe, given what had happened, Kuczynski or his wife could now be persuaded to part with it. After all, he had almost certainly stolen it.

Stolen. Now the ghost of a plan began to formulate in his mind. What if Eliachim of York's story was indeed the genuine article—looted by the Nazis from some Jewish library, as so many valuable artifacts were during that period—and then somehow ended up in Kuczynski's house in Cockfosters; and what if he, Russell, were to...to rescue this stolen masterpiece from its illegitimate custodian and offer it, if not to the descendants of its rightful owners then at least to some Jewish museum somewhere...

But how would he get it from Kuczynski, who wasn't even answering his phone? He would somehow have to get him to let him into the house, and then Russell would either persuade him to give it up or even...well, he would just have to take it.

That couldn't be theft, could it, since taking something from someone to whom it didn't belong in the first place couldn't be stealing. And if anyone asked him why he hadn't discovered Kuczynski's true identity earlier, he could say something vague about always suspecting he wasn't quite as he seemed, or something like that.

Yes, yes, that would be by far the most elegant solution. His mind returned over and over again to his first meeting with Kuczynski, the sullen hostility of his wife, his first sighting of the manuscript.

Now Russell felt a righteous anger beginning to burn inside him. He was the victim in all this; yes, this Kuczynski, this imposter, this thief had singled out Russell as merely the latest of his Jewish targets. Why, surely anyone would have fallen for such an elaborate and infernal ruse. Nazi. Murderer. Monster.

He could wring his neck.

20

HE STOOD OUTSIDE Kuczynski's house, ringing the bell continuously. No reply, but deep in the house Russell thought he heard a door slam. He had that familiar, disconnected sense of having been here before. His head swam. Not now, he thought, no panic feelings now, please, no. He had to do this. Had to.

He wondered about shouting up from the street; but that would only draw attention to himself. He rummaged for a notebook in the shoulder bag he habitually carried, wrote a note, tore it out and put it through the letterbox. Then he sat on the garden wall to wait. Breathe in, slow, slow; now out, slow, slow.

She must have been standing just inside the door all the time, because within a couple of minutes the door opened. Veronica's face was red with anger and hatred.

"After all you've done, you're now blackmailing us?"

"I've done nothing other than help your husband. If he really is your husband. And I'm certainly not a blackmailer. I'm not the criminal round here."

She thrust the note at him. "Threatening to tell the police about that book is blackmail."

"So why do the police frighten you? Surely the book can't be stolen property?"

She glared at him, but then dropped her eyes.

"Your husband owes me an explanation."

"He owes you nothing," she spat. "You brought us bad luck. You brought us the police."

"Nothing to do with me, I promise you. Your husband brought me here. Now I want to know just what he was playing at."

"Go away and leave us alone."

She started to shut the door but he stuck his foot inside it. He yelled in pain, but pushed the door back against her. She was very slight and it jammed her against the wall. In the gloom of the hall, he saw Kuczynski hovering.

"If you don't let me in," shouted Russell, "I'll make sure this whole shitty street hears all about you. If necessary I'll knock on every door and tell them myself."

Afterwards he marveled at his own sangfroid.

Kuczynski motioned to his wife. She stood still, radiating hostility, as he shuffled into his front room and Russell followed.

"I know what you want from me," said Kuczynski, breathing heavily.

"Just explain all this to me. I'm totally bewildered." Russell spread his hands and adopted an expression he hoped suggested he was pained but listening.

"Vot they saying, I didn't do. The Germans did it all. They make me scapegoat. I vos Polish patriot."

He sat crumpled in his armchair like a used banknote. He looked down fixedly at his knees. Try as he might to see him in a new light as a war criminal, Russell could only see instead a very old man.

"They say you took part in a Nazi massacre."

"I never Nazi. Is filthy lie. Poles wictims of Nazis. Wictims of communists as well. This massacre, communists said Poles did it, put Poles through political trial, beat Poles until they confessed to stop torture. They said Jews burned in barn. I never burned nobody."

"Burned in a...They put you on trial?"

He made a dismissive gesture with his hand. "No trial, I vos in hospital when trial happened. I had breakdown because of all that happened to us, all I saw. But vos nothing left here." He put his hand to his head. "Nothing I remembered. All wiped out."

All forgotten? "So how do you know you weren't involved?"

"I remember later. When I recover and come to UK."

Convenient, he thought.

"No life in Poland under communists after vor. England wery good to me but now they make terrible mistake."

"You...You lied to me. You tricked me. Made me believe you were a Jew."

"No lie. But you brought police."

"What are you talking about? I never said anything to the police. How could I? I knew nothing about you, never heard about this massacre."

"British police not like communists. British police wery polite. But they just doing what government tell them. British government want to show they tough against immigrants, Polish pipple. Want to show also they nice to Jewish pipple because so much criticism of Israel. They got rich donors, got to keep them happy. So this win-win for them. But I never do what they say. Some nasty person gave wrong information. Maybe communist. Police don't tell me vot evidence they have, don't tell me nothing. You know police, you put them on TV, you friends with them."

It was of course preposterous from start to finish. Persecution of Poles, indeed. Russell hated the whole anti-immigration thing, of course; but this arrest was obviously nothing to do with that at all. And was Kuczynski suggesting that Russell should somehow intercede with the police on his behalf?

You've got to be kidding, he opened his mouth to say; but then it dawned on him. A bargain. Kuczynski was making an offer: Eliachim's story in exchange for a quiet word in the ear of the police and the charge then dropped.

Well, if that was the way he thought it worked, then clearly he had never really left Poland at all. But what Russell now had to do was play along with him, to suggest that he did indeed have this kind of influence so that he could get the manuscript in return.

"Well yes, I do know a number of police officers."

"So it *was* you."

He swiveled in his chair. He hadn't realized Veronica had followed him in and was sitting tensely at the table on the other side of the room.

"I didn't say that at all. I just said I knew some officers. Very different."

He glared at her and turned away. Kuczynski was now looking at him steadily. Russell took a deep breath.

"You've first of all got to tell me why you pretended to be a Jew."

Kuczynski sighed deeply, shifted in his chair and closed his eyes.

"Is painful for me. You see, I swear to God, I love Jews. What British police don't know, we all got on wery well together, Poles and Jews, no problem at all until communists come."

Russell was confused. "The communists? You mean, in 1945 after the war? But we're talking about *during* the war, 1941."

Kuczynski sighed again. "Now I have to teach you history of Poland. When war started, Soviet Union and Germany made deal..."

"Yes, I know that, the Molotov-Ribbentrop Pact..."

"...so Poland diwided, communists on one side, Germans on other. My town went back and forward like blessed yo-yo: first German for few months, then communist, then German until end of war when communists took over again.

"My country...she went through much suffering. Many families destroyed: millions were killed. Poland wictim twice over, by Nazis *and* communists. But Bolsheviks were worst. They were...real devils. They decided who was to live or die on basis of how you made living. Those marked for liqvidation were businessmen, priests, rail station managers. Peasants on the land, these vere protected, although they too liqvidated if showed were loyal to family, to church, to Poland.

"Russians sent many, many thousands of Poles in cattle trucks to Russia, to Siberia, to labor camps, to prison. Deportations started vinter 1940. First to north Russia. Many died, old people, babies, because of extreme, extreme cold.

"Second deportations started April 1940 to Siberia, Kazakhstan. My own father, he vos farm manager, he vos sent to Kazakhstan, my brother and my mother, all sent to prison camp. Russian soldiers, they came with bayonets in night, dogs started barking, soldiers broke down door. I ran out back door, hid inside vell. No one come to help, all neighbors too scared, if help they too deported. I never see family again."

He blew his nose loudly. Veronica sprang up and hurried over; he waved her away.

"Jews were Bolsheviks. When communists marched into our town, we see Jews welcoming them with open arms. The baker, he was Jew, he put out for them table with red cloth with bread and salt. But the Poles, we hated communists."

"So you hated the Jews too."

Yes, thought Russell, that figured, hadn't the Jews always been called commies, just like his own father. But they'd only joined the party to fight the fascists.

Suddenly, he understood. The Nazis had wanted to do away with the Jews but had been indifferent to the Poles, other than those who resisted them. So the Poles had no real issue with the Nazis. But Stalin had deported the Poles to populate the empty Russian wastes, just like other troublesome ethnic groups. So the Poles hated the communists with a passion—and the Jews were caught in the backwash. As usual.

"They talk about killing Jews, massacre. But Jews help massacre Poles. Bolshevik Jews. Jews vorked for NKVD, Bolshevik secret police. They helped Bolsheviks kill thousands of Polish partisans, Polish patriots.

"I vos partisan fighting Russians. Ve hid in forest. The Bolsheviks, they vere devils. They kill thousands of us. They arrest partisans, promise them to go free, then arrest them when they lay down arms. They torture them in prison, kill them, send hundreds of thousands to Siberia. In Katyn forest in 1940, 15,000 Polish officers shot dead by Bolsheviks in one single action. Another 10,000 the Russians shot in other places in Poland.

"That vos massacre. But covered up for years, said Germans responsible. No one brings Russians to justice. But British now try to arrest me, claim I guilty of killing Jews. Vy they do this? Maybe because of Jews in government. Jews always vanting to say Polish antisemitism. Jews alvays vanting to make black name of Poland. Vy else accuse me?"

A sinister Jewish conspiracy. Of course.

"In 1941, I vos seventeen when Germany vent to vor with Russia. Was great relief to us when Germans arrived. No more deportations to Siberia. Pipple gave Germans flowers as they marched into our town. And they helped Germans uncover all who helped communists."

He paused, and wiped his face. It glistened with sweat. He sat silently for a while, lost in his thoughts. Then he looked at Russell, pleading with his eyes.

"Ve had to do votever we could to surwive. Votever it took. You have no idea. you cannot know vot is like, not you do just to keep alive another day, another week."

He looked away again. A tear glinted as it rolled slowly down his cheek.

"It was Germans who killed Jews. Not Poles. There is monument in town that says so. Is carved there in vords in stone. You can go see it with your own eyes."

He swallowed hard, several times, as if there was a constriction in his throat. Russell glanced round at Veronica, but she just stared back, grimly.

"That day...the day that this...this thing happened, this thing in barn, they make me do something, but not that, not that..."

"Who made you? And do what?"

"They threaten me with gun...the Germans would kill me if I didn't do it. Every Jew they rounded up in town square. We had to make young ones pull down statue of Lenin that Bolsheviks had put up. I only gave communists taste, small taste, of what they did to us.

"I vos afraid of these German murderers. I had good reason, believe me. When communists first came in, I hid in woods six months among partisans. But then communists found me, accused me of being part of anti-Soviet underground. So I did deal: they let me stay on farm, and I gave them...information."

"What kind of information?"

Kuczynski's eyes were expressionless. "Details of area they found useful. I don't know vy," he shrugged. "When Germans came in, communists did not destroy all their documents. So I wery frightened Germans think I vos Soviet collaborator."

Russell stared at him. How many people must this man have betrayed to the communists? Of course, he would have been terrified that the invading Nazis who swept into his town would have thought he was a Soviet collaborator. Because he had been.

Now he understood. Fascists, communists—the Poles were under the thumb of both. Both had tortured them, jailed them, killed them. The Poles did what they needed to do to survive. Kuczynski had collaborated with the hated communists to stop them killing him. That had made him terrified of the Nazis when they arrived.

"So...you did what the Nazis wanted to get them off your back?"

Kuczynski looked away again for a long time. But making Jews pull down a statue didn't sound like a war crime.

"The vor, it changed everything," he said, heavily. "The Jews and us, before the vor ve all got on fine. Other places in Poland, not so good. But in our town, no problems. We called each other by first names; we gave them food, they took water from our vells. We were in and out of each other's houses all the time. Why not? The town it vos mainly Jewish. Most of the houses, Jews lived there."

He paused again. It seemed as if he was gathering his strength to continue.

"There vos one family, Jews, who I knew. Ajzensztejn. Boruch and Symma."

He almost whispered their names. Then he swallowed hard.

"They wery good to me. I vos orphan boy; my father sent away, my mother dead. Boruch and Symma, they looked after me ven I vos hiding from Bolsheviks. They gave me dinner, mended my clothes, almost adopted me. I vent there Friday nights. I can still smell challah bread baked that day, see candle lights, hear songs they sang round table. They taught me Jewish customs, even prayers. Boruch, he vos tailor, and he showed me quality of fabrics, how to look after them."

He looked down at his knees again.

"There vos one daughter. Blume. She vos 16, so beautiful. I vonted...ve vonted to be, you know, boyfriend and girlfriend, but she could not...her parents...it vos because I was not Jew."

Now Kuczynski started showing signs of real distress. He wiped his eyes and rocked back and forth. When he resumed, he seemed almost to be talking to himself.

"The same day Germans made Jews destroy statue, that day they did more terrible things. The Gestapo rounded up all Jews, beat them with clubs and pushed them all into barn. There were dozens of Germans, dozens of Gestapo. By the end of day, all of them dead. All Jews of town. Boruch, Symma, Blume...all of them. Gone."

Tears now streamed down his face.

"And you? Where were you while all this was going on?"

"I didn't see much...but I heard...ve all heard screaming, terrible screams..."

He was obviously lying.

"And afterwards? What happened then?"

He wouldn't look at Russell but now kept his head lowered. "I had such guilty feelings. Blume...maybe I could have done more to save her. They knew...they knew something bad vos going to happen. For days before, Germans had been killing Jews in nearby willages. There were rumors, terrible rumors...I didn't believe them, I brushed it all aside, but Boruch, he vos vorried.

"One night he said he had big thing to ask me. He give me big box. Inside were all waluables, silver plates and candlesticks and goblets they used for their Jewish ceremonies."

Russell followed his gaze to the locked cabinet. Of course.

"Vos also smaller box inside. He told me inside was holy book, been in Symma's family many generations. Wery old, wery precious. He asked me to hide it all in safe place in case something happened to them. I took it all and buried it on my farm.

"After vor, when communists inwaded Poland and started killing Poles and sending so many this time to Russia, I got out and came here as refugee, with box Boruch gave me. I dig it up. I keep it all safe all this time."

It was all just too pat, thought Russell. So much had been left out. Questions swirled inside his head.

"Joszef is actually a hero."

Veronica had moved forward silently and was now perched on another armchair. Her eyes never left Russell's face.

"He rescued all those precious things from the Germans, even though he was running for his life from the Gestapo *and* the communists. What he's only been through. And now the government has the nerve to try and prosecute a sick old man, drag his reputation through the mud."

Now Kuczynski looked at Russell again. His expression was blank, inscrutable.

"I not vor criminal. I wictim of Germans, Bolsheviks, now blessed British too. I carry scars, here."

He pointed to his head.

It was true, thought Russell, that he had not sold any of the valuables he had brought from Poland to make money out of the tragedy he had witnessed. If, though, any of that tale was true. This whole fantastic story about his friendship with the tragic Jewish family—who had conveniently all perished—burying their valuables on his farm, his feelings for the daughter Blume...all of this might well be a pack of lies too. How could be believe it? Kuczynski had thoroughly deceived him, after all. He wasn't going to fall into that trap again.

"What were you doing in the synagogue? Why did you pretend to me you were a Jew?"

Now the old man's expression changed again: it was the look on his face Russell had seen in the early days as he worked on Eliachim's manuscript. It was a look of cunning, greed—and a great coldness. He gripped the arms of his chair and leaned forward intently. His eyes seemed to bore into Russell's skull.

"The Jews, they hold all secrets of vorld."

His voice was now little more than a hoarse whisper. Russell had to crane forward in his own chair to hear.

"I ask myself, what they have I don't have? These Jews—they not normal people. They run vorld. They run America, all banks and finance houses, Goldman Sachs, TV, politicians, journalists, doctors, lawyers. Top judges, all Jews! Movie directors! All Jews! Wherever you look, Jews in background pulling strings. Even blessed Royal Family, they also have Jews."

Really? But he was in full flow.

"So is vorld full of Jews? Are there many millions, billions of Jews in vorld? No! Wery, wery few Jews in vorld. But still they control it! Even when no Jews around at all in country, they still control it. This is most amazing thing. Jews, they should have been viped out long, long ago. Everywhere in history they been attacked, killed, driven out of homes, country after country after country.

"In Poland before vor vere many, many Jews, three million. In my town were mostly Jews. By end of vor, all gone, almost every one. Wiped out. In Europe two out of three Jews killed. Any other people, they would have vanished from face of blessed earth. But still Jews run vorld. Still more powerful than anyone else. Still tvist America round little finger. Is not amazing fact? So from vere they get this power?

"In Poland I know them, I look at them, ask what they do so different from me. I learn their language, their songs, their holy ceremonies. But I vos not one of them. I could not be one of them. They were different, separate, special. I felt deep inside me they were special. Vy should they be more special than me? They vere not better people than me, is good and bad in all of us.

"I go to priest in town and ask him why Jews are so special. He say to me, Jews killed our savior, they killed God. That's why they special, they belong to devil. But I not believe this. I good Catholic, I go to mass, but this make no sense. Because I see whatever done to them they still love God. I see they have special line to God. They don't have priest who talk to God, they do talking themselves. And such talk. As if they know him. As if he family.

"I see when Germans attack them, humiliate them, treat them worse than dogs, even when do things to them so terrible I cannot speak about, they still pray to God. After they are killed, their families still pray to God. When they put body in ground, they don't scream and shout for vengeance. They don't curse God. They praise him.

"And I see how God protect them. Sure many, many Jews killed. But I watch, afterwards, as Jews don't disappear but get even stronger, how whole vorld looks to them. Look at science, look at medical inwentions, look at hi-tech. All Jews! So why he protect them like this? Why he listen to them? Why he not listen to prayers of Polish people that they not suffer so much? Why Jews have such special place in his heart?

"I think and think but I cannot answer this qvestion. I think, if I do what Jews do, do what I see them do in Poland, maybe God make me special too. So I go to synagogue to be part of them, to learn from rabbi, to get holy blessing.

"And all the time I look at book I brought from Poland, that Boruch told me was holy book, and I know secret of Jews must be in it. Because is miracle that book surwives so long, with so many killings and burnings and destructions. But book still here. And I think I chosen to look after it. And when I see you, I realize this too was meant to happen, that you sent to me to unlock secrets of book, secret that explain why Jews chosen by God."

Kuczynski slumped back in his chair. There was a silence. The only sound was the ticking of the clock.

Russell sat, stunned. The whole mad, infernal logic was now laid out before him. How could he have failed to understand the signs? Treating Eliachim's manuscript like a holy relic—no Jew would ever have done that. And a deep-dyed anti-Semite...no, wait, he had taken all the signature obsessions of antisemitism and turned them into a kind of Jew-worship. Believing the canard of the global power of the Jews, he actually wanted some of that for himself.

His head was spinning. Focus, he thought. The manuscript. Crazy and outlandish as Kuczynski's story seemed, the looted property seemed the most plausible part. However Kuczynski had come by it, his admission that it had belonged to a Jewish family in the area made Russell believe that the manuscript was genuine and not a forgery. He just had to retrieve it.

"I may still be able to help you."

"You see I not vor criminal? You see I cannot be, that Jews vere my friends?"

Kuczynski's eyes lit up eagerly.

"I can certainly see that you were faced with some, ah, very difficult and complex situations," Russell volunteered.

"So you tell your police friends is all big mistake? You tell them they got wrong man?"

"If you give me the book. I might be able to use it to argue your case."

"He can't," said Veronica suddenly. "He's got rid of it."

"What! What! Got rid of it? How? What do you mean?" cried Russell, leaping to his feet.

"What you done, stupid cow!" shouted Kuczynski, lunging forward in his chair. "Now he never speak for me to police!"

"You imbecile, he was never going to speak up for you to the police," said Veronica coldly. "He was just playing you along. As he has done from the start."

She lit a cigarette. Her hands were steady.

"I told you he was trouble, didn't I, but you wouldn't listen. You and your obsession with that bloody book. I told you it would bring us bad luck. You should've burned it years ago."

"What! You've burned it?" Russell was beside himself.

"What you gonna do, tell the police about it?" sneered Veronica.

"Not burned, no. But now where you never ever find it. Ever." said Kuczynski, almost as if talking to himself.

"Now get out," said Veronica, "before I throw you out the door myself."

In his pocket, he fingered his iPhone on which he had recorded Kuczynski's confession.

21

HE PACED UP and down. He couldn't concentrate. At night, he was finding it hard to sleep; a succession of images processed through his mind as soon as he closed his eyes—Kuczynski, Waxman, the hooded thugs with the flashing blade, his father.

What was happening to him? At every stage, events were conspiring against him. Why wasn't anything working out anymore? He thought about the workman in the church, about the thugs outside the mosque. No no, no way that workman could have been right.

It was unthinkable. Go down that road, start thinking like that and Russell would end up turning into Michael Waxman. The youths who chased him down the street were probably just bored, out of work, the disadvantaged. The thing about alcohol was just a pretext, an excuse for a bit of violence. It meant nothing more than that.

To think otherwise, to allow himself even to entertain the possibility of the otherwise thought, was to go over a personal precipice spinning into a vacuum.

He couldn't possibly allow himself to think like that because of the kind of people who did. The reactionaries, the uneducated, the narrow-minded. People like Elliott. Ugh! And once he thought like them, even on one single issue, that would be it as far as his own friends were concerned. He would just cease even to exist in their minds, he would become an un-person. But worse even than that, he would stop being a decent human being. He would find himself in some circle of hell.

The reason he was so unsettled, so panicky, was that he suspected that precisely such a process had already started. And that was making him frantic.

He looked in the fridge. It was empty, apart from some bottles of Budweiser, a half-eaten tub of hummus and a yogurt past its sell-by date. He went out to the local mini-market to get some food for supper.

At the checkout, his phone rang. It was Alice. He held the phone to his ear while with the other hand he tried to stuff his items into the bag.

"You do know that Rosa is now coming out with one weird idea after another, thanks to you."

No, he didn't know.

"She thinks abortion is wrong in most cases, sperm donation is anti-family and she's not going to have sex until she gets married."

"Well, *I* haven't told her any of that."

"It's this zealot rabbi you introduced her to. He's been brainwashing her."

"Really? Sounds more like she's thinking of becoming a Catholic."

"Oh that's right, just joke about it. Nothing's to be taken seriously with you, unless it's about *you.* I suppose you don't care your daughter will be seen as some kind of freak, to be bullied and become a laughingstock at school. Of course, I know what this is really all about; she's just getting at *me.*"

"Maybe she just doesn't like the example she's been set. I mean, what's so terrible about respecting herself and caring about family life?"

"What's happened to *you* all of a sudden? Sound like you've gone all Moral Majority. Why have you become so right-wing? Why have you become so *Jewish*?"

The bag he was balancing as he filled it with groceries toppled over. Eggs and a jar of mayonnaise smashed on the floor and spattered his trousers and shoes. *Shit.*

"There's nothing right-wing about the truth," he heard himself say, as he waved helplessly at the bored checkout girl. Oh no, maybe he really was turning into one of them. And just imagine if Alice or anyone else discovered he had actually been in cahoots with a war criminal, who if he wasn't actually a Nazi was as close as dammit. He went hot and cold at the thought. It was unthinkable.

"And if she really is being bullied, shouldn't you be doing something about it?" he said weakly into the phone. But she had already hung up.

22

DETAILS ABOUT KUCZYNSKI in the newspapers were scarce. Where might he find out more, he wondered miserably. He Googled "war crimes" on his laptop. There was a story from 2010 about how Scotland Yard had been criticized for disbanding its specialized war crimes unit. He clicked on another story which said the unit's caseload had now been taken up by a group of senior detectives inside SO15, the Yard's counterterrorism department.

SO15—he'd known an officer quite well who had gone to that unit, although he hadn't spoken to him since he'd been poached from hate crime. He scrolled through his contacts directory. Yes, there he was: Chief Superintendent Ian Avery. Praying that he had not changed his cellphone number, he dialed it.

Avery answered. Bingo. Good to hear from Russell again, long time no see and all that and what could he do for him? Yes, he was indeed one of the officers handling war crimes. Well they could all do without it, quite frankly—after all it was hardly the same priority as the war on terror, was it, and they were all stretched enough in the unit as it was, what with all the cuts.

"Frankly, I don't think this guy Kuczynski's even going to be charged," he said. "Quite a lot of sensitivity among the powers-that-be about being seen to persecute such an old man. We could've done without the reptiles getting hold of the fact that we'd fallen over him. Now we'll probably be hung out to dry whether we prosecute or don't prosecute. But really, we're not talking Heinrich Himmler here; this guy was a minnow."

"So what did he actually do?" Russell's heart was in his mouth.

"Seems he lived in a Polish town that flipped back and forth during the war between Germany and the Soviet Union. Jedwabne, it was called. It started out briefly under German occupation, then fell under the Soviet Union when it joined forces with Hitler in 1939, and then when that fell apart the Nazis took over the town in 1941.

"What happened then was almost beyond belief. Under the Nazis, half the town went and murdered the other half. More, in fact, because more than half the town was Jewish. It was all totally horrific. They rounded up all the Jews and herded them into a barn, where they proceeded to burn them alive. When it was all over, just seven Jews remained alive in Jedwabne. Seven.

"No question this was a very great war crime. But this guy Kuczynski's role just isn't clear. After the war, the Russians put a number of people on trial for the barn. Kuczynski wasn't one of them, but that doesn't mean anything. The trials were a farce."

"What, political show trials?"

"No, quite the opposite, in fact. The Russians were sloppy, couldn't have cared less, because the victims were Jews. Stalin also wasn't very keen on them, you may recall. So there was a total abuse of process, defendants beaten until they confessed, prosecutor even getting the date of the atrocity wrong."

"So what makes you think Kuczynski was involved at all?"

"It was the Simon Wiesenthal people, you know, the group in Switzerland that goes round bringing Nazis to book, who alerted us to him, said he'd been involved and that he was living in the UK."

"But what evidence can there be against him after all this time—especially if all the victims died in 1941?"

"Yup, that's the problem. The Wiesenthal people themselves have just one witness, a very good one, in fact, pretty reliable, I'd say; but this witness for some reason is very reluctant, indeed refusing, to come and give evidence in court. This witness, would you believe..." Avery paused, "is Kuczynski's sister. Lives in America. Somewhere in Virginia."

His sister! Kuczynski had never mentioned having a sister. Russell tried hard to remember. He'd mentioned a brother, an older brother, who had been jailed by the Communists, but had never mentioned a sister, let alone that she was still alive and living in America. Why not?

"Uh...curious...why should his sister suddenly come forward and inform on him after all this time?"

"And why should she then seem to take fright and refuse to follow through by coming to give evidence against him?" agreed Avery. "Makes very little sense at all."

Another secret that Kuczynski had been keeping bottled up, thought Russell. Maybe this sister would know something about the manuscript. Maybe she could tell him if Kuczynski's story about how he had gotten it was true, and whether or not the book was a fake. He had to get to her.

"Uh, Avery, could you do me an enormous favor and let me have the sister's name and whereabouts?"

Avery was wary. "Why, you thinking of making a show about this guy? Can't do anything till the trial's all over, contempt of court otherwise, you know that."

Russell swallowed hard. "Sure, sure, don't worry about that. Erm...thing is, doing something not on him but pre-war Poland, the experiences of people under first communism and then Nazism, and so, well, this woman sounds just up my street. Not many of that generation still alive, after all, and so she'd provide invaluable firsthand evidence. Not often you can get hold of that!"

"Ah, I see. Bit of a change from your usual fare of bashing HMG, har har. Well, okay then—but you didn't get it from me."

23

HIS PHONE BUZZED. Another text from Alice.

now Rosa saying wants to change name!!!

Shit, he thought. His daughter was renouncing her father. Alice had poisoned her against him. She was abandoning Wolfe for...

to what?
Ruth
Ruth?
biblical yr fault next she'll be bloody converting
at least same initial so less confusion?
brainwashing you failing fatherly protection exposing yr daughter to raving lunatics appalled

He texted Rosa.

what's with name change?

yr people r my people remember?

Dimly, he recalled the Biblical story in which Ruth left her Moabite background to join up with the Hebrews.

anyway rosa crap name who wants to be called after raving communist loon
so whats with new boyfriend?
honestly!! friend not boyfriend Udi teaching me hebrew.

What was wrong with Alice, he wondered; not for the first time.

24

THE HOUSE WAS in West Virginia, near Charleston. He hired a car, and drove from his hotel in Washington through lush green forests. His GPS took him into an area where the houses were large and set well back from the road with well-kept, deep front lawns, separated from each other by up to half a minute of driving. Not for the first time, Russell marveled at the sheer size of America. Here they had land, space. Here there was room to breathe.

It was a large, low, well-kept, grey clapboard house with the windows and verandah picked out in white.

A woman answered the door dressed in a pink overshirt and black trousers. A pair of black-framed spectacles hung from a chain round her neck. Early sixties, he guessed. She had a round, open face that half-smiled at Russell inquiringly.

"I wonder...would it be possible to speak to Mrs. Peterson? Mrs. Zofia Peterson? I am Russell Wolfe from London."

"London?" The woman looked blank. "Is she expecting you?"

Russell drew a deep breath. The first hurdle. "Not exactly. But I think she'll want to see me. I have some information which will be of great interest to her."

The woman put on her glasses and looked carefully at Russell. "What exactly do you want with my mother?"

"I'm, um, I'm a researcher into...here...here's my card." It said Pollyanna Productions, but what the hell. "I'm...I'm doing research into the different regimes that controlled Poland during the war, the Nazi/Soviet pact? Stuff like that."

The woman's face cleared. "Ah, yes, I see. Did the Old Comrades suggest you come to see my mother?"

Old comrades? Russell's face froze in a smile. "Old comrades indeed!" he said brightly.

"Do come in, please. My mother is always happy to hear from the Comrades."

She ushered him into a neat and cozy living room. He perched on the edge of an armchair covered in a flowery chintz.

"My mother is asleep. I'll bring her down in a minute. Can I get you some tea?"

"That would be lovely."

He sat and looked around him. The walls were crowded with family pictures, frame after frame of smiling, open-faced children. There were also embroidered samplers bearing meticulously stitched mottos saying "Home Sweet Home," "The Lord is my shepherd," and "I am the way, the truth, and the light."

Russell's heart sank.

There was a tinkling of cups, and the woman returned with a tray set with tea-things and a plate of what looked like homemade tea bread.

"My mother will join us shortly. She is very curious about having a visitor all the way from London. I'm Stacey, by the way."

There was a pause. "You have a splendid house," said Russell.

"Why thank you. May I just say," said Stacey shyly, "I just love your accent. You British have such a way of speaking. So classy."

There was another pause. "While we're waiting," said Stacey, rummaging inside a small bureau, "since you're a researcher, maybe you'd like to take these for future reference? You might be interested."

She handed him some leaflets. They were advertisements. One was for *Homeschoolers' Success Stories: 15 Adults and 12 Young People Share the Impact that Homeschooling Has Made on Their Lives!* The second was for *The 31st Annual Virginia Homeschool Convention: Three Days that Will Change the Life of Your Family!* The third promised *The A-Z of Homeschooling: Everything You Need to Know to School Your Child for a Fulfilled and Wholesome Life!*

She sat on the edge of a chair, looking intently at him.

"We homeschooled all our children, all seven of them. Now we are fighting to make sure that universities accept these qualifications. They're actually of a higher standard than what's produced in regular schools. But they're always trying to make out our children aren't properly socialized, or something. What nonsense."

"That's quite an achievement, er, homeschooling seven children," he said politely. He didn't know anything about it, but his instincts told him it was something he probably wouldn't like.

"Well I was a teacher, so of course that helped," said Stacey. "That's how I knew about all this terrible propaganda being pumped into the kids in the classroom, all this explicit and perverted stuff about sex, every single kind, you can't imagine, and such indifference to things like drug-taking and discipline. So unwholesome. You just have to protect your children against that, don't you. Do you have kids?"

The door opened slowly and an elderly woman came slowly into the room, leaning heavily on a walking frame. Stacey jumped up to help her.

"I can manage," said the woman in irritation, waving her away. "Don't fuss."

"My mother is very independent," said Stacey with a little laugh. Irritation there too, Russell thought, oh yes.

Stacey poured tea for her mother into a sturdy glass mug, and wrapped her fingers round the handle. The old woman nodded curtly and shakily raised the mug to her lips.

She looked steadily at Russell. He could see the likeness. The same rawboned, East European peasant face. But she was smaller and slighter. And her eyes, the same slanting, Mongolian eyes, were bright and focused. Despite her physical frailty, there was intelligence there, and a certain stillness that seemed like strength.

"So you are from London? The Comrades sent you?"

Russell dropped his eyes in what he hoped would be taken as a sign of appropriately discreet assent.

"You are Polish?"

"No, I'm a researcher...er, researching...historical events in Poland. I thought...the comrades thought...I thought you might be able to help me."

"Historical events? I don't think I can help you."

Her eyes became veiled, wary. This was the moment. He breathed in deeply.

"I have information about your brother, Joszef."

There was a silence. Stacey sat up, startled.

"Uncle Joszef? The one who died in the war?"

Zofia sat still, her mug trembling slightly as she clasped it between her hands. Her eyes never left Russell's face.

"Leave us."

"You quite sure, Mom?" Stacey looked from her mother to Russell and back again. No one said anything.

"Well, all right then," said Stacey reluctantly. "Just call if you need me, okay?"

She patted her mother's hand. The door clicked shut behind her.

"You have seen him? The Comrades took you to him?" Her body, hunched awkwardly in her chair, had become rigid with tension.

"I know where he is. Yes." Pace it carefully now; lead her along, don't allow her to put up those defenses.

Her face was like a mask, apart from those eyes boring into him. He wondered if she had Parkinson's.

"I thought he was dead. All these years, I heard nothing. Then a few months ago, I suddenly found out he was alive."

"The Comrades."

She nodded slightly. "One of them wrote something, a memoir, about resisting the Soviets. I knew him back then, of course. We were all hiding in the woods together. You form a bond in such a situation. We keep in touch with each other. They send me bits and pieces from time to time. So they sent me this memoir. And at the end they wrote that Joszef was living in London."

"Must have been quite a shock."

"The past comes back to haunt you. You want to forget, but it won't let you."

"Did you get in touch with him?"

For a moment, he saw Joszef on her face. A flash of something guarded, cunning even. She looked away for the first time since she had sat down.

"No."

With an effort, she lifted her mug of tea to her mouth.

"They must have been terrible times."

Careful now. Sympathetic, but not prying.

"You don't know. No one can know."

Her eyelids drooped, and she bent her head towards the mug. He sat very still.

"What people are capable of. You don't know. You can't imagine until it happens. And then you can't believe it. Don't believe it."

Her voice was clear and high; her words, if a little slow, precise. An accent, but a perfect command of language. The younger sister, but cleverer. Ah yes, he thought. A distance between them; a resentment.

"Was that why you went to the Simon Wiesenthal Foundation?" he said softly.

She did not look up. When she spoke again he could hardly hear her.

"The British must prosecute him, jail him."

So it was her. Whatever Kuczynski had done, she knew.

"Why don't you give your evidence to the British police, then? They can't jail him without you."

She was silent for a while. Her eyes remained lowered. "What do you want from me?" she whispered eventually. Her head remained bent towards her cup.

He leaned towards her. Should he take her hand, perhaps? No, too forward. Be attentive, empathetic, but not too keen.

"I'm researching war crimes trials, the decisions behind these prosecutions, whether there are limits to them because of age or illness. That kind of thing. I've spoken at some length to your brother. Now I wanted to hear your side of the story."

"You have spoken to him? You are working for the British police?"

She raised her eyes to his. She was startled, but not wary. He thought he saw a flicker of interest, even eagerness.

"I'm a researcher. It's important to make sure I've got all the facts right. This is a historical record I'm researching. But some things your brother told me, they don't make sense."

He put his iPhone onto the table between them.

"What he said to me, it's all on this phone. His voice is on this, talking to me."

She gazed at the device as if her eyes might melt it. Then imperceptibly she pulled back.

"I don't want to say anything."

But she wanted to hear that voice, Russell was certain.

"You want him put in prison, don't you? But you don't want to give evidence yourself. I don't know why you don't want to do that, but I expect you have your reasons and that's ok with me."

She was listening to him attentively now.

"I think I can help you. The police need the information you have about your brother. They need to know what happened, what he did. You are the only person who can tell them. I can act as your go-between. I need your information for my own research, but I don't need to use your name. And I can pass on to the police the information you give me. That may well enable them to prosecute your brother without dragging you into court."

It would be her voice on the recording, of course, but he didn't need to point that out to her.

She was obviously torn.

"May I just play you my conversation with Joszef? I promise, if it's too much for you I'll put it away and say no more about it."

She listened to the recording without expression, her eyes closed. Only the rapid rise and fall of her frail chest offered any suggestion of emotion. He played it all except for the end of the conversation where Kuczynski had mentioned the book. Too risky to let her hear that; she might think he was a gold digger.

After the recording ended, there was a long silence. She remained utterly still, with her eyes shut.

"This was not the truth," she said, finally. She shook her head. "You have to understand..." Her voice tailed away. "To hear that voice, after all these years, to bring it all back...This is very painful for me."

"Of course it is. Would you prefer..."

She waved him away, swallowed and started talking.

"The Soviets took my father, my mother, my eldest brother Pyotr, sent them to labor camps, Siberia."

"The Soviets?"

He was briefly confused. Then he remembered.

"This was, what, 1939, the alliance between Hitler and the Soviet Union?"

She nodded.

"The Soviets invaded Poland. We all hated them. It was chance that made us their prisoners. The war started, and then a few weeks later suddenly the border shifted. We became part of Russia. Just like that.

"So the Russians came to our town. They were very cruel. They took hundreds of thousands of us prisoner; tortured them, jailed them, transported them to places where they were never seen again. My parents, my brother. I live it all again in my mind every single day.

"Came in the middle of the night, beat on the door with their fists, the dogs barking, barking. I can still hear my mother screaming as they dragged them away. I was sixteen, Joszef a year older. We hid in the well in our yard. Afterwards we ran into the forest and the partisans looked after us."

She closed her eyes. Russell stiffened. Would she carry on, or would this all be too much for her? Surreptitiously he checked his iPhone to make sure it was still recording. When she spoke again he started guiltily, but her eyes were still closed.

"We were all partisans, the resistance against the Soviets. How could we not have been? They destroyed our family.

"We hid in the forest. Blackberries grew wild there. We crammed our mouths with them. To this day I cannot bear the taste of blackberries. We lived in camps; we had a bakery, a school, a laundry, even a primitive kind of clinic. Our group was accused of stealing a cow, but we didn't have to. The farmers gave us food. Everyone detested the Russians. We prayed for deliverance from them. Then things changed.

"The Soviet secret police tracked down the underground. They came into the forest and surrounded our camp and attacked us and killed a lot of partisans. The Russians took a lot of casualties too because our side, the partisans, we fought back with great courage. And shortly after that the Soviets declared an amnesty for all partisans who came out of hiding and identified themselves. I thought it was a trap, but Joszef told me no, we can go home now.

"So later that year, as the leaves were falling from the trees, we went back to our house. I trusted Joszef. I was very naive then. But not for long."

Now she twisted and untwisted her fingers. She was becoming agitated. The silence seemed to crackle between them.

"Next door to us was a Jewish family. We knew them so well. All my life, we were in and out of each other's houses. That was the thing, the terrible thing...there were so many Jews in our town, it was a Jewish town almost, all of us had Jewish neighbors, all of us got on with each other so well, never a problem..."

She shook her head slowly, from side to side, as if trying to shake out of it some intolerable memory.

"The Ajzensztejns. A lovely family. Boruch, he was a tailor, and Symma, his wife. We never had enough to eat, but however little they had they would give us: some fresh eggs, half a loaf of bread, a few carrots or onions.

"Boruch would mend our clothes. He made a little brown jacket for Joszef and a cap from the leavings of the material. He would sit at his sewing machine every day, whirring away. We would sit and watch him, Joszef and I; and he told us stories, such stories, about the spirit world and about the golem and the dybbuk, you know, how someone is taken over by someone else's soul and what comes out of their mouth is that soul's voice? And he would do the dybbuk's voices and I would shriek with terror.

"I would watch Symma as she cooked, my God what with, none of us had enough to eat, but somehow she managed to produce on a Friday such a chicken soup I can still smell, and the challah bread she baked, the special Friday night loaves, the fragrance of that bread. And she showed me all the laws they had to keep, the separate dishes for meat and dairy, how when she made her dough for the Friday loaves she would reserve a piece in honor of the Almighty."

So that was how Kuczynski knew so much, he thought.

"At home, it was so very different. Religion to us was a cold and drafty church once a week, plaster statues of the Virgin that were said to weep—however long and hard I stared I never saw such a thing. And all these terrible warnings about hell and damnation, sin and guilt. Everything was guilt. So miserable. So grim. But Boruch and Symma's house was full of such joy and laughter. Their religion, their God, was in every single thing they did, all the ordinary, routine, everyday things were somehow made special, had a kind of glow that somehow raised that whole family above the harshness of the lives we all led."

"And did your brother feel the same way?"

She fell silent, and a shadow seemed to fall across her face. Family. She had said family. Yet she had made no mention of the daughter, the girl whom Joszef had loved and who had loved him.

"Our parents were good Catholics. They went to confession every week, they prayed to the Virgin, they looked up to the priest. Father Pawlicki. The Jews were our neighbors and our friends. But Father Pawlicki preached that the Jews had killed Christ and were damned for all eternity. They were the people of the devil.

"Our father would sometimes make remarks about how the Jews were not to be trusted, how they might appear on the surface to be like us but how they were always scheming to steal all our money. Joszef was very close to our father. He would sit listening to Boruch's stories as he sat at his treadle; but then afterwards he would make sneering remarks about the Ajzensztejns, about their peculiar ways and how they weren't really like us at all. Of course, there was another reason why my brother kept going there..."

She checked herself. Russell slowly wiped his hands on his trousers.

"When the Communists came, and they were so hated, people said a lot of them were Jews and that the Jews of our town were supporting them. This was true, but also not true. Plenty of Jews, pious Jews like the Ajzensztejns, knew the Communists were not their friends. But there were bad feelings against the Jews. There was a tension.

"It wasn't just because of the Communists. Before the war—well, before the Nazis and the Cossacks made their deal—there was violence against the Jews in our area. Savage. A Jewish woman was killed; a few days later someone in a neighboring town was shot to death. Rumors flew around that the Jews had taken revenge. In an instant there was a mob ready to commit murder. The Jews would have been set upon then and there, but the rabbi went to the priests and begged them to do something. God help me, the priests could have stopped it, all of it, all this butchery of the Jews. Because in our area this thing was done not by Communists, not by Nazis, but by Poles."

Russell hardly dared breathe. But he felt confused. The Jews had been their friends, she said, in and out of each other's houses. Yet the Poles had repeatedly attacked them. How could this be?

She paused again, apparently lost in a reverie. She was back in Poland, reliving whatever it was she had been through.

"An informer gave my father away to the Soviets. This we knew. Joszef said the informer was a Jew. Was that true? We never knew. But from that moment, Joszef's attitude changed. Now he was openly hostile towards the Jews. And there was a cynical edge to him. Harder.

"It troubled me, he'd always been a bit on the wild side, but it was not uppermost in my mind. After all, we were now both fugitives from the Russians, living with the partisans in the forest.

"But I couldn't understand why suddenly we were able to go back home. The Cosssacks were rounding up partisans. Yet we could come out of hiding. The danger to us seemed to have disappeared. But why?

"After we went back, Joszef seemed different again. He seemed, I don't know, to have grown a sense of self-importance.

He strutted, that's the only way I can put it. I was nervous; partisans were being discovered and picked off, shot or transported. But no one touched us.

"You know, when something is really, really bad, so bad it will break your heart, you so much don't want to believe it you'll swallow anything.

"One day a Cossack came to our house. I was terrified, but he sat with Joszef. My brother told me to bring them both tea. When I brought it to them they were talking quietly together. As if they knew each other. And then, all of a sudden, I understood. Everything became very clear. I was shocked, I can't tell you how I felt. I said to him, how can you do this, how can you possibly do such a thing? These are our comrades, we are all fighting for the same cause. But he just sneered at me, told me not to be so stupid. I saw then he had become very cruel."

Russell heard again Kuczynski's voice, heard him falter. Yes, he thought, his suspicion had been correct. Kuczynski had been a Russian informer. He had betrayed the Polish partisans to the Russian invaders. Just as someone had betrayed his own family to them.

She slowly raised her cup to her lips again. When she spoke again, she wouldn't meet his eyes.

"You have to understand, in those times everyone was out for himself. Just to survive."

Apart, of course, from the resistance members Kuczynski had betrayed, Russell thought.

Now she became agitated. Her breathing became more rapid and the knuckles of her fingers, twisted together, turned white. Her voice became quieter. Imperceptibly, Russell leaned forward in his chair.

"The Ajzensztejns had a daughter. Blume. Just the one: they thought they couldn't have any children and then she was born to them late. A miracle child.

"Blume was my friend. She was extraordinary, an exotic creature to me. One in a million. She was very lovely. Full of fun and gaiety, even in those times. Witty: her intelligence just shone through. And gifted: she played the violin, melodies of such sadness and sweetness I had never heard. And Boruch and Symma would sing as she played, songs of such longing. I didn't understand many of the words, but they touched me in my heart.

"My brother...he was very attracted to Blume. Of course she wouldn't look at him. She was a proud Jewish girl. She told me she was afraid of him. The way he looked at her, it made her very uncomfortable. He was very persistent. One day he held a kitchen knife to her throat as he told her he loved her, then said he had been fooling around. Love!"

She grimaced.

"He had no idea what that was. Really, I think looking back he had no feelings for other people, that there was always something missing there. Even before. Anyway..."

She swallowed several times. Now her voice was so quiet he had to strain to hear her.

"Blume was resisting him. She was very strong, he knew he couldn't wear her down. So...so he told her he would denounce her parents to the Soviets as partisans unless she slept with him."

Again Russell was confused. "And were they? Were the Ajzensztejns partisans?'

She waved her hand impatiently. "It was a lie. Boruch and Symma did nothing at all against the Russians, the very thought of it, they were totally outside politics. But Joszef didn't care whether it was true or not. He assumed all the Jews were communists anyway. He said it just as a weapon to get his way with Blume.

"Blume knew it was a lie, of course. But she was terrified of Joszef. She knew he had credibility with the Cossacks. He told her how many partisans he had helped send to the labor camps or to be shot. She thought if he denounced her parents to the Soviets they would believe him. So she gave herself up to him."

Russell thought of Kuczynski weeping in his living room as he had told him about Blume. Christ, he'd assumed there had been some kind of forbidden love affair. Star-crossed lovers, a Polish Romeo and Juliet; or Eliachim and Duzelina. His stomach heaved. God help him, he had even allowed himself to make a comparison with himself and Alice.

"I was told all this only later. Afterwards." Almost imperceptibly, Zofia rocked herself back and forwards in her distress. "Blume just seemed to disappear; I didn't see her anywhere. Nor did I see Symma and Boruch. The invitations to their house just stopped. I asked my brother what was going on, but he just shrugged. He didn't seem curious. I was worried the Cossacks had taken them, but he told me not to interfere in case it made us look bad. In any event, I had other things on my mind. The Soviets left and the Nazis arrived..."

"This was 1941? When the Nazi-Soviet pact collapsed?"

She nodded, faintly. "The Soviets were replaced by the Nazis. For the second time we were occupied by barbarians, but different ones. That June, when the Nazis marched in, they were greeted as liberators by our town."

"Liberators?"

"Sure. So much suffering under the Soviets, you see."

"Was that how you saw them too? As liberators?"

She looked at him steadily. Her skin was like creased parchment, but her eyes were still a deep cornflower blue.

"You are an Englishman. You have the luxury of never having had to live under occupation, never having to work out how to survive from day to day under a cruel regime. Communism, fascism, what was the difference to us then? We died under both."

She closed her eyes as if weary. He waited on tenterhooks. When she spoke again, it was as if she was speaking from somewhere far away.

"To begin with, that first day when I saw the Germans arrive, yes, yes, I felt relief. I heard the cheering of the people, and I allowed myself to dare to think, maybe, just maybe we'll be safer now. But then that day, later that day, that very same day, I saw...I saw..."

There was a catch in her throat. She composed herself.

"I saw in the main square one, two, three members of the Soviet militia, the men we had so much feared; and next to them three Jews, there was the baker who had put out a table with a red cloth to welcome the Soviets when they arrived, I knew him well, and two other Jews. The six of them stood there, they'd been beaten, they were bleeding, surrounded by Germans; but in front of the Germans stood local people from the town, holding clubs, thick clubs. One of the Germans was calling out, 'Don't kill at once, make them suffer slowly...' "

She stopped again.

"Did you recognize any of the men doing the beating?" he asked softly. Of course, he knew already. Kuczynski had been part of that mob.

She sat with her hand over her mouth. He himself felt transfixed by her horror, scarcely daring to breathe.

When she resumed, it was almost as if she was talking to herself.

"War is terrible. But this was something else. It was... incomprehensible."

She spread her hands, palms upright.

"People were as if possessed. Farmers, the local carpenter, the blacksmith, the grocer. I knew them. But now it was as if I had never known them at all. People who had been neighborly, hospitable, polite—now they were transformed, worse than wild animals. There was...there was what I can only describe as a blood lust. A desire for extreme violence, a horrible excitement to crush and maim and mutilate.

"There were no longer any boundaries, there was no reason for them to do these things. A young Jewish mother managed to jump from a train taking prisoners to the death camps, jumped with her two small children. Twenty or so partisans, the kind of people I had been with in the forest when we hid from the Soviets, they beat to death this mother and her children with sticks and clubs. Just for the pleasure of killing Jews. What had this poor girl ever done to them? Nothing. She was already a victim of the Nazis. But it was Poles who murdered her."

She shook her head slowly from side to side.

"It was chaos. Poland was now under Nazi occupation, and the Nazis were now killing thousands of Poles. But the Soviets were also still killing Polish partisans, even though they were all fighting the Nazis. It made no sense..."

Once again she seemed to be talking to herself.

"You think you are a good person. You think there are good people and there are bad people. That's a luxury, to be able to think like that; it's self-indulgence. There is no good and bad, no black and white. Under that kind of pressure, people simply go mad."

She looked up, and in her eyes he saw such desolation he had to look away.

"Poland had become a vortex of absolute evil. And the Polish people turned on the Jews. Over the following days, just in our part of the country, pogrom after pogrom. Thousands of Jews murdered by Polish hooligans. They went and asked the Germans, should we kill them? They actually asked them for permission to kill. Imagine.

"The Germans were themselves beating up and killing Jews, taking away their cows and stealing their property and giving it all to the Poles. They forced the Jews to burn all their holy scrolls and books and to dance around the burning piles. The Poles would sometimes send the Germans to beat and murder the Jews. But mainly it was Polish people themselves who did these things. The Germans just stood back and watched.

"We all heard this was going on in the towns nearby. The mob was becoming more and more wild, more and more bloodthirsty. Terrible, terrible things were being done: beheadings, people being buried alive. It was like a hysteria, a mass hysteria.

"Joszef...Joszef was very excited. The Jews were getting what they deserved because they were all communists, he told me. I said to him, what makes you say such a thing? Father Pawlicki told me, he said. Father Pawlicki said it was time to settle the score with the people who had murdered Christ."

"But the communists were against Christianity."

"Sure. But whatever evil there was in the world, the Jews were behind it. That's how they thought, the Poles. That's how Joszef thought. I tell you, it was a madness. *That* was pure evil.

"Our town though had been quiet. Jedwabne had been calm. So Jews fled there from the places where these pogroms had been happening. The bishop promised he would protect the Jews in Jedwabne, that he wouldn't allow such things to happen there. But my brother was telling me something very different. He was...he was horribly excited. So I knew something terrible was about to happen in our town. We all knew. Everyone knew.

"That day, that terrible day in July, from dawn onwards, a mob from local villages started gathering in Jedwabne. They were talking to the Gestapo, cooking it up together. The town council signed an agreement with the Gestapo, an agreement about what was going to happen. What the Poles were about to do.

"Some men came to our house, men we knew: all louts, thugs. They knew my brother Joszef. They were carrying pitchforks and clubs. I heard one of them say, 'It's starting,' and my brother pulled on his jacket and picked up an iron bar. I held on to him, I begged him not to go, but he threw me off. I would have followed him, I knew what he was capable of, I'd seen it, I would've run after them to stop him, but I hesitated..."

She paused and wiped her eyes with her hand.

"Later that day, he burst through the door like a thing possessed. His hair was wild, his clothes covered in blood and soot, his face streaked black with dirt. He was dragging a sack. He had been drinking, I could smell it, but this wasn't drunkenness. It was...it was like a kind of ecstasy, almost a religious transfiguration. Except it wasn't that, it was demonic, it was from the devil himself.

"He started to shout in a kind of triumph, like a madman; and you know, I couldn't stop myself thinking of these stories Boruch would tell us about the dybbuk. Well it was like that.

He wasn't my brother anymore, he didn't sound like my brother, this terrible, terrifying voice coming out of his mouth as he stood there shouting..."

He spoke as gently as he could. "What had he done?"

She twisted her hands together. "I had a friend, a very good friend: Julia. She worked for the Germans as a secretary in the gendarmerie. She told me afterwards what happened, she saw some of it and the Germans told her the rest. They had stood there throughout, the Germans, just watching what was happening and taking photographs."

She shook her head slowly from side to side, as if trying to shake away the memory.

"All the Jews were told to assemble in the town square for cleaning duty. All day long the Poles beat them to death, hacked their heads off, raped the woman and massacred them with their children. No one could run away; the Poles cut them off and slaughtered them. It was a frenzy.

"Everywhere they were beaten, knifed, mutilated. Everywhere they were forced to sing and dance as they were cut down. One old man—they set fire to his beard. They were made to topple a statue in the square, a statue of Lenin, and under a hail of blows to dig a hole to bury the pieces, and they made them sing as they dug the hole; then they were butchered and thrown into the same hole.

"Then they lined the Jews up, four in a row. They were all ordered to sing and they were herded and beaten into a barn. Sleszynski's barn. Some young men stood nearby playing instruments. The more the Jews screamed, the louder they played. They poured kerosene around the barn, threw the rest inside and set fire to it."

She swayed in her chair with her eyes closed. He thought, maybe he should call a halt. He could scarcely bear to listen. But now she drove herself on, her voice flattened into a kind of relentless drone.

"During that day I heard terrible screaming from next door. I made myself look out of the window. I saw them dragging off the Ajzensztejns: Boruch, Symma, Blume. They may already have killed them, they were being dragged along, they looked bloody and lifeless. I have always hoped, given what was ahead of them, that they were already dead."

He recoiled. "The barn?"

"They went to the Jews' houses and dragged out the babies and the sick and threw them into that inferno. They roped some children together, stuck them on pitchforks and threw them onto smoldering coals. At the end of that day, no Jews were left in the town."

She stopped talking and sat very still. The silence reverberated in his head. He wished he could go and lie down. When he spoke, he found his voice was trembling.

"And when your brother came back? What happened then?"

In the silence, the ticking of the clock sounded very loud. She sighed very deeply.

"I said the Ajzensztejns had been very good to us. We were often in their house. They invited us to share their table on Friday evenings. Then they would bring out their best china and cutlery, it was gold plate I think, and some beautiful silver things, goblets and candlesticks, a spice box and other things they used for their rituals. These were very fine, quite intricately carved with filigree and what have you, and old, they were heirlooms handed down through generations.

"Joszef used to say, bet they're worth something, all those things; that always made me feel uncomfortable, the way he said it. Calculating. The Ajzensztejns also had a lot of books, religious books; Boruch was quite learned in that way, and I think Symma knew a lot too. This seemed to worry my brother for some reason; maybe he was jealous, but he seemed to think there was something troubling about the fact that they were so learned, that they knew so much.

"One Friday evening, Boruch showed us a book that was very old indeed, so old it was kept in a special cloth. He didn't open it, showed it to us inside its cover and then put it away. Boruch told us this was a very precious book, it had been in his family hundreds of years and had survived even through terrible times when the family had been attacked or had to flee.

"My brother pestered Boruch to show him this book, to tell him what was in it, but all Boruch would tell him was that it was about a faraway land. This made Joszef even more curious. He wouldn't stop talking about it, about what was in it, what faraway land. I said to him, it's just an old book, what interest can there be in that? But he thought it was like a kind of talisman, that it had some kind of magic that would keep safe anyone who owned it."

Russell thought his heart might jump out of his body, it was thumping so hard.

"That terrible day, when Joszef burst through our door, he was dragging a sack. Inside were all the Ajzensztejns' valuables, the silver candlesticks and goblets, the gold-plated cutlery. And the book. He waved that book in the air. That's why he was so triumphant. He had gone back to their house and looted it. Well everyone was doing it. Everyone was looting the Jews' houses because they assumed they were all of them as good as dead."

There was clearly something else. He waited.

"I said by the end of that day no Jews were left. Well, that wasn't quite true. That morning, when the attacks had already started, there was a knock on my door. Blume was standing there with a baby in her arms, wrapped in a shawl. She held the baby out to me; I never want to see again such desperation, such anguish. 'There is no time,' she said urgently. 'Please take her. Take my baby. Please, please.'

"I was stupefied but I took the bundle. 'Her name is Haia,' she said. 'She is your niece.' She kissed the baby's head, so tenderly it broke my heart, and then she threw her arms around me. I felt her whole body shuddering. Then she was gone."

His mind flew back to that morning in the synagogue, when Joszef had silently wept.

"Did Joszef know?"

"Of course he knew. And when he came back and looted the house, he looked for the baby. To kill her too. He burst through that door like a creature possessed. His face at that moment will stay with me until the end of my days. I looked into his eyes and saw the devil himself.

"I screamed at him to get out. I picked up a carving knife and ran towards him. I swear I would have run it through him. I had a strength at that moment, I cannot say where from. I tried to fight him but he was too strong; he clubbed the knife out of my hand. Next thing I knew I was on the floor, my head all bloody, and he had gone."

"With the sack?"

"With what he'd looted, yes. But I'd hidden the baby in the well, the same well where Joszef and I had hidden from the Soviets. I climbed in and got her out, put her in a basket and ran from the house. There was a family across the fields—good, decent people I knew—who took us in. But it was too dangerous to stay, too dangerous for them. Poles who hid Jews were being betrayed by other Poles, murdered. And I knew my brother would come looking for me. And for the baby.

"We were smuggled out in a hay cart and then passed from one member of the Polish resistance to another until we were put on a boat to Sweden. From there we made it to America.

"From that day to this I have never been back to Poland. I made a new life here. I had an American husband, American children, grandchildren. You can't ever forget; but you can lock all the memories away, grow a new skin. When I was told Joszef was alive after all this time, it as if someone had ripped that skin off my body."

She sat quietly now, looking out of the window as if lost in a memory. The sun, now low in the sky, streamed in. Dust motes danced in its rays.

"My son-in-law is a veterinarian," she said, with her gaze still fixed on the window. "He makes a good living. He is a decent person. I have wanted for nothing, and I'm grateful. Grateful to America. Here a person lives free from fear. Do you have any idea what that means?"

No, he had to admit to himself, he had never known that kind of terror, what it felt like to be hunted. Yet fear was his constant companion. But fear of what? He thought of his father, spending his whole life in terror although he lived all that life in the safety of Britain. Terror of other people, terror of new experiences, terror of disease.

Russell stared at his crumpled paper napkin. He was once again sitting at his parents' plain, dour, wooden fifties' dining table, with the food sticking in his throat and the fork slipping through his fingers as he surreptitiously eyed his father toying with his dinner.

His father thought he was dying. He had been diagnosed with a chronic bowel disease but he was convinced he had been lied to and that he had cancer. His terror had been infectious. His mother seemed paralyzed by it, and Russell was miserable with fear.

His father's moods had affected him badly. But Jack had lived until he was 80, and so what had so frightened Russell as a child had been fear itself. The fear that his father's nightmares would become real and smash Russell's world. His demons had been phantoms, he thought; but still, he had run away from them, taken refuge in a different world. He felt embarrassed and ashamed.

"We brought up Haia as our own daughter."

He looked involuntarily towards the closed door. She shook her head. "Stacey is her sister. Her adoptive sister."

She was certainly still sharp. Her gaze, now upon him again, was fierce.

"Haia knows nothing about what I have just told you. Nothing. She has no knowledge of who her father was. And she must never know."

Was that directed at him? Would she now fill in the final piece of the puzzle?

"Of course. An amazing story. I'm sure that I...that I wouldn't have had the courage. And Haia is now...where, exactly?"

The silence hung between them.

"And your brother? Did he...does he now know about Haia?"

Zofia's eyes remained closed.

"I had no interest in ever contacting him."

He thought about that for a moment.

"Did he ever try to get in touch with you? Through the comrades?"

She stiffened slightly. He held his breath.

She was weary now. When she spoke again her eyes remained closed, almost as if she was speaking mechanically, as if no longer possessing the strength to keep hold of what she knew.

"I heard nothing from him until a few weeks ago. Out of the blue, I received a parcel. It was the book, the old book he had stolen from the Aizjensteins, the one that had so obsessed him, why, I have no idea to this day. He had kept it all this time. Now, after he was arrested, he sent it to me with a letter. Not a word asking how I was, or regret about the past, or any curiosity about my life; nothing. Just a final act of malice."

"Malice?"

"The book had brought him bad luck, he said; now you can have it. That was all he wrote."

"I see. So...so you've got this book now?"

She looked at him steadily. Oh God, he groaned inwardly, had his tone given something away?

"I'm, er...my research...I'm particularly interested in lost Hebrew literature..."

Zofia grasped her walking frame and hauled herself painfully to her feet.

"I am tired now," she said, and turned slowly towards the door. He watched in despair as she shuffled across the carpet. No! So close!

The door clicked shut behind her. He heard a murmuring outside, her daughter exclaiming about helping her to her room and Zofia sounding irritable. In a few minutes, Stacey reappeared through the door. He stood up awkwardly.

"Well, you had a nice long chat with Mum, didn't you," she said brightly. "Did you get what you wanted?"

"Get...?"

"Was she useful, did she give you the information you need for your research?"

"Oh...Yes, yes indeed. Really helpful, and totally fascinating."

"You did well. She doesn't really talk about...about those times. Not surprising, is it. What she went through hardly bears thinking about, does it."

How much did she know?

"She was obviously very brave. She told me a little about what happened, about your sister..."

"Haia? Yes, quite a story isn't it? Rescuing a Jewish baby like that and then escaping with her in a hay cart across the border; well you just can't imagine it, can you. Not your own mother."

"A...a Jewish baby?"

"Yes of course, didn't she explain? She knew this Jewish family, and there was some kind of terrible attack in which they were all killed, but Mum was able to rescue the baby and escape with her, something about hiding in a well; and that was Haia. Look: this is her, and this, obviously when she was much younger."

He looked at the photographs. There was one of the whole family, with five tow-haired, freckle-faced, laughing children, and a slightly older teenager wearing glasses and with her long dark hair in a ponytail, smiling shyly. The next was of the same girl, now in her twenties, he guessed, with her face framed by dark tumbling curls.

"What a beauty," he said softly, as if to himself.

"Oh yes, she had all the boys after her, for sure, back then," said Stacey with a slightly grim little laugh.

"And so where does she live nowadays?"

"Nowadays? Oh, in the holy land!" Stacey's voice dropped respectfully.

"The...what, Israel?"

This he had not expected at all.

"Wonderful, isn't it! I'm so jealous! It's where Our Lord will return at the end of days, which is why it's so precious to us because that is where all the unbelievers will be converted to the one true faith and then there will be peace all over the earth. So Haia is doing holy work. And of course, she herself is one of the chosen. So she is really special."

Jesus, he thought. That's all he needed, Christian fundamentalist wackos.

"Keep in touch much, do you?"

"Quite a bit. We do FaceTime now, which helps. She has two children; her husband passed some years back. I miss her. And I think she misses all the things we have here that we take for granted. I'm always sending her bits and pieces—she loves to read American magazines. My mother sent her a book only the other day."

A book. He thought quickly. He had one final card. He couldn't afford to drop it.

"You know, I'm really very interested in your homeschooling idea. I think it's got a lot going for it. I'd love to test the water for it back in Britain."

She clapped her hands into a steeple and pressed her fingertips to her mouth in excitement.

"You really think there'd be some interest? Gee, that would be just wonderful! What we need, what would make such a difference, is for a school to give us its backing. That would sure make all the folks who say we're just some kinda weird nutjobs brainwashing our kids with creationism and suchlike to pipe down! D'ya think you might get some school interested? Oh, I'm so excited! Here, why don't you sit down and I'll make some more tea and tell you some more about it."

Half an hour later, after he had enthusiastically accepted a pile of books about homeschooling to show to his contacts in the university world, he started gathering his things together in order finally to take his leave. He was so thrilled to have met Stacey as well as her remarkable mother, he told her earnestly. They had so much in common and he had learned so much.

And of course, he said as casually as he could, he'd see what he could do about homeschooling, but Stacey had to understand that it wasn't his area of expertise, which was really a very narrow aspect of East European history, specifically standards of literacy and education amongst the pre-war Jewish community in Poland, the kind of books they read, that sort of thing.

"Well, how funny you should say that," smiled Stacey as she helped him on with his coat, "because that book I told you my mother sent Haia the other day? Well, apparently that had belonged to Haia's parents but my mother only unearthed it recently; apparently she had forgotten she had it, and so she sent it straight on. Can't think why, though; it looked pretty old and tatty."

He almost stopped breathing. His heart was pounding fit to burst.

"Really? Well, I'd love to take a peek at that; sounds like it might be just the thing to fill in a few crucial details in my research. You know, just so happens that I'm due to be visiting Israel very soon. Maybe I might visit Haia? I'd love to meet her, having heard so much about her."

"You are? Why, sure thing! She runs a riding school for disabled children. Somewhere in the Judean hills. Just how romantic does that sound?"

She reached for a pad and wrote an address. "I'll tell her you're coming. I just wish I was going with you to that blessed land. You'll have such a great time."

Halfway out of the front door, he said: "Well, what a stroke of good fortune that we met."

Stacey gasped his free hand and stared into his eyes. "Not good fortune at all. It was God's work that brought you to us."

He fled.

25

"OOH, I'D LOVE to come with," said Damia.

They were sitting cozily in the flat in Stockwell. She had cooked a vegetable biryani that was now steaming in its dish on the table. There were bright rugs on the floor and gaily colored cushions on the sofa. Jazz played softly in the background. Outside, the rain streamed down.

It was remarkable, he thought wonderingly as he opened a bottle of red wine, how quickly his life had settled into such a comfortable pattern. It felt as if he had been with Damia forever. Emboldened by the ease between them, he had taken a deep breath when he returned from Virginia and told her everything; all about meeting Kuczynski, about Eliachim of York, and about the shattering news of Kuczynski's real identity and what his sister Zofia had told him.

When he had finished he looked at her timidly, braced for her scorn. She sat staring at him for a while, her expression inscrutable. Then she threw back her head and burst out laughing.

"That was some mistake you made!"

For a second, he felt offended. Then something in him relaxed. He started to laugh too. He felt all the shame and anxiety drain away. It was going to be all right.

"But my God, Russell, what a fantastic story! Eliachim and Duzelina! It sounds like a fairy story, and yet it's all true!"

"I just feel such a total fool."

"Mmn, no; not *total.*" She caught his eye and they both started laughing all over again.

She was very practical and direct, he was discovering; she didn't waste time on what wasn't useful.

"We have to work out how you're going to approach the daughter, this Haia," she said as she ladled out the food onto his plate. "It's a delicate situation."

"We?" Did she think she was coming too?

"I think I have to go there alone, you know."

She nodded. "Sure, but we have to have a strategy. You've just got to get hold of that book again. You're right, it would make a fantastic story. A dead cert for BBC2, I'd say. Lots of historic pictures, and you walking round York telling the story, and we'd have actors silently representing Eliachim and Duzelina, all lit like a medieval painting. It will be fabulous. So what will you tell Haia to win her trust?"

He hadn't got a clue, he thought. But her enthusiasm had fired him up for the challenge. She chewed thoughtfully for a while.

"You tell her the truth," she said finally, waving her fork in the air; "but not the whole truth. You tell her that you're researching Jewish cultural life in pre-war Poland..."

"For TV?"

"Mnn, no, leave it vague; and that her mother told you about this book which sounded as if it would help your research, te tum te tum, and of course you don't let on that you've already read half of it but it would be so helpful if you could borrow it to study it; and well, after that you just play it by ear."

"I promised the mother I wouldn't let on to Haia about Joszef."

"You don't have to say anything about him at all. Put him out of your mind. For now, all that's happened is that you're doing research and you met Zofia and the sister. Your sole focus is that book."

He felt a wave of relief. For the first time that he could remember, he felt looked after.

"You're very good at this," he said admiringly.

She came and sat on his lap, and put her arms round his neck. "And well done you," she said softly, "for finding out about the book in the first place and working out what it says. No small achievement."

Absurdly, he felt as elated as if he had won a prize.

26

THE PHONE RANG in the middle of the night. In his sleep-befuddled state Russell heard Alice's panicked voice.

"It's Rosa. She's in the hospital. Overdose."

"*What!* How, what happened? How is she?"

"She's okay, she's fine, they pumped out her stomach, I got to her in time, she made sure I noticed, left the empty pill bottles where I was bound to see them, she wasn't serious, just another bloody cry for attention..."

"Jesus, Alice, she's *fifteen years old* and she took an *overdose* and you're trying to *minimize...*"

"I'm not minimizing anything!" Alice's voice rose and she started to wail. "You just don't know what it's like trying to manage her, all on my own..."

And whose fucking fault is that, he thought furiously.

In her hospital bed, his daughter looked like a little Gothic wraith. Pinioned beneath a white cotton blanket, with her black hair startling against the crisp white pillow, her face was almost as pale as the bed linen. He pulled up a chair beside her bed. She looked at him and started to cry. He put his arm round her and she clung to him with surprising force.

"Don't give up on me! I don't want you to leave me again!"

He was perplexed.

"Hey, I'm not leaving you. What makes you think I am?"

He could hardly hear her between sobs.

"She's gonna stop me seeing you."

"What, *Mum*? She can't do that. Anyway, why would she want to after all this time?"

"She's gonna take you to court..."

"What?"

"...and say you're an unsuitable parent and can't be trusted to be with me. Says it's child abuse."

He was startled. Despite everything, Alice had never used that trick of making false allegations of sexual abuse against him in order to deny him contact with Rosa.

"Says you're a bad influence, that you've helped me get brainwashed by Rabbi Daniel and she's stopped me seeing him *and* Udi and now she's saying I can't change my name and it's all your fault because you're harming my human rights..."

"*What* rights?"

"...my right not to be brainwashed by religious nutjobs which is what she calls them."

Russell was almost speechless. It was hard to say which was the greater, Alice's stupidity or her wickedness.

"But Udi's not even religious. Is he?"

"She says he's a child-killing apartheid Nazi. 'Cos he's Israeli."

"But isn't he still at school?"

"William Ellis."

"Is all this why you...?"

She nodded imperceptibly.

"Dad, I hate her, she's crazy, I wanna live with you. Can she do it? Can she get a judge to stop me seeing you?"

There was a fresh burst of sobs.

He hesitated. The truth was, he just didn't know what she was capable of doing. In any sane world she wouldn't be given the time of day. But then he thought about Michael Waxman and his assault.

There was something else he had to tell Rosa. He sat on her bed and took her gently by the shoulders.

"Now listen to me, munchkin. Your mother is not going to stop you seeing me."

She brightened. "Promise?"

He took a deep breath.

"Promise. I just won't let her do it. This whole thing is ridiculous. I will put a stop to it as soon as I can. But first I have to go on a trip."

"A trip? Where? How long?" Rosa became alarmed.

"Israel. A few days, maybe a few weeks. I'm not sure."

"Take me with you! Please, please!"

Of course he had been expecting that.

"Can't do that, munchkin. I've got a job to do. And you've got to get back to school. But I will bring you back something nice from there, if you promise me you won't do anything like this ever again. Because if you do, then we really won't be able be together, will we. And when I come back, I'll settle all this nonsense once and for all. Deal?"

Rosa hesitated. She looked at him. Then she made a face and put up the palm of her hand.

"Deal," she said.

They smacked palms together.

"Dad?"

"What?"

"You haven't called me munchkin since I was, like, five. Before...before everything went bad."

He stroked her hair. "But I've never stopped thinking of you like that."

She smiled sleepily.

When he left her, he sat for a long time in the reception area. He stared unseeing at the melee of visitors and patients coming and going. Then he took out his phone and punched in a number.

"It's me," he said. "For once, just shut the fuck up and listen to what I am about to say. I have just visited our daughter. It is clear to me that you drove her to try to take her own life. If I hear that you have forbidden her to see anyone or change her name, or if I hear you have either taken action to stop her seeing me or threatened her that you will do so, I will personally ensure that you are publicly exposed for the child abuser that you are so that no human rights litigant will henceforth touch you with a ten-foot pole. As no decent person should. Unfortunately, you happen to be our daughter's mother. For once in your selfish, narcissistic life, behave like one."

Next, he called another number.

"Of course we'll keep an eye on her while you're away," said Rabbi Daniel. "Sam will visit her this afternoon."

He punched in another number.

"Hold on, I'm coming straight round," said Damia to the weeping man at the end of the phone.

27

IT WAS THE quality of the light that first struck him, as if a grey film had been lifted from his eyes. The blue of the sky, the green of the leaves, the white stone of the unexpectedly attractive airport, all seemed to possess an incandescent clarity that for some reason made him suddenly, inexplicably cheerful.

The flight to Israel had not been an altogether comfortable experience. He had thought he was safe enough travelling British Airways. The first shock was the number of Hassidic Jews on the plane. A group of them, in prayer shawls and with *tefillin* strapped to their foreheads and arms, were even praying and swaying at the departure gate. The desk staff were paying them no attention. Russell stared at the scene in squirming embarrassment.

On the plane, he watched uneasily as more and more Hassids poured on board, trailed forlornly by dowdy wives in ill-fitting wigs and long skirts, staggering under the weight of babies and surrounded by pale, whiny, bespectacled children.

The men uploaded oversized wheelie bags and outsized hatboxes containing *shtreimels*, their furred Shabbat headgear, into the overhead luggage bins. These unsurprisingly very soon filled up, causing harassed flight attendants to first suggest and then insist that cabin bags had to be moved into the hold. Luggage duly piled up in the narrow aisles waiting to be moved, blocking the passengers still streaming on board from getting to their seats. Voices were raised.

Russell observed this growing mayhem with a grim sense of validation. You see! You see! This is what you have to expect, he told himself.

The rest of the plane seemed to consist solely of people speaking in the adenoidal tones that grated so badly, further blocking the aisles as they greeted friends and family with whom they felt the need to share lengthy news bulletins trumpeted at ear-splitting volume. Russell looked round desperately. My God, he thought, I am completely surrounded.

Sitting next to him was a young woman, engrossed already in a book. Gradually Russell became aware of an extra commotion. A Hassid was standing truculently next to the third and empty seat at the end of the row. A flight attendant was quietly asking various passengers if they would mind moving. The answer was obviously in the negative.

"I'm afraid I can't find anyone sitting next to a man who is willing to swap," she said to the Hassid, flustered. The Hassid remained immobile, impassive.

Russell couldn't believe his ears. What, refusing to sit next to a woman? No!

The plane was ready to depart. The Hassid remained standing in the aisle. "You'll have to sit down now, sir," said the flight attendant, indicating the seat next to the young woman. He didn't move. Another flight attendant appeared. "Sir, the captain will not take off until you sit down," he said in a loud voice. "If you don't do so immediately you will be removed from this plane."

Finally roused from her book, the young woman glanced up, startled. The Hassid still didn't move. Another flight attendant appeared; there were now three of them staring at him. The passengers fell silent at the drama. Suddenly a young man approached. "I don't mind swapping," he said, "and there's a man sitting next to me."

"That was very nice of you," said the young woman as the boy sat down. He shrugged and smiled.

"It was really no problem. Live and let live?"

He looked like a student, in jeans and a T-shirt.

"You'd think I had leprosy or something," said the girl with a sniff.

"Disgraceful," said a woman in a cut-glass English accent from a seat behind him. "They should have thrown him off the plane. Behaving like that! Gives us all a bad name!"

Russell shrank into his corner. He stared sightlessly out of the window and hoped everyone could see that he was absolutely not a part of any of this. Hideous! And they hadn't yet even left Heathrow. If it was this bad on the plane, what was Israel going to be like?

He soon had his answer. He had been advised to take a *sherut*, or shared taxi, from the airport to his hotel in Jerusalem. It turned out to be a ten-seater van around which milled a great crowd of people with mountains of suitcases. A man who seemed to be in charge barked something at him he didn't understand. He stared back helplessly.

"Where you go?" shouted the man.

"Jerusalem," said Russell. "Where in Jerusalem?" shouted the man more loudly, exasperated by such an imbecile.

He gave the name and address of his hotel. The man jerked his thumb at the van, snatched up his suitcase and hurled it into the back. Russell climbed in and found a seat, sweating. Were they all on such a short fuse here?

It appeared they were. An argument broke out between the driver and a knot of people trying to get into the van. Shouting ensued. Suddenly, the group moved like an amoeba on speed towards a second *sherut* that had pulled up behind the first.

Russell was wedged in between an overweight sweaty man and a woman with a carrier bag on her lap digging into his ribs. The last seat was finally filled, the driver climbed into his cab and the van set off.

The woman called out a question in Hebrew to the driver. He responded sharply and with another question. An argument developed. The woman started shouting and waved her arm angrily at the driver, clipping Russell round the ear. The driver jammed on his brakes, reversed the van through the terminal approaches all the way back to the taxi stand and gestured to the woman to get out. She screamed back; he shouted louder. Finally, she left. A young backpacker got on and took her place. They set off once again.

The other passengers excitedly discussed the drama. The non-Hebrew speakers wanted to know what had happened. "She wanted to be dropped at the entrance to the city and was insisting on a reduction in the fare," said an elderly man near the front. There was much shaking of heads.

Clearly, they were all quite unhinged in this country, Russell concluded.

The driver turned up the radio at deafening volume. It was a news bulletin. The *sherut* fell silent. The Israeli passengers listened intently; the others listened uneasily to the Israelis listening. There was an almost audible sigh of relief when the driver turned the radio back to the music that had been playing.

Russell gazed out of the window. They were beginning to climb towards Jerusalem. Flat, neatly ploughed fields gave way to majestic hills dotted with white stone and terraced with bushes and trees. At one point along the roadside he saw what looked like the skeletons of old army vehicles.

"Look," said an American passenger to his wife, "these are from '48 when the Arabs cut off this road. In those days it was the only way in and out of Jerusalem. There were battles here, massacres of Jews."

"Nothing changes, does it," said the wife with a sigh.

The hills rose steeply on either side of the road. The phrase "sitting ducks" lodged itself uncomfortably in Russell's mind and wouldn't fade.

They rounded another bend and suddenly there it was ahead of them, on top of a distant hill: the city itself. Russell gasped. He was unprepared for the sight. The sun was setting, and the pale stone of the distant city seemed to be glowing like pink gold. A long, white jagged column slanting upwards on the horizon pointed like a crooked finger towards the sky.

The *sherut* wound its way through one Jerusalem neighborhood after another, depositing passengers at their various destinations. Every few minutes there was yet another breathtaking view, with golden pink villages glimmering atop the undulating, white and green Judean hills.

There were new neighborhoods with pristine, red-roofed houses in creamy stone; there were many poorer areas where shabby apartment blocks had washing draped over rickety balconies along with the occasional blue and white Israeli flag. Everywhere the houses and apartment blocks were jammed up against each other. The city seemed to have no room to breathe, Russell thought; it felt as if it were being stifled. And in these shabby neighborhoods, the streets teemed with the black hats and long skirts of the ultra-orthodox and their myriad children. My God, he thought, they are absolutely everywhere.

The stone finger pointing skywards turned out to be the pillar of a futuristic bridge strung like a giant harp. Underneath and beside this soaring statement of purpose and optimism, the city sprawled restlessly in a perpetual motion of scurrying black hats and perpetually hooting cars.

To his relief his hotel, in the center of the city, seemed full of normal people. It was a small, boutique hotel with pleasant young staff and modern fittings. For the first time in ages he slept a deep, dreamless sleep. In the morning he filled his breakfast plate with fresh bread and pastries, eggs, smoked fish and fruits from the ample buffet and ate in the hotel's tiny patio garden.

Apartment blocks hemmed it in but here a small oasis had been carefully and lovingly created. Lemon and clementine trees were in sweet, fragrant flower. Tame sparrows hopped hopefully near his chair; a tortoiseshell cat sat in the early morning sun washing herself. It was quiet in the garden; he heard birds calling to each other in the trees. He breathed the soft, scented air. A deep tranquility stole over him.

Haia lived on a *moshav*, a collective industrial farm, in the Judean hills. The taxi-driver who he flagged down outside his hotel eyed him in his mirror as they set off.

"American?"

"Er, British."

"Ah, Britain! Liverpool football club! What a team! What I give to go to England to see them play! You see them play?"

There was a flash of white teeth in the mirror. His skin was like brown leather; he might have been an Arab but for the small black skullcap perched on his shining bald head.

"Well, er, no..."

"No? You live London? London not far from Liverpool! You don't go Liverpool football club?"

Russell wished the driver would stop engaging with his rearview mirror. Cars seemed to be coming straight at them while the driver conversed with his reflection and waved his hands around.

"Don't people ever, uh, slow down here?" said Russell faintly after a four-by-four coming the other way seemed to have narrowly missed shaving off the door where he was sitting.

"Ach, this is Israel, you just stick to the middle of the road and eventually the other fellow gives way," said the driver, taking both his hands off the wheel now in an expressive shrug.

The taxi suddenly emerged from a tunnel into sunlight so dazzling it seemed to explode onto his retina as the hills and valleys rolled away below and beyond them into a shimmering distant horizon.

The beauty of it almost took his breath away. There was something poignant about these hills, with their white stone and terraces of olive trees and the occasional simple village clinging to their slopes. He thought of England, its soft, rolling landscape clothed in carpets of green dotted with cows and sheep. But these stony, thorny outcrops seemed somehow exposed and vulnerable, as if bared to their fundamentals and open under the sky.

The house was up a dirt path. The car bumped along past a sign with a picture of horses and stopped outside a jumble of buildings. The driver jerked his thumb in their direction.

"You want to see sights, you call me, ok?" He thrust a card at Russell. "I drive you, cheap price, I take you everywhere, I show you off beaten track, anywhere you want. You want?"

He finally roared off in a cloud of dust.

28

AT THE END of the jumble of buildings stood a low, shabby house. As Russell approached, he heard the sound of a cello; Schubert, he thought.

He knew it was Haia as soon as she opened the door. The likeness was quite shocking: the same large-boned, peasant face—and yes, the same dimple in the chin. But the eyes were from somewhere else: huge, dark velvet pools. He stared at her in the doorway, momentarily paralyzed by the burden of the secret he now carried.

"You are Mr. Wolfe?" she said, and extended her hand. "You are welcome. My sister has told me all about you."

She smiled warmly, and then he saw it—something sparkling, vivacious, even teasing. "So full of gaiety," Zofia had said. He caught his breath. She was plump, with full, glossy lips and snowy white hair pinned into a tight plait on the back of her head. Her skin was smooth, remarkably unlined for a woman in her seventies. She was wearing a full-length embroidered kaftan and gaudy plastic earrings in the shape of fruit.

A cello was propped against a grand piano. Paintings were crammed onto every wall. The house was dark and full of bric-a-brac. She saw him looking.

"My late husband and I collected art. Whatever we could afford, you know. Come! Let me show you."

She led him through the house, into rooms and up and down stairs, all the time delivering a breathless running commentary on the pictures. "My late husband had an eye for artistic talent, well he was very talented himself, he wrote poetry, he would spot these wonderful artists when they were just starting out so of course their work was very cheap back then, well who knows what all this is worth nowadays."

She served coffee, black and in eastern-style tea glasses. He choked on a mouthful of grounds.

"It's Turkish; you are not used to it."

It was a judgment. He waved away her concern with what he hoped was sufficient insouciance as he spat out the grounds into a paper napkin.

"You play?" He motioned to the cello and piano in order to regain the initiative.

"A family trio: my grandson on piano, my daughter on flute."

He was confused. "I thought you ran a riding stables...?"

"Oh I do, well I did, I started it, you see, I trained as a psychologist and of course I rode, back in Virginia, and I realized that riding was excellent therapy for trauma or depression. So I started my riding school for children with these difficulties. Now my daughter runs it; I'm not quite as spry around horses as I used to be. But I also realized that music is therapy too. So we take our trio to play to communities where there's a lot of trauma. There's no shortage of that round here, I'm afraid."

He found himself under a sharp quizzical gaze from those dark pools. "You know Israel well?"

"Uh...first time here, actually."

"Ah! You are not Jewish?"

"Um, well, yes, yes I am. Sort of."

"Ah!!" There was a pause. Her eyes asked a question which he had no intention of answering. He looked down at his knees.

"Your research must be very important to you then, to have brought you all this way."

Her gaze had not left him.

"What did you say your field was, exactly?"

Look up, he told himself, look into those pools openly and frankly.

"The culture of pre-war Polish Jewry," he said firmly, assuming an earnest and, he hoped, suitably scholarly expression. "Your mother thought that a book she had sent you would be of use to me. But I'm only a lowly researcher, really. Grateful for anything that comes my way."

"I'm surprised she has any idea what it is," said Haia. "Frankly, I don't really know why she sent it. She said she had been clearing out her cupboard and came across it at the bottom of a trunk. She's not actually my mother, by the way, she's my adoptive mother. Said the book had belonged to my parents, she hadn't realized it was there, didn't want to throw it away and thought I should have it. But it just seems to be some broken-backed old thing; I can't even read what's in it. Seems to be in Hebrew but I can't make head nor tail of it. All very strange. I do hope this behavior doesn't mean she's dying."

Russell hastened to assure her that Zofia had been in very good health when he saw her. He had also been very pleased to meet her sister. To his surprise, Haia rolled her eyes.

"The Christian visionary. Thinks I'm going to have a ringside seat at the Second Coming."

He was puzzled. "You're not...I thought you were brought up as part of the family, same as everyone else?"

She shook her head emphatically. "No, no, I am a Jew, a Jew from birth. My parents were murdered in Poland during the Shoah."

He struggled to keep his expression neutral.

"My adoptive mother knew my parents. Apparently she was quite friendly with my real mother. When my parents were murdered she managed somehow to smuggle me out of Poland to America. She was an atheist, although my adoptive father was a Christian, and she was determined to bring me up to know about my Jewish identity. She was very passionate about that, remarkably so."

"Did she tell you much about your...your parents? About what happened?" he asked cautiously.

She shook her head sadly. "She told me a little about my mother, that she was a great beauty, apparently, and very musical. But she didn't like to talk about it and, well, I knew the memories were just too painful so I never asked. I think they were both taken away, to one of the camps, but I just don't know. I think my mother—my adoptive mother, Zofia—just wanted to forget Poland, even the fact she was Polish. She wanted to make herself into an American, become a new person altogether."

"The past is a big gap for me too," he said. "My grandparents were also from Poland but I don't even know from where. My father never spoke to me about any of that. Well, to be frank I never spoke to him about anything very much."

She nodded sympathetically. He forgot, for the moment, why he had come there. He found himself telling her how little he knew about what he was supposed to belong to. He told her about Alice, about the rupture with his father.

She put her head on one side and gave him a long, appraising look. "That can be very difficult," she said softly. She sighed deeply and poured some more coffee. "For a long time," she said eventually, "I didn't know what I was. I just always knew what I *wasn't*. Zofia was very determined that I should know my 'identity'."

She made quote marks in the air with her fingers.

"She told me all the time that I was a Jewish child, that I was very special and that I should never forget what I was. But I didn't know what I was. All I knew was that I was apparently not really American. I wasn't like my adoptive parents, my sister. Certainly not like my sister. She got religion very badly when she was a teenager. Did she try to convert you? She tries to convert everyone. When she tried to convert me, that's when I decided what I was. That was when I decided to go to Israel."

"So...so are you religious? Jewishly, I mean."

Clumsy! he winced.

"Good heavens no," she laughed. "Not in the slightest. Although my daughter is. Where she got that from I really don't know. Maybe it's in the genes."

In the genes. He decided to risk probing a bit further. There was something he suddenly wanted to know, and she could tell him.

"My daughter likewise," he said slowly. "But with her it's even more curious, being the child of a mixed marriage. What makes a child identify with one parent rather than another?"

Her face assumed a professional expression. "No simple answer to that, really," she said thoughtfully. "Depends on so many different factors. Push as well as pull. Some kids react against one or the other parent, and so despise what they are; for others, the parent is a role model and so what they are shapes the kid.

"For me, in a way, history was destiny. I was brought up to identify with my people, with their ancient story. My family, my real family had been destroyed. So I came to live here, to be with my wider family. For me, history didn't end with the horror that killed my parents. To be where my people are even today still fighting for their right to exist, surrounded by madmen just like in the 1930s—that has given my life meaning."

He blinked away sudden unexpected tears.

"To be honest, I never knew much about my family, nor about Judaism, I'm ashamed to say."

"It's never too late to find out," she said. There was a distinct gleam in her eye. "You have biography but no history. I have history but no biography. We're a good match, aren't we?"

She left the room and returned with a cardboard box. She opened it and lifted out an object wrapped in blue velvet.

"Is this the kind of thing you are looking for?"

She held it out to him. He could hardly breathe, his heart was pounding so hard. Carefully, he unwrapped the velvet. He felt beneath his fingers the familiar roughness of the book's end-boards. He saw that she saw his hands were trembling.

"Could be," he said casually, as he gently opened its pages.

"What do you think it might be?"

He pursed his lips and funneled a long breath. "Well, could be a kind of diary, or travelogue maybe, of the kind that was not uncommon in earlier times..."

"Really? How much earlier? How old might this be?"

"Ooooh...well now, possibly...well, really quite old."

"So might it be valuable?"

Here we go again, he thought. But he couldn't mislead. He was already entangled enough by secrets. Yes, he said, it might be really quite valuable. Then again, it might not.

"How extraordinary. I wouldn't have given it a second thought. But how do you know this, so quickly?"

Again, that piercing stare.

"I've, ah, made quite a study of the kind of books Jews either write or possessed in Europe, some of them going back a very long way. And I can see immediately..."

He swallowed hard. "...I can see immediately why you didn't understand the Hebrew. Because although the letters are Hebrew, the words are French. Norman French. It's a transliteration."

"French!" she said in amazement.

Now, he thought, right now.

"Very common in the medieval period," he said in his most confident voice. "Jews of that time would never write in the language of holiness. So they used the demotic vocabulary of the time. I...I have experience translating such texts. If you like, I can do that with this. If you're interested, of course."

He showed her the frontispiece and translated for her, Eliachim of York. He could see she was taken aback.

The door opened and into the room burst a young couple, laughing together as they entered. They stopped uncertainly when they saw Russell and drew back.

"My granddaughter, Shira," said Haia, recollecting herself. "And this is her partner, Ido. This is Mr. Wolfe from London, who's going to make us all rich."

Russell winced. The young people looked bemused. Haia explained.

"An heirloom!" said Shira. "From family you never even knew, *savta*. That's so spooky! Like a voice from history."

She was wearing jeans patterned with metal studs, high wedge-heeled red sandals and a black sleeveless top with straps that crossed over at the back. Hooped silver earrings dangled below fashionably cut straight dark hair. There was a dimple in her chin.

Shira and Ido were from Tel Aviv. Shira was an interior designer; Ido was in high-tech. It appeared they visited Haia quite frequently in order to go riding.

"How's this gonna make you rich?" asked Ido in disbelief. He was wearing a black T-shirt and black jeans. His clear plastic-rimmed spectacles, which had thick silvery metal arms that stuck out straight behind his ears, perched below a skull that was closely shaved. He stood, chewing gum, his head tipped sideways looking at the book, his thumbs in the back pocket of his jeans.

"I don't think Ido can relate to anything that's not online," teased Haia, "let alone something that may be centuries old."

"Yeah, but how you gonna monetize this?" persisted Ido. "I mean, you gonna sell it? What's it worth?"

This last inquiry was directed at Russell. He spread his hands helplessly.

"Sell it?" exclaimed Shira. "But it's an heirloom! It's the only thing that connects *savta* to her family!"

There was a silence. Haia flapped her hands dismissively.

"This is all putting carts way before horses. First we have to know what the book actually says. Which Mr. Wolfe is going to help us do."

He breathed out slowly. So at least that hurdle was now overcome.

The sun was going down. Haia opened a bottle of cold Chardonnay. Shira brought in olives, dishes of avocado dip and hummus, and delicious little nutty crackers. Russell began to feel a lot better.

Ido flopped down in an armchair, draping one leg over an arm.

"You come from London? I'd love to go to London," he said wistfully. "Camden Market! English pubs!"

"Princess Kate!" said Shira. "What's she really like? Have you met her? Why's she so thin? Does she have an eating disorder?"

"Now, Ido," said Haia severely. This was obviously an all-too familiar refrain. "You know right here is where there are the opportunities for you. It's the high-tech capital of the world."

"We're being stifled here," said Shira. "So claustrophobic. You feel you're going to go mad unless you get out."

Haia clucked disapprovingly. "But you're in Tel Aviv. You have the sea there, you have young people, you have culture."

"But it's hopeless," Ido said in sudden passion. "The government is terrible. No one's got any money, the country is owned by a handful of oligarchs, you have to go to Cyprus to get married if you want to escape the clutches of the rabbis..."

"But you don't want to get married. You have chosen to live together," objected Haia.

Ido ignored this.

"Nothing moves, nothing changes. Month after month, year after year, no solution in sight. No one wants to do it, to make the peace, to make the compromises. We just get by from day to day hoping for some...miracle. As if! Are we going to have war forever?"

"The settlers are untouchable," said Shira. "Okay, I know, I know; Aunty Yael. Even so. While the settlers are there, nothing will be solved."

"The Prime Minister is definitely the problem," said Ido. "He's so hardline! Someone has to take the initiative here! We can't carry on just doing nothing. We have to come out of the territories. We can't rule over the Arabs like this. What we're doing to them is terrible, the suffering at the checkpoints. Pregnant women, old people, forced to wait for hours in the heat. We keep building in the territories, no wonder the world hates us. Soon they'll boycott us, isolate us. In London, don't they already hate us?"

'There is, certainly," said Russell cautiously, "a lot of feeling that Israel killed so many children in Gaza, that it was out of all proportion considering that hardly any Israelis were killed. That's why some people say Israel committed genocide."

Shira and Ido both looked at him in astonishment.

"They say that? But that's obscene, ridiculous! How can they possibly say such a thing?"

"This was war, a totally justified war, not genocide! Genocide is what they're trying to do to *us*! They fired thousands of rockets at us!"

"In Tel Aviv we were in shelters all the time. That's why we don't have more casualties, because we have shelters to go to!

In Gaza they don't build shelters but put their children on top of the building so they'll get killed!"

"Gaza is completely different to the West Bank! We left Gaza years ago, every last Israeli settler was dragged out of there. They're just trying to kill us because they want us dead. They built tunnels so they could get into kindergartens and kill little kids!"

"Are people in Britain really saying we mustn't defend ourselves? Would they just sit there and do nothing if London was being rocketed? What do they say about the thousands of rockets fired at us? About the fact that now we're being stabbed and shot every day, just because they want to kill Jews?"

"Erm, well none of that is actually reported," said Russell.

Their mouths dropped open.

Russell felt confused. Hadn't they just been denouncing their government as the problem?

"The young here have been brought up to think Israel is just another country like any other," said Haia, refilling Russell's glass. "They're all on social media, they're plugged into Western music, watch Western movies. They think of themselves as just like young people in the West. They expect Israel to be treated exactly the same as any other country. They have never been taught that Israel can never be like any other country."

Shira and Ido both looked at her in horror.

Eliachim's story (3)

But look now upon those Gentiles who call themselves Christians. They are ignorant even of their own language, being unable to read the simplest document or write their own name. They do not follow the laws of reason but place their faith instead in devils and witches, in necromancers and conjurers.

Yet they treat us as their slaves for we are not free men. They milk us for our money like the cows in the barn. And then when the time comes for them to honor their debts they turn upon us for the manner of our faith. They whip us like dogs and slaughter us because we refuse to worship their idol. They tell us most falsely that we killed their god. Yet they do not scorn to take our gold, and then they blame us for the debt which they tell us brings them fast to ruin and shows the evil and avarice of our race.

But it is we who have been punished by the most greedy and improvident king, who takes from us sums that greatly and unjustly exceed the demands placed on other subjects in his realm.

As the king neared his death, the waters of hatred rose up even higher among the barons and the priests on account of the debts that we were owed. The leader of these barons was one Richard Malebisse, may his name be blotted out for all eternity, who was in debt to my master Josce for many thousands of marks, as were other mighty nobles whose names shall also live in infamy.

They spoke against my master and spread false reports that tarnished his good name. But who would yet have imagined what was about to be unleashed.

In the Frankish lands, many of our number were slain with great savagery at the hands of the bloodthirsty Christians. And everywhere the people murmured against us with charges that shouted out to the heavens for their baseness and injustice.

These miseries and terrors increased yet a hundredfold when the old king passed away and the land was ruled by his son, who they say has the heart of a lion but in truth has the fangs of a snake.

In the year of the coronation of this king, great evil fell upon us. Many folk came to bring tributes at the crowning at the great abbey in London, including my master Josce and Benedict his associate in the house of finance in our town of York.

Alas the wretched day that the King received the crown of this wicked and faithless land upon his head. For the members of his accursed court spread false report that our people were sorcerers come to put a spell upon the King. Some including my master Josce and Benedict his associate entered the abbey; whereupon a great roaring broke forth from the multitude, and they set upon the members of our faith and dragged them from the church and beat them and slit their throats and hewed them into pieces.

Many fled from the massacre but the mob pursued them into the houses of the Jews and murdered every one they saw and performed abomination upon their wives and then they burned their houses to the ground. From house to house they stormed in a frenzy of bloodthirstiness, shouting "Kill the Jews! The King has commanded it! Kill the destroyers of Christ!" And the slaughter continued throughout the night and until the following afternoon.

From these horrors my master Josce escaped and made his way back to our town of York.

The king was much displeased by these events because he knew his coffers would empty if those who were so punishingly taxed were no more. So he proclaimed a law for the peace of the Jews throughout England, and there was quiet as we mourned our blessed martyrs. But our respite was short, and an evil greater than anything we had yet suffered was about to befall us.

29

RUSSELL CAME TO the house every day to finish translating Eliachim's story. He sat in a corner of Haia's living room. She brought him mint tea and cake she had baked herself. Sometimes she sat and played her cello. Would this disturb him, she asked solicitously. On the contrary, he found its plangent sadness matched his mood. He recognized some of it—once he thought he detected Elgar, but was too shy to ask—but other pieces stirred in him much deeper memories: buried Yiddish melodies and half-remembered snatches of liturgy. He felt his father, his grandmother, hovering in the room like yearning shadows.

Strangely, it soothed him.

"So what's it all about?" asked Haia curiously.

"It's a kind of love story," he said. But it was turning into something else.

"How romantic," said Haia, picking up one or two of the books he had brought with him: Middle English and Anglo-Norman dictionaries and reference books, histories of the

Jews in medieval Europe. She turned them over slowly in her hands and gave him a quizzical glance.

He felt himself blushing, and was alarmed. She waited.

"I...your mother...Zofia...I had a bit of an idea what this book might be," he mumbled.

She nodded slowly. He could see she thought something didn't quite add up. But it didn't bother her enough to do more than fleetingly wonder.

He was troubled, and she noticed. He was working feverishly, driven not just by the fear that at any moment he might once again have to abandon the task but by the tumultuous story unfolding before him, word by word.

"You're very caught up in this," she said, wonderingly. "It all seems very intense for a love story."

He snapped his laptop shut and looked at her.

"It's about a country and a people I never knew," he said, slowly. As soon as he said it, he realized there were two peoples in that country whom he didn't know. He sat back and puffed out his cheeks. So which people *did* he know? To whom did he now feel he belonged?

"You know," said Haia, "I lived in America, and when I came here I didn't realize what made the fit so good 'cause I didn't know anything else. See, the people there have the same outlook on life as the people here. Straightforward. Transparent. What you see is what you get. Sometimes it's a bit too much in your face. But when I meet up with Brits, that's when I feel like I'm meeting a foreigner. Their language is...well, opaque, it's veiled. They speak in riddles half the time–metaphor, irony, saying the opposite of what they mean. You do it too."

He raised an eyebrow.

"Oh, most definitely. The self-deprecation, for instance. 'I am but a lowly researcher,' when it turns out you arrive in a stranger's house in a foreign country toting a whole library of medieval lexicography."

Her voice sounded severe, but her eyes were crinkled in a smile.

"In any case," she said, "I'd have thought most Brits can't recognize their own country anymore. It's all over, isn't it? Britain, I mean, and Europe. They're finished."

He bridled.

"Of course it's not over," he snapped. "Britain remains what it always was. It just has different kinds of people in it, which is fine." But in front of his eyes swam the image of himself running for his life down Cable Street.

"Anyway," he said defensively, "it's your granddaughter and her boyfriend who think this country isn't worth staying in."

Haia shook her head despairingly. "It's becoming a serious problem. Who would have thought we Jews would have so neglected the education of the young. But we have. They just haven't got a clue what this country really is all about, how unique it is, and how uniquely it is seen and always will be seen. They can't bear it, you see, the young. They see the isolation and they hear the vilification and the lies and they think it's not natural for people to be so hated, it must be our fault, something we've done. But this is how Jews have been treated since the very beginning. Whatever we do, we have to do it alone."

He stared at her, transfixed. It went against everything he stood for, everything he believed in. And yet, when he thought of Eliachim, when he thought of Michael Waxman, when he thought of Haia's own father, for heaven's sake, it was as if a pixelation began to resolve itself into a recognizable image. An image from which he recoiled.

"And that's very, very hard. Not just for the young, for all of us. Look, I was trained to deal with children who had been abused. We did what we could to undo the harm that had been done to then, to help them heal and live a normal life. But it was very hard for them because they had never known anything other than living in the shadow of the abuse. The stronger ones developed strategies to deal with it; that helped them survive rather than be destroyed. But those very strategies meant their lives were abnormal. They survived, but as dysfunctional people.

"So it is with this amazing place. It has never known what it is to be a normal country, to live in peace and security: not one day, not ever.

"This isn't a country like Britain or America. This is an armed camp. Everyone here lives with their hearts in their mouths. All the time. Everything here is geared to the next attack on us, the next desperate defense against an enemy just down the road who never stops trying to kill us. Just because we exist. This is a people who have never known anything other than surviving against the odds, against the psychotic hatred of millions of people. With no prospect of it ever stopping because that hatred, that madness, is deep inside a culture; and now with much of the West kicking us in the head too. And then people expect Israelis to act normal, to behave as if everything can be settled over a nice cup of tea and a cucumber sandwich?"

He wanted to tell her she was wrong, that the situation could be sorted so easily, it was so obvious; the words dissolved in his mind into a fog. She didn't look or sound like a zealot. She was intelligent, cultured, gentle. He liked her; he enjoyed being with her. Could he have been wrong about all this? Could so many people, hundreds of thousands of them in Britain and Europe who thought like him, all his friends and colleagues, all thinking, concerned, educated, compassionate people like him—could they all really be so totally wrong? It was inconceivable.

"But you chose to live here," was all he said.

She looked pensive. "It was certainly a strange decision. I was an all-American kid, and, after all, plenty of others also had a tragic Holocaust back story. But I had no front story. See, I was told I was a Jew. But the thing was, I couldn't actually be a Jew in America. I was raised in a Christian family. My sister wanted to save my Jewish soul for Jesus. I wasn't drawn to practice Judaism; the religious stuff meant nothing to me. Israel was the only place where I could be a Jew just by being me."

No no no, Russell wanted to shout, of course you can be a Jew in America or Britain without religion. That's exactly what he was, wasn't he? He was brought up as one. He looked like one. He had all the cultural baggage–guilt, neurosis, concern for human rights. How absurd to suggest you had to have all this nationalist stuff as well.

So why did he feel so uncomfortable?

"But it's tough here," Haia went on, "no question, very tough. We pay a heavy price."

She paused, as if unsure whether to continue.

"When my son was born—my first child, Noam—I thought that by the time he grew to be a man there was bound to be peace here, that he wouldn't have to go into the army, to serve in a war. Now one of my grandsons, Amitai, nineteen years old he is, well he's a commander of a unit which is sent into the Palestinian murder tunnels to sweep for booby traps, for bombs and mines. Imagine. Another grandson, Calev, all of 20 years old, also my daughter's son, he's in a crack commando unit so secret we have no idea where he is; we just know he's likely to be in danger. We haven't seen or heard from him for months now. My daughter doesn't sleep at night."

She shook her head sadly.

"And this never-ending nightmare splits families. My son Noam—you met his daughter here, Shira—well, Noam's a hot-shot lawyer at one of the most swanky law firms in Tel Aviv. He's very left-wing; he was involved in the Oslo peace negotiation, another world now, the process by which we all thought finally, finally the Arabs would agree to let us live; and he's never changed his views. He refuses to visit my daughter Yael because she lives over the green line, in one of the settlements. As a result Yael won't even speak to him. He won't even come here now in case he sees her."

"Can't you smooth things over?"

She sighed deeply.

"Noam is just too angry. Angry with Yael, angry with me, angry with everyone."

"Angry just because of the settlers?"

There was a pause. When Haia spoke again it was with obvious difficulty.

"My husband, Aryeh, was a wonderful man. A pediatrician who specialized in treating children with cancer."

"And a poet and art collector too?"

She nodded. "He was a very rare human being. So talented, so humane. A sweet man, entirely taken up with giving of himself to others. Second Intifada, he was eating pizza in a cafe in the center of town when a Palestinian came in and blew the place up. Suicide bomber, so-called. He murdered seven people in the cafe that day, including my husband. He was sitting close by the guy, didn't stand a chance. Frankly, I don't know quite what it was that we buried."

Her voice was flat, matter-of-fact. Russell gazed at her, horrified. Suddenly he saw her quite differently. The room, the furniture, the pictures on the walls, everything in that moment seemed frozen, as if time itself had stopped. And he was back standing at the foot of the bed, with his father there but not there, feeling then as he did now that strange sensation in his head, as if he had stepped outside himself.

Her life, her heart, her very being had been shared. He had been a good man, a great man, a man who had made a difference. In a split second, though, he had been erased.

"I'm so very sorry," he said finally. She looked at him, and he flinched from what he saw in those dark pools.

"It's often the living whom we mourn most, isn't it. Noam, our son Noam, he took it very badly. He kept going over and over it in his mind, why Aryeh had gone to the cafe that day, why that particular cafe, why he hadn't been sitting in another seat; totally pointless, obviously. He just couldn't accept it. Of course you can't ever come to terms with such a thing, not completely, but you can learn to park it so that it doesn't take you over, doesn't destroy your life. Noam couldn't do that. His anger, his grief just consumed him. And he felt guilty..."

"Guilty?" Russell was startled.

"Sure. Because he was still living and Aryeh was not. Aryeh had been such a wonderful, exceptional person, Noam felt he himself should have been blown up that day, not his father. But the pain of all this was just too great. The monstrous fact of this murder, and all the others who were being murdered or terribly injured, dozens and dozens of them blown to pieces in buses and hotels and amusement parks, all the parents who lost their kids and all the families shattered forever, and the fact that it was going on and on with no end to it—well, he just couldn't bear it. He couldn't bear the fact that the Palestinians were just never, ever going to stop this—never going to *be* stopped. He had to find someone else to blame for it all, someone over whom he felt he could have some control.

"So he became fixated on the settlers, and on the governments that built the settlements. He became obsessed by them, convinced that if only they weren't there the murders and the attacks would stop. And anyone who disagreed, anyone who supported the settlers—he thought they were themselves helping produce more attacks and more murders."

"Including Yael."

"Of course. And including me. I was very distressed that he wouldn't talk to Yael. I knew he was in pain. So I tried to reason with him. The result was that he accused me of taking Yael's side, taking the side of those responsible for incubating mass murder. And then he refused to talk to me too. He won't come here, he won't speak on the phone. I see him fleetingly at family events, but I haven't seen him properly, to talk to properly, for years. It's as if he's cut me out of his life. In a way, that's even worse than losing Aryeh. It's a kind of death in life, if that's not being too melodramatic."

Her voice caught. The tears welled up in Russell's own eyes. He heard his mother's voice: "It's as if you are dead to him." But it was Russell who had had the door slammed in his face; or was it? And then he heard Beverley, angry Beverley, accusing him, saying no, it was he who had abandoned his father. And his head swam in confusion. Which way round was it? Who had been to blame? Were they perhaps both to blame? How he wished his father was still there. Because now it could never, ever be put right.

Once started, Haia clearly was finding it hard to stop.

"Losing Aryeh," she said softly, "well that was hard, of course. But we had had a good life together, and he was of a certain age. But Noam, well, there's the grief; and it's ongoing. Y'know, I stare at his picture, this middle-aged, brilliant, powerful lawyer. My Noam. Because I can't put the two together, the eager little boy in his shorts and knee socks who was so open and so loving, and now this big man who is so remote, so wound-up, so angry. And I wonder, where did my little boy go? Because this man, this Noam, seems like an entirely different person."

He had almost stopped listening. Jack now stood just behind her shoulder, with his characteristic stoop, looking away. What did I do to you, Dad, said Russell silently to himself. What were you: the frightened *nebbish* that I knew, or a war hero? Were you both? Could you be both? He hadn't ever really known him at all, had he, and now he never would. His father's shape dissolved into a mist.

She shook herself slightly, as if in reprimand. "I'm sorry. I didn't mean to unload all this on you. But...well, somehow you remind me of him."

"You have to find a way to talk to your son," he said.

Eliachim's story (4)

The king assembled his followers for the pilgrimage to take the holy city of Jerusalem from the Saracens, with cries of bloodthirsty vengeance against all those who denied the divinity of the crucified one who has caused the world to err. This enraged the citizens not just against the Saracens but against all who do not bow down to their idol.

All the envy and hatefulness that the barbarians had stored up against us burst forth in a frenzy of killing as they struck against us again and again, burning and looting and dishonoring our daughters before putting them to the sword. They tore down the stairways and destroyed the houses. They plundered and ravaged.

This barbarism spread like a contagion throughout the land. Scarcely a week passed without some new horror. In Stamford, in Norwich, in Lincoln and in Bury, our people were butchered with swords and with arrows and lances, with stones and with fire, even children of tender age. These were scenes the like of which we do not permit even inside our slaughterhouses: women with their breasts or ears sliced off or their children sheared from their bellies, men with those parts formed for the sacred duty of procreation stuffed in their mouths, souls burned alive inside their houses.

They were slaughtered in this inhuman fashion and dragged naked through the streets and the marketplaces, which flayed the skin from their bodies and left them as torn and bloody carcasses. But in the cursed town of Dunstable, all the Jews saved themselves from massacre by submitting to be baptized, which is a worse calamity even than the slaughter, for it commits the sin of idolatry, for which God's wrath is visited upon all the house of Israel.

When we heard of these terrible events all our bodies shook with terror. Not a soul among us walked from our houses without fear for our lives or our faith. Alas, our fears were as nothing compared to what was about to befall us.

30

MOST OF THE work at the stables was done by Haia's daughter, Yael. One day, he sat for a long time over Eliachim's manuscript, unseeing and with his head in his hands. Haia quietly put a mug of tea in front of him.

"Difficult?" she said, looking at him contemplatively, her head tilted to one side.

"Mmn. Well, not really. Just a bit hard to concentrate. Was wondering about my daughter, in fact. How she is. A bit vulnerable, you see."

Haia nodded. "They can be such a worry." She sat quietly, drinking her coffee.

"You haven't seen our riding school, have you," she said after a while. "I think you'd find it interesting. And it would be a break from this. You need a break. I'll get Yael to show you round."

Yael came to collect him. The riding school was a short distance from the house; she motioned to him to get in her car, a dusty jeep with a large dent in the side.

She was reserved and quiet. He wondered if she resented having to show him round. She was tall and slim, dressed in a long-sleeved cream top and black leggings under a loose black skirt. Her hair was concealed by a startlingly colorful headscarf tied in a tight knot on the nape of her neck.

She opened the glove compartment and he saw a pistol lying there. She noticed him do a double-take.

"I live in bandit country," she said with a laugh.

"Doesn't it worry you?" he said.

"Not as much as it probably worries you," she answered.

Was she spoiling for a fight? She had only just met him.

"Why should it worry me?"

"Because you're British, and the British hate us."

He decided it was time to be diplomatic.

"I expect it's a very spiritual experience for you, to live there."

She twisted her face into something between a smile and a grimace.

"Cheap housing. That's the real reason."

He couldn't stop himself.

"Because it was land that belonged to someone else?"

Her knuckles whitened on the steering wheel, although her voice remained calm.

"Only in the sense that it belonged for a while to squatters, or thieves. My town is as legal as Tel Aviv, or London for that matter."

She paused for a few seconds.

"How long has your family been in Britain?"

"My family? Er...hundred years or so. Less, some of them."

"My town, Neve Ya'acov, was built in 1924 when the Arabs sold the Jews the land. Sold it to them. You know: contracts, money. Just like you buy a house from someone in London. But here we Jews were actually coming *back*. We'd lived there when it was Judea. No Arabs then. No Islam. Not even invented. Then there were Arab pogroms, and then Jordan stole it from us in '47 and drove us out. So, just who do you think has the greater right to live in their house—you or me?"

She looked at him coolly. His mind raced. Her question was ridiculous. How could there possibly be any comparison? The response to her was so obvious. He just couldn't be bothered to think of it now. Why should he?

The jeep pulled into the stables. Russell climbed down, irritated. He could do without such lectures from right-wing zealots. Presumably her riding school would be full of kids from such families.

He stepped carefully over piles of manure and breathed in the acrid smells of hay and animal. Yael paused to caress and croon over the horses leaning their heads over their stall doors, and to talk to young members of staff who were busy saddling and unsaddling on the cobbled yard. Russell jumped as the horses snorted and tossed their manes. Nervously, he gave them a wide berth.

His eyes widened as they approached the field where instructors were taking the young riders through their paces. About half of these children were Arab.

A woman sat on a bench with a small boy, around eight or nine years old at a guess. The woman was young. She wore tight white jeans and pink stilettos; her eyes were dramatically outlined in thick black liner and mascara. Her hair was concealed beneath a pale blue Muslim scarf which reached below her shoulders. She looked bored. The child hung his head and scuffed his shoes in the dirt. She spoke to him sharply. He didn't respond but hung his head even lower. Exasperated, she sighed and started scrolling on her cellphone.

Russell and Yael stood by the fence on the perimeter of the field. Now Russell could see that all around parents were standing or sitting on benches watching their children at their riding lesson. Several parents were dark-skinned.

"Many Arab children come here?" he asked in surprise.

"Sure," she said. "They come from all over; Israeli Arabs from east Jerusalem, Arabs from Judea and Samaria, even from Gaza. They don't have this kind of riding therapy where they are. And there are a lot of very traumatized kids out there, Israeli and Arab. Bombs, terrorism, war—this all has a terrible effect on children wherever they come from. So the Arab kids ride here side by side with Jewish kids. The horses don't discriminate."

She smiled impishly, and suddenly her long, severe face was transformed.

A couple of children on horseback were being led by instructors slowly round the field. Another horse stood quietly while an instructor talked insistently to the child sitting in the saddle. Even at a distance, Russell could see that the child, a girl, was rigid with fear. After a while she started to wail, with a high-pitched cry of terror. A man sprang up by the fence, presumably her father, and danced from foot to foot in agitation as the child continued to wail. The instructor carried the child down off the horse and brought her over to her father. An intense conversation then took place between the three of them.

"Have *all* these children been traumatized by what's going on here?" he asked.

"Not at all. Some of them have other problems in their lives, much more mundane but no less damaging, the usual stuff like abusive parents or family breakdown, even things like dyslexia or eating disorders. It's all helped by learning to ride."

"How so?" He was intrigued.

"All kinds of ways. It makes the child feel kind of powerful, in control. Sometimes that's the first time in their life that the kid has felt that. To master a big animal, to get it to do what you want, that's no small matter. It makes them more sensitive; they get to know real fast that hurting an animal won't get them very far; they might even get a kicking. If they want the horse to do something, they learn they have to be gentle and attentive to how the horse feels. For kids who think violence is how things get done, that's a revelation. And we teach them to groom the horses, to look after them. To care for another living being. Again, sometimes that's a first for them."

She really cares, he thought. Despite himself, he was impressed.

The wailing child was now back on her horse. She was still wailing, but now she was being led slowly round the field. They stood silent, watching. Gradually, she quietened. Her father, hunched tensely on a bench, buried his face in his hands.

"Terror, being terrified, is crippling, a real disease," said Yael thoughtfully.

He stared at the horses processing slowly in front of them. He tried to imagine himself on the back of one of them.

He wanted suddenly to confide in her.

"You don't have to live in a war-zone to feel it," he said.

She looked at him sharply.

"But you help spread it," she snapped.

"What? Me? How?"

He felt physically winded.

"You think we don't know here what people like you say about us, how you think? Here we're trying to defend ourselves against madmen trying all the time to kill us, living just down the road from us, teaching their children to hate us, people like these..."—she gestured around the stables—"...knowing that in Britain, in Europe, people like you are blaming us for trying to stay alive. It's as if you really do want us dead."

"Oh come *on*..."

"What, you don't think they don't play up to your own prejudices? You think they don't notice that the more they kill us the more you hate us? You really don't think that, when they hear the BBC parrot their lies, when they hear you provide a megaphone for their hatred and hysteria, they don't feel validated when they slit our throats?"

"Actually, mainly there's just indifference," he said uncomfortably. "Most people in Britain never even think about it. Or else they're just sick and tired of hearing about it."

"Really. You think we're also not tired of this war to the death, the hatred and the fictions that get us murdered?"

"Why is this all so black and white? Are you really so whiter-than-white? Maybe some of the violence is because of things Israel has done. Maybe the Palestinians feel you're as aggressive towards them as you feel they're aggressive towards you."

"My father died," she said quietly, "because people like you filled the minds of his killers with the lie that we are responsible for their misery. They've made themselves victims of their own aggression; and so have you."

He was trembling all over. Of course she was wrong. So very, very wrong.

That night, he dreamed about Alice. She was smiling at him and saying something he couldn't hear. He woke up feeling an acute sense of dread, and wondered why.

***

Eliachim's story (5)

In this most terrible year 4950, in the month of Nisan as we prepared for the great memorial to our deliverance from Egypt, there came an evil beyond compare in the cursed city of York.

When news of the massacres of our holy martyrs reached the barons who were in great indebtedness to my master Josce, they resolved with great wickedness to obliterate their debts and the lenders along with them, and all their families and community alongside. Richard Malebisse and his squires all did conspire most foully to annihilate those whose only crime was to have lent them sums of money that they did require and to worship the one true God.

One night when there was fire in the city by an unknown hand and all was confusion, some of this most cursed company broke into the house of Josce's associate Benedict of York, who had died of his wounds after the massacre following the coronation of the King. They most cruelly slaughtered his widow and all his household, seized all his property and set fire to the building.

When news of this abominable deed reached my master Josce, he was filled with foreboding. He gathered his household and sent urgent word to others of our community to make all haste with him to the castle.

The constable of the castle, William de Badlesmere, had often sheltered Jews from the mob on the word of the sheriff of the city, who was entrusted by the King to ensure that no harm should befall those who furnished so much of the finances of the realm.

Outside we heard the foul shrieks and oaths and the blood-thirsty stamping of the mob and smelt the burning of timber, and our hearts failed us. We put our holy books and our possessions into bundles and made haste to the castle along with Josce and his wife and his sons.

Now the constable protected the hundreds of souls who had put themselves at his mercy, placing them in the tower of the castle on the top of the mound so that they might remain safe in a very strong place.

But the Lord's face remained turned away from us. A few nights later a great calamity arose when the uncircumcised, enraged by the flight of Josce and his followers, cruelly slew all those left in Josce's house and set it on fire with all still left within it.

A great and terrible shout went up from the mob when this grand house, which was like a small palace, was consumed by this conflagration. As the flames leapt into the sky, so the greed and bloodlust of the mob took added fire from the sparks. Waving their clubs and their swords and their spears and roaring for vengeance for the crucified one, they ran to the house of every Jew and pulled the inhabitants from their beds and with their knives to their throats told them to submit to the water of idolatry or else be put to death.

Some were baptized into that blasphemous faith but others bravely stayed true to the one God and many deeds of heroism by our blessed martyrs were recorded. They stayed steadfast and refused to embrace the one who was crucified, for which they were hewn into pieces and even buried alive.

The next day the constable left the castle on business, we knew not where. Then the people started saying to one another that he had gone to betray us, that he would deliver us to the mob so they could steal all our possessions.

The sheriff gave orders to recapture the castle from the people of the covenant who were sheltering there. But when word went out that the castle was barricaded, the mob seized their clubs and their spears and their knives and surrounded the castle in a frenzy for blood, throwing rocks and fiery bolts at the walls of the tower and bringing a monstrous beam of timber shod at the end with iron to batter down the gates.

A shout went up for the priests to join the holy work against the children of Satan, and they flocked like the crows of the air with their vestments flapping and with their blasphemous books held on high as they pronounced their evil decrees against the followers of the one true God, roaring with a sound that would freeze the dead: "Destroy the enemies of Christ!" and stirring the blood of the mob into an ever greater frenzy of murderous rage.

When the children of the covenant saw the savage multitude beyond the castle walls, they rent their garments and wept and cried out to heaven that they had been forsaken. Others fell on their faces and prayed, and said to one another: "The will of God is being done. Let us be strong and accept our fate bravely and embrace it with joy as the proof of our faith."

Upon these words the sons of Josce and other young men spoke hotly to our elders thus: "What, are we men of upright bearing or are we as low as the worms? Should we meekly surrender to those who deny the oneness of God? Are we to pass into the next world on our knees or with our heads held high?"

Now there rose men of high standing in our community of souls. With great bitterness they spoke against our hot-blooded youth, charging that they had caused the unbelievers to rise up against us through their insults and recklessness. The salvation of our people could never lie in war-like acts upon our tormentors. Such deeds would only serve to enrage them still further. We should rather be silent and show neither our hand nor our faces to our besiegers but remain out of sight. This would perplex our assailants and after a period their rage would die down like a fire that had consumed all its wood.

To which some of our number murmured assent, while others cried out that it was through just such accommodation by our great ones that the people of the Lord had revealed their weakness to the bloodthirsty; and still others were amazed and knew not what to think, so great was their terror and confusion.

But I was already suffering the torment of the damned. For was it not I who had brought these monstrous acts upon the heads of my people? Had I not brought down the wrath of heaven upon all of us, so great had been my sin?

31

WHEN HE WASN'T working at Haia's house, he walked around Jerusalem. He wandered in and out of museums and markets; he sat in pavement cafes alongside girl soldiers, barely older than Rosa, filing their nails and drinking cappuccinos with their guns slung over the backs of their chairs; he scrutinized the many plaques commemorating British rule, the war of independence and more recent terrorist attacks.

He saw his father everywhere. Frequently he would do a double-take at an elderly man with Jack's gait, the shape of his head, his eyes or his mouth. Every time, he felt compelled to look at their faces to make sure. So many were so very similar; every time, he felt an absurd lurch of disappointment.

He walked into the Old City, through the dark, winding alleyways of the souk with its Arab traders standing in their doorways picking their teeth, sizing him up for a sale of a carpet or tourist trinkets. Up several flights of steps he found himself on a promontory overlooking a hill lined with yet more of the white rocks that were such a distinctive feature of the landscape. He looked more closely, and gave an involuntary gasp. They weren't rocks. They were gravestones. From a distance, the looked as if they were part of the very ground itself.

He stood for a long time at the excavations of the ancient Jewish Temple, lost in thought. He was taken aback by these finds: the royal seals and coins from the time of King David, the ritual baths, the foundations of an entire street of shops which had adjoined the Temple wall. He felt directly, through the soles of his shoes, the connection going back more than two thousand years. Incredible, he muttered to himself. Here was actual evidence of...well, what, precisely? It was as if he couldn't quite clear a blockage in his mind; nor could he say what form it took.

Despite himself, he was charmed. The city was in turn magnificent and chaotic. It was so unlike any other city he had ever known. There were no skyscrapers, no glittering avenues of shops. This was no temple of consumerism; it was instead like walking backwards into history. Every street, every building in that beautiful pale stone seemed to have a story.

Something else seemed strange. What was it? Ah yes, that was it. No advertising in the streets, he suddenly realized: no billboards or advertisement hoardings, and so no pictures of fast cars or women in underwear or sexually suggestive slogans. How refreshing, he thought.

One warm night, he was walking along a winding lane on the edge of a park when he heard music, loud music, a rock band playing somewhere. He followed the sound as it got louder and louder. In the near distance, the ancient walls of the Old City were strung with white fairy lights. Through a wire fence, he looked down into a huge open space between the park and Old City walls. Illuminated on a stage by colored strobe lighting, a singer backed by a band was belting out rock songs in Hebrew. In front of him, thousands of ecstatic young people packed into banks of seats were belting them out with him, waving their arms in the air and singing every word.

He passed a knot of young people on the path who were also singing and dancing, enjoying the free concert down below. Half the city must be hearing this, he thought in wonderment. The pounding beat, the joyous, abandoned singing and dancing, the music of the carefree Western youth being sung in this ancient language of piety beneath the twinkling, magical walls of this ancient civilization—it was all quite enchanting. He had a physical sensation of something falling away from his shoulders, as if he was emerging from a chrysalis. He found he was smiling. The young people on the path gyrated; he danced alongside them.

He was nearing the end of Eliachim's story. One morning, he looked up from his books and saw through the window a young soldier standing in the garden, praying. He was about 19 years old. This must be Amitai, he thought: Yael's son, the one who cleared mines and booby-trapped tunnels: home on leave.

He was, Russell noticed with envy, a boy of exceptional beauty, tall and powerfully built and with a majestic profile. Perched on top of unruly dark curls, which not even an army haircut had quite tamed, was a small, flat, blue and white knitted *kippah*. Over his army fatigues, his broad shoulders were draped with a *tallit*, or prayer shawl. As Russell watched, he pulled the *tallit* over his head so that his face was obscured as he gently swayed back and forth in his prayer.

He was touched by this strong, muscular soldier with his gun now propped up against a tree, this boy not yet out of his teens who would once again soon be pitting his own life against who-knew-what horror, showing such trust and faith in something beyond all that, and which he was certain would never abandon him. As Russell stared at him, he realized he was jealous. He thought about his father as a soldier, the father who had apparently acted with the heroism of which he was certain this boy was capable—the father he never knew. He tried to imagine his father in that terrible battle in Normandy, and failed.

And by effacing himself in his *tallit*, by obscuring his head so that all that could be seen was the white of the prayer shawl over his khaki trousers tucked into thick black boots, this boy himself turned into something eternal, an image stretching back thousands of years. It was as if Russell was staring at a Jew praying in Temple times, or even earlier. The feeling was visceral, it was overwhelming, and he didn't like it at all.

Eliachim's story (6)

Now I choke upon scalding tears to write these words. My fingers tremble so severely with the foul memory of what they must now transcribe that the letters themselves are in revolt against their very formation.

It was on the eve of the great Sabbath before the Passover that the hand of the Lord unleashed an evil to cause the angels themselves to hide their faces in grief and confusion.

The children of the covenant huddled in the castle looked down upon the ferocious multitude gathered beyond the castle walls. The besieged had no strength for want of food.

Then a great groan rose up from our people as we heard a sound like the rumbling and cracking of the earth itself that grew ever louder and more terrible, accompanied by the redoubled shrieking and stamping of the mob. And we observed with shaking limbs that there drew ever closer to our citadel the mighty engines of war to lay siege to our fortress.

In huge carts they were dragged to the castle walls. There was the great ballista, the giant crossbow that would hurl huge stones or arrows or flaming torches; there were infernal catapults that would crush buildings to heaps of rubble. And there were assault towers that would allow the bloodthirsty mob to climb the walls once they had been thus breached and surely slaughter every last holy soul who was huddled inside.

Now a great moaning and sighing arose, for there was not a single man or woman in that sacred assembly of martyrs who did not understand that at last they were staring straight into the pit. They fell to the ground and sobbed and rent their garments. The little children screamed for terror at the sight and sound of their parents so distraught. And then I saw my beloved Duzelina, her face as white as any shroud, gather into her arms her small brothers and sisters and hide their faces for comfort in her shawl.

Then all that assembly of martyrs formed a great and solemn council; whereupon the holy sage Rabbi Yomtov of blessed memory stood and addressed them with fateful and terrible words. "Men of Israel," he said. "The God of our ancestors in whom we place our most perfect and unquestioning faith now commands us to yield up our lives in the defense of His holy law and His commandments. We are about to enter the valley of the shadow of death and there is no way we can prevent our departure from this world. The blasphemers and idolators are determined to slaughter us. All that remains for us to decide is how we shall face this in the manner that best proclaims the glory and oneness of God.

"If our enemies take us alive they will taunt us and humiliate us and inflict upon us unspeakable cruelties and torments before they end their diabolical sport with our slaughter. Should we then sit here and wait for those who would destroy not only our lives but the honor also of our faith? We are a people of sacred purpose. We must turn this evil into the glory of God by taking our own lives in His great name."

He then sat and put his face in his hands and wept. Then the elders of our people debated earnestly his words one with the other, even as the hammering and grinding of the construction of the great siege engines beat its infernal din beneath the castle walls. For others brought forth the contrary words of others amongst our sages. These laid down that in the fateful choice between death and transgression none shall trespass upon the sanctity of life save in the event of three demands; which are idolatry, abomination of the flesh and the taking of human life.

If we are forced with a blade at our throats to steal another's cattle or to break a solemn oath, then our sages instruct us to commit such transgression for the greater purpose of preserving the life that the has been bestowed upon us. But if we are so threatened in order to abandon the word of the one true God, or to lie with another man's wife or to commit foul murder, then we are commanded to embrace death.

So spoke the supporters of Rabbi Yomtov. But yet others scarcely less learned spoke otherwise and called forth the words of the sage Rabbi Ishmael, who had ruled that the children of Israel should choose idolatrous worship over death. For if man did not live, what purpose would be served by the holy commandments other than as an empty mockery of the word of the Lord?

In this way did those who sought to avert the horrible decree argue with all the skill of their craft. But straight came the reply from Rabbi Elijah who was in that company second only to Rabbi Yomtov in learning and piety, and who said our lives are not to us like our cattle or our houses or our gold to do with as we would wish but are given to us so we can sanctify the name of God.

Then Rabbi Yomtov rose once more from the meditation of his heart and spoke these words to the holy congregation of martyrs. "Our enemies are fast upon us. Before the sun sets once more and the stars rise again in the firmament the castle will be taken. Let us therefore delay no longer but most speedily do the will of our Creator. We must every one of us harden our hearts for this holy task so that none shall spare neither himself nor his sons nor his wife nor the babes at her breast. Each shall slaughter the other according to our rituals and the last remaining shall slaughter himself by piercing his throat or his belly so that the idolaters sully none of our house by their abominations.

"We shall leave this place of darkness for the shining light of paradise. May the merciful and compassionate one hear our prayers and avenge the blood of His servants, and save us from the waters of idolatry and abomination."

Then Rabbi Yomtov of blessed memory asked all who were in disagreement to seclude themselves from that place. Most stayed, and they gathered all their possessions with great weeping and sorrow and burnt all that which the fire would consume.

But I fell to the ground in great perturbation of spirit and tore my clothes and prayed to the Lord yet again for forgiveness. For I knew this was all my doing, that this was punishment for my sin. Yet I had but fourteen summers, and I was not yet prepared for the life everlasting and to sit on a throne in the company of angels. I had a great love of this world that God had created, the buds and the blossom that even then were bursting from the trees, the sound of the lute and all those pleasures which are as music to the senses, of which in truth I had scarcely partaken.

But then came near to me my beloved Duzelina, whose once rosy lips were now as white as parchment; and she fell to her knees before me, and between piteous sobs beseeched me to slaughter her before turning the same knife upon myself, so that even though we were never to be one flesh in this world our blood would be commingled and we would be united in the world to come.

I could not commit such an unthinkable act. I told her of my grief and guilt, and further of my fervent wish to cling to life and to the last vestiges of hope; and I implored her to put her faith in

God's great compassion and mercy that through the miracles at His command He would avert this horror.

At these words she sprang to her feet, and with flashing eyes declared in a firm and ringing voice that it was wrong to question the will of God. Those who did His will would leave this world of darkness for shining bliss, and would exchange all that which crumbles into dust for the paradise which lasts for all eternity.

With this she fell once again to the ground and sobbed and lamented. My brothers made a canopy of their prayer shawls above us both, and I pronounced the vow that I took her according to the laws of Moses and all of the house of Israel; and thus married, I embraced her most tenderly. She caressed my face and we murmured endearments between our sobs, before she tore herself from me and vanished back into the inferno where her family prepared to sacrifice themselves to safeguard the holy name of God.

And now there followed scenes of horror. With the fires still blazing from the burning of their possessions, and the din of the siege engines growing ever louder along with the shouts of the bloodthirsty mob, all of the men cried out that they could delay no longer for the enemy was fast upon them. Let us make haste, they said with one firm voice, to deny the foe his blasphemous victory. Let those who have knives examine them so they be not nicked or blemished, in accordance with our rituals of purification, and then pronounce the blessing for slaughter before cutting the throats of this holy congregation and then plunging the knives into their own bodies.

And then the men wrapped themselves in their prayer shawls, and most tenderly embraced their wives and took their children in their arms and covered their bodies with kisses and shed tears over their dear ones, who in turn clung on to them and wept upon their necks.

Some lay down upon the ground and threw their arms around their wives and their little ones and stretched out their necks for others to perform the melancholy office of execution. Others themselves plucked up their courage and cut the throats of their sons, their daughters, and their wives before running their knives through themselves and falling upon their slain families. Dear God, they slaughtered each other; husbands upon wives, grooms upon brides, brothers upon sisters, mothers upon the infants at their breast.

Alas, alas, my own flesh and blood were slaughtered before my eyes. My father slaughtered my mother and then ran his knife across his own throat. My brothers slaughtered their wives and then Jechiel stretched out his neck to Aharon who straight after plunged his knife into his own body. But now hear, all you generations that stand confounded by these terrible deeds, of the fate of my sister Zipporah and her four sweet young sons. Zipporah was upright and pious, and said to her women friends not to spare her children lest the Christians should take them alive and bring them up in the false religion of idolatry. But when she saw the knife that was to slaughter them she screamed and fell on her face and cried out, "God of our fathers, why have You thus forsaken us?"

Then she took the knife herself and checked it for blemishes and pronounced the benediction for slaughter, and said to her companions to hide the smallest children lest they saw their brothers' deaths and ran away. One by one she cut their throats; but the youngest, Ezekiel, saw his brothers were slain and screamed, "Mother, mother, do not slaughter me" and hid behind a door. His mother, distraught with weeping, cried out "You too I cannot spare," and dragged him from behind the door and slaughtered him. Then she lay down with her dead children tucked beneath her sleeves and stretched out her own throat to the knife. When her husband Eleazar saw all his beautiful children slaughtered in a row like sheep he screamed aloud in agony, and ran his knife through his own stomach so his entrails spilled onto the ground.

Why did the sun rise the next morning upon such slaughter? Why did the heavens not shroud themselves in darkness and the stars lose their brightness?

I fell to the ground and lay there all night long. I could not weep; my body was frozen in horror and guilt. For was it not I who had caused this horror beyond imagination? If anyone should have lost his life it was surely I; and yet I was alive, cursed by my love of life to spend the rest of it in a living hell.

At daybreak, those few who remained huddled together shouted from the battlements the report of the massacre, and threw the dead over the walls. May the Creator forgive them, they cried out to the uncircumcised that God had saved us from the slaughter to embrace the Christian faith, as the horror had convinced them of the truth of that religion. The treacherous leaders of the mob, may they be cursed for all time, promised clemency and so our company opened up the gates of the castle at last.

But as soon as the gates were open the mob burst in and butchered the remnant with great ferocity and cruelty. They smote them with clubs, pierced them with knives and spears and arrows, cut off thumbs and ears and sliced open bellies. I was struck repeatedly with stones and fists and knives and burned by flaming torches; but by some miracle was spared worse injury. I fell to the ground among the corpses thrown from the battlements, which were piled up so high they formed a mountain, and feigned that I was dead as the massacre raged around me.

I lay there all day in that horror without moving. At nightfall a laundress came and bore me to her home where she concealed me and bound up my wounds. From there I was smuggled in a cart to a Jewish home in Lincoln, and from there transported among sacks of potatoes to my kinsmen in London.

All my dear ones lost! I still feel upon my cheek the brush of that soft skin and hair that smelt of honey that now I will never feel again. My beloved is in paradise among the heavenly hosts, and my father and mother and brothers and sister and all the many others who were so foully massacred by the Christians, may their bones be ground up with giant millstones. My heart is broken into pieces. How can the god of mercy have done this to his children? Only because of the great wickedness with which I desecrated his name.

These last several nights have been quiet, thanks be to God, and they say the King himself is much displeased on our account and has given instruction not to touch the hairs on our heads. But which man can place his trust in such promises when the priests whip the population against us to a frenzy of hatred and murderous intent?

Now I am in hiding and in fear for my very life. I am of sound constitution so that my crushed and beaten body has once again become whole. Yet I am sorely afflicted by great agony of mind from which I fear in truth I have half lost my wits. Where can I go that will afford me refuge? Am I to be punished by having to wander this earth from sea to sea? For wherever we settle, there the people become inflamed against us by their preachers pronouncing their blasphemous falsehoods and hatred. I am sheltered in the house of my kinsmen, but in their eyes I see only fear and misgivings. For there is no house however mighty its owner, however thick the stone of its walls, which can protect us from these barbarous Christians and their impiety and jealousy, may they and their descendants be cursed for all time.

In the morrow I shall entrust my being to the shelter of the most Holy One. For I am to be dressed as a woman, being slim and yet beardless and, they say, delicate of feature; and thus disguised am to be smuggled abroad, back to those very Frankish lands from which my ancestors were forced to find refuge not six decades hence but where they say the terror against the children of Israel has been quieted in recent times.

But are we destined to be forever in perpetual motion, batted back and forth like shuttlecocks across lands and oceans in a ceaseless voyage in search of refuge across the face of the earth? For how long will it be before the Frankish lands too will succumb once again to the murderous hatred that never ceases to consume us? The whole of Europe is in flames before the advance of the Christian pilgrims who go to take the holy city of David from the Saracens, and who under the banner of their idol behave with unfathomable savagery towards all those who refuse to wear the convert's shift and proclaim the blasphemy of the Christian heresy.

I look down the endless procession of years and I see only yet more savagery and more infamy. This chronicle which must pass from generation to generation will stand as witness to the infamy of the Christians and their surpassing cruelty towards the children of the covenant.

As the time of my departure draws near, I am filled with dread and foreboding. My heart knocks, the palms of my hands grow damp and the food burns in my throat. Yet in my anguish I will nevertheless pronounce the blessing before departure and place my faith in the compassion of my creator, that he will preserve me and keep me safe so that I can henceforth carry out His commandments which I have so desecrated.

May the name of the Holy One, blessed be He, be glorified and exalted, extolled and honored, adored and lauded above and beyond all the blessings, hymns, praises and consolations that are uttered in this world. May He who makes peace in His high places grant peace for us and for all the house of Israel. Amen and amen.

32

RUSSELL SLOWLY CLOSED his laptop. It was done. He felt numb, drained. His mind was in a tumult. He had managed it. Despite everything that had happened, now he had a completed manuscript. He should have felt elated, but he couldn't stop thinking about Eliachim.

This was no longer a story of unrequited love. Until then, he had thought of the Crusades as events that happened in Europe and the Middle East. Terrible things had been perpetrated by the knights with their red crosses; but all that had happened a long way away and had nothing to do with him. It had been a fight between Popes and Saracens, right?

But now, beneath his hovering fingers had unfolded a barbarism that had been unleashed in England—and the victims of these unspeakable acts had been the Jews. Gentle, bovine England had turned into a riot of frenzied psychotics. Yes, he knew the Jews had been thrown out of England in, what, the thirteenth century, wasn't it. And yes, he knew there had been wars of religion, when people had been burned at the stake. But those had been between Catholics and the Protestants. Yet here Eliachim was describing Jews being burned alive, Jews being disemboweled and Jewish babies impaled on the end of Crusader swords.

He thought of those warm, sun-dappled summer Sunday afternoons watching the cricket on some green in Datchet or Burnham Beeches, with the Ford Popular parked on the verge and Alan Freeman on the transistor radio playing the top twenty, and with Jack sighing in deep contentment, "Y'know, there isn't more beautiful countryside anywhere in the world" from all his vast experience of Adriatic seaside resorts. Or stating periodically, shaking his head slowly from side to side with the deep portentousness of the thought he was about to utter, "No doubt about it, England has been very good to us Jews."

Which England? The England of all those disembowelers and baby-impalers, who had extorted and butchered his own people? But then Jack would hardly have known about that either. And what had he even known about the Britain in which he had lived, really known? He had been in it, but never of it. He had never been part of any institution, never played the game of social or professional advancement, never read Dickens or George Eliot or Orwell, never gone to a Promenade concert or joined a pub darts team or even adopted that defining characteristic of English society, owning his own house. The most that could be said of that relationship was that England had left him alone.

So why was it only now, with the revelation that Jews had been slaughtered right here in England simply because they were Jews, that Russell was so horrified? Why had he previously dismissed the wars of religion in Britain as of no interest to him? Was it because he had thought of them as merely between one set of Christians and another—not part of his own story? And so what did that say about what he himself was? Did it mean that, all those years when he had asserted fiercely that no, Jews were bloody well not merely "tolerated" in Britain because they were as British as anyone else, he had after all not felt himself to be, deep down, the thing he had thought he was? And if he wasn't thoroughly British through and through, then what was he?

To have done what they did, to have had that degree of faith, that unbreakable commitment to what they were that it superseded life itself; he kept returning to this in his mind.

He tried to imagine himself on top of that tower, to imagine what it was like to slit the throats of those you loved most, what it would feel like to slice through the soft flesh of your own neck.

Eliachim had not described terror. He had described horror and guilt. Guilt because he thought he was somehow the cause of the catastrophe; guilt that he couldn't go through with it because the will to live in him was just too strong. That wasn't fear. They hadn't been terrified, he suddenly realized, because, unlike himself, they accepted that death was part of life. They didn't try to fight it. The fear, Russell now understood, came from the refusal to believe, the attempt to deny the inevitable. The panic came from denial. Their strength was rooted in acceptance.

And now he saw something else. This apparent act of collective fanaticism was in fact an act of love. To love, you had to be attached, he thought; and to be attached you had to have someone or something to be attached to. He wasn't attached to anything. He had snapped all his moorings.

Yes, that act of collective suicide was a horror. But again, he felt a stab of envy mixed in with the revulsion. They had belonged to something that joined them all together, something they treasured beyond life itself. They had been bound by a shared sense of love.

To whom was he bound by such love, he wondered morosely. His wife, his father, his sister: all estranged. And he could now see that his share in Britain had been conditional all along.

It wasn't conditional on his origins being in British culture. It was conditional on his not being a Jew. Because now he understood that to be a Jew was to be part of the Jewish people. And that particular sense of peoplehood was not permitted in Britain. It immediately made you suspect.

He hadn't seen it at first because he had never wanted a share in that peoplehood. And he still didn't want it. But he was saddled with it regardless, because he had stuck up for others who happened to be like him. Out of a sense of simple justice, and a respect for the truth. But if you were a Jew, you weren't allowed to do that, because it couldn't be about justice or truth. It meant "you people" were "all sticking together."

No other people provoked such a reaction, he thought in wonderment. And it was impossible not to make the connection, not to see the thread linking Eliachim and Michael Waxman and Haia. And his father. For the first time, he felt that thread running through himself. And he knew it could never be snapped, however hard he might try.

Haia fussed around him. "Poor thing, you're exhausted," she exclaimed. "What you need is some R&R. How about giving yourself a day off and I fill in some more of those gaps in your education you're so worried about. I'll drive you down to Masada. You'll really enjoy it, I promise."

They drove south into the desert. He had anticipated sand dunes. Instead, rocky cliffs stretched into the distance. Occasionally he glimpsed groups of Bedouin with their camels by the side of the road, waiting for tourists to stop and pose.

His thoughts returned inexorably to the story he had now completed. He had said nothing about it yet to Haia. He needed first to process it all in his mind.

He had finished the translation. The book would cause a sensation. He anticipated no problem from Haia about getting it authenticated and published. It was what he had dreamed of for so long now, making his name with a unique contribution to scholarship, to history. He had managed to overcome all the problems and setbacks, the shattering blow about Kuczynski which had almost capsized the entire project, successfully navigating Zofia and Haia. So why didn't he feel more exhilarated?

They stopped to stretch their legs and he walked well away from the road, scrambling stiffly over stones and boulders.

The earth beneath his feet was almost red. The cliffs towered around him, gaunt and majestic.

Despite the heat, he shivered. The silence was profound. The world, it seemed, had altogether retreated. He thought about London, Damia, Beverley. It seemed so far away. In this silent, empty landscape he felt a different world gently enclose him. It was as if a host of shadowy figures were hovering all around him. His breathing slowed and he felt the tension draining out of himself. He felt himself cradled by beauty, and by a deep sense of connection. Reluctantly, he picked his way back to the car.

They walked up Masada to the fortress at the top. The path was steep and winding, and crowded with tourists. "That's cheating," said Haia, cheerfully pointing at the cable car that slowly swung up and down the mountain.

The sun beat down out of a deep turquoise sky. The path was merely roped off from the precipice and the barrier felt insecure when Russell grasped it. There wasn't much room in places for people to pass as they came down the mountain. He wiped away the sweat that was pouring off his forehead and neck.

As they walked up, Haia decided to fill him in on the history. At the beginning of the great revolt against Roman rule, a group of Jews had been besieged in the Masada fortress. This had been built by Herod on no fewer than three rock terraces; an amazing feat of engineering. She pointed these out as they climbed. Russell merely grunted and didn't look up. He didn't feel like admiring the feat of engineering. He was concentrating on putting one foot in front of the other. He had looked down over the rope barrier and had felt his head sickeningly swim.

Reaching the top at last, he didn't feel any better. His head was thumping. He was sweating and shivering at the same time.

They walked around the summit fortress and admired the remains of the palace, the bathhouse, the mosaics.

"Of course they were zealots," said Haia reflectively, "but even so it was quite something for a bunch of Jews to hold out here against the Romans for as long they did. Three years, it was; and then the Romans managed to scale this tremendous height and it was all over. But to kill themselves like that *en masse*, every single one of them, so as not to be taken alive; unimagineable, isn't it."

This was the example, thought Russell. This was what Eliachim and the Jews of York had all had in the front of their minds when they were huddled on top of Clifford's Tower. And so the thread of belonging stretched even further back than he had thought. History, this history at any rate, merely repeated itself over and over again. There was no end to it, no break from the terrible past, no possibility that the pattern would fade away. How could this be endured?

Now he understood how essential it was to remember. It wasn't people who lived on; it was what they stood for that was eternal. It was the collective memory that had to be preserved and defended against the barbarians scaling the cliff-face. Now he understood the full extent of Eliachim's anguish. It wasn't just the horror he had witnessed; it wasn't even his belief he had somehow been the cause. It was that he had betrayed his tribe.

"Dad," he whispered. "Dad, I'm so sorry."

He stood near the edge of the fortress under the fierce sun and looked out across the great desert plain that stretched out beneath him. In the far distance, on the other side of a broad river, lay the kingdom of Jordan. The river, the sky and the vast rocky expanse below all seemed to be shimmering in a blue haze. It was so beautiful, he thought. The throbbing in his head was worse. The haze danced in front of his eyes like twinkling blue pinpricks of light. He felt again that terrible compulsion to draw ever nearer to the edge. He swayed a little. Then the ground upended beneath his feet and he was spinning.

33

HE WAS AWARE of light, a white light. He opened his eyes a little, but the whiteness was blinding so he closed them. When he opened them again he tried hard to focus. The white light resolved itself into a fluorescent tube in the ceiling. A machine was bleeping next to his ear. Cautiously, he moved his head. The bleeping was coming from a heart monitor. A cannula in the back of his hand attached him through a tube to a drip hanging on a metal stand.

So it had finally happened, he thought. This time he really was dying. Strangely, he felt very calm.

He heard nearby the by-now familiar guttural tones of Arabic. In the next bed lay a young Arab. Around him crowded men in Arab headdress and women in full-length *chador*. One of the women saw him staring. He attempted a smile. She turned her head away.

A middle-aged Arab man in a white coat and with a neat grey beard came and stood at the end of his bed.

"So you've come back to us," he said, and smiled. He lifted a clipboard from the end of the bed and thumbed through the notes attached to it.

"Are you...are you a doctor?" said Russell.

The man smiled again. "Allow me to introduce myself. I am Dr. el Arish. I am a consultant cardiologist."

Russell gripped the white cotton blanket covering him. "Have I had a heart attack, then?" he said weakly.

"No, your heart is absolutely fine," said the doctor. "Of course, we've been monitoring it closely. Good news is, everything else seems okay too. You're in reasonable shape. Need to lose some weight, but still."

"Where am I?" said Russell, confused.

"You are in Soroka."

"Sirocco?" Why was he in an Arab hospital? "Am I in the West Bank?"

Now the doctor laughed. "You are in Israel, of course." He separated the second syllable: Isra-el. "You were at Masada, remember? You collapsed there. Soroka is the nearest hospital."

An Israeli hospital? With Arab patients, Arab doctors? Russell was bewildered.

"You've been unconscious for several hours. A mystery, really: we can't find anything wrong with you. We'll do more tests of course, now that you're awake."

An orderly brought a wheelchair to take him down to X-ray. He was black, with the delicate oval face of an Ethiopian. A small kitted *kippah* was clipped onto his hair.

Outside the ward door sat a soldier with a machine gun. The orderly noticed Russell staring at him as they passed.

"That guy in the bed next to you," he said, bending down to talk quietly into Russell's ear as he punched the button for the lift, "He's Hamas. Was on his way to blow up a kindergarten but the bomb went off early and he blew himself up instead. Lost a leg, apparently."

Russell was aghast. A terrorist killer in the next bed! Christ alfuckingmighty. The guard on the door was hardly a reassurance. What the hell was wrong with this country, that it didn't keep such people separate but instead treated everyone the same?

Back in the ward, Russell nervously stole another look. The boy, he now saw, was young: around seventeen at most. He was still asleep, his mouth open underneath a faint suggestion of a moustache. Wires and tubes protruded from under his blankets, attached to a battery of bleeping monitors, drips and bottles. Nurses in white smocks and trousers came and went, checking the monitors and reading the printouts that regularly chattered into life.

There were now only two people by the boy's bed, both young men, swarthy and unshaven. They stood up to go. As they moved towards the door of the ward, the guard outside swiftly rose and gripped his gun with both hands. They passed through the doorway and disappeared towards the lifts.

In due course, another doctor appeared at the foot of his bed. He stood flipping through Russell's notes without saying anything. Then he moved to the head of the bed and produced a medical flashlight. He flashed it in Russell's eyes and then took his pulse, all still without saying a word. Russell read the tag hanging on a lanyard round his neck: Dr. Mikhail Ostrovsky, Neurology.

"Turn your head please. Now other way."

A thick Russian accent; the voice abrupt, impatient. He wrote busily on the clipboard. Then he started to move away.

"Er, excuse me..."

The doctor paused and came back. He frowned down at Russell.

"Could you tell me...have you found anything?"

Dr. Ostrovsky stared at him. "No meningitis or encephalitis. No sign of brain tumor, no evidence of epilepsy." He shrugged. "A mystery," he said sarcastically. "Now I have to see patients who really are sick." He turned and strode out of the ward.

Russell burned with indignation. The implication he was some kind of malingerer stung. He had apparently been unconscious for hours, for God's sake. There was clearly something very wrong with him.

He dozed off uneasily. He felt something brush against his bed and opened his eyes. A young woman was peering down at him. Dr. Noa Ben-Dror, he read on her lanyard.

"What kind of doctor are *you*?" asked Russell wearily.

"General physician," she replied, smiling. She took his pulse. "How're you feeling now?"

Her Israeli-accented voice was soft. She was slim, with full lips and warm brown eyes.

"Can anyone here tell me what's wrong with me?" said Russell testily.

"We've found nothing," she said.

"How is that possible? I was out cold for hours, apparently."

She put her head on one side and looked at him quizzically. "These things happen sometimes. Particularly if you are under a lot of stress. Sometimes the body just needs to take time out and regroup. We'll keep you in overnight for the final results of all the tests, but if they're normal you'll be able to go." She patted his arm sympathetically.

The Hamas boy was being moved in his bed out of the ward. They both watched as the guard stood up again, gripping his gun.

"Is it normal here for terrorists to be treated alongside Israeli patients?"

Dr. Ben-Dror looked at him coolly. "This is a hospital. We leave politics at the door. If a patient needs treatment, we treat him, we save his life, whatever he has done. Same treatment, same triage system, everyone treated equally according to their level of need. Sometimes we have Arab terrorists lying here alongside their victims. And by the way, some of these terrorists are Israeli Arabs, Israeli citizens. This boy though, he is not. He comes from Gaza."

"And his family who were here, also from Gaza? They're allowed into Israel too?"

She raised an ironic eyebrow. "Sure. Unless they're not allowed; if the crossing is closed because of the terror. Crazy country, this."

"There was a heart doctor who did some tests on me...el Arish or something..."

"Yes, what about him?"

"He's an Arab, right?"

"Of course. We have many Arab doctors here, many very distinguished ones including professors and heads of department. You have a problem with that?"

She had drawn back.

"No no no no no, not at all, quite the contrary..."

"You are surprised? You didn't think Arabs work alongside Jews here? Ah, you come from England, yes?"

She looked at him now as if light had suddenly dawned.

"Mahmoud el Arish is a terrific person, a really nice guy. You should talk to him about it, he won't mind at all."

The next morning, the Hamas boy still hadn't come back. Dr. el Arish materialized soon after breakfast.

"Good news," he said, smiling. "You're all clear. We found nothing at all. Just watch those stress levels."

"What do you mean?"

"You're carrying way too much anxiety. Not for me to pry, but you need to find ways of losing it somehow. Believe me, we have a lot of experience of that here."

"What's happened to him?" asked Russell, motioning to the empty space next to his bed.

"He's been moved to intensive care." The doctor dropped his eyes discreetly. A vein throbbed in his temple. There was a pause.

"Whereabouts do you come from?" Russell hoped his tone was as neutral and conversational as possible.

"Kalandiya. A so-called refugee camp. Near Jerusalem. That's where I was born and grew up."

"So-called?"

He shrugged. "Look, I got out. It's a terrible place, a place for losers. It suits certain people to keep us permanently as losers. I was very fortunate. I managed to get an education. I studied in Cairo and then in Prague. It opened my eyes. I learned a number of things I wouldn't otherwise have known. I learned how to think.

"And now I work here where I'm just a regular guy. An Israeli Arab. Actually, you know, these days I prefer just to call myself an Israeli. I look at these guys who are brought in here, kids like this, I listen to the way their minds have been twisted, and then I look at the rest of the Arab world and I give thanks to God that I am here in Israel and not there. These people who hate the Israelis, they have no idea what real oppression is."

"This boy..." Russell gestured to the empty space, "he's very young to have done what he did."

The doctor slowly shook his head. Now Russell saw that his eyes were unfathomably sad.

"Many of them are much younger. They're taught from the cradle to kill: to kill Jews. I should know: I was taught like this. We're dealing with a complete madness, total evil. I can hardly bear to think about it. That's why what we do here is so good. We don't think about what our patients may have done.

We don't think about anything except treating their wounds or diseases and making them better. We bring a little bit of goodness into the world, all of us here, Jew and Arab, Muslim and Christian, Druze and Kurd, everyone. This is what co-existence looks like. This is what sanity looks like."

He had to ask.

"What do your friends, your family make of you working here? Do they also think like you do?"

He flinched at the doctor's answer. "They call me a traitor to my people. They have disowned me."

"So where do you feel you now belong?"

Dr. el Arish shook his head sadly and sighed.

34

BACK IN HIS hotel in Jerusalem, he texted Damia.

Eliachim now finished story spectacular am totally exhausted

Brilliant well done excited to read it have you got agreement to bring it to London

Gathering nerve to broach it

Say you need to authenticate and there's money in it

Tried that once before with less than total success

Be brave

When he turned up again at Haia's house, she gave him a long hug. "You gave us a bit of a fright, didn't you. So glad you're ok, after all. I would've stayed at the hospital, but they kept me informed by phone."

He gazed at her. She had cared about him.

"We have much to discuss," he said. "I've finished the translation."

She inclined her head in a gesture of congratulation. "Well done! We must celebrate your achievement."

She busied herself with getting out glasses and opening a bottle of wine. "So now you'll publish it?"

"It's not quite so simple. I need to get it authenticated by experts who will confirm that it really is a manuscript from the 12th century. That means people need to come and look at it here..."

"...or you need to take it back with you to England." She finished the sentence for him. "That's okay." She nodded at him benignly.

He stared at her again. She showed no more than sympathetic interest, as if what he was proposing was nothing to do with her.

"It's a really amazing story," he said. "It was written by a young boy who witnessed the mass suicide of medieval English Jews who were being besieged by Christian fanatical killers. Very much like what happened at Masada. I think it's a really important manuscript. It will cause a sensation."

"I'm very happy for you," she said. "I'm happy that the world will see it. It's an important contribution to scholarship."

He was bewildered. "This is a joint project, of course, you and me together. The book belongs to you, after all. I'll send you the translation for you to read. You'll see then how powerful this is."

She left the room and returned with the book. She drew it out of its velvet cover and softly turned it over in her hands.

"This book was in my family for hundreds of years," she said reflectively. "Maybe they knew the story it told; maybe they didn't. We'll never know now how they came to possess it; we'll never know the story behind the story now, will we. They're all dead. Everyone is dead."

"It will probably make you—and me—quite a lot of money. There'll be a lot of media excitement over it." Maybe that was what was troubling her.

She was quiet for a few minutes, looking at the book. Then she gently folded it back into its velvet cover. "My life here is very settled," she said finally. "I know what I am here. To a large extent I have constructed it myself. I have only the fuzziest picture of what came before. Some of that picture is made up of images I have had to invent for myself. I don't want to see them dissolve, to find that I have to look at a whole new set of images by poking around in the past. I'd rather leave it alone."

She looked at him steadily. What was she trying to tell him? She took the book and handed it to him.

"Take it. I'll read about it with enormous interest when you place it in some university library, when you make this great contribution to knowledge. Who knows, maybe I'll even read the story itself one day."

"But it's yours," he stammered.

"No it's not. It belongs to the ghosts of the past. Let them rest in peace. You've done all this work on it; you deserve to get some benefit from it."

He took the book from her. His taxi was waiting outside. She walked with him to the door, and as he turned to say goodbye she gripped both his arms below his shoulders.

"Let him go," she said softly. He hung his head and she pulled it towards her. He buried it in her shoulder.

He got into the taxi and drove off, his mind in a tumult. He had done it. He had pulled it off. He had got what he wanted, and on better terms than he could ever have imagined. He would get the manuscript authenticated, of that he had no doubt. Damia would get its story told on TV. It would make him some money, maybe quite a lot of money. More important, it would make his name. Rosa would be proud of him. Alice would be dumbfounded. He would become a sought-after commodity. It was all now working out just as he had dreamed.

So why did he feel so wretched?

As if someone else was speaking, he heard himself say, "Stop the car. Go back."

After a lot of exclamation and hand waving by the driver, and not before Russell had to pass over a wad of shekels, the car turned back. Haia opened the door and look at him quizzically. Gently but firmly, he pressed the book into her hands.

"Whatever you choose to do with it," he said, "even if you never read what it says, it belongs here with you."

Then he turned abruptly and left, before he had the chance to lose his nerve.

35

HE LOOKED OUT of the aircraft window as the white skyscrapers of Tel Aviv fell away beneath. The city got smaller and smaller and then there was only the sea and the sky.

Home. He was going home. He felt relieved and strangely bereft at the same time.

It was as if he had stumbled into an enchanted kingdom. It had been magical, mysterious, spellbinding. But it hadn't been real. He wasn't part of that, and could never be so. He had not been amongst his own. How could he have been? It was all so deeply foreign to him. The high emotion, the black and white view of the world, the naive unsophistication of the people, the sheer Middle Eastern-ness of it: life as a bazaar, always ducking and weaving, every transaction a bargain, all sharp elbows and patronage.

He thought, once again, of his father. He was certain Jack would have hated it, and for the same reasons. The in-your-face rudeness, the indiscipline on the roads, the sheer incomprehension of the very concept of the queue. It was all the opposite of what his father had most loved about England:

the restraint and the stoicism, the formal manners, above all the bloody miserable grey dampness of the place. That was what had made him feel safe. That was the England to which Russell knew he too belonged. It was part of him; it had formed his character. He could no more renounce it than sever one of his own limbs.

And yet he felt nevertheless that he had indeed left his heart behind. He had been deeply touched in places inside himself he never suspected even existed.

To live permanently in the shadow of war, to endure the relentless attacks and the murder of loved ones—it didn't alter what he thought about the politics of the place, not at all, but the human side had brought him up short. He had been moved above all, he realized, by the everyday and the mundane. The things he found so tedious in England now took on a heroic dimension. Day by day they managed somehow: loving, working, squabbling—my God, how they all argued—bringing up their children, dealing with the terrible shocks life delivered them but finding consolation and purpose in everyday things.

And now he saw something else too. He saw his father in a different light. Indeed, he was now able to think about his father without flinching. It was enough that he had survived as an ordinary man. He didn't have to be heroic. He had endured. He had taken the knocks and had just carried on, without fuss. His life had not needed noisy purpose to have meaning.

He thought of all the dramas of his own life and felt ashamed. His reputation had meant so much to him. Now he saw it as an empty vessel. He had wanted to leave Eliachim's story as his memorial, his legacy. Foolish, he thought. Books had no intrinsic value. Books could be burned. It was people in whom ideas lived on; other people. Rosa. And he knew now that his father lived on in him.

He felt bereft at having left Eliachim's manuscript behind, but not because he regretted the decision. He felt he had lost a friend, a companion who had accompanied him for so long and who had reached out his hand through the centuries to usher Russell into a world to which he had never known he belonged.

Now he was unsettled and he knew he would remain so. He was going home, but what did that mean? Where did he now fit in? Not in Israel, that was for sure; but did he fit in England anymore?

He heard Yael's voice, mocking and bitter about Britain; he thought of Kuczynski and Eliachim and the boys who had chased him down the street and Waxman being attacked by the green bandannas, and he recognized with a panicky dread that he had crossed over some kind of line.

How comforting it would be, he thought as the plane crossed the Channel, just to turn his back on it, to move to the society he had just left, which, for all its many perils and irritations, would take him in without any questions, accept him unconditionally. How easy it would be to sink into it gratefully, to accept an uncomplicated identity, to give himself up to the intoxication, the tremendous romance of a history reclaimed and redeemed.

Easy; but for him, impossible. Everything would work out all right in Britain. It had to.

Nothing had really changed, had it. The Kuczynski thing had been unfortunate, but anyone could make a mistake. Those Muslim boys had been upset because, well, it had probably been tactless of him to have been drinking in the street. Waxman had really been asking for it; he couldn't have been more provocative.

Good God, he thought, he'd been beginning to think like a right-winger himself. Having Islamophobic thoughts, and letting Yael get under his skin like that! A *settler*! He had been carried away by emotionalism, by sheer human sympathy, but she was just defending the indefensible.

Yet images kept flooding his mind. The young Israelis dancing in the street. The Arab children at Yael's riding school. The teenage soldier Amitai praying alone in the garden with his gun propped against the tree.

Eliachim in torment, about to flee to France and then to who knew where.

He got down his bag from the overhead locker to put things away before landing. He fingered the gifts he had bought for Rosa: a volume of poems by Yehuda Amichai, a book of photographs of Jerusalem and an Israel Defense Force T-shirt. The books had been recommended by Rabbi Daniel. The T-shirt had been Russell's own impulse. He had smiled in amazement as he found himself buying it. Rosa. She would come and live with him. He wanted her near him now.

The plane dipped over the Thames. He pressed his face to the window and looked down upon the great, familiar landmarks of his life, now so small and diminished. He gazed at the brown river snaking below; he spotted the Dome and Canary Wharf and Tower Bridge, and the wide green spaces of Richmond Park and the tower blocks at Roehampton; he observed tiny cars streaming along ribbon-like roads, oblivious of their insignificance; and then he saw the houses and gardens of English suburbia, rushing up to meet him.

36

"AFTER ALL THAT effort. So why on earth did you go back?"

She was put out, Russell knew. Well you could hardly blame her.

"I can't really explain. It just felt wrong to take it from her. Even though she was alright about my taking it. It still felt... somehow exploitative."

Damia chewed pensively on a fingernail. "Do you think she knew?"

"About her father? Not specifically, no. But she knows something isn't quite right about her story. She didn't want to find out. She didn't want to disturb the ghosts. I think I was worried that's what I would somehow do."

The unquiet ghosts, though, were in his mind. He was restless and couldn't settle down to anything.

Abandoning the book had left him with an alarming gap in his life. He had been banking on it to release him from the trap in which he had somehow got himself snared. Now that route was closed off because of the whole damn Nazi thing.

"We've been given a transmission date for the East End program," said Damia brightly. Even that couldn't shake his mood. "We've got to map out your script," she said. But he wasn't interested in the East End anymore.

"You need closure," said Damia one evening, finding him sitting staring into space.

He realized she was right. It wasn't actually the book, though, that was making him so unsettled. It was Kuczynski. He needed to speak to him again. He needed to confront him with what Zofia had said.

"I'm going back to see him."

"I'm coming with you," she said. "Moral support. You'll need it.

37

THIS TIME HE only had to bang on the door once before it opened. He was shocked at Kuczynski's appearance. Gone were the dapper blazer and cravat. He was disheveled and unshaven, in a grubby polo shirt.

There was no sign of Veronica. Kuczynski shuffled wordlessly into the front room where Russell had spent so many hours working on the manuscript. Russell was shocked again. The room was in a state of disarray. Dirty plates and cups were stacked up chaotically, on the table, on the footstool, on the shelves. Rumpled clothes were strewn on the floor along with packaging that had been ripped open, newspapers, plastic rubbish bags full to bursting. A mattress and bedding were also on the floor near the door. It looked as if Kuczynski was barricading himself into this room every night.

There was a rank smell that turned Russell's stomach. Damia perched on the sofa and opened her bag. She took out a handkerchief and kept it pressed to her nose. Kuczynski looked her up and down with a sneer. Russell knew what he was thinking. His blood boiled.

"You lied to me. How many Jews did you kill that day in Jedwabne?"

"I didn't kill no one, vos Germans, Nazis, vos war, vos all madness."

"Don't give me any more of this rubbish. You were going to kill your own daughter, your baby girl. You stole from the Ajzensztejns and then you tried to kill your own child. What kind of monster are you?"

"I have no child, no daughter."

"You and Blume weren't 'in love' at all, were you. You raped her, you threatened to tell the communists her parents were partisans but that was a lie to get her to sleep with you. You blackmailed her and she had your child and then you tried to kill the baby. Were you part of the mob that killed Blume too? Did you kill Baruch and Symma? Look at me, you piece of filth."

Kuczynski kept his head down.

"Is lies, all lies, why you come to persecute old man?" he whined.

"I have spoken to Zofia."

Now Kuczynski raised his head. He looked at Russell in amazement. Then after a pause his expression became calculating.

"Ach, she's bitter. Her boyfriend was partisan shot by Soviets. She blamed me, vy I don't know. She's not right in head. She make up stories. She should be in home." He made a circular movement at his temple with his finger.

"I saw her. I went to America and met her. There's nothing wrong with her mind. Her memory is very good. She told me you stole the Ajzensztejns' valuables and looked for the baby to kill her. Then you hit Zofia."

"I was given waluables for safe keeping. There was no baby." His voice rose and he smacked the arm of his chair.

"You were in the square that day. You told me you made the Jews tear down the statue. Then you helped club them to death."

"We were made to do it, the Nazis would kill us otherwise, you don't know...They were communists. That was justice."

Well which was it then, he thought, intimidation or justice? Russell smelled weakness. Kuczsynski was beginning to lose coherence.

"They were Jews in that square. You killed them because they were Jews."

"Why you care so much?" said Kuczynski in a sudden passion. "All of a sudden you care? Is because you are communist also. Vy you persecuting me? You hate Jews. Yes, you. I hear this. You love Palestinians. Palestinians, they hate Jews. In the vor, we knew the Arabs in Palestine were vorking with Hitler. Now they say Israelis drink Palestinian children's blood. You don't say nothing against that, only against me, Polish patriot. Palestinians say Israelis are Nazis, they committing genocide. You also, you think Israelis Nazis. So Nazis not so bad after all, no? Ve all do bad things as well as good, no one has monopoly of virtue, yes? I heard you say it with my own ears. So vy you care so much? Suddenly you think you make money from book, so you become Jew!"

Russell gasped.

"I *am* a Jew! My family was murdered in Europe by your friends because they were Jews! I am *anti-Nazi*! I am *anti-racist*! I am *against* fascism, *against* antisemitism! I am against everything that you are!"

The charge was ludicrous, obscene. Only right-wingers were antisemitic. Only right-wingers were Nazi supporters like Kuczynski. The idea that the Palestinians were Nazis! They couldn't be; they were the *victims* of Western imperialism and Jewish nationalism. Left-wingers like himself simply couldn't be antisemitic. Anti-racism was in their very DNA. Kuczynsi's thinking was utterly twisted.

So why did he feel so threatened? He glanced at Damia. She seemed to be fiddling with something inside her bag.

"You sent Zofia the book. I saw it. I finished the translation."

Kuczynski seemed physically to recoil, as if he had been hit. He tried not to look as if he was desperate to know. But he started to tremble.

Now Russell leaned forward and dropped his voice. He had a weapon and he was going to make damned sure it hit its target.

"You wanted to know the secret of the book, the secret of the Jews, why God loves them so much they survive everything that's been thrown at them. Well I found it, the secret of the Jews."

Kuczynski was so still he seemed to have stopped breathing.

"The secret is that there's no secret. The Jews don't have some hidden path to God's heart. The book says their God abandoned them. So why have they survived and prospered more than any other people? Because there have always been people like you to make sure they remember who they are. They have been persecuted, tortured, exterminated by people like you. No other people has ever suffered such malice. You singled them out for unique treatment and so the result was they knew they were unique. They can never ever forget what they are, because people like you have made sure they can never forget. That's why with every attack, every pogrom, every attempt to exterminate them they grow stronger than before.

"There's no comfort for you in that book. On the contrary: it shows you are cursed to have caused the Jews to grow ever more powerful. It says that you and others like you are condemned to a living hell where what you tried to exterminate only grows in strength. That book damns you for all time."

Kuczynski rose from his chair, shaking. His face was contorted with fury. "Get out!" he screamed as he advanced upon Russell. "Get out! Get out!"

Russell and Damia fled.

38

HE WAS BEYOND exhausted. He felt as if he'd been run over by a truck. "Perhaps I'm coming down with something," he said weakly.

Damia said it was just reaction. She took him back to her flat, poured him a whisky, gently undressed him and ushered him firmly into bed. He slept deeply and dreamlessly.

In the morning he felt better. He couldn't stop turning over in his mind, though, what Kuczynski had said to him.

"He said I hated Jews."

"What does it matter what he said, a man like that? It's obviously absurd."

Of course it was. Yet he thought of Waxman, and his "evidence" of the Palestinians' Nazi imagery and their role during the war as Hitler's Middle East legion. He had dismissed it all as Zionist propaganda. He thought of all those people, just like him, who wanted to defend the oppressed and make a better world and for whom supporting the Palestinian cause was what defined them as decent and good. They couldn't all be wrong, could they? They couldn't all be supporting genocidal Nazi Jew-haters, could they? Impossible!

Yet he couldn't dismiss Kuczynski as easily as he could dismiss Waxman. For Kuczynski was not a Zionist. Kuczynski wasn't trying to blacken anyone in order to promote the Jewish cause. Kuczynski hated Jews. Yet Kuczynski had said pretty well what Waxman had said. And Kuczynski had better cause than most to know.

"Is it possible to be a good person and yet believe bad things?" he asked.

Damia pondered this as she buttered another slice of toast. "Yes," she said finally, "but only if you don't know they're bad. Once you know, you have to stop believing them."

But what if you choose not to find out? he wondered.

"You realize," said Damia, "that you've now got a great story to tell."

He looked at her. He didn't get it. "I can't tell Eliachim's story anymore," he said, baffled.

"Forget the book. Kuczynski! He's the story now. The inside track of a war criminal! You can tell how he was first of all anti-Soviet and then a Soviet informer and then took part in the massacres and stole from the Jews and then hid in England for all these years."

"But...but what about Haia? I gave my word..."

"You don't have to say Kuczynski was her father. Just talk about how he betrayed the Ajzensztejns, and how he thought all Jews were communists. It'll coincide with the trial verdict, and it will be sensational!"

It was true; he had the recording of Zofia detailing Kuczynski's role in the massacre at Jedwabne. He had given her his word that he would hand it over to the police, which he had duly done. But there was nothing to stop him from publishing her testimony.

He could contrast Kuczynski's self-serving excuses to him with Zofia's chilling denunciation of her brother. He would reveal that this was the testimony that had brought the British police to Kuczynski's door. He would be taking the reader inside a mind made monstrous by the twin evils of Nazis and Soviet communism. The program would be hailed as an original contribution to the study of the two great totalitarian systems of the 20th century.

He would be fêted as the sleuth who had brought back to the British police the testimony that finally ran a Nazi war criminal to ground. And he would also feel that finally, he had done something of which his father would have been proud. More than that: he would feel he had avenged his father's memory.

Of course, Eliachim's story would have to remain hidden. But burning Jews alive in 1941 probably needed no further embellishment. And anyway, the major selling point, the aspect which would hook viewers, was Zofia's heroic rescue of the infant Haia from otherwise certain slaughter. And there was a ready-made story for that which obscured Kuczynski's parentage. Russell would repeat the lie that Haia herself believed—that both her parents had been slaughtered as Jews.

On that basis, he might even be able persuade Zofia to appear on the daytime TV chat shows that would undoubtedly be beating a path to his door.

He felt excited again. Things were now going to be fine. He didn't need Eliachim's story after all.

His phone buzzed on the kitchen table. He was busy making coffee so he put it on speakerphone. It was Ian Avery, the war crimes officer from Scotland Yard. He was just ringing to thank Russell so much for the audio of Zofia's testimony about her brother, absolutely invaluable and so it was obviously a pity it had been overtaken by events.

"What events?" said Russell, after a small pause.

"Haven't you heard?" said Avery. "It's been on the news: Kuczynski hanged himself last night. Relief for us, frankly; gets everyone off the hook of having to prosecute a poor old man, yada yada yada, and frees up us chaps to catch the villains that matter."

"He *hanged* himself?" repeated Russell faintly. "*Last night*?"

"Yeah, seems his wife had left him, house in a terrible state, it all must have got to him. Interesting isn't it how even war criminals do apparently feel shame, maybe even guilt; who knows what goes on inside a mind like that."

Russell did know. It wasn't shame or guilt. It had been a verdict more devastating than anything a court could hand down.

But now his main protagonist was dead. There was no longer any opportunity to put him on the record. For the second time, Russell faced the collapse of a story because he himself had made the principal evidence unavailable.

"What now," he said to Damia helplessly.

She looked at him impishly for a moment. Then she got up from the table and brought over her own phone. She laid it on the table between them and clicked the play button. Kuczynski's voice, alternately whining, petulant and angry, filled the room.

"We were made to do it, the Nazis would kill us otherwise, you don't know...They were communists. That was justice."

"On we go," said Damia.

Yes, Russell would indeed go on in the life he was leading because there was no alternative. But he was different nevertheless. He could no longer deny it.

He couldn't stop thinking about what Kuczynski had said to him. Those venomous words kept reverberating in his head. They had stung him badly because, try as he might, he could not escape the fact that they were true.

Appalling as it was, Kuczynski had hit home when he had accused Russell of siding with the people who hated Jews. Worse than that, hadn't he hated the Jewish part of himself?

It was unbearable to be bracketed with the likes of Kuczynski. Ridiculous. Preposterous. Yet when he looked back, he couldn't deny there was something in it. He thought of Yael, of her bitter accusation that he was somehow responsible for her father's murder. More than something.

But that was what he had been like in the past. He was a different person now. Indeed, when he looked back to before it had all happened, he felt as if he had stepped out of his own skin.

Had it started with Eliachim of York? Or had it all begun earlier, at the moment he saw his father lowered into the ground? He had been angry and confused when Jack had died. Now, though, he recognized that his passing was also a form of release. Maybe his father's death had permitted him to be open to what Eliachim was telling him. Or had Eliachim performed some ghostly alchemy that had allowed him finally to separate from his father in peace?

Whatever way round it was, Eliachim had somehow pried open a crack in his heart; and other stuff, surprising stuff, had flowed in. The hard, bitter edge of him had softened. What once had so threatened to overwhelm him that he shut it all out for fear he would disappear beneath it no longer terrified him. He saw now it was possible not to hate what he had come from but to accept it, and also to see what people could love in it. Indeed, he had come close to loving it himself.

And Russell knew that he had been changed forever. Yet he also knew that the world he inhabited would not allow him the space to make such a change. He understood that his tolerant world would only tolerate him on condition that he was like everyone else in this one crucial respect—that he did not make them feel he had something they wanted, even if they had no idea what that something might be. He understood, finally, that the emotion lurking beneath the veneer of comradeship was not fear or contempt or disdain, but jealousy.

So now he was stranded between two worlds. Strangely, that somehow felt appropriate. Had he actually become, he wondered wryly, the rootless cosmopolitan of anti-Jewish caricature?

The change in him didn't mean he had turned into Waxman. He saw that now. He still believed in all his old ideals. None of that had altered; it didn't need to. The world, he realized with relief, wasn't binary. There was good and bad everywhere.

This was new to him. He perceived that he had been living under a constant fear: the terror that any deviation in how he thought, however small and insignificant, would inescapably consign him to isolation and worse on the opposite side to virtue, a bad person to himself as well as to others.

Now, though, he knew he was an outsider and would always be so. In the world he had assumed was his own, he would merely be tolerated on certain conditions. Well stuff that, he thought. It no longer mattered that he might not fit in. He no longer wanted to fit in amongst people with such objectionable attitudes. Attitudes, moreover, that went against every principle they were supposed to stand for. Principles he still stood for. He had thought they were all on the same side. That had been his profound mistake.

Yet he also knew that he was now in danger. If he let on at all, if he started exposing the Jewish part of himself then his colleagues, his friends, those who controlled his livelihood would all close ranks against him. He could not afford to let them see any change in him at all. So he would go under their radar. Outwardly he would be the same: liberal, worldly, cynical. But inside he would be a different person. Inside, he would be exploring and developing a part of himself that had been suppressed for too long.

He looked across the table at Damia, humming as she licked marmalade off her fingers. There was nothing hidden about her, he thought wonderingly. She was exactly as she seemed; and she believed others were too, unless they showed otherwise. He loved that innocence about her. And she accepted him as he was, without any conditions.

Only now did he realize how shattered he had been when Alice had left him. Now he felt as if he wasn't worthless after all; he really could be loved by someone for what he actually was. He thought of Rosa with a pang. Only if you feel you are truly loved, he thought, can you then yourself love in turn.

"Did you mean what you said to Kuczynski?" Damia asked suddenly.

"Said what?"

"That the Jews only continue to exist because of what people like him have done to them?"

She was looking steadily at him.

"I used to think that. I don't think it anymore."

"Good," she said. "It didn't sound very nice. And you still haven't told me..."

"I know. I will, I promise."

First, though, he had to find out for himself. Where Eliachim had pointed, where Rosa was pointing, that's where he wanted to go too. But now he wasn't alone. There was someone who would come on the journey with him.

"Hey," he said.

"Hey yourself," said Damia softly.

He rested his elbow on the table and raised his hand. She leaned over and rested her palm on his. He smiled.

ACKNOWLEDGMENTS

THIS BOOK IS a work of fiction crafted around two events that actually happened: the massacre of English Jews at Clifford's Tower, York, in 1190 and the atrocity committed against the Jews of Jedwabne, Poland, in 1941.

Although my characters are fictional, I have tried to reproduce as faithfully as possible the details of these actual events. Accordingly, I drew widely upon a number of sources.

Principal among these are the two pioneering books about the Jedwabne atrocity by Jan Gross, *Neighbors* and *Golden Harvest.*

I also drew upon an interview with Anna Bikont by David Mikics, published in *Tablet* magazine on 25 October 2015 as "The Day We Burned Our Neighbors Alive."

For details about the York massacre, the Crusades and the Jews of medieval England, I consulted among other works the following:

- The Medieval Sourcebook:
    - *Ephraim of Bonn: The York Massacre 1189-90*
    - *Albert of Aix and Ekkehard of Aura: Emico and the Slaughter of the Rhineland Jews*

- *Soloman bar Samson: The Crusaders in Mainz, May 27, 1096*
- *Jewish Perspectives during the Crusades*
- *A History of the Jews in England*, by Cecil Roth

For information about the Polish partisans, I consulted "The Last Rising in the Eastern Borderlands: The Ejszyszki Epilogue in its Historical Context," by Marek Jan Chodakiewicz and "My Childhood Story" by Krystyna Balut (née Martusewicz).

Finally, it is customary to acknowledge the influence of someone "without whom this work would not have been possible." In the case of this novel, that is no exaggeration. It would not have been started, let alone finished, without the patient, expert and unfailingly generous encouragement of Luigi Bonomi, whose faith in me and in this novel was a game-changer. To him should accrue the credit for this book; any mistakes are my own.

ABOUT THE AUTHOR

THE BRITISH JOURNALIST Melanie Phillips is Britain's most controversial champion of national and cultural identity. Her weekly column currently appears in *The Times of London*; she also writes for the *Jerusalem Post* and *Jewish Chronicle* and is a regular contributor to BBC TV and radio. Her bestselling book *Londonistan*, about the British establishment's capitulation to Islamist aggression, was published in 2006. She followed this in 2010 with *The World Turned Upside Down: the Global Battle over God, Truth and Power*. You can follow her blog and all her work on her website, melaniephillips.com. This is her first novel.